SPECIAL MESSAGE TO READERS

THE ULVERSCROFT FOUNDATION
(registered UK charity number 264873)
was established in 1972 to provide funds for research, diagnosis and treatment of eye diseases. Examples of major projects funded by the Ulverscroft Foundation are:-

- The Children's Eye Unit at Moorfields Eye Hospital, London
- The Ulverscroft Children's Eye Unit at Great Ormond Street Hospital for Sick Children
- Funding research into eye diseases and treatment at the Department of Ophthalmology, University of Leicester
- The Ulverscroft Vision Research Group, Institute of Child Health
- Twin operating theatres at the Western Ophthalmic Hospital, London
- The Chair of Ophthalmology at the Royal Australian College of Ophthalmologists

You can help further the work of the Foundation by making a donation or leaving a legacy. Every contribution is gratefully received. If you would like to help support the Foundation or require further information, please contact:

THE ULVERSCROFT FOUNDATION
The Green, Bradgate Road, Anstey
Leicester LE7 7FU, England
Tel: (0116) 236 4325

website: www.ulverscroft-foundation.org.uk

THE TEASHOP GIRLS

It is early 1940 and World War Two has already taken a hold on the country. Rose Neville works as a Lyons' teashop Nippy on the Kent coast alongside her childhood friends, the ambitious Lily and Katie, whose fiancé is about to be posted overseas in the navy. As war creates havoc in Europe, Rose relies on her close ties with friends and family. When Captain Benjamin Hargreaves enters the teashop one day, Rose is immediately drawn to him. But as Lyons forbids courting between staff and customers, she tries to put the handsome officer out of her mind.

ELAINE EVEREST

THE TEASHOP GIRLS

Complete and Unabridged

MAGNA
Leicester

First published in Great Britain in 2019 by
Pan Books
an imprint of Pan Macmillan
London

First Ulverscroft Edition
published 2020
by arrangement with
Pan Macmillan
London

A catalogue record for this book is available
from the British Library.

ISBN 978–0–7505–4779–6

Published by
Ulverscroft Limited
Anstey, Leicestershire

Set by Words & Graphics Ltd.
Anstey, Leicestershire
Printed and bound in Great Britain by
T. J. International Ltd., Padstow, Cornwall

This book is printed on acid-free paper

To all seaside landladies who,
like Flora Neville, created such
happy memories for so many families.

Prologue

September 1926

Flora Neville pulled a pearl-tipped hatpin from her best black felt hat and placed both onto the bed. It had been a tense day, and she was glad to be home and back to work; there were sheets to bring in from the line, where they'd been hanging a good part of the day, and there was dinner to prepare for the guests. A quick glance at a dainty ormolu clock standing in the middle of the walnut tallboy reminded her Rose would be in from school shortly. Flora needed to be back in her work clothes with today's events firmly locked away, so no one would know where she'd set off to when she boarded the first train up to London. Furthermore, the nature of the business that had her kitted out in her Sunday best on a Thursday, and her usual sunny disposition replaced with a sad, thoughtful expression, should be known only to her and never told to a living soul. Some things should be forgotten, she thought to herself. She wouldn't deny, though, that it had been pleasant to stop for a cup of tea and a toasted teacake in a Lyons Corner House along the Strand after her appointment with the solicitor, Mr Bartholomew, and then catch a train from Charing Cross back to Ramsgate and home.

For once she'd enjoyed being waited on by

1

delightful waitresses who showed her to a vacant table and took her order. It made a change from being the one looking after her boarders at the Sea View guesthouse. She sat watching as the young women dashed here and there, taking orders and carrying heavy trays laden with food and drinks. They all had ready smiles and were so polite. However, she was surprised so many people would call out the word 'Nippy' to get their attention.

'Why do they call you Nippy?' she'd asked as her tea was brought to the table.

'It's our new name,' the dark-haired young waitress explained. 'It's supposed to be because we nip about all over the place,' she giggled.

'How strange. Surely they could call you something more in keeping with your smart appearance?' Flora said as she reached for the milk jug.

The girl smiled. 'I don't mind it one little bit. They used to call us Gladys, and as that's my old gorgon of an aunt's name, I much prefer to be a Nippy.'

'Oh, I see,' Flora said as she poured her tea. 'Who decided to make the name official?'

'Lyons had a competition to find a new name, and that's how we came to be Nippies.'

Flora smiled back at the girl. 'How interesting. Nippy is a much better name, and so memorable.'

She thought about the busy Nippies as she sipped her tea. Hopefully the documents Flora now held in her black leather handbag would mean that her ten-year-old daughter, Rose,

2

would never have to work as a waitress. When Rose grew up there would be money enough for her to train for a position in an office until the day came for her to marry and have a family to care for. Yes, that would be a very pleasing situation indeed.

★   ★   ★

Flora shook herself from her thoughts as she ran a brush through her soft brown hair and frowned at a few grey threads running through the gentle curls. 'Time waits for no one, especially you, Flora Neville,' she muttered before twisting her hair back into a severe bun at the nape of her neck and fixing it with a tortoiseshell clip. 'Now, what to do first?' She smiled at the pleasantly rounded face staring back at her from the mirror.

She hung her coat in the wardrobe and looked at an envelope she'd placed on the bed as she walked into the room. Kneeling down, she reached under the double bed and pulled out a battered suitcase. Opening the stubborn catches, swearing under her breath as one caught her fingernail, she delved inside and pulled out a smaller leather case. Taking a long chain from around her neck that held a delicate brass key, she unlocked the smaller case. She gently touched a pearl cameo brooch and a small ruby ring, stopping to think for a moment about the past and how different her life had been. Then she placed the envelope she'd collected from Mr Bartholomew inside. 'At least he kept his promise,' she whispered, before locking the case. Looking around the room, she put the chain and the key into a small porcelain jar on her dressing table and pushed her secret safely back under the bed.

1

January 1940

Rose Neville shivered as she hurried up the street towards the Ramsgate branch of Lyons teashop, hugging the straps of her black leather handbag and gas mask holder close to her side in case they slipped off her shoulder and were lost in her haste. She dreaded the day she would need to use the ugly gas mask; like so many in the small Kent seaside town, she hoped the war would be over before they saw enemy action. So many people were using the words 'phoney war', but as her mum was fond of saying, she could feel it in her water that something would happen before too long, and she wanted to be prepared.

Rose wasn't keen on the early morning starts, especially with a cold wind blowing off the nearby seafront and snow threatening to fall again. Her pert nose was frozen cold even though she'd wrapped a bright red knitted scarf across most of her pretty face. Waving to an old school friend who was opening up the doors of a nearby cafe, she thanked God she was working for the prestigious Lyons teashop chain, who even had posh Corner Houses in London. So much better than the small cafe where staff did little more than fry eggs and serve mugs of tea all day long. Not only were Lyons staff taught how to serve food and be the best waitresses, but they wore smart uniforms and went by the name of Nippies. That couldn't be said for any other waitresses, she thought, feeling proud. Why, she'd even been trained in London, just as other Nippies had.

'Hey,' a voice shouted from close behind her. 'Didn't you hear me calling for you to wait?'

Rose stopped suddenly and turned as her friend Lily barrelled into her. 'Oops, sorry, I can't hear a thing wrapped up in this scarf. Aren't you cold?' she asked, seeing Lily's coat flapping open and her hair flowing free while she held a green felt hat in her hand.

'I was late getting up and I've run all the way. My hat blew off back at the corner. I've lost my hatpin,' she added, seeing Rose shake her head in despair.

'Again? You'd lose your head if it was loose,' Rose said. 'Now stand still while I do up your coat, or you'll catch your death . . . ' She froze as the words came tumbling out. What an idiot she was. 'I'm sorry, Lily. That was thoughtless of me.'

Lily brushed a tear away that had been threatening to fall. 'Don't be daft. You didn't mean anything by it, and my mum would have said the same if she'd been here. In fact, she'd have made sure I was out of bed on time and had some breakfast inside me before I set off for work. And she'd have told me off for not getting dressed properly,' she added, giving Rose a quick hug. 'Tell me off as much as you want. No doubt I deserve it. Now, let's get to work before the old dragon reprimands us both for being late.' She grabbed hold of Rose's arm and hurried her along the street.

'All the same, I should be more thoughtful,' Rose said as she trotted along, trying to keep up with her friend. 'It's only been three months since your mum . . . '

' . . . Died?' Lily finished Rose's sentence. 'It's been two months, three weeks and four days,' she said, stopping by the door of a shoe shop and turning to give an over-bright smile to Rose. 'But who's counting?'

Rose felt awful. Lily's mother had been taken ill so quickly and faded away almost before their eyes. Apart from a stepfather, her friend didn't have any relatives to turn to, and she had been determined to carry out her mother's last wishes to keep a roof over her husband's head and care for him as best she could. Rose didn't care much for Lily's stepfather, but she knew that her friend would do her very best for him, just as she too would have carried out the wishes of her own mother. Not for one moment could Rose imagine losing her mum, Flora, who meant the world to her — but if it should happen, she would honour her mum's memory and follow her wishes until her dying breath. It would be all she could do for the woman who had brought her up single-handedly since Rose was ten years of age and who had never once complained. Flora had never spoken of her past life, but Rose had a feeling that she had worked in London, as she seemed to know streets and buildings there when they were mentioned by visitors to the Sea View guesthouse. However, if anyone asked about her early life Flora would say very little, and would quickly change the subject.

7

Rose was shaken from her reverie as the Lyons teashop came into view and she spotted someone on the doorstep. 'Surely Miss Butterworth hasn't got someone outside cleaning windows in this weather?' she said as they hurried closer.

'I wouldn't put it past her,' Lily huffed. The early morning shift hadn't started yet, but they both knew the grumpy woman who managed the Ramsgate branch would stop at nothing to keep her Nippies working hard. 'She's a dragon! She had me cleaning the shop front five minutes before I was due to clock off. I swear it's because she heard me telling Katie how much I was looking forward to our trip to the pictures.'

'You got there by the skin of your teeth,' Rose commiserated. 'At least you managed to see Johnny Johnson in that Clive Danvers B movie. I hope they make a third film, as Johnny is such a good actor.'

Lily grinned. 'He's easy on the eye, too.'

'Why, Lily Douglas, what a thing to say,' Rose exclaimed, although she agreed with her friend. 'Oh look, I do believe that girl outside the teashop isn't cleaning at all. Come on — let's go see what's happening.' She started to hurry, ignoring the flurry of icy snow now stinging her eyes. Lily had no choice but to keep up.

As they reached the grand facade of the teashop, Rose could see that the young woman was leaning against its glass window. She was shivering, and had tears running down her face. 'My goodness, whatever is the matter?' Rose asked with concern. 'Is there anything I can do to help?'

The young woman shook her head, causing auburn curls to tumble from beneath a black beret, before cuffing her eyes with woollen mittens that had seen better days. 'I'm just being daft, and I'm freezing cold,' she said, giving Rose a brief smile. 'I have an interview with the manageress at nine o'clock and I left earlier than I should. Now I'm too afraid to go inside.'

'Your nerves got the better of you, and now you're half frozen as well,' Rose said as she took charge. 'What you need is a hot cup of tea and a chance to warm up before you meet the Dra . . . before you meet Miss Butterworth,' she corrected herself, not wanting to frighten the young woman even more before she'd as much as stepped over the threshold of the smart-looking Lyons premises.

'I can't sit in there drinking like a customer. I'm not dressed . . . ' The girl faltered, looking down at her coat that had seen better days. 'I've done the best I can for my interview, but as for sitting with posh people, I'm just not sure. Besides, I've only got a few coppers to last us until my husband gets paid.'

'You're married?' Lily said, looking shocked.

The girl jutted out her chin and glared at Lily. 'I'm seventeen, and old enough to be a wife. My mum said it's better than being an old maid.'

Rose felt her face start to twitch. She suddenly felt quite ancient, even though she was only six years older than the girl. 'You can come into the staffroom for your cuppa. You don't have to pay,' she added, seeing a shadow fall over the girl's face.

'And Lyons isn't posh,' Lily added as she

9

pushed open the door to be met with a cloud of warm air. 'It's a friendly place for one and all.'

Rose ushered the girl into the teashop and through to the staff quarters, where she sat her down with a cup of tea poured from a large brown china pot kept under a red tea cosy. She placed a bun onto a tea plate and put both in front of the girl. 'The bun may be a little stale as it's left over from yesterday, and before you ask, you don't have to pay a penny. Eat up while I get changed into my uniform, and then I'll let Miss Butterworth know you are here.' Her tone made it clear that she didn't expect any arguments. 'I've not seen you around the town before, and I've lived here all my life,' she added.

'We came down here to live with my husband's mum. I'm from the East End of London,' said the girl proudly. 'I've brought me mum an' little brother with me. We was told it would be safer down here once the war kicked off, which it's bound to do before too long.'

'Well, I hope you will like living here,' Rose said, thinking how brave it was of the girl to up sticks and move from the capital down to the other side of Kent. 'I've always found everyone friendly around here.'

The girl gave her a grin. 'I like living by the seaside. Me mum's tickled pink to be able to walk along the front and take in the sea air — she says she feels like one of those toffs that used to come down here when it was the posh thing to do. It's supposed to be good for you, so hopefully it'll help Mum's bronchials.'

'I do hope it helps your mum. Yes, Ramsgate

used to be very popular for the upper classes to visit to take the air. We aren't quite as popular these days, but holiday-makers still come down and until the war it was a busy town. Nowadays we see more soldiers than families. Now, drink your tea before it gets cold,' Rose said before heading to the room where the girls changed their clothes and kept their coats and bags.

'Blimey, married at her age. It makes you think, doesn't it?' Lily remarked as she stepped into her black waitress dress before checking her stocking seams were straight. 'Do my shoes look clean? I should have given them a good going-over last night, but I fell asleep on my bed.'

Rose stepped back and looked Lily over. 'You look fine. And as for the girl out there — who's to know if she didn't have to get married on the quick, or that her husband's not out of work? She looks frightened half to death, poor kid. She'll need a bit more backbone if she wants Miss Butterworth to hire her. As for going to London to be trained . . . '

'You've got a point there. I found it bad enough staying in that hostel for young women, even though the three of us were there together learning the ropes. By the way, where is Katie?'

'She's on a later shift today, so we'll see her at midday.' Rose said, checking her white cap was pinned on correctly, and that the Lyons badge was lined up correctly and not skew-whiff. It was something Miss Butterworth checked when she inspected her staff.

'As long as she's still coming to the dance with us this evening,' Lily said as she dabbed lipstick

11

onto her lips and gave a small smile into the cracked mirror hanging on the wall. 'It will be good to go out and have some fun, and listen to you sing.'

Rose grinned. 'It will. Now, I must take that young girl to Miss Butterworth. I hope she gets taken on — it looks as though she could do with the job. I'll see you at the coal face.'

Lily laughed. 'Not that we get much chance to chat, with my workstation being way across the tearoom from yours.'

Rose went back to where the young girl was picking crumbs from her plate. 'I'm just going to let Miss Butterworth know you are here, and then I'll fetch you.'

'Oh, I didn't recognize you in your uniform,' the girl said. 'You do look very smart.'

Rose smiled. 'If you are accepted, then you will be wearing the same uniform — that's unless you're put to working the kitchens, or trained to be a Sally.'

The girl giggled. 'A Sally? Whatever are they?'

'Did you see the women serving customers at the counter at the front of the teashop?'

'I saw a lady selling teacakes and bread.'

'Yes, well, they are Sallys. They do tend to be taller, though. It's to do with reaching into the window display and across the counters, I suppose . . .'

'There's no chance I'll be a Sally, then. I'm shorter than you.'

Rose laughed. 'That's true. By the way, what is your name? I'll need to tell Miss Butterworth who is waiting to see her.'

12

'My name is Grace Gibbons,' the girl said, holding out her hand.

They shook hands, and Rose hurried out of the staffroom. She had her own workstation to get to once she'd notified the manager. Stepping into the teashop, which was already busy with early-morning customers, she felt a tinge of pride as she looked across the rows of tables dressed with crisp white tablecloths and set with silver cutlery. Overhead, brass light fittings hung from chains, enhancing the polished tea urns and stainless-steel teapots lined up waiting to be filled with steaming hot tea.

She felt the usual thrill run through her, knowing she worked for a chain of teashops that were held in such high esteem throughout the country. Joe Lyons may have had his grand restaurants and Corner Houses up in London, but down here on the very eastern tip of the county of Kent, the smaller teashops were just as important and equally impressive.

Straightening her back, Rose tapped on the door to Miss Butterworth's office and waited to be told to enter. Her mind wandered to the dance she was attending that evening, and the songs she hoped to sing when Silvano Caprice called her to the stage. If only her life had been different and she had been able to pursue her dream of singing with the big bands; perhaps even touring with them, and maybe one day her voice being heard on a 78 rpm record. However, things like that hardly ever happened to girls like her; and how could she even think of leaving Ramsgate and her mum? she thought, chastising herself. How would Flora cope running the Sea View guesthouse on her own if Rose were to go running off to pursue her dreams? No, she'd have to make the most of her life and just sing when invited. But a girl could dream, she thought sadly as a stern voice from inside the office called for her to enter.

'Excuse me, Miss Butterworth,' Rose said as she stood in front of the manageress's desk. She spotted Mr Grant, the area manager, pushing the last remnants of a toasted teacake into his mouth before brushing a scattering of crumbs from his expansive chest.

'Yes, Neville, what is it?' Miss Butterworth snapped, looking up at a large clock on the wall. 'Spit it out. I have appointments to deal with.'

'I wanted to let you know that a Mrs Gibbons is here for her interview. I've left her in the staffroom having a cup of tea, as she was frozen stiff,' Rose answered, thinking it would be a good idea not to mention she'd also given Grace a bun.

'Hurry up and show her in,' Miss Butterworth said, looking away to continue her conversation with Mr Grant.

'Before you go, Miss Neville . . . ' Mr Grant said as Rose reached for the door handle. 'May I ask if it was your idea to check the Nippies' gas masks each morning?'

Rose took a deep breath. Was she in for a telling off? 'Yes, sir. I noticed some of the Nippies were having problems attaching their gas masks to the back of their belts, so I suggested that they paired up with others on the same shift

14

to help each other. I didn't think it was worth mentioning,' she said, giving her manageress an apologetic look. Miss Butterworth looked askance.

'You did very well, Miss Neville, very well indeed,' he said, looking her up and down. 'Had you thought about furthering your career with Lyons?'

'No, sir — I mean . . . I do like my job here in Ramsgate. I'd never thought of doing anything else,' she replied, pushing her dreams of singing to the back of her mind. It wouldn't do to mention them or she'd not have a job at all, as Miss Butterworth would soon show her the door. She always made it clear that she was the boss, and the Nippies could easily be replaced.

'Keep it in mind, Neville,' Mr Grant said, giving her a dismissive smile.

Rose hurried to the staffroom, wondering what Mr Grant was going on about. The more she thought about it, the more she wondered if she could be a manageress — or perhaps work in another part of the Lyons empire? Yes, if the opportunity were to arise to further her career, she'd grab it with both hands.

★　★　★

Flora took a sharp intake of breath before raising her fist skywards at young Charlie Stubbs. The scruffy lad was perfecting his aim, armed with a large round stone, egged on by a gang of identical-looking lads. 'You throw that and you'll feel the back of my hand so quick, you'll not know what hit you.'

15

Charlie cuffed his dripping nose with his sleeve and glared sullenly at Flora, allowing the stone to gently fall from his hand. 'Well, she's a spy. I heard me dad say all foreigners are.'

Flora shook her head in disbelief. The Stubbs family were notorious in that part of Ramsgate, and it wasn't for the eloquence of their speech or the generosity of their nature. 'Don't talk so daft, boy.'

'If they speaks funny like her, then they must be spies,' he answered back, raising his chin defiantly, pointing to what looked like a bundle of rags on the ground nearby. 'We don't trust the likes of them,' he added proudly.

She tutted and gave him a stern look. 'Your father wouldn't know a spy if he found one in the bottom of his pint pot. Now, you and your mates help me get this poor woman onto her feet, then you can run off home to your beds. It's far too late for a child your age to be out alone. Why, there might just be a proper spy around the corner waiting to kidnap a boy and take him off to Germany to fight for that Hitler.' She tried not to smile as young Charlie looked fearfully around before tearing off as fast as his legs would carry him with his gang close on his heels.

It was time Sean Stubbs took his children in hand, Flora thought as she moved closer to see what poor soul Charlie had been stoning. Charlie and his many siblings had turned feral since their mother, Eileen, had run off with a sailor when his ship had anchored off the Kent coast and he'd come ashore looking for entertainment. The last Flora heard, Eileen was

16

plying her trade in the East End and the sailor had copped it on some foreign sea. By rights Eileen should be home caring for her kids, but no doubt Sean Stubbs would kill her if she ever came anywhere near the town again. He'd been heard saying so on many occasions — as if he didn't approve of women whose virtue had ended up in the gutter, even though he was acquainted with more than a few of them himself.

Flora leant closer to the ragged figure. She could see it was a thin-faced woman, huddled close against the wall, trembling with fear as blood ran from a cut on her high cheekbones. Her first thought was that the poor wretch needed feeding up, put in some clean clothes and with the luxury of a bath, she would be most striking. Her hair was pulled back tightly under a scarf, but it looked thick and dark. Yes, in the right circumstances this lady would be most handsome. At the moment, though, she already had a bruise forming around one eye. 'You're going to have a right old shiner there come the morning.'

The woman shied away from Flora, pulling a blanket up to her chin.

'Come on, my love, no one's going to hurt you. My house is just up the road a bit. Let's get you cleaned up and sort out that nasty cut, shall we? No doubt you'd like a hot drink too, eh?'

The woman muttered a few words of thanks, but they were lost on the wind that whipped in from the sea. Flora detected a foreign accent, but she had no idea of where the young woman

17

came from. That would have to be a question for another time. Lifting a small suitcase she'd kept close to her side throughout her ordeal, Flora helped her to her feet. 'Don't you worry about speaking, my love. Just you hang on to me, and we'll have you home and safe in no time.'

The woman leant heavily on Flora's arm as they slowly covered the few yards along the harbour front before turning the corner towards the steep slope up Madeira Walk that led to the Sea View guesthouse in Albion Place. Flora felt a harsh wind on her back from the sea as the tide came in at an angry pace, and flurries of harsh snow made it hard to see ahead. Everything and everyone seemed angry these days, she thought as she fought to keep the woman on her feet. Those boys were just the tip of the iceberg. There again, who wouldn't be angry, what with this bloody war and what Adolf was up to? she thought, as she placed the suitcase at the top of the three steps leading to her front door before fishing around in her pocket for the key. 'Let's get you inside and put the kettle on shall we? Everything will feel better once we've had a cuppa.'

'That's your answer to everything, Mum.'

Flora turned to see her daughter, Rose, reach for the suitcase and follow them into the warm hallway of the guesthouse. 'You're home early, love.'

'Only a little,' she said. 'Who is this, then? Have you picked up another waif and stray?' she grinned.

'I . . . I am Anya,' the woman said slowly as she looked around the large hallway with three oak doors on the right and a wide carpeted staircase on the left that swept upwards, curving to the right before disappearing out of sight. 'You have . . . you have a good home. I feel the warmth . . . the love.'

Flora beamed in delight. 'Thank you, Anya, I agree with you. There has been much love in this house.' She gave her daughter a hard glare as she spotted a fleeting grin appear on the girl's face, knowing from experience that Rose was likely to pull her leg at any time. 'Let's get you through to the kitchen, and then you can tell me why those boys were throwing stones at you.' Flora took Anya's arm and steered her to the door at the end of the hall.

'Not the Stubbs kids?' Rose asked as she helped her mum guide the frail woman.

Flora nodded, her lips set in a thin, angry line. 'I'm going to have a word with their dad. It's happening far too often. Look at the nasty cut on this lady's face. I may even have a word with PC Denning so he can keep an eye out for the children. They're little blighters in the blackout. As for getting them down an air-raid shelter when the sirens go off with these false alarms — I've all but given up blowing my whistle to get their attention.'

'Mum's an ARP warden,' Rose explained as she saw their visitor's confused frown. 'She will make sure everyone is safe if we ever have an air raid.'

Anya thought before nodding her head. 'She is very good at caring for people, I feel. She helped me very much.'

'Call me Flora. 'She' sounds like something the cat dragged in,' Flora said before leading Anya to a comfortable chair by the stove that Flora kept burning all day long, using scraps of driftwood collected on her walks along the beach; not that she was able to do much of that anymore, due to the shoreline being off limits to the locals since the army arrived to protect the coastline. 'Here; sit yourself down while I put the kettle on the hob. Then I'll take a look at that cut on your face.'

'Mum's a dab hand at first aid, too,' Rose said, taking off her hat and coat and throwing them onto a spare seat. 'She took a course as part of her ARP training.'

Anya followed Rose's movements with wide eyes. 'You are a maid?' she asked, taking in the formal black dress with its row of buttons down the front and neat collar and cuffs.

Rose hooted with laughter. 'God, no, although it feels like it sometimes; I'm a Nippy at the Lyons teashop up the road. A waitress,' she added, seeing the foreign woman's frown. 'You're not from round here, are you?'

'That's enough of that,' Flora scolded. 'There'll be enough time for questions once I've cleaned up this pretty face and we've had a cuppa.'

Anya blushed. 'I thank you. No one has ever said I am pretty before. Not even my husband. He says I am handsome woman,' she added quickly, seeing the smile fall from Flora's face. 'He is a good man, and that is why I am here.'

'Well, as far as I'm concerned you are a beauty, and I'll not have anyone say otherwise.

20

Now, let's help you off with your coat and make you comfortable. The kettle's about to boil, so if you can warm the teapot, Rose, I'll get Anya seen to, then she can tell us all about herself and how she came to be in such a pickle.' Flora went to a cabinet and pulled out an enamel bowl and a clean piece of rag, not seeing the shadow that swept across Anya's face. She added the water Rose had left in the kettle and checked it with her finger. 'That seems to be about right,' she said, dipping the cloth in the liquid before gently dabbing at the cut on Anya's face. The woman looked straight ahead, biting her lip just a little. 'Sorry, love. It will sting just a little, but we'll soon have you as right as rain. I'll put a dab of Acriflavine cream on the cut once it's clean. Now, why were those nasty kids picking on you?' she asked.

'I asked if they knew of any . . . what you say . . . lodges?'

'Lodgings, do you mean?' Rose asked, putting down a cup of hot steaming tea where Anya could reach it before perching on the arm of her chair to listen to what the stranger had to say.

'Yes, that would be it . . . lodgings. The taller boy, he said rude words to me and then picked up a stone to throw at me. He called me a Nazi and a spy. I am not either of these things. I have papers to show who I am, if you would like to see them?' She looked to where her small battered suitcase had been left near the kitchen door.

'I'm sure you're not,' Flora fussed as she pulled back Anya's hair that had fallen loose to

21

check if there were any cuts she'd missed. 'I must say you have the most beautiful hair. It is so thick and dark.'

'I thank you. My husband he say it is as dark as the night.'

'He seems to have a way with words.'

'He does.' She smiled gently and nodded to Rose as she passed her tea. 'He writes many words in books. I have his journal in my bag. I couldn't leave it behind,' she said, her eyes taking on a faraway look once more as she sipped from the cup. 'This is very good tea. Not so, how you say . . . the wet and warm kind.'

Flora laughed. She knew exactly what Anya meant. 'I pride myself in always having a decent cup of tea for my guests. Now drink up, there's another in the teapot. I'll get you something to eat in a minute.' She'd noticed how thin the woman was under her threadbare navy-blue cardigan.

'I cannot eat your food,' Anya said, looking alarmed. 'You must keep it for yourself. When I have finished my tea I will be going. You have been more than kind in helping me and cleaning my wound. I must be going to find a lodge . . . lodgings,' she added as Rose attempted to correct her.

Flora crossed her arms and stood in front of Anya. 'I'll not hear of any such thing. We have a room going begging here. It's no more than a box room, but you are welcome to it.'

'You would take me into your home without you know who I am? The nasty boy may be right. I may be a spy, but I can assure you I am no

Nazi,' she added with a shudder. 'You are generous woman, but I cannot take your charity.'

Rose hooted with laughter. 'It's not charity. Mum runs a boarding house. Lodgings,' she added, seeing Anya frown. 'She takes in paying guests.'

'I prefer to call Sea View a guest house,' Flora said, giving her daughter a prim look.

Rose chuckled before draining her cup and getting to her feet. 'I must have a wash and change my clothes. There's a dance at the Margate Winter Gardens this evening, and I've been asked to sing with the orchestra.'

'I wondered why you were home so early,' Flora sniffed, appearing not to approve. 'You'll get the sack before too long if you keep coming home in your work uniform, my girl.'

Rose shook her head, causing her shoulder-length blonde curls to ripple across her shoulders. 'The teashop is too understaffed for Miss Butterworth to give me the sack. Besides, she also let Lily and Katie leave early, as it was quiet. Would you like me to show Anya up to the room?' she asked, knowing how to keep her mum sweet.

Flora nodded. 'You'll find clean bed linen in the airing cupboard. Can you make up the bed, as I have the evening meals to finish?'

Anya noticed Rose's downturned expression. 'Please, I can make a bed. I have no wish to make you late for your dancing and singing.'

Flora sighed. Her daughter could charm the birds from the trees. 'That's very kind of you, Anya. When you've unpacked your things, please come back down to the kitchen and I'll have a meal ready for you.'

I'd also like to know a little more about you, she thought to herself as she turned to the task of peeling potatoes for their evening meal. There was food enough for Anya, regardless of whether she had a penny to her name. Flora would not see someone go hungry if she could help it.

★　★　★

Anya ran her hand over the freshly washed sheets. It had been a long journey, but she was now here and soon, with much luck, she would have answers. Her few items of clothing hung in the small wardrobe, and a hairbrush and bible lay on top of the chest of drawers. She could be happy here, and Flora and Rose Neville seemed very pleasant people. If only she had more money. Her next priority would be to find work. Yes, she needed to work to be able to stay and complete her mission. There was so much she needed to do, and after all this time her goal was almost within sight. She sighed as she thought of her past life and how different it was to be here in England. Poland was her home, and always would be; but for now she would concentrate on what she had to do and make the most of her circumstances.

A polite knock on the door brought her back to the present. 'Yes, who is it please?' she asked.

'It's only me,' Rose said as she entered the room and looked about her. 'I hope you will be comfortable. This was my room when I was a child. You can see the harbour from here,' she

24

said, going over to the window.

Anya joined her and they stood silently shoulder to shoulder, watching out over the dark sea lit by a pale moon. 'It is beautiful,' she whispered.

Rose glowed with pride. She loved her hometown, with its tall Georgian houses and the busy fishing port. It retained its charm even as locals prepared for the possibility of invasion, covering their windows with heavy curtains to cut out the smallest chinks of light — sometimes actually painting over the glass panes, so that if enemy aircraft should fly overhead they'd have little chance of seeing anything below. Rose's mum had been out day after day, carrying out her ARP warden duties with diligence, advising residents on how to prepare for any form of enemy attack. If Adolf should come, they would be ready. Why, even the boy scouts, who hadn't been evacuated, had been roped in to fill sandbags and distribute them to homes and businesses.

Giving Anya a sideways look, taking in the white skin and large grey eyes, Rose wanted to ask what had brought the woman here, but she knew it would appear rude. Perhaps in time Anya would share her story. 'You look tired,' Rose smiled in sympathy. 'Don't forget Mum said she'd have a meal for you; then perhaps you could put your head down and have a sleep?'

'Head down?' Anya frowned.

'It's something we say here in England. It means put your head down on your pillow and go to sleep.'

25

Anya thought for a moment before giving Rose a warm smile. 'I like that very much. Yes, I will be putting down of my head very soon. The day has been a long one. I think your language will be hard to understand.'

Rose sat down on the bed and laughed. 'It certainly is, but you put us to shame — we don't know one word of your language. Polish, is it?'

'Yes, I am Polish.'

'Poland is such a long way away. Whatever bought you to England?' Rose asked, completely forgetting that she had decided not to ask questions just yet.

'Yes, it is a very long way away . . . ' Anya said, gazing back out over the sea.

'You must miss it most terribly,' Rose said, knowing she was pushing for an answer.

Anya pulled the curtains together and turned to give Rose a bright smile. 'No, I no longer miss Poland. Now, tell me about your singing and dancing. I do like your pretty dress,' she said, stopping Rose from adding any further questions.

'This old thing? Why, I've had this for two years now. Miss Tibbs added a little lace trim and altered the neckline for me, so it looks as good as new.'

'Miss Tibbs?'

'She's one of our boarders and has lived here for years. You'll simply adore her — we all do. She used to be a dressmaker until she retired and closed her workshop. Now she does bits and bobs for neighbours and friends, which is very handy now rationing is starting to grip us all.

26

From what we hear, it won't be too long before even new clothing will be thin on the ground.'

'Bits and bobs . . . ?' Anya frowned. 'I think I have a lot to learn.'

Rose chuckled. She did like the polite Polish woman and hoped they'd become friends, even though it seemed strange her turning up as she had. She thought of the many foreign servicemen who came to the Lyons teashop while she was working. It would be lovely to share a few words with them, to make them feel welcome. 'Perhaps you could teach me something to say in Polish?'

Anya hesitated. 'Perhaps it is best we speak in English. Not everyone welcomes a foreign tongue. Now, again, I ask you to tell me about your singing?'

Rose shrugged her shoulders. She didn't like to talk about her dreams, especially to someone she'd just met. 'It's nothing much. Where we go dancing, they sometimes ask if anyone can carry a tune, and my friends pushed me up onto the stage. Carry a tune means to be able to sing a song,' she added, seeing a questioning expression cross Anya's face. 'I'll try to be more careful in what I say, as I can see it is a problem for you to understand me,' she said.

'No, please never do that,' Anya implored her. 'I must learn. I want to learn. It is important I learn.'

Rose thought Anya seemed surprisingly keen to learn the language, but she resolved again not to ask why. If the woman had secrets, who was she to poke her nose in and interfere? All the same, she must remember to tell her mum about the conversation. 'Shall we go downstairs and have that bite to eat? I don't have long before I need to be somewhere else.'

Anya smiled. 'Yes, a bite to eat would be very nice indeed and I understand you need to be . . . what you say . . . somewhere else,' she laughed. Rose took her arm and they headed down the two flights of stairs towards the sound of plates being put out on a table as Flora dished up their meal.

'It's only bubble 'n' squeak,' Flora said as she pushed the plate in front of Anya. 'But the hens have come up trumps, so we have a fried egg each. Miss Tibbs isn't back from her church meeting, so I'll feed her later.'

'Oh, Mum. Not fried food again. My dress and hair are going to smell like a chip shop. No one will dance with me,' Rose said, poking at the food with a fork.

'You can take it or leave it,' Flora huffed. 'I've got too much on my hands to pander to you, young woman. You don't find our guests complaining, and they pay for the privilege of living here.'

Anya, who had been tucking into her meal with relish, laid down her knife and fork and reached into her pocket, pulling out a small leather purse. 'Here, I must give you money for my food,' she said. 'What will it be?'

'It can wait,' Flora scolded. 'Get on with your meal before it goes cold.'

'If you are very sure,' the young woman said with a shy smile. 'I do not wish to . . . how you say . . . be beholden. I was very lucky that you came to rescue me.'

28

Rose, who had pushed her plate aside and was peering into her powder compact to top up her lipstick, gave Anya a questioning look. 'Where was you off to when those horrid little boys attacked you?'

'I was looking for a place called Margate. Do you know it?'

'Know it? It's where I'm off to this evening, dancing to the Silvano Caprice band.'

Anya's eyes lit up. 'Is this place — Margate — very far away? The bus driver was not helpful and would not tell me. I could not see any signs, and he told me to get off when the bus went no further.'

'P'raps he thought you was a German?' Rose said, running the red lipstick over her top lip and smiling into the small mirror.

Anya looked dismayed. 'But I am Polish. Anyone can tell that. I hate the Germans,' she added vehemently. 'They ruined my life.'

Flora had been thoughtful as the two girls spoke. 'What I don't understand is how you got here? Thanet is not such an attractive area to visit these days, since the war started; and January is no month for a holiday by the sea.'

'I met a man in London. He told me that for the right money, he could get me to Margate. He was a strange person and tapped his nose a lot when he spoke to me.' She demonstrated the action, adding a wink at the same time. 'He also wanted much money from me, but I gladly gave it, as I so much need to be here.'

'Hmm, he sounds like a bit of a spiv,' Flora said. 'How did he get you here?'

29

'I know not what is a speev, but I travelled in a lorry until we approach Thaneet, where the driver told me to hide under old sacking until he drop me off and told me to find a bus. Then I am lost, and you rescue me — for which I thank you once again.'

'Mum, do you think Anya has broken the law?' Rose asked, looking worried.

Flora was thoughtful. 'I don't know, but as movement is prohibited in and out of Thanet, I do believe there will be some explaining to do. I'll take you to the police station tomorrow and we can find out. I take it you do have identity papers?'

'I am legal. You wish to see?' Anya asked, reaching for her handbag.

'There's no need. Perhaps if we say you are a friend who has come to visit, they will be happy for you to stay here. That's unless you really do want to go to Margate?'

'I will stay here if I may. If the policeman says I can.'

'What's this about the police?' A large red-faced woman in a boiler suit entered the kitchen and went to the stove, rubbing her hands together to warm them. 'Has someone broken the law? Been caught smuggling Germans in on a fishing boat, have you?' she guffawed.

'Nothing so serious, Mildred,' Flora said as she rose to her feet to pour a cup of tea for the woman. 'Anya, this is another of my lodgers. Mildred, meet Anya.'

Anya held out her hand, which the older woman took and pumped up and down

30

enthusiastically. 'I am not German,' she said warily.

'If you were you'd not be welcomed here, I can tell you, but any friend of Flora's and all that . . . ' Mildred said, picking at the food Rose had left on her plate. 'Is there any more of this going begging?' she asked, taking the seat Rose had just vacated.

'I've got some keeping warm in the oven. It'll only take a few ticks to fry an egg. Have you had a busy shift?'

'You could say that. Some lads on a boat out of Margate had a mine caught up in their nets. By the time the navy mine disposal team arrived we'd helped to tow it out to sea and cut it loose. They'll no doubt blow it up soon, so prepare yourself for a bit of a bang.'

Flora put her hands on her hips and scowled at the rotund woman. 'You'll get yourself killed one of these days, and no mistake. Why you can't get yourself a nice job that any female would be pleased to do, instead of messing about with them fishing boats, I just don't know. Now go and wash your hands, or I'll not be putting any food in front of you. You're worse than any man.'

Anya gave a small smile. This household was not what she had expected at all. 'You go fishing, Mildred?' she asked, thinking how big the sea had looked when she arrived in the town just this afternoon.

'And a lot more,' Rose giggled as she took her coat from a hook on the kitchen door. 'I won't be late, Mum,' she told Flora, giving her a kiss.

'Make sure you're not, and be careful in the

31

blackout on that bicycle. Your knee has just cleared up after the last time you come a cropper. Where are you meeting Lily and Katie?'

'Aw, Mum, I'm not a little kid anymore. Don't fuss so.'

'I'll fuss and worry about you until I draw my dying breath,' Flora said. 'It's what mothers do.' She gave her daughter an indulgent smile and glanced at Anya, who had placed a hand on her stomach as she gazed into space, lost in her thoughts.

I know that look, Flora thought to herself as she placed Mildred's fried egg on top of the plate of hot bubble and squeak. It looked as if the next few months were going to be interesting . . . very interesting indeed.

2

Rose pushed into the crowded ladies' toilets and headed to a large cracked mirror over a washbasin. 'Just look at the state of my hair! I don't know why I bother, I really don't. I must look an absolute fright.'

'Here, use my hairbrush. You're lucky — your curls will soon bounce back into shape,' Lily Douglas said as she passed a small tortoiseshell hairbrush from her clutch bag before delving back inside for a lipstick. 'I don't know why we had to cycle here. I swear I swallowed a fly,' she added, checking her teeth in the cracked mirror and wiping off a speck of red lipstick. 'As for cycling in falling snow . . . ' she moaned to no one in particular. 'Here, Doris, I thought they was supposed to be changing this mirror. A girl can't see herself for cracks; especially in this crowd.' She gave a rotund woman next to her a sharp poke in the ribs. 'Here, watch it, won't you?'

The cleaner carried on scrubbing round the washbasins with a grubby cloth. 'The boss says it isn't worth it, as it's bound to crack again. Besides, all this talk of bombs and what have you — what's the point?' she added darkly.

'Aren't you a bundle of joy,' Lily said as she slipped the lipstick back into her bag. 'Are you done with that, Rose?'

Rose handed back the hairbrush and grimaced as she looked at her hair in the offending mirror. 'It doesn't look any better. I should have pinned it up but I couldn't find any kirby grips, and wearing a woolly hat did it no favours. There's me about to go up on the stage to sing, and I look as though I've been dragged through a hedge backwards. Perhaps I should say I've got a sore throat and will have to give it a miss?' she added sadly. 'I bet Helen Forrest never has problems like this before a performance.'

Lily sighed. 'Helen Forrest is a star, not a Nippy from Kent. For goodness' sake, come here and turn round,' she commanded, opening her bag and pulling out a couple of hairpins. 'I've always got a few spare.' She deftly brushed Rose's hair before folding it into a neat pleat at the back of her head and fastening it with the pins. 'Now, turn round to face me.' She looked at her friend with a frown before fluffing up the loose blonde curls on top of her head. 'Give me your lipstick and powder,' she added as she threw the brush into her bag. 'Hurry up, or the band will start without you.' She swiped the red lipstick over Rose's lips before putting a little onto her finger and dabbing each cheek. Swapping the lipstick for the powder compact, Lily rubbed in the colour and added a liberal amount of powder over Rose's cheeks. Stepping back as much as possible in the crowded room, she cocked her head to one side. 'Here, Doris, do you think she'll do?'

Doris stopped her scrubbing and looked carefully at Rose's face before giving a long sigh.

'As pretty as a picture. You'd give that Betty Grable a run for her money, take my word for it.'

Rose shook her head and gave a laugh. 'Oh, I don't know. The pair of you could give me a big head if I didn't know you were joking. Come on, Lily. Katie has saved us a table, but by now she could be hanging onto it for grim death. I spotted the girls from Woolies coming in just behind us and they'll be after a table. I don't want them shoving Katie out, even if she has put our coats on the seats.'

Rose led the way across the busy ballroom. All around her were men in uniform, and even a few women. She couldn't tell which service was best represented, but it looked like a close thing between the RAF and the navy. Talk at the Lyons tearooms was that they'd see more of the army any day soon, and anyone with a room to spare would have billeting officers banging on their front doors with the intention of foisting a soldier or two onto the unsuspecting family. Perhaps that was why her mum had been so quick to offer the box room to Anya, she thought as she waved to the leader of the band. He indicated he wanted her up on the stage, and she gave him a thumbs up.

'He's a bit keen,' Katie said as Rose sat beside her.

'I was only invited to sing a couple of songs during the whole of the dance,' Rose huffed. 'If he wants me up there for the evening he's going to have to pay me. I bet his regular singer hasn't arrived.'

'Stick to your guns,' Lily said as she joined

them, putting a tray of drinks on the table. 'These are from the sailors over by the bar,' she added, watching Katie to see if she picked up on her friend's words.

Usually the quietest of the three chums, Katie jumped to her feet and gave a shriek that had people around them looking to see what the problem was. 'It's Jack,' she cried, hurrying over towards where a sandy-haired sailor was pushing through the dancers to reach his fiancée. Katie fell into his arms and, oblivious to anyone watching, allowed him to sweep her off the floor and swing her round before they stopped to kiss.

'There goes love's young dream,' Lily said with a touch of sarcasm as she reached for a half-pint glass of light ale and took a deep draught.

'Oh, don't be so cynical. Katie loves Jack, and it's obvious he adores her too. I just hope they name the day soon, so that she gets to walk down the aisle before he's dragged off somewhere overseas and they don't see each other again for ages.'

'And if he don't come back she's going to end up with a baby and be stuck in a small room somewhere, hardly able to support herself, let alone a nipper. It's not as if she has any family to care for her, is it?'

Rose looked at her. The three friends had been close since they started school together, and it was Lily who'd always seemed the most worldly wise even though she'd hardly set foot outside of Thanet, let alone Kent. She had ambitions — not like Rose and Katie, who were happy to live in Ramsgate and work at the tearoom. Even with her friends Rose wasn't prepared to share her dream of being a professional singer, as it was just that — a dream.

Katie had been brought up in the local children's home. If it hadn't been for her two friends sticking by her and Rose's mum, Flora, kitting her out in hand-me-downs, the child would have had nothing to call her own. The three girls had even started work as Lyons Nippies on the same day, and travelled together to London for their formal training.

'Don't deny her a bit of happiness,' Rose said to Lily. 'She deserves some, and if worse comes to worst, we will be there to help her out. None of us know how this war's going to pan out, so let Katie have a bit of fun while she can, eh?'

'Blimey, you sound like your mum,' Lily laughed as she opened a packet of Player's cigarettes and offered one to Rose. 'Here, have one of these. I got them off a soldier who came into the teashop. He said it was by way of a tip.'

Rose refused the cigarette, making it clear she wasn't amused her friend was accepting gifts from customers, as it was against the rules laid down by their employer.

Lily ignored Rose and continued with her opinion. 'Blimey, your mum will be clucking round Katie before we know it if she does get herself married and up the duff.'

'Mum's not that bad. She just likes looking after people, and they do appreciate it. Look how many have stayed on at Sea View since the war started.'

Lily snorted with laughter. 'Her lame ducks,

do you mean? They know what side their bread's buttered. She'll not be rid of them that easily.'

Rose felt uncomfortable. She didn't like to hear Lily speak about her mum's lodgers in such a way. When she thought of Miss Tibbs, who'd lived with them as long as Rose could remember, and Mildred, who could fix anything from a dripping tap to the engine on a fishing boat, it was as if they were part of her family. Joyce Hannigan, with her young daughter, Pearl, rented two rooms at the back of the house and they had fitted perfectly into the group of residents from the day they arrived. Rose thought they were a delightful family. Then there was Mr Cardew, who kept himself to himself and even took his meals in his room these days; Mum only ever saw him to collect a dirty plate and hand over his washing. Tell a lie, Rose smiled to herself — he does pop in to the kitchen on a Friday evening to hand over his rent money. She wondered what he would think of the new lodger.

'What's tickled you?' Lily frowned.

Rose shrugged. 'Nothing much,' she replied, but knew that Lily would wheedle it out of her. She could never keep a secret from her friend. 'I was just thinking about our new lodger. Mum's given her the box room. She's not from around here,' she added thoughtfully.

Lily's eyes lit up. 'Really? Is she a foreigner? You know they picked up some chap the other week, charged him as being a spy then carted him off to the Tower of London?'

'Oh really, Lily, I despair! You should know

better by now than to listen to our customers' gossip. Much of it has no basis in truth. Besides, Anya is Polish — and don't look like that,' Rose added, noticing the way Lily was starting to sneer. 'I don't know what's come into you lately. You're either biting people's heads off, or you're picking holes in everything. You used to be a barrel of laughs, but not these days.'

It was Lily's turn to shrug her shoulders. 'If truth be known, I'm fed up with my life. There's nothing to do apart from go to work and come home again. This war is becoming boring. I thought we'd be able to have some fun with so many servicemen in the area, but so far I've not seen any fun at all. If that Polish person was a spy, at least it would add some excitement to our lives.'

Rose shook her head in despair. She'd noticed lately that Lily wasn't the life and soul of the party the way she used to be. No doubt this was down to the sad loss of her mother. 'But we're having a good time tonight, aren't we? And you always seem so cheerful when we're serving the customers? You've been out a few times with the soldiers we've met. As for Anya being a spy, we have enough strange people living at Sea View as it is. That Mr Cardew fair gives me the creeps, the way he moves around at night. I can hear the floorboards creak while I'm in my bed.'

Lily reached for her cigarettes and lit one, not thinking to offer them again to Rose. She was too caught up in her own thoughts to respond to her friend's comments about Mr Cardew. 'If I don't smile at the customers at work, I get told off. It's a fine line between being friendly and being over-friendly at Lyons.'

Rose knew instantly what Lily was referring to. 'I think chatting to those army chaps was seen to be over-friendly by Miss Butterworth. A smile is one thing, but perching your backside on their table and sharing a risqué joke was taking things a bit too far.'

'I didn't mean anything by it. Blimey, there wasn't even time for one of them to ask me out before Miss Butterworth came running over! Then she blamed me for them walking out without paying for their meal. It wasn't my fault they called her Miss Prissy Knickers, was it?'

Rose felt her face twitch as she tried not to smile. Lily was her own worst enemy at times. 'Anyway, we're having a nice time this evening, aren't we?' she said brightly.

Lily drew deeply on her cigarette and blew smoke circles into the air. 'If you say so. But cycling to a dance hall with the snow blowing in our faces and then paying for our own tickets isn't exactly glamorous, is it? If those squaddies hadn't stopped and given us a lift we'd have been in a right state by the time we got here.'

Rose knew Lily had a point, but now wasn't the time to discuss such things. She hadn't felt comfortable being hauled into the back of a lorry and having so many 'helping hands' assist her.

Out the corner of her eye, she could see the bandleader looking in her direction. She was needed on stage before too long and didn't want to leave her friend in a bad mood. 'Perhaps we could get the bus next time?'

'I suppose so, or better still we could have some of those sailors pick us up. Katie could put a good word in for us,' Lily said, looking to where Katie was standing with Jack's arm protectively round her shoulders as they chatted to his mates.

'I'm not sure Katie knows any other sailors. Are you forgetting she knew Jack before he joined the navy?'

Lily looked even glummer. 'I wish I could just run away to London. At least I'd see some nightlife.'

'Well, with no money or job you'd see the wrong kind of nightlife, and God knows what would happen to you then,' Rose said, getting to her feet. 'I've got to go — Silvano Caprice is waving at me to get over there and sing.'

Lily snorted with laughter. 'You mean Sam Coggins with his trumpet? Everyone knows he's made up some fancy name just so he sounds like an American bandleader. You want to watch him or he'll get his wicked way, and then where will you be? I've heard too many stories about him for them not to be true. Just you watch yourself.'

'Silvano or Sam, I don't care. At least I get the chance to sing on a stage. You aren't the only one who wants to enjoy herself,' Rose snapped as she turned to push her way through the crowd on the dance floor. Everyone was trying to get closer to the stage, knowing it was time for the entertainment to start.

'Ouch! Watch out,' a male voice exclaimed as Rose stumbled against a soldier and tried not to tread on his toes without success. He caught her

41

as she lost her footing, and for just a few seconds he held her securely until she'd righted herself.

'I'm sorry,' she apologized, trying to move on. She could hear the first few strains of the melody.

'It's no trouble, I'll live,' he said in a rich, well-spoken voice, causing her to look up into the deepest steel-grey eyes she'd ever seen in a man.

'I . . . er,' she started to say, stumbling over her words. For some reason she couldn't quite catch her breath. The warmth of his hands on her arms was all she could concentrate on, apart from those eyes. 'I've got to go. The bandleader's waiting for me,' she apologized.

On stage, Silvano was announcing that a Ruby Norris was about to sing. Rose pulled away and pushed her way to the stage, hurrying up the few steps to stand in front of the band. Silvano gave her a hard stare before nodding to the band and raising his trumpet to his lips. She'd cut it fine, getting to the stage only just before her part of the song began. As the notes from the trumpet faded away she started to sing, her sweet voice soaring over the crowd of dancers, who stopped to watch and listen.

'*You made me love you* . . . ' Rose put her heart and soul into the song as she'd never done before. Each word resonated through her body. She could drift away on the lyrics: in her mind she was no longer in Ramsgate, but singing in a posh London hotel. Or even on stage in America with a big band accompanying her, like she'd seen so many times in the movies. When it was

Silvano's turn to play a refrain, she closed her eyes and dreamt of those few moments when the soldier had held her captive. As she started to sang once more her eyes scanned the room for him, but she couldn't see him amongst the sea of uniforms. 'You know you made me love you . . . ' she pleaded into the audience as she sung the last few words of the song. Could she fall in love that quickly, was it possible?

To thunderous applause, Rose started to leave the stage, but she was caught by Silvano behind the curtains that led to the steps down to the dance floor. 'Not so quick,' he said, grabbing her roughly around the waist. 'I thought me and you could go for a drink later? I've got a good bottle of whisky back at my place. We could share it . . . '

Rose flinched. There had been rumours about Silvano and the women he chased going all the way back to their schooldays. To say he would love them and leave them was an understatement. 'I'd rather not, if you don't mind. Unless you want me to sing again tonight, I'll go back to my friend,' she said, pulling away.

'Be friendlier, Rose, and you can sing your pretty little heart out,' he said, pulling her closer.

Rose snorted with laughter and pushed him away. 'My friends are waiting for me,' she said firmly, trying not to let him see how he made her skin crawl.

Silvano shrugged his shoulders. 'I'll stop asking one day, and then you'll be sorry,' he called to her departing back.

She ignored his words and headed back to the

table, where Katie and her fiancé had joined them along with a couple of Jack's sailor buddies. They all congratulated her as she sat down and took a sip from her glass.

'Blimey, girl, you was good tonight, even if everyone thinks your name is Ruby.' Lily patted her on the back, her earlier grumpy mood forgotten. 'Anyone would think you was singing to just one bloke in the audience.'

Rose chuckled. Was it that obvious, she wondered? 'Silvano is playing well this evening, and it helped me get into the mood of the song,' she said.

Lily laughed. They'd all known Silvano since they were at school, and she couldn't get used to his stage name. However much she tried, he would always be Sam Coggins to her. 'He ain't no Harry James, but he can play a trumpet OK,' she begrudgingly acknowledged.

Rose wasn't listening. She was still replaying those few moments after bumping into the soldier with the steel-grey eyes.

★ ★ ★

Rose was aware of Miss Butterworth glaring at her back as she slipped off her coat and went to the tiny staffroom mirror, which hung from a piece of old bootlace on the wall of the little room. She pinned her white cap in place and checked for stray hairs, then looked down to make sure her shoes were not scuffed and a ladder had not mysteriously appeared in her black stockings. She was trying to breathe deeply

44

as she awaited the telling-off she knew was coming. She didn't have to wait long.

'Miss Neville, I believe you wore your uniform home yet again. What do you have to say about this?'

Rose gave a big sigh and turned with the brightest smile she could muster. Inside she was seething. The old battle-axe was picking on her yet again. 'I needed to stitch a couple of buttons that had come loose,' she replied, crossing her fingers behind her back. She hated to lie, but sometimes there was just no way out of it.

Miss Butterworth thought for a moment, looking Rose up and down as she did so. 'Are you sure you haven't shortened your uniform as well? Come to my office at once so I can measure the length,' she added, turning round and marching swiftly from the room.

Rose followed obediently, knowing that to argue would have been futile. Without blowing her own trumpet, she knew she was good at her job and got on well with the customers. Miss Butterworth also knew that, and there lay the bone of contention. Clarice Butterworth should have retired long ago, but with war looming, the area manager had requested she stay on in her job and be promoted to oversee the teashop staff. So many of the male managers were either being called up, or were keen to do their bit for King and Country and were volunteering for the services. Before her promotion Miss Butterworth had served in the kitchen area, and it was only by length of service that she had beaten Rose to the job of manageress. She was more than aware that

Rose would be a popular choice for manageress amongst the staff.

'Stand still,' she commanded as Rose wriggled to pull the drop-waisted black dress down as much as possible, muttering that it had shrunk in the wash. Miss Butterworth held a wooden ruler from the hemline to the floor.

'It's as I thought. This dress has been turned up. Do you have no shame?' she sneered, only inches from Rose's face. 'Lyons is a respectable company, and will not have its female staff behaving like harlots while working under their roof. Take a spare dress from the storeroom and change your clothes this instant. You will have to work late to make up for your time, and you will also let down that hem in your own time and bring it back to show me first thing tomorrow morning. Now, hurry along.'

Rose bit her lip to stop herself answering back as she hurried from the room. She'd not altered her dress, and Miss Butterworth would have seen as much when she looked at the sewing-machine stitching around the hem. Rose's hand stitching left a lot to be desired, and it would have been obvious to Miss Butterworth when her nose was so close to the fabric.

Rose had planned to go to the picture house with Lily this evening to see *Jamaica Inn* — she had longed to see the film ever since she'd read the book. She knew she'd be late now. She would have to tell her friend not to wait for her after work, so she hung about close to the office door, as Lily would be passing by with food for the tables on her workstation.

As she lingered she could hear murmured conversation from inside the room, where a younger Nippy had gone in as Rose came out. Suddenly the door opened again and the girl came rushing out in floods of tears, heading for the staffroom. Rose hurried after her, not wishing to see anyone in such distress.

'Whatever has upset you so?' she asked as she caught up.

'Miss Butterworth told me I was the worst Nippy she had ever seen. She told me I was scruffy and no good at my job,' the girl said, wiping her eyes with a handkerchief.

Rose frowned. 'It's Clara, isn't it?' she asked, looking at the girl hunched up against the table.

'Yes. I started last month. I didn't think I was *that* bad at my job. I've not dropped one plate this week so far.'

Rose gave a little chuckle. It was a new Nippy's worst fear to break a plate. 'No, you're not a bad Nippy at all. Why, from what I heard, you passed your training course with flying colours.' And there lies the problem, she thought. Clarice Butterworth was down on any staff member who might possibly do better than herself.

'I did do rather well. I worked really hard, because I wanted this job so badly,' Clara said with a watery smile. 'She also said I'd stitched a button on wrong,' she added, looking down at her uniform with its neat row of buttons down the front.

Rose could see the problem at once. 'Ah, you've used white thread instead of red. Lyons are particular about the style of our uniforms,

47

and as silly as it may seem, we have to use red thread to attach the white buttons to our black dresses.'

The girls both laughed together as Rose pulled open a drawer under the table. 'Here — we keep some needles threaded with red cotton for emergencies. There's also some black darning thread in case we snag our stockings. A few quick stitches will carry us through our shift, so we don't get told off. Let's sort out that button now, shall we?'

Rose quickly removed the offending button and reattached it while the young Nippy gave grateful thanks. 'Now, run along to your workstation before you get told off again. If you become upset at all, you can speak to me anytime.'

'Thank you, Rose,' Clara said, and hurried from the room.

Rose tidied up the sewing threads and went to follow. She was pulled up short by the sight of the area manager, Mr Grant, standing by the door looking thoughtful. 'Sorry, sir — I'll get back to my workstation at once.'

'Not so fast, Miss Neville. Do you often help out the younger staff?'

Rose took a deep breath. No doubt this was where she got in trouble for not serving her customers. 'It took no time at all, sir, and the poor girl was upset. She'll be fine now. I had just come from Miss Butterworth's office myself, so was close by.'

He frowned. 'Why would you be seeing Miss Butterworth?'

'She'd noticed the hem of my waitress dress was the wrong length. I have to stay after work to correct it,' Rose explained, trying hard not to make it look as though she was telling tales out of school.

'Your hem looks perfectly fine to me,' he said, looking stern. 'Perhaps Miss Butterworth was mistaken on this occasion. I take it you had plans for this evening?'

Rose was puzzled by his question. 'Yes, sir, I was meant to be attending the picture house with my friend to see *Jamaica Inn*.'

'Then you leave your shift at the right time, and enjoy your evening. I took my wife to see the film the other night and it was most splendid. I'm sure you will enjoy it.'

'Thank you, sir — but Miss Butt — '

'You leave Miss Butterworth to me, Miss Neville. Now run along to your workstation — and well done for helping that young lady. Most commendable.'

'Yes, sir,' Rose whispered, and hurried from the staffroom.

'There you are,' Katie hissed as Rose bumped into her friend in the seating area of the teashop. 'We've had a bit of a rush on, and I'm doing my best to cover your tables as well as my own. Where have you been?' she asked as she cleared a nearby table that had just been vacated by two women laden down with shopping bags.

'The old trout caught me. I swear she's got it in for me.'

Katie was sympathetic. 'Do try to keep on her good side. I heard she might be leaving us soon. Her sister is poorly and has no one to care for her.'

'It can't come quick enough as far as I'm concerned,' Rose said, wiping the table with a cloth and helping Katie to lay out fresh cutlery. 'She's had it in for me ever since she was promoted — doesn't miss a chance to put me down or make me work late. I really don't know why.'

'She knows she got the job because of her age rather than her ability to serve customers, and she's noticed that you're good with the staff *and* customers. Just bide your time. It'll all come out in the wash.' Katie gave Rose's arm a friendly squeeze before lifting the heavy tray to take back to the kitchen. 'Oh, there's someone wanting a word with you over there. I sat him at one of your tables and mentioned he might have to wait,' she added with a grin.

Rose's heart skipped a beat. Perhaps it would be the handsome army captain with the gorgeous grey eyes. She knew he didn't know her name, let alone where she worked, but it didn't stop her dreaming. Straightening her cap and rubbing the toe of each black shoe in turn on the back of her legs to remove any dust, she pinned on her best smile and headed towards her section of tables. They were set behind a marble-effect pillar and a large brass pot holding an enormous fern. There was already a couple waiting to be served, with the man tapping his fingers on the table in an impatient manner. Rose quickly took their order, discussing what was available from the tariff card. Although the war had already brought food shortages, thankfully restaurants were still unaffected, so there was a good selection for Lyons customers. After quickly taking their order to the counter, Rose hurried back to her section of the tearoom.

Through the fronds of the fern she could see a gentleman's back — and he was wearing the jacket of an army officer. Could it possibly be her mysterious captain? Nodding to a man who had just been seated to indicate she had seen him, she circumnavigated the large potted plant and stopped dead in her tracks as she recognized the officer. 'Oh, hello, Silvano. What are you doing here — and why are you in uniform?' she asked, as she felt her heart sink into her shoes.

'Sit yourself down. I have something to say to you,' he said, indicating the chair opposite.

'I'm at work, if you hadn't noticed,' she hissed. 'Apart from which, I really don't have a thing to say to you after the way you acted the other night.'

'Come on, love; I thought you liked me enough to spare a few minutes of your precious time. I've got something important to put to you.'

Rose looked over to where Miss Butterworth was now presiding over the cash register. The small desk set on a raised plinth meant her boss's beady eyes didn't miss much that went on in the teashop. She was admonishing Lily over something, so had her attention away from the other Nippies busy working at their assigned tables.

'Hurry up and say what you've got to say. I could get the sack if I'm not careful,' Rose hissed, sliding into a seat opposite Silvano. 'I'm hoping you will start with an apology, followed by an explanation as to why you're in that

51

get-up. You know it's an offence to impersonate an officer. But knowing you, you'd impersonate Adolf to get attention.'

Silvano gave a big sigh. 'If only you'd stop your wittering on, I'll tell you my news.'

Rose stopped talking and glared at him.

'Right, I know I'll never hear the end of it if I don't say sorry for the other night. I had things on my mind, as you can see,' he said, indicating his uniform jacket with a flourish of his manicured hand.

'That was no excuse for forgetting my name, then pawing me like that. It's not as if you pay me for singing with your band. So I want something out of our deal,' Rose pouted.

'And that's why I'm here,' he said, leaning across the table and taking her hand to give it a squeeze.

'Well, tell me then, and hurry up about it,' she said, glancing from left to right in case someone was watching. She didn't feel it was quite proper for him to be hanging onto her hand like this in a public place. She tried to pull away, but he was holding on tight.

'Have you heard about ENSA?'

Rose nodded. 'Who hasn't? Every Night Something Awful,' she grinned.

He ignored her comment. 'I've been invited to organize a touring party to entertain the troops,' he said proudly.

'I take it you were called up?' she said. She knew he lived in fear of joining the services, which would put paid to his leisurely life along with the wheeling and dealing he was partial to.

52

Silvano wriggled in his seat. Rose knew him far too well. 'You could say they made me an offer I couldn't refuse. My group of entertainers will be touring France before too long. That's why I wanted to speak to you.'

Rose's eyes lit up. With a bit of luck, Silvano's replacement as bandleader would give her more opportunities to sing. She might even get paid enough to stop working at the Lyons teashop. 'Hurry up and tell me, before my boss catches on that I'm not serving my customers,' she hissed, at the same time crossing her fingers that he was the bearer of good news. There again, if she was offered a job with the new bandleader she could tell old Butterworth where to shove her job. Deep inside Rose still yearned to sing for a living, even though she knew it didn't make sense for girls like her to do such work.

'I'm taking the band with me on tour. So if you sign up with ENSA, you may well find yourself with me all the time — if you get my drift?' Silvano said this in the silky way he usually saved for the women who flocked to the edge of the stage when he was talking to his audience. He rubbed the palm of Rose's hand with his thumb, holding on tightly as she tried to pull away. 'You and me could see the world together,' he winked seductively.

Rose understood only too well what he was suggesting, and with a mighty tug she freed her hand from his grip and stood up quickly. The sudden movement caused her chair to topple over with a crash.

All she'd ever dreamt of was being a singer for

53

one of the big American bandleaders like Harry James, or perhaps Tommy Dorsey. Silvano wasn't a bit like Harry James, but a job with him could be a stepping stone to greater opportunities. However, Rose had standards, and would not stoop to running off and living in sin as his mistress. News travelled fast in Ramsgate; not only would her name be tarred for life, her mum's reputation would be ruined too. She'd not do that to Flora in a million years. She'd heard talk that Silvano was already father to more than one child, although he always strenuously denied such things.

'What do you take me for, Sam Coggins?' she shouted, reverting to his proper name. 'I'm not some flighty bit who'd drop her drawers at the mention of travelling with you. You'd best take yourself off to the stage door and pick on some unsuspecting girl. I'm no strumpet, and you should know that, being a local lad.'

Silvano looked around him in panic. It was well known that he had done his best to shake off his birth name, and that he came from humble beginnings as the son of a fisherman. 'Shh — someone might hear,' he said as he nodded and smiled at the people seated at a nearby table.

'For Christ's sake, keep it down,' Lily hissed, hurrying over from behind the bakery counter. 'Old Butterworth will hear you! And the mood she's in, she'll be giving you your marching orders. It isn't worth it for the likes of him,' she whispered, giving Silvano a dirty look before noticing he was in uniform. 'You know you can get nicked for impersonating an officer?'

'You can shut your mouth for a start,' he sneered, standing up to face her. 'I came in here to make a proposition to Rose, and it's none of your business.'

'We know the sort of propositions you make, Sam Coggins, and Rose isn't that kind of a girl. Now, be on your way before I call the coppers.'

Silvano pushed past the two girls and walked briskly from the teashop.

'And you forgot this,' Lily shouted, running after him and throwing his cap out the door.

Rose righted the chair and sat down. She felt as though the bubble holding all of her dreams had popped, leaving her feeling empty and more than a little sad.

Lily returned to her friend, looking worried. 'Butterworth's on the warpath, so look lively.'

Rose knew she was in trouble going by the thunderous look on her boss's face. She could see no way of wriggling out of it.

As Clarice Butterworth was only a few feet away, Katie appeared with a glass of water. 'Excuse me, Miss Butterworth, this is for Rose. She became rather faint after that customer made rude suggestions to her.'

Lily tried not to smile as she went along with Katie's story and picked up a menu from the table to fan the face of a stunned Rose.

Miss Butterworth looked between the three girls, suspecting they were up to something. 'You do look flushed, Neville. You're not . . . er . . . you're not with child?'

'No, she isn't,' Lily and Katie both said in unison.

'Rose is a good girl,' Katie added, jutting her chin out in indignation.

'I think she should go home and rest,' Lily suggested, helping Rose to her feet. 'She's no help to anyone in this state.'

'Get your things,' Miss Butterworth snapped. 'And I want you back here bright and early tomorrow morning. We have Mr Grant, the area manager, visiting again for an inspection, as well as a new salesman from head office. I want the tearoom looking spick and span.'

Rose nodded without saying a word. If the truth were known, she did feel faint, but it had more to do with her disappointment at not being able to sing with the band anymore. Katie took her elbow and guided her around the potted palm to go to the staffroom. 'I'll see you at the cinema this evening,' she whispered to her friend.

It was Katie's turn to look glum. 'There's no point. The theatres and cinemas are all closed. A customer just informed me; she said it's for the duration of the war. It could soon be the dance halls as well.'

Rose groaned to herself. The day was getting worse by the minute. No singing, and now no pictures and no dancing. She'd started to wonder what it took to become a nun when she spotted the man sitting at one of her tables. It was the army captain with the lovely grey eyes. Because of Silvano, she had missed the opportunity to finally speak to him. He looked up as she walked past the table and gave her a knowing smile. Please don't say he'd been sitting there and overheard all of her conversation! She was far too embarrassed to stop and have a few words, instead dashing to the staffroom for her coat before leaving by the kitchen door.

3

Rose pulled her coat around her and huddled against the wooden bench as she stared out to sea. It was bitterly cold, and she knew it would be best if she headed home and had a cup of something hot to warm herself up. But Mum would be at home; she wasn't due at the ARP station today, unless there was a sudden air-raid warning. There'd been so many false alarms lately. The last thing Rose wanted was to be quizzed as to why she wasn't at work.

She pulled her felt hat down to try and cover the tips of her cold ears. As usual, she'd left her knitted scarf and gloves behind at home when she'd hurried out the door, not wanting to be late for work.

Her life felt as grey as the day. There was hardly anyone about, and the few ships outside the harbour seemed to be waiting silently for something to happen — just as she was. She didn't even have her singing to look forward to, now that Silvano was heading off to entertain the troops. Perhaps she should join him after all, she thought as she chewed at a fingernail and contemplated her dreary future. No, that wasn't an option, a small voice inside her head told her sharply. He was only after one thing. Look at the amount of times she'd had to duck out of his grasp back-stage when she'd sung with his band.

If she were alone in digs and he started his funny business, God only knows what would become of her. She just had to face it; she was stuck here for the duration of the war. No doubt she would end up an old maid, like Miss Tibbs and Mildred Dalrymple. A small sob caught in her throat, and before she knew it she was sobbing into her handkerchief.

'I say, I do hope there's nothing wrong?' a kindly voice enquired.

Rose looked up, and her heart immediately skipped a beat. It was the grey-eyed army captain. He looked as handsome as he had in the fleeting moments she was with him in the dance hall. Broad shoulders under his greatcoat and a twinkle in his eye, even though he looked concerned. Trust her to be red-faced and not looking her best. She felt a terrible mess.

'I didn't mean to startle you,' he said, showing concern. 'I'll be on my way and leave you to your thoughts.'

'Please don't go on my account,' she said, not wanting him to disappear in case their meeting had been a dream. 'I'm just feeling a little sorry for myself. It's been a rather tiring day. Please — take a seat,' she added, indicating the other end of the long bench on which she was perched.

'I take it your boyfriend upset you. I couldn't help but overhear some of your conversation in the teashop,' he added, seeing her startled expression.

'No — no, it's not like that at all,' she faltered, feeling shocked that he thought she was in some way attached to Silvano. 'That man is . . . a nasty

59

piece of work.' It was one of her mum's favourite sayings.

'Please excuse my bad manners. I'm Benjamin Hargreaves . . . Captain Benjamin Hargreaves,' he said, holding out his hand after removing a glove.

Rose trembled as they shook hands. 'I'm pleased to meet you. I'm Rose Neville,' she replied in a quiet voice, no more than a whisper. She was feeling quite overcome by this man. She'd dreamt of him holding her hand, if only for a few seconds.

'Rose Neville,' he said thoughtfully. 'Singer, Nippy and the woman who breaks men's hearts.'

She felt her cheeks start to burn. 'Are you making fun of me?' she asked indignantly.

'No, not at all,' he said, raising his hands as if to fend off her fury. 'Are you not aware of how men watch you when you sing? Especially the band leader who is so enamoured of you,' he added, his face twitching as he tried not to laugh at her affronted expression.

'I just like to sing,' Rose replied. 'The music and the words take over. I feel as if I'm someone else — I can tell a story, and serenade all the servicemen and women who are far from home.'

Benjamin watched her as her eyes took on a faraway expression. There was something about Rose Neville that fascinated him. A brave woman who could step onto a stage and sing her heart out in front of hundreds of people, and more than captivate him — and the next moment put someone like Silvano Caprice in his place. What puzzled him was why she was a waitress, albeit for the well-known Lyons chain. 'You certainly love to sing,' he said, not wanting to break the spell. 'So why are you working as a waitress, if you don't mind me asking?'

Rose shrugged her shoulders. 'It's a job I enjoy, and besides, there's only me and my mum. A singing job would no doubt take me away from her. It wouldn't be fair, not with everything in life being so uncertain. At least I can sing and be a waitress. I'm only really happy when I sing,' she replied, giving him a shy smile. 'You will think me daft, but I've never told anyone that before,' she added.

'Then I take it as an honour that you've shared such a confidence. But I must say, it seems a shame you aren't making your living as a singer. You are as good as the women who front the big bands in London and America.'

'You've heard them and seen them?' Rose gasped in delight.

'Before the war my work took me to America a few times, and I was fortunate enough to hear Bing Crosby and also Ella Fitzgerald. Then recently, in London, I attended a concert where Vera Lynn was entertaining the troops. Believe me when I say, you sing as well as they do any day. I'm not pulling your leg, if you'll forgive the phrase. I really mean it.'

Rose's eyes shone. 'Please tell me . . . did you hear Helen Forrest sing? She's my favourite.'

'Sadly not, but I do have a couple of her records, and I agree with you. She can belt out a song.'

Rose laughed, and Benjamin smiled as he saw

the woman beside him blossom as she relaxed in his company. 'I'd love to hear her sing. It would be magic.'

It was magic when I heard you sing, he wanted to tell her; but he thought it too forward to say aloud. 'You'd go down a storm in London singing with the big bands.'

Rose shrugged her shoulders. 'As I said, I don't want to leave my mum on her own, especially to run off to have fun — and it would be fun,' she added wistfully. 'No, I'm happy here.' She spoke as if confirming something to herself, shaking her head until her felt hat was in danger of flying off.

'I'm sorry,' Benjamin said. 'I had no right to ask you such a question — we've only known each other a few minutes. I do apologize. Look, do you fancy a cup of tea? I don't know about you, but I'm frozen to the core, and I swear this snow is getting heavier by the minute. It will engulf us if we aren't careful.' He gave Rose a gentle smile. 'Would you join me?'

Rose only took a minute to decide. She was in no rush to let go of this delightful man she'd been dreaming about since that night at the dance. 'I'd love to; but we'd best not go to Lyons teashop, as I'm supposed to have gone home sick.' She grinned as he held out his hand to help her to her feet.

'You're not really ill, are you?' he asked as he tucked her arm through his and they strolled along the seafront, past the barbed-wire fencing that stopped the public getting down to the sea below the harbour wall.

'I was upset by what happened, but I'm not ill. That was Lily's idea to get me out of trouble with Miss Butterworth. I'm not really one for getting out of working, Captain Hargreaves,' she added, worried in case Benjamin thought she was the sort of person who would wriggle out of doing a day's work.

'I didn't think that for one moment. And you must stop calling me Captain — I'm Benjamin. In fact, I prefer Ben, so please, let's drop the formal names.'

Rose grinned. 'I will, and I'm Rose, plain and simple.'

'Rose, you're anything but plain.' He smiled down at her as they stopped in front of a small cafe. 'Will here do?'

'It will do just fine,' she beamed back as he opened the door and led her into the steamy interior. 'Oh dear!'

'Is there something wrong?' he enquired as she stopped dead in her tracks. 'It's not that chap Silvano, is it?' He looked around at the tables where people sat chatting. 'We can go somewhere else, if you wish?'

'No, I'm happy to stay here. I spotted someone who stays at my mum's guesthouse. Miss Tibbs is a darling lady, but she will be home and telling Mum that I'm courting and all sorts before we've finished drinking out tea.'

'Does that bother you?' he asked, pulling back a chair for her to sit down.

'No . . . but the ladies who live with us are awfully keen to see me walk down the aisle. I only have to be seen with a man and they can hear wedding bells and smell orange blossom.'

'Then let's give them something to talk about,' he said as he bent over and gave her a brief kiss on the cheek.

Rose froze in her seat. Goodness knows what would get back to her mum now. She put a hand to her cheek and thought how gentle his lips felt on her skin, then gave herself a shake. For heaven's sake, he was joshing. The kiss meant nothing, nothing at all. She picked up the piece of card that constituted a menu and tried to concentrate on the words. If she looked to the right, she just knew Ben would be watching her. Look left, and Miss Tibbs and her cronies would have put down their knitting and be twittering on about whether Flora Neville knew her daughter had snared herself an army captain — and her just a plain and simple Nippy from a Lyons teashop!

'Why the glum face?' Ben asked as he removed his army greatcoat and hung it over the back of an empty chair. 'I say, I've not put you on the spot with the old lady, have I? I wasn't thinking,' he said apologetically. Inwardly, though, he was pleased to have kissed Rose, as he'd been aching to do since he first met her.

'Don't worry about it; Mum will understand. It's not as if I'm a child. Why, some of the girls I went to school with are married and have children. My friend Katie is engaged to a sailor and hopes to be married soon, before he is shipped off to God knows where.'

Ben was thoughtful and stared at the menu Rose passed to him without reading a single word.

'A penny for them . . . ?'

'Sorry?'

'A penny for your thoughts; you seem to be miles away,' she said with a frown. 'Was it something I said?'

Ben forced himself away from his thoughts. 'It's me who should be apologizing. Tell me, who is your friend's fiancé serving with?'

Rose frowned. 'I have no idea, beyond him being in the Royal Navy and something to do with a medical unit. Katie's relieved he won't be caught up in any fighting.' She watched Ben's face closely. 'You think differently, don't you?'

Ben nodded slowly before looking to left and right to see if they could be overheard. 'Every man will be caught up in the fighting, as your friend puts it. Look, I shouldn't be saying this. It's not as if we know each other very well.'

'I did step on your foot,' Rose said, trying to put a smile on his serious face.

The smile appeared for a second, then disappeared. 'If I were you, I'd advise your friend to marry her sweetheart while she can. We never know what's on the horizon, and . . . '

' . . . And it is better to have some memories. Is that what you're saying?' Rose finished his sentence for him.

Ben's face broke into a gentle smile, creating small laughter lines around his eyes as he reached across the table and took both her hands in his. 'You are right. Better still not to fall in love in wartime and leave broken hearts behind,' he said, a shadow crossing his face fleetingly.

It's far too late for that, she thought to herself,

65

although she wondered what had happened to change his expression. 'I agree. Perhaps friendship is best for everyone until Herr Hitler's been sent packing.'

'Are you two lovebirds going to order something?' an elderly waitress said as she shuffled over to their table with a notebook and pencil in hand. 'If not, can you be on your way, as I've got people waiting.'

'A pot of tea for two, and perhaps two slices of your gypsy tart, if we may?'

'It will have to be one thin slice, and you can share. We can't get the sugar, yer know,' she huffed as she shuffled off towards the counter, putting her pencil behind her ear.

'Welcome to Ramsgate,' Rose grinned as she pulled away from him, knowing the spell was broken — for now.

★   ★   ★

'Pass that tray of loaves to me, Katie,' Lily called to where her friend was arranging rock buns amongst the cardboard display cakes that stood behind a glass screen in the window of the teashop. 'The area manager's going to be here before too long, and Miss Butterworth will give us what for if the place isn't spick and span.'

Katie handed over the heavy wooden tray. 'Here, take the other end before I drop it. She'll have our guts for garters then,' she grinned.

'You look blooming happy considering the long day we've got ahead of us,' Lily said as she stepped back to admire the food laid out in the

66

window and along the shelves behind the counter. 'Has it got anything to do with your Jack and a certain wedding, by any chance?'

'It might have, but I'm not saying just yet. Wait until Rose is with us, then I'll share my news, otherwise I've got to say it all over again. Do you want me to go outside to check the window display in case something's not right? You know what the old dragon's like. I swear she keeps a tape measure in her pocket to make sure we line the buns up straight.'

'Go on then, but look snappy. There's a queue forming out front already. Don't let any of them in,' Lily called as Katie unlocked the door. Lily took out a small dust-pan and brush and carefully brushed away any crumbs from the food she'd been laying out. It wouldn't do to have Miss Butterworth on their backs this early in the morning just because they forgot to sweep up crumbs.

Katie nodded hello to a few of the customers she recognized in the queue. 'We will be open soon,' she smiled before wiping down the window ledges and stepping back to inspect the white-painted shop front with the gold lettering that distinguished Lyons teashops from other tearooms. The snow had stopped falling but it was bitterly cold, and Katie wasn't going to hang about to catch her death. Everything looked spick and span — although Lily hadn't lined up the scones neatly . . . Satisfied the shop front looked as sparkling and smart as the Nippies who served inside, she went back to her duties.

'I've laid out the tables on both your workstations, girls,' Rose said as she approached the serving area at the front of the shop, where customers would go to purchase bread, cakes and other provisions rather than to sit and dine in the restaurant section of the tearooms. 'Where is Janie? She's usually here by now. What is it with these Sallys being late all the time? It's not right that you have to do her work as well as your own. Miss Butterworth has already added three extra tables to each of our workstations due to staff shortages. It is such a shame Miss Butterworth didn't hire that young woman, Grace. She seemed nice. No doubt her face didn't fit.'

'I don't mind,' Lily said as she straightened up, rubbing her back before pushing a wisp of hair back under her starched white cap. 'At least the job gets done. Miss Butterworth said that one of the girls from the kitchen could serve if Janie hasn't arrived by the time the shop opens. I offered to do the job myself, but the old so-and-so said I was being lazy wanting to sell bread and cakes rather than serve customers — then pointed out I'd not been trained to be a Sally. I quite fancied it myself. Thanks for laying out my tables; it would have been touch and go whether I was ready before the doors opened.'

'Could you see me waving at you?' Katie huffed as she came back into the teashop. 'There is a row of scones all over the place on the bottom shelf. You'd best get them sorted out before you-know-who notices, or she won't stop going on about it all day long.'

'At least when she's moaning at me she's leaving the other girls alone,' Lily laughed.

Rose giggled. 'Blimey, you'll be asking for a

68

medal next for services to teashops. Look out, here she comes. Let me give you a hand taking these wooden trays back to the kitchen.'

Clarice Butterworth approached. 'Miss Neville, Miss Donavon, Miss Douglas: stop all this loitering. I'm about to open the shop, so please get to your workstations immediately.'

Rose almost bobbed a curtsey as she took the other end of the pile of wooden trays to help Katie carry them to the kitchen. Behind her she could hear Miss Butterworth admonishing Lily for having a crooked cap and bread-crumbs on the front of her black uniform. 'Does she never stop moaning?' she asked Katie. 'Just for once it would be nice for her to say something pleasant.'

'I would faint from shock if she did,' Katie said as the two girls checked each other over, making sure their uniforms were correct and their caps were securely pinned without a hair out of place. 'Come on, let's get to our stations. I've checked the work rota; we all have the same tea break. Don't be late — I have something to tell you,' she added with a secret smile.

For the next couple of hours the girls worked hard. The teashop was short-staffed, with some of their colleagues having volunteered for the women's sections of the armed services and a couple of the younger women deciding to take work at the nearby Manston airport. Miss Butterworth fussed about, watching over the waitresses, making sure customers were served and not left waiting for their food. Rose kept watching the door in the hope that Ben would appear again. She didn't even know for sure

69

where he was billeted. Her mum had mentioned that many servicemen were being put up in the empty rooms of guesthouses that once upon a time were rented by holidaymakers visiting the seaside towns of Ramsgate, Broadstairs and Margate. News was that billeting officers would be visiting all houses shortly, looking for empty rooms in which to put up soldiers and officers. Rose just hoped that the servicemen who moved into Sea View would be a decent sort and would fit in with the motley group of people who had made the guesthouse their home. Her heart skipped a beat as she wondered what it would be like to live under the same roof as the handsome Benjamin.

'Miss Neville, you have customers waiting. Please stop daydreaming and do the job you're paid to do,' snapped Miss Butterworth. 'With the area manager due to call any time now, I don't want my staff putting a foot out of step. If we were not so short-staffed I'd be giving you your marching orders,' she sniffed before moving on to Katie to berate her for spilling hot tea over a crisp white linen tablecloth. It had splashed close to a customer, who jumped up in alarm. Katie was horrified at what had happened and was apologizing profusely. Miss Butterworth snapped at her, 'Show your customer to an empty table while we have this mess cleared up.' She turned to the customer, giving her a charming smile and offering her a free meal for the inconvenience.

Rose watched with concern, knowing that the cost of the food would come out of Katie's pay packet. At that moment she hated Miss Butterworth as she had never hated anyone before.

Every penny counted for Katie, who lived alone in a small rented room over the chip shop in the middle of Ramsgate. She was saving hard for her wedding to Jack.

'It's almost time for my break.' Katie bravely said to her boss.

'Clear this mess up and go; you obviously care more for your own comfort than you do for our customers.'

Katie lowered her head in shame and headed to the staffroom, taking with her the dirty tablecloth, which she threw into a laundry bin. Rose stepped in to take the customer's order of toasted teacake and coffee before following her friend. She noticed Lily was not on the shop floor, so must be in the staffroom already. Thank goodness all Nippies covered for each other, or they would never have a break. With around twenty serving staff on the floor at the busiest times of day, the girls were fortunate to be able to meet for a chat over a meal.

'Blimey, she's more of a battle-axe than normal. Why do you think that is?' Rose said, joining her two friends at a small table after kicking off her shoes and sitting down. 'Ah, that's better.'

'She must be worried about her sister. For all her bullying tendencies, she obviously cares for her,' Lily said as she passed a plate of Spam sandwiches to her friends.

'Do you think she will take time off to care for her?' Katie asked hopefully.

'We should be so lucky,' Lily said as she bit into her sandwich.

One of the Nippies from another table leant

71

over to speak. 'My boyfriend, who delivers the baked goods each morning, told me that the manageress of the Margate teashop has been transferred. It seems she is moving to London to work at one of the larger corner shops.'

'Lucky cow,' Lily said, putting the remains of her sandwich back on the plate. 'I'd give anything to work in London; it always sounds so glamorous. Did you know that the staff up there have their own sports and social club? I've even heard that film stars pop in for a cup of tea, and sometimes something stronger. They have proper orchestras playing in the big corner shops as well,' she sighed. 'It's a million miles away from life in Ramsgate.'

'What would you do in a sports club? You're not exactly the sporting type, are you?' Rose said.

Katie giggled. 'I've heard Lily can be quite social at times.'

'Here, less of your lip,' Lily said, giving her a playful nudge. 'I do nothing the pair of you wouldn't do — which reminds me, what is it you wanted to tell us, Katie?' she asked, taking no notice of her two friends as they looked at each other with smiles and raised eyebrows.

'We've named the day,' Katie beamed, 'and I want you both to be my bridesmaids.'

Rose felt relief flow through her body. Since Ben's words she had been worried that Jack would go off to war and something terrible would happen, leaving Katie wishing she'd married her childhood sweetheart before waving him good-bye. 'Go on, tell us when it's to be?'

'Christmas. It will give us time to plan, and as

we are being told the war could be over by then, we will have a double celebration.'

Rose sighed. Her friend was naive in so many ways. It was hard to believe all three girls were close in age. 'Lovely — but from what Mum has told me, they said the very same thing in the last war, and look how long that lasted. If I was you I'd grab hold of that lovely man and rush him up the aisle before he gets shipped off.'

'I agree with Rose. Jack could find some foreign beauty and before you receive a Dear John letter he will be married with half a dozen kiddies — or dead and buried,' Lily added without thinking.

'No, I don't believe either of you. Jack promised me we would be together always.' Katie started to sob. 'How can you both be so horrid? I thought you would be happy for me.'

Lily rushed round to comfort Katie, while Rose passed a clean cotton handkerchief across the table.

'There, there, no need to get so upset. Please don't take any notice of what I said. Was it Jack who wanted to wait?' Lily asked as she hugged Katie.

'No, he was all for popping off to a registry office and doing it on my next day off. But I want to marry in church and have a wedding I'll remember all my life,' Katie sniffed. 'I thought that if we saved up a bit of money it would pay for a nice dress — and we'd have time to find a small flat or a couple of rooms to rent. I didn't think for one minute that the war would interfere with my life.'

'My dear, this war, for however long it lasts, will turn our lives upside down whether we want it to or not,' Lily said. 'Look at all the women who lost their loved ones in the last war and haven't remarried. Some never had the chance to marry at all and remain spinsters to this very day.'

Lily's words had Katie crying once more. It was only the girls on the next table getting up to return to their workstations that prompted Rose to look at the clock. 'My goodness! Miss Butterworth will have our guts for garters. Just look at the time,' she exclaimed, picking up her cup and knocking back the remains of her tea. 'Yuck, it's cold. Come on, you two.'

Lily and Katie followed Rose from the staffroom, heading down the long narrow corridor that led from the staff and kitchen area to the more opulent-looking cafe and shop. Katie wiped her eyes and did her best to calm herself.

'Look, why don't you both come round to my house this evening and we can chat about things? If money is the only thing holding you back from marrying Jack, perhaps we can come up with a solution. We can have fish and chips so as not to bother Mum providing us with a meal. It will be my treat.'

'That sounds like a plan,' Lily said as Katie gave a watery smile and nodded her head as way of thanks. 'Look out — I can see Butterworth with a couple of chaps. Straighten your stocking seams, girls!'

The three friends quickly checked their uniforms before stepping into the bright lights of the shop. Rose always got a thrill from seeing the brass fittings on the counters and white porcelain light fittings hanging from high ceilings. With their crisp white table linen, shining cutlery and smartly dressed Nippies dashing here and there, who could fail to be impressed with the teashops owned by J. Lyons & Co.? Even the smaller seaside teashops like the one in Ramsgate had an air of importance about them. The Ramsgate teashop was quite a small affair compared with the London Corner Houses or with the teashop in nearby Margate, which had a first-floor terrace overlooking the sea. Rose had worked there several times when they'd been short-staffed and had thoroughly enjoyed herself in her new surroundings.

'Miss Neville, can you spare me a few minutes, please?' Miss Butterworth called out as Rose headed to her workstation. Rose looked towards Lily, who had also heard their boss's words; she nodded to indicate she would cover Rose's tables.

'Of course, Miss Butterworth,' she answered obediently, following her boss to the small office close to the kitchen area. Two men were already squeezed inside. She recognized Mr Grant, the area inspector, and was introduced to a Mr White, a younger man who it seemed was to work under Mr Grant overseeing orders and sales in the teashops around the Kent coast. Rose wondered why she been called into the office, imagining something must be wrong; but try as she might, she couldn't think of a thing — unless it was that argument with Silvano the other day. Lyons didn't like their Nippies to answer back to customers. Well, if she was here to get the sack, what could she do about it? No doubt she could find another job around Ramsgate, although she didn't relish working in an ordinary cafe after her prestigious job in Lyons.

Mr Grant cleared his throat with a small cough. 'Miss Neville, I wish to put you in the picture about the management of this teashop — and also the one in Margate. I believe you are aware of the other establishment?'

Rose frowned. Whatever did he mean? 'Yes, sir. I worked at the Margate teashop when several of the girls went down with influenza.'

'Good, good,' he said. 'An opening has appeared for the position of manageress at the Margate shop. Ordinarily I would have offered the position to Miss Butterworth, as the Margate teashop is larger than this one. However, as Miss Butterworth will be leaving shortly, it seems foolish to move her for a few weeks. I wish to offer you the position, Miss Neville — as long as you complete your manageress training course in London, that is.'

If Rose hadn't been surprised by the turn of events, she was now. Standing with her hands clasped behind her back, she was able to pinch herself, and tried not to flinch when it hurt. No, she wasn't dreaming. 'I'm sorry to hear you are leaving, Miss Butterworth. You will be missed.'

Clarice Butterworth stared at her with beady eyes. They both knew Rose was not telling the truth. 'My sister is poorly, and I'm needed to nurse her. Mr Grant has allowed me extended leave, for which I am most grateful,' she said with a smile towards the area manager.

'I hope your sister's health improves soon,' Rose said, before turning to Mr Grant. 'Could I not stay here as manageress?' she asked, and at once realized she sounded most ungrateful. 'It's just that I would have thought someone older, and with more experience, would have suited the Margate teashop. It is twice the size of this teashop, what with it having the upstairs veranda.'

'We have someone coming down from London to take on the position temporarily until we know whether Miss Butterworth is returning. We value our staff at J. Lyons & Co.,' he said, puffing himself up. 'The person stepping in only has experience of smaller teashops, so it seemed prudent to train up someone who knows the area and would become a permanent member of the management team. We are giving you an opportunity to go far in this company. By the way — are you planning to marry?' he asked, peering to look at her left hand in search of a wedding or engagement ring. Both hands were still hidden behind the skirt of her dress.

Rose waved her bare left hand. 'No, sir, no ring and no boyfriend. I'm footloose and fancy free,' she said, trying to ignore the smile spreading over Mr White's face. 'Not that I'm . . . er, I mean I'm not one for . . .'

'I think we know what you mean, Miss Neville. Shall we move on?' Mr Grant said with another small cough. 'Perhaps Miss Butterworth could drum up a pot of tea while we go over the small details?' He pulled out a chair at the desk for Rose.

Rose dared not look Miss Butterworth in the eye as she accepted the seat. There would be hell to pay for this if she didn't take up Mr Grant's offer and move to Margate.

4

'Well, I'll be blowed,' Flora remarked as she listened to what Rose had to say. 'Fancy them thinking that highly of you and sending you to Margate! I'm so proud of you, my love.'

'Thanks, Mum,' Rose said as she stirred her tea. They were chatting at the kitchen table and for once, they were alone.

'You look thoughtful, love. Are you not sure about this promotion? Is it about going up to London for the training course? I know you were nervous when you went to learn how to be a Nippy but it turned out all right in the end, didn't it?'

'It's not that, Mum. I'm just wondering if I'm doing the right thing . . . '

Flora observed her pretty daughter. At times she looked so like her father. She'd spotted it when Rose got fired up about something. A certain way with her hands and a tilt of the head . . . Perhaps Rose was changing her mind about being a Nippy? She'd been shocked when, along with Lily and Katie, Rosie had declared she wanted to work for Joe Lyons in his teashops. For a while she'd thought that meant going to work in London at one of the big Lyons Corner Houses. Flora had been more than a little relieved when she heard the girls intended to stay in the Thanet area. If things had turned out

79

differently, her plans for her only child would have meant a proper career, perhaps in an office. 'If you would like to do something else with your life, I'll support you,' she said. 'Is there anything . . . ?'

Rose took a deep breath. Now was the time to say how much she loved to sing. 'Mum, I'm probably being daft, as the offer of this manageress job is such a great opportunity for me to earn more money — but I've always had a dream . . . '

Flora closed her eyes fleetingly. She had dreaded this moment. She'd ignored comments from friends, when they'd heard her daughter sing at parties and dances, that Rose should be on the stage. But if Rose's yearning to sing was as strong as her own desires had been when she was young, what could she do to stop her? 'You mean, to be a singer?'

'Yes. Do you think it's a silly idea?'

'No dream is silly, my love, but I feel you'd be missing a great opportunity if you turned down this job offer. How many young women of your age can say they are in charge of a teashop? Why not enjoy singing as you do now, when you go dancing?'

Deep down, Rose was disappointed, but she knew her mum had a point. No doubt Flora's advice was because she didn't want to see her daughter leave home, especially during wartime. She decided she wouldn't bother mentioning it again.

Flora watched Rose's thoughtful expression and prayed the girl wouldn't argue. She'd never

80

told Rose, but she had once performed on stage and led a gay life in the music halls. Until she'd met Rose's father — then her life had changed forever.

'Forget I said anything, Mum. I was just having fanciful thoughts. It's the shock of being offered that job. Shall I make us another cup of tea? By the way, where is everyone? It's very quiet here, considering you have a guesthouse full of residents.'

'Round and about. They'll all be back home for their dinner, don't you fear. I was given a rabbit and made a pie. I've only got the crust to make in a while. Mr Cardew is up in his room; I heard him banging about earlier. Goodness knows what he's up to now.'

'He's a strange one. With his room above mine, I've lost count of the times he's woken me up with the floorboards creaking.'

'Oh dear, we can't have that with you about to be taking on an important job. I'll have a word with him when he brings me his rent money.'

'Don't worry, I've got used to it. We don't want to upset him and have you lose the rent money if he leaves. By the way, I've invited Lily and Katie round tonight for a chat. Katie's talking about getting married, and we want to make some plans.'

Flora's face fell. 'Oh dear, I'm not sure I've got enough to feed the two of them as well. I suppose I could boil a few extra spuds . . . '

'There's no need, Mum. I'm treating them both to fish and chips to celebrate my promotion. That means I won't want my dinner,

81

so more for the guests.'

Flora nodded absent-mindedly. 'We'd best make sure your bicycle is checked over as you'll not want it letting you down. Or were you thinking of catching the bus to Margate each way? It's more than a couple of miles each day. Mind you, the bus has been a bit on the unreliable side recently . . . '

Rose took a deep breath. 'Mum, there's something else I've not told you. I'll be living in Margate. With the long shifts and having to be available most of the time the teashop is open, Mr Grant told me I'm to live close to the premises. There's a flat nearby — we can both go and take a look, if you'd like?' she asked cautiously.

Flora bit her lip and reached for the teapot, pulling off the knitted cosy and putting her hands around the brown earthenware pot. 'No need to make more tea. This is wet and warm and more than enough for another cup each.'

Rose slid her cup and saucer over the table towards her mum. 'Don't be too sad that I'm leaving home. I'll be over here on my days off. And they have a telephone, so if you need to speak to me you can ring me from the box on the corner of the road. You are all right about this, aren't you?'

Flora gave her daughter a watery smile. 'I'm so pleased for you, Rose. I just never expected you to be taking off for pastures new like this. With me having to billet those soldiers and not having you around to give me a hand like you usually do, I'm going to be pressed for time, what with my ARP work and all.'

'Excuse me, I do not wish to interrupt you. May I make a drink? It is cold out there. I'm thinking we could have more snow,' Anya said as she entered the room and went to the stove to warm her hands. 'That feels much better,' she added, rubbing both hands together.

'Sit yourself down here and I'll make a fresh pot,' Flora said as she got to her feet. 'You must tell me how you got on today. Any luck with looking for a job?'

Anya looked downcast. 'I'm very sad to say I have not been lucky. But I'm trying very hard, I promise you.'

'I don't doubt you for one minute, my love,' Flora said, putting her arm around Anya's shoulders and giving her a squeeze. 'Why, you're frozen half to death. Don't you have something thicker to wear than this dress?'

'When I have a job I will be able to purchase clothes to wear; I have only a few clothes in my small suitcase. My other possessions were stolen while I was travelling. I still have money to pay my rent,' she added quickly, in case Flora thought otherwise. 'I sewed some into the hem of my coat.'

'That was clever of you, Anya. It was very brave of you to travel across a strange country on your own — and how awful to then have someone rob you,' Rose said, looking concerned. 'I think we should tell the police.'

'We did that when I took Anya to the police station to see if she had to register with them,' Flora said as she banged the kettle on the stove.

'We were told there was not much hope of retrieving her possessions. I could wring the neck of whoever it was that stole from a woman on her own who is a visitor to this country. It leaves a bad taste in my mouth, I can tell you.'

'What kind of work are you looking for, Anya?' Rose asked.

'I will do anything — I am not proud. I just need to survive while . . . while I decide what to do next. I am allowed to work here. The kind policeman told me I could,' Anya said with a weak smile.

'I wonder if Miss Butterworth would take you on at the teashop,' Rose said thoughtfully.

'And wear a pretty dress like you?' Anya said with glee.

'No, it would be in the kitchens, and only part-time; but it would be a way to earn some money while you looked for something else,' Rose said, giving her an encouraging smile.

'I don't think you need look elsewhere. I could do with a hand here, and I'd gladly pay you and give you bed and board thrown in,' Flora said. 'That's if you are interested?'

'You want me to help you here in this beautiful house?'

'It wouldn't be anything much. Just helping me with the laundry and cleaning to keep our guests comfortable. With Rose going away, I will have lost a pair of hands.'

'You are going away?' Anya asked, looking between Flora and Rose. 'I am sorry to know this.'

Rose's laugh tinkled around the kitchen.

84

'There's no need to look sad. I'm going to be living in Margate, and I will be the manageress of the Lyons teashop that overlooks the beach. You and Mum will have to come and have tea there one day, as my treat. I want you to look at where I'll be working. Now, I must dash off and get the fish and chips or Katie and Lily will be here and no doubt very hungry.' Rose got up to go. 'Oh, and I have a cardigan you can have. It shrank a little in the wash and no longer fits me. Can you get it for Anya please, Mum? It's the green one with the embroidered rosebuds down the front. You'll find it in my chest of drawers.'

Flora nodded her head as her daughter hurried out. She knew the cardigan that Rose spoke of, and it hadn't shrunk at all. She was such a generous girl. Making the fresh pot of tea and taking it to the table, she spotted Anya put a protective hand across her stomach. 'You can tell me to mind my own business if you like, but I need to ask. Are you having a baby?'

Anya glanced down at her hand and snatched it away. Looking sad, she gazed up at Flora. 'No, I am no longer with child,' she answered, not saying any more.

★ ★ ★

Rose pulled the collar of her coat up around her ears. Anya was right, it was certainly turning colder. She prayed there wouldn't be any more snow. Not now, when it was almost February. She'd be starting at the Margate tearooms in a couple of weeks, after she'd been up to London

85

to undertake her management training. The thought gave her a little thrill. Perhaps there would be time to take in a show, and even go to a dance and listen to the singers? That's if the government had truly decided to reopen the cinemas and places of entertainment. It would be a drab old war if they didn't.

Marching down Madeira Walk at a brisk pace, she crossed the road and headed towards the fish and chip shop. There was only half an hour before Lily and Katie were due to arrive, so hopefully she wouldn't have to wait long if the fish needed frying . . . She sighed as she spotted the queue. It would be a miracle if she was back at the house before her friends arrived. She'd been so deep in thought after talking to her mum that she'd also come out without her gas mask; it was still hanging on the back of her chair in the kitchen. Just my luck if we get gassed right now, she muttered to herself. And me with a new job and some excitement to look forward to.

She was deep in thought until a woman ahead of her in the queue gave her a nudge. 'Excuse me, love, there's a man up the front trying to catch your eye.'

The woman alongside her screeched with laughter. 'He can catch my eye any day of the week,' she cackled as her mate joined in with the laughter, causing many in the queue to turn round to see what was so funny.

'Rose, what was it you wanted? I've forgotten,' she heard from the front of the queue.

She peered through the row of people. It was Ben waving to her. 'Fish and chips three times please,' she beamed.

'That's right,' he called back. 'I'll forget my own name one of these days.'

She stepped out of the queue and waited for Ben to join her, trying hard not to meet the suspicious eyes of others who were queuing.

'Here you go,' he said, passing her three portions wrapped in newspaper. 'Mind how you hold them, they're rather hot.'

'Thank you,' she said, holding them close to her body and enjoying the heat from the packages through her coat. 'I feel rather awful for jumping the queue like that.'

Ben shrugged his shoulders. 'No one died. Besides, this way I get to talk to you rather than have those old girls listening to every word we say. Can you spare five minutes?'

'I'm sure I can — I can put them in the oven to warm when I get back. There's a bench down there,' she said, nodding to a wooden seat facing out over the harbour.

'It's not very romantic, is it,' Ben said as they sat down.

'Oh, I don't know. It's rather magical to see the moonlight shining through the snow onto barbed wire, and the few fishing boats bobbing in the water.'

'Perfect for the Luftwaffe,' Ben said, causing them both to look skywards.

'Don't say that.' Rose shivered. 'Do you think they will bomb us down here in Thanet?'

'It's only a matter of time before this war heats up. Then it could be hell, especially with Manston Airport on our doorstep. I believe the enemy did drop bombs here in the Great War, so you never know.'

'Shh,' Rose hissed, looking from left to right dramatically. 'Walls have ears.'

'My dear girl, apart from the fact we are nowhere near a wall, everyone in Ramsgate knows that Manston Airport is just up the road,' he chuckled.

Rose knew he was pulling her leg and chose to ignore him. 'Eat your chips before they get cold,' she admonished him.

'I'm taking them back to my digs,' he said. 'It's my turn to provide dinner. What about you — are you treating your mum?'

'No, she's cooking for the people in our guesthouse. These are my treat for my friends, Lily and Katie,' she said before clamping her hand to her mouth. 'I need to pay you,' she exclaimed, reaching into her pocket for her purse while trying not to let the parcels slip from her hands.

Ben raised his hand to stop her. 'No, let this be my treat. You can buy them next time.'

'There may not be a next time,' Rose blurted out without thinking.

Ben didn't answer and focused instead on a small boat heading out to sea.

'What I mean is, they are transferring me to Margate,' Rose said, stumbling over her words in order to correct the way she'd spoken.

Ben visibly perked up. 'Have you been so naughty that they're sending you away?' he laughed.

Rose laughed with him. 'It may appear that

way to you, but in all honesty, I am a good Nippy and I know my job. I've been offered the job of manageress at the Margate teashop. It means we may not bump into each other so often,' she added sadly.

'I don't know; Margate isn't far away, and I may need a change of scenery. Don't forget, we met in Margate. My toes remind me of this from time to time.'

Rose felt a warm glow inside her at the thought of seeing Ben when she started work in Margate. 'It won't be for a few weeks, as I have to go to London to train for my new position,' she said excitedly.

Ben was thoughtful. 'Have you been to London before?'

'Yes, just the once, when I was younger. I went to train to be a Nippy, along with Lily and Katie. We didn't go anywhere as we were too scared to wander further than where we were staying,' she laughed at herself. 'It sounds funny me saying that now when I'm dying to see so many things on this trip, and the war likely to stop most of it.'

'It needn't interfere too much. What is it you want to do?' he asked, moving closer to allow another couple to sit at one end of the bench, as she started to speak.

'I've always wanted to see a musical performed on the London stage. I've seen plenty of seaside shows, but it's not quite the same thing. I dream of seeing the famous stars I read about in the magazines. Do you think I'm being silly?'

'No, not at all. Is there anything else you'd like to see or do?'

'Well . . . you know I like to sing, but I've never been to a proper dance. I don't mean the ones round here. I mean the ones where women wear beautiful dresses and the band is one I've heard of. If I never sing with a big band, I would at least like to watch and hear how it's done by the professionals,' she sighed.

'That's a dream and a half,' Ben said thoughtfully.

Rose got to her feet. 'That's enough of my daydreaming. I must get this food home before my friends arrive. And by the way this snow is falling, it's not going to let up for a while,' she grinned, looking up into his face where softly falling white flakes were starting to settle on his cap.

'I'll walk you,' he said, taking her arm. 'You've probably left your torch at home as well as your gas mask. We can't have you stepping in front of a bus, can we?'

'How did you guess?' Rose chuckled.

'From what I've seen, many young women use their gas mask case like a handbag. I noticed you checking to see if you had it when I first saw you in the queue at the chip shop.'

'Nothing much gets by you, does it?' she laughed. 'I go this way, up Madeira Walk. Mum's house is at the top over there, the one with the blue front door. Not that you can see that in the dark — and mind yourself, as this snow is getting slippery.'

'There's enough moonlight for me to see what I need to see,' he said.

Again Rose felt a thrill run through her as they

walked up the hill in companionable silence.

As they approached Sea View, the door opened and Flora appeared. 'There you are, Rose. Lily and Katie have arrived, and I wondered what had become of you. You can never be too careful in this blackout. Look at what happened to poor Anya. Oh . . . ' she trailed off as she spotted Ben.

'Mum, this is Captain Benjamin Hargreaves. He's a friend. I bumped into him in the chip shop and he walked me home as I'd forgotten my torch,' Rose explained, thankful that it was dark and Flora couldn't see her cheeks, which were beginning to feel hot.

Ben stepped forward and shook Flora's hand. 'It's a pleasure to meet you, Mrs Neville,' he said. 'I'd best be on my way now.'

'Oh please, you must come in for a drink. Would you like to eat your meal with us?' she said, noticing he was carrying a newspaper-wrapped parcel of food similar to her daughter's.

'That's very kind of you, but I must be on my way. My friends will be waiting for their supper. I wish you a good evening, Rose,' Ben said, before turning and walking away.

'Goodnight, Ben, and thank you,' Rose called out as he disappeared into the snow. It seemed to be falling more steadily now.

'I'll need to put these in the oven for a while,' Rose fussed as she walked past her mum into the house, waiting for Flora to close the door and pull the heavy curtain over it to block out any light and draught from under the door.

'He seems very nice, from what I could see,' Flora said, following Rose to the kitchen. 'Where

91

did you meet him? I hope he wasn't a customer at the teashop. We don't want you getting into trouble now you're being promoted.'

'Mum, I know the rules,' Rose sighed. 'I met him at a dance the other week and then again the other day. I doubt I'll ever see him again,' she added quickly before heading into the front room to greet her friends.

'I think you will, my girl.' Flora spoke to the empty room. 'I can feel it in my water, and I'm not usually wrong.' She gave a shiver as a feeling of foreboding swept over her and she grasped the back of a chair. 'Please God, don't let history repeat itself,' she whispered as she thought back to a time when she was younger than Rose was now, and had fallen in love with a man in a uniform.

★　★　★

'I couldn't believe it. Old Butterworth's face was like thunder when she came out of her office. I thought you'd got the sack for sure. Are you sure you aren't making it all up?' Katie asked, after Rose had told them the ins and outs of what happened in Miss Butterworth's office.

'Talk about coming up smelling of roses,' Lily laughed. She felt no malice towards her friend. 'I'm so pleased for you, and on top of that, old Butterworth is leaving.'

Rose stopped collecting the plates from their meal and sat down. 'I think it's rather sad that she can't work and has to go to look after her sister. From the little I've learnt, they only have each other. Fancy being in that position. If anything should happen to her sister, she will be alone in the world and not have a penny to her name unless she can return to work. It doesn't bear thinking about,' she said, looking downcast.

'Rose, you are too soft for your own good,' Lily joshed. 'That woman has never made any attempt to make friends with anyone and seems to enjoy making our lives hell. Don't waste your breath on her. Now, get rid of those plates as I have these we can look at,' she said, pulling a pile of magazines from her bag and placing them on Katie's lap.

Katie picked up one of the magazines and flicked through it. 'Why are you showing me these?'

Lily turned a few pages and pointed. 'Look — this is all about how to have a wedding, and this one is how to make your own wedding dress . . . It seems very simple.'

'If you can sew it does; I'm going to save up and buy one. That's one of the reasons for getting married later in the year.'

Rose got up and lifted the tray of plates. Perhaps now was the time to say something? She took the tray over to the sideboard and went back to her friends. 'Katie, what does Jack say about all of this?'

Katie gave a sweet, dreamy smile. 'He said he'd go along with whatever I decided. He knows a wedding day is for the bride. He'd be happy if we dashed down to the registry office and got it over with in a few minutes.'

Lily was horrified. 'Do that and people will

start to talk. Why, they will think you're in the family way. You don't want a reputation, do you?'

Katie shook her head sadly. 'That's another reason I want a nice wedding in a church, with you two as my bridesmaids. You're the closest thing I have to family — not counting my Jack, of course.'

Rose knelt down in front of her friend and took her hands. 'Katie, what if Jack gets taken overseas before then and, God forbid, something happens to him? Wouldn't it be better to have that memory of a wedding and all that it entails?' she said gently. 'Why, if you married now you could have a baby by Christmas. It would be your new family — you, Jack and your own child. Think of that. It would be something to remember him by if . . . if anything should happen.' Rose faltered over her last words. It didn't bear thinking of what this war could do to couples.

Katie snatched her hands away, looking horrified. 'Nothing is going to happen to Jack. I keep telling you, it will all be over by Christmas. Besides, Jack said he'd take care of that side of things, so there won't be a baby for a while,' she added shyly. 'That's a man's responsibility.'

Lily raised her eyebrows at Rose over their friend's head. 'I overheard someone in the teashop saying that the reason there are so many troops on Thanet at the moment is because they are being shipped over to France and beyond before too long. That means your Jack could be amongst them. They are bound to be sending them out by ship, and with Jack being a sailor . . . '

'I heard something similar. A person I know

94

said we should live for today, as we have no idea what will happen in the future,' Rose said, trying hard not to upset Katie.

Katie stared wide-eyed at her friends. They could see she was taking in what they were saying. 'I'd never forgive myself if . . . But what about the arrangements and everything?'

'We could help you. That's if you want us to?' Lily said. 'Rose, would your mum have the wedding breakfast here? There won't be many of us, and she has that big dining room. I reckon we could get a discount on food from good old Joe Lyons, don't you?' She looked desperately at Rose for suggestions.

'I reckon so, and I do have an idea for your wedding breakfast, but I'll need to speak to someone first before making rash promises. Is that enough for you and Jack to think about bringing the wedding forward?'

'I suppose so,' Katie agreed. 'But we'd need somewhere nice to live as well . . . '

'What's wrong with the room you rent at the moment? If Jack does go off to war, you can look around while he's away and make a nice home for him to return to. What do you say?' Rose didn't add that with many rooms being taken over by the military, Katie might have a problem finding something cheap and cheerful in which to start her married life. Hardly a day went by without a customer in the teashop moaning about billeting officers knocking on their door.

Katie nodded her head slowly. 'It does all make sense,' she agreed, 'but I'd need to discuss it with Jack first.'

Rose grinned at her friends. 'I'll go and make us a cuppa, and then we can make some plans for you to tell Jack about,' she said, picking up the tray and heading to the kitchen.

'Give that tray to me — I'll rinse those plates through while I'm doing this lot,' Flora said as she stood by the white stone kitchen sink. Miss Tibbs was nearby, with a tea towel in her hand. 'Are you having a nice chat with your friends?'

'Yes, it's nice to get together away from work. Mum, can I ask you something?' Rose perched on the edge of the large wooden kitchen table.

'Fire away,' Flora said.

'It's Katie. She's thinking of getting married.'

'That is lovely news. Her and Jack have been courting for quite a while now. I'll pop in and congratulate her when I've done here. When is the happy day to be?'

'Soon, we hope — it doesn't pay to leave things too long now we are at war.'

'I agree with you, dear,' Miss Tibbs said. 'I know many a spinster who wished she'd married her beloved before he went off to fight the war to end all wars. Not that it did,' she sniffed.

'Oh, that's awfully sad to hear. Did you lose your sweetheart during the first war?'

Miss Tibbs' laughter filled the room. 'No, dear, I couldn't be doing with the noisy, messy creatures. I much preferred the company of my lady friends when I wasn't working.'

Rose felt her face twitch and dared not look at her mother. Miss Tibbs was a darling and much loved by all who lived at the Sea View guesthouse. She was like the grandmother that

Rose never knew. 'I was wondering, Mum . . . '

'You were wondering if I could help out?' Flora smiled.

'Would you? That would be just great,' Rose said as she jumped to her feet and hurried over to hug Flora. 'She doesn't have a mum to help organize the wedding. Could we have the wedding breakfast here, do you think?'

'I don't see why not,' Flora said. 'It won't be the first party this house has seen.'

'Perhaps I could contribute something to her trousseau?' Miss Tibbs suggested.

Rose kissed her cheek. 'Katie would just love that. She was looking at pictures of wedding dresses just now. Would you, with all your expertise in the dressmaking world, be able to advise her?'

Miss Tibbs cocked her head to one side as she thought about Rose's request. Rose could see the elderly lady was taken with the idea. 'As you know, I was trained as a tailor rather than a dressmaker, but I have a feeling I might just have a little something stored in my chest up in the attic that belonged to my late sister. Come along and help me, Rose. We mustn't keep the bride-to-be waiting.'

Rose beamed as she followed Miss Tibbs. With luck and some help from her friends, Katie would have a lovely wedding to remember.

Flora watched her daughter leave the room and smiled to herself. A wedding in the family of friends would be something to look forward to in these dark days. She'd watched Katie grow from the frightened young girl Rose took under her wing that first day at school, and seen her blossom into a beautiful young woman. Katie had been a part of this family for as long as she could remember, but she had always refused to move into the Neville home, wishing instead to forge her own way in life. At least they could give her the send-off she deserved as she set out on the unknown road to married life. Flora looked down to where she'd been unconsciously twisting her own gold band. At least the girl wouldn't be setting out with lies and deceit hanging over her head; they were a heavy cross to bear, as she knew only too well.

* * *

'Miss Tibbs, this is absolutely lovely,' Katie said as the older woman held up the most beautiful lace wedding gown any of them had ever seen. 'However can you bear to lend it to me?'

'It's no use to man or beast packed away in my chest. At least you will have a beautiful day, and I'll be able to revisit my memories of when Lucinda walked down the aisle. You look so much like her, my dear. It will be painful for me to watch, but I know my dear sister would have wanted another bride to enjoy wearing the dress we so lovingly made between us.'

Rose reached into her pocket for a handkerchief, noting that Lily was already sniffing into hers. Katie, however, was jumping up and down for joy. 'This is so wonderfully kind of you. What happened to your sister? Was she let down at the altar, or did she die young in childbirth?'

Miss Tibbs gave a belly laugh. 'I have no idea what became of her. She was only married to Cedric two years before she ran off with his brother. I thank the Lord she was never blessed with children; think of the shame that would have brought on our family! One of the few times we spoke after that, I asked her what she would like me to do with this beautiful wedding gown. Her answer was unrepeatable.'

Flora felt herself starting to grin as she saw the open mouths of the three girls who had been swept up in the story of the wedding gown before having it dashed at their feet. 'Then this time the dress will bring much luck to Katie and her beau. Why don't you slip it on? We'll see if it will need altering. It has survived very well, Miss Tibbs.'

'It was packed with love and care in tissue and lavender bags. The dress knew its time would come.'

Rose shivered, and hoped that Katie would have more luck than the first owner of the dress. 'What became of your sister's first husband?' she asked.

Miss Tibbs' eyes took on a faraway look. 'Cedric was a most handsome man. He never married again, and he died of a broken heart in 1918. Some said it was Spanish influenza, but I knew he pined for over twenty years hoping my sister would return. Why don't I help you into the dress? I have some pins in my room. Help me find them, Katie, then we can make a start on the alterations down here in the warm,' she said.

The heavy wooden door closed after them, and Lily started to roll about on the stuffed sofa, holding her sides as tears ran down her cheeks. 'Oh my, do you think Miss Tibbs held a torch for the lovelorn Cedric before he died from unrequited love?' she said, before blowing her nose and trying to compose herself.

'It is more likely the story has been embroidered over the years. Miss Tibbs can be quite fanciful at times. Whatever you do, please don't let her know you have been laughing. She would be mortified. I do wonder if she was saving the dress for you, Rose?'

Rose shuddered. 'I do hope not, Mum.' Second-hand dresses carry second-hand tears, she thought to herself, though she wouldn't have said so in front of her friend. 'I'm bigger built than Katie, so the dress most likely wouldn't have fitted me. However, I do wonder if the dress is as old as Miss Tibbs has said, as it doesn't look as heavily boned as a gown from that time,' she said, examining the dress closely. 'Perhaps this was something she made for a woman who never married? Even so it is beautiful,' she said, running her hands across the lacy fabric and touching the delicate pearl buttons on the cuffs. 'It's a dream wedding gown and I hope that one day Miss Tibbs will make one for me,' she sighed.

'Perhaps we can worry about that when the time comes for you to marry,' Flora said. 'It's not as if there's a groom on the horizon, is there?' she added, fishing for a response from her daughter. The answer came from another source.

'If she doesn't make a habit of stepping on his feet, there could well be a handsome army captain who is quite keen on our Rose,' Lily grinned, and Flora smiled. The young woman's words made her think once again of her own past, and the path she'd taken.

5

'Have you got any fags on you? I've run right out, and I'm not up to going down the road to get some more.'

'What, again?' Lily asked as she pulled off her coat and gas mask, hanging both on a hook on the hallstand. She wrinkled her nose. 'Have you been frying onions? This place reeks of burnt lard. Can't I go out for the evening without having to come back to your mess?'

'That's no way to speak to your father. Look out, or I'll take my belt to you.'

'But you're not my father. And considering it's me that pays the rent and everything else around here, I think it's about time you got off your fat, lazy backside and sodded off.' Lily put her hands on her hips and glared at George Jacobs. 'And if you raise even one finger to me, I'll call the cops. I'm not some frightened kid anymore, and now Mum's gone, I don't have to mind what I say.'

Lily ignored the moans coming from where he sat, in the only armchair in the room. She set about opening windows, letting in the cold night air along with a flurry of snow. She was careful to mind the blackout, and didn't give a damn if her stepfather was feeling the drop in temperature. She did her best to keep out of the way of his wandering hands when he'd had a few too many, and had taken to putting a chair against her bedroom door after his uncomfortable drunken advances. She was a grown-up now, and didn't have to put up with what he'd done when she was a kid. To this day she slept with a knife under her pillow. Anyone outside of her home would only see that kindly Lily was still taking care of the man her mum had married in a moment of pity, who had claimed to be an invalid. Although weak, her mum had been a caring woman. Lily would not let anyone know about the animal living under her roof. If only she could meet somebody and run off to marry him, it would solve all her problems. She envied her friend Katie, who was about to embark on a new life. Even Rose had a caring mother, and Lily envied them both, although she was not one to show it. It was a shame that George Jacobs was too old to serve his country. She knew he'd been approached to join the Local Defence Volunteers, and Flora Neville had suggested to Lily on more than one occasion that perhaps her stepfather, as he liked to be known, could help out at their ARP unit.

She looked at the dirty plates in the sink before putting a kettle onto the hob, then using a brass poker to stir up the ashes enough to heat the water. She'd make herself a cuppa and use the rest of the hot water to clean up his mess. He could go swing if he expected a meal at this time of night; as far she was concerned, he could go without. It must have been the couple of drinks she'd enjoyed at Flora's house to celebrate Rose's news that had given her the courage to stand up to him. Lily knew she had to do

103

something, as his drunken ways were getting worse. She was often afraid to go home after work, never knowing what to expect. Perhaps she could join one of the services, or move away — she'd heard there was good money to be made working in munitions. She contemplated the idea as she stacked the dirty plates in the sink. It made her sad, as she loved the town where she'd grown up; as much as she moaned each day, she was very happy working in the Lyons teashop alongside her friends. With Rose off to manage the Margate teashop, the future would be very different, but she clung onto the knowledge that she'd still see her chum outside of work.

With her mind far away as she tackled the dirty crockery and pondered her future, she didn't hear George coming up behind her. Before she knew what had happened, he'd grabbed her around the waist and pushed her against the hard, cold stone sink. She was trapped. You bloody fool, she thought to herself as she struggled, you should know what he's like by now. 'Stop it, George. I've told you before — leave me alone!'

'Be nice to me, Lily. You know you like it really,' he slurred into her ear.

'I don't, and you're hurting me! Please let me go, George,' she pleaded, more than a little frightened. The more she wriggled, the more he grunted as his hands pulled her skirt up around her waist.

'Don't, George, don't — this isn't right. Mum wouldn't have liked you doing this to me.'

'Your mother isn't here. I'm a man and I demand my rights,' he said as he pinned her arms to her sides with the strength of just one of his own, while pulling at her undergarments with the other.

'Please, God, no,' Lily prayed aloud as she felt the breath being forced from her body. She closed her eyes, trying to block out what was happening, whilst willing herself to think about how she could escape as George grunted and groaned. The stench of stale sweat and beer, coupled with the lingering smell in the kitchen, made her retch. Blood pulsed in her head, and she knew she was about to pass out. What would happen to her then?

At that moment, George loosened his grip in order to reach for the buttons at the front of her dress. Lily felt the fabric of her best frock tear and froze as he leant over her shoulder to look at her exposed breasts. He panted close to her face, and again she heaved in disgust at the smell of his unclean body. She felt herself freeze as his body slammed into hers again and again before shaking and groaning, then slumping against her. Unable to control herself, Lily was violently sick in the sink.

'You dirty cow,' he snarled, pushing away from her in disgust. 'No man will want you if you act like that.' He did up his trousers and staggered back to his armchair.

Lily took a few deep breaths, trying to regain her strength. The heavy poker lay beside the stove where she'd left it. She reached out; it would take just one hefty blow and she'd be free of George Jacobs forever. Try as she might, her legs could hardly hold her upright. Fortunately, in those few seconds as she reached for the poker, common sense prevailed. She would go down for God knows how long for his murder. It would ruin her life forever. She was better than that, she thought to herself, looking to where the man had collapsed into his armchair and was already starting to snore. Without thinking twice, she straightened her frock as best she could and set about clearing up the mess. She had to get away from this house — and soon. Before it was too late, and she did something she'd regret for the rest of her life.

★　★　★

'Whatever is wrong with you? You look like something the cat dragged in,' Rose said as she hung her coat in her locker. She'd never seen Lily in such a state: her eyes, puffy with dark shadows underneath, looked blankly back.

'I didn't sleep very well,' she mumbled as she stepped into her black uniform dress.

'Neither did I, with all the thoughts of Katie's wedding running through my head. I do hope Jack agrees with the plans.'

'He's a man, isn't he?' Lily said bitterly.

'Are you all right?' Rose said, looking concerned for her friend.

'I'll be fine,' Lily snapped. 'I just want to be left alone. Tell Miss Butterworth I'll be out in a minute; I just need to finish changing into my uniform.'

Rose placed a hand on her friend's arm. 'Are you sure you're all right? Perhaps you should go home, if you're feeling unwell?'

Lily shuddered. Home was the last place she wanted to be. She had spent the night huddled under her bedclothes, afraid George would burst through the door and attack her even though she'd wedged a chair against the handle. When dawn broke she'd dressed as quietly as she could and, carrying her shoes, crept slowly downstairs, trying to avoid the steps she knew creaked and the loose floorboard in the hallway. Once the front door was open she'd fled as if her life depended on it, ignoring the freezing snow that had started to fall again. 'I said I'll be all right,' she said to Rose, trying to muster a smile. 'You go on. I won't be long.'

Rose nodded and left the room, although she looked back to where her friend was buttoning up her black dress. There was something wrong; she just knew it.

Lily went to the small washbasin set in the corner of the room and ran her hands under the cold water before splashing her face. It felt good. Cupping her hands, she scooped up the water and drank thirstily before it ran through her fingers. She felt heaps better just for doing that. Digging into her handbag, she pulled out a comb and ran it through her hair before checking her face in the mirror above the basin. 'You'll do,' she muttered to herself as she squared her shoulders and headed to where Miss Butterworth was giving the girls their daily orders.

' . . . Please take care of the salt cellars; there

were complaints yesterday that some were empty. Ladies, I don't need to remind you that incidents like this lower the high standards in Lyons teashops and will cause customers to go elsewhere for their meals. There are plenty of other cafes and hotels our customers could give their patronage to.'

Katie nudged Rose. They both knew it was a customer on Lily's table who had made the complaint. 'Yes, Miss Butterworth,' they all chanted.

Clarice Butterworth looked down at her notes. 'It was also observed that one Nippy had not replaced her order book and was seen writing an order on the palm of her hand. Please ensure right now that you all have an order book that will last your complete shift. Remember, I know everything that goes on in this teashop and slips like this will not be tolerated.'

Every Nippy without fail checked she was carrying an order book with plenty of clean pages. These hung from the waistband of their uniforms.

'Finally, I wish to notify you all that I shall be leaving the Ramsgate branch once my replacement arrives. Miss Neville is also leaving to take over management of the Margate branch. We do have some vacancies at both teashops that we hope to fill before too long. In the meantime, I'm asking for a concerted effort to cover all tables so our customers are not inconvenienced by the shortage of staff.' Miss Butterworth checked her watch. 'Your shift is about to start. Do your best to maintain standards, ladies,' she said as she dismissed them.

'Blimey, old Butterworth could be a danger to

us all if she worked for Hitler,' Lily sniggered as she joined her friends. 'She doesn't miss a thing.'

'You seem a bit brighter,' Rose said, cheered by her friend's jovial banter.

'I'm all right,' Lily assured her, making a mental note not to bring her troubles to work or have her friends be concerned for her. It would do no good, and she couldn't stand the pitying looks. This was her lot, and until she could make changes in her life she would just have to be more careful.

'I'm going to meet Jack this evening,' Katie whispered to them as she hurried by with a tray of salt cellars and pepper pots. 'Cross your fingers and hope that he agrees to the plans for the wedding.'

Her friends both crossed their fingers and held them up to show their support.

'I think she is fussing unduly,' Rose smiled. 'Jack loves her to bits and will agree to anything she wishes. By the way, do you fancy going dancing this evening? I'm not sure what band is playing.'

Lily grimaced. She didn't fancy having men bump into her or run their wandering hands all over her if she agreed to dance with them. 'I don't fancy that. How about going to the pictures?'

'That's fine with me. I'm so relieved the government decided to open the cinemas and dance halls again. The war is bad enough without us missing out on having a bit of fun! I'll get a newspaper in my break and see what's on, shall I?'

Lily nodded her head. At least being out for the evening meant her stepfather would be dead to the world by the time she got home, and with luck she'd be able to avoid him. She blamed herself for what had happened the previous night; she should have had her wits about her. Hopefully it wouldn't happen again. 'That sounds good to me. Shall we go straight from work? That way we'll see the B film as well. I hope it's one of those spy movies with Johnny Johnson in the starring role.'

Rose gave her friend a smile. 'I look forward to it.' She reached out and gave her friend's arm a gentle squeeze. 'I'm glad you've got a smile on your face again.'

Lily smiled back, knowing her friend's kind words could easily make her cry. 'Best we get to work, or Butterworth will be on the warpath. You aren't a manageress yet,' she said.

* * *

Rose checked that the tables in her workstation were ready and waiting for the first diners of the day. Table linen was clean, and cutlery laid out correctly at each place setting. After Miss Butterworth's warning words, she'd made sure that every salt cellar and pepper pot was full. She remained deep in thought as she greeted customers and handed them the tariff card, chatting politely about the meals available that day while she carefully wrote orders down on the pad attached to the waistband of her apron.

Rose smiled and was courteous, but her mind

remained elsewhere. There was definitely something wrong with Lily today, she thought as she carried a tray containing plates of pie and mashed potato to one table, placing the food in front of her customers. Lily could be down at times, but Rose had always thought this was due to her mother having died so recently. Today, though, she seemed different. Rose also wondered about Ben. Would she see him again before she set off to London to train as a manageress? She felt close to him even after such a short time, and hoped desperately that he felt the same. He had such a calm and comfortable air about him considering he was an army captain. Although Rose knew little about the ranks in the army, she'd always thought that a captain was someone special. Surely he had to be someone important to be in charge of men, especially during wartime? To find him queuing in a chip shop seemed a little unexpected. And his interest in her — a waitress who served tea for Joe Lyons, and liked to sing when she had the chance — puzzled her, too. The thought that perhaps he was leading her on crossed her mind as she removed dirty plates from tables and presented her customers with their bills. How was she to know his true feelings?

Rose's tummy started to rumble, and she hoped it wasn't too long before her meal break. She'd just decided to lay two empty tables ready for new diners when she noticed someone being shown to a table in her section. It was Ben, and he was alone. Her heart skipped a beat; a small tingle of excitement ran up her spine. He could have asked for a table anywhere in the tearoom, but he'd chosen one she was in charge of — that must mean something?

'Good morning, sir; may I show you the meals we have today? I can recommend the sausages, or perhaps a teacake?'

'Thank you,' he said as he browsed the tariff card. Without looking up he added, 'I just had to see you before you left for London. Have you made your travel plans yet?'

Rose poised with her pen over the order pad, aware that Miss Butterworth never missed a thing. 'I should know this afternoon, when our area manager visits. I thought he might have been here this morning, but he's been delayed by the weather. Why do you ask?'

'I'll be in London myself this coming week, before . . . before we are shipped out.'

'Oh . . . ' was all Rose could say. She'd not given a thought to the handsome army captain leaving Thanet.

'What time do you finish work? Would it be possible for me to take you to dinner?' he asked, before adding, 'I'll have the rarebit, thank you, Miss.'

Rose wrote down the order with trembling fingers. To think she'd been dreaming only minutes earlier of never seeing him again, and here he was asking to take her to dinner. 'I'm afraid I promised to go to the pictures with my friend this evening,' she whispered disappointedly. 'Could we meet tomorrow evening?'

'I'm afraid tomorrow evening is too late for me,' he said, looking up into her eyes.

It took only a moment for Rose to make up her mind. 'I can go out another time with my friend. I'd love to dine with you, thank you.' As she took his order to the counter to hand it over, Rose spotted Lily working on her station at the back of the teashop. However would she explain that she wouldn't be able to accompany her this evening? Something wasn't right with her friend, and here she was letting her down. Rose felt terrible. What could she do?

Lily couldn't wait for one o'clock and her meal break. She'd had the morning from hell. Already she'd had to change her apron after a young child had spilt soup over the tablecloth as well as herself and Lily. She'd had to dig deep to not only keep calm, but to smile sweetly and assure the harassed mother it wasn't a problem. If the child had been hers she'd have beaten him soundly and taken him home to his bed, she grimaced as she cleared up the mess. If she had her way she'd never marry, let alone have a child if they were all like that one.

'Are you having a bad day, Miss?' a man's voice said from behind her as she returned to her workstation, wearing her clean apron and having washed the sticky soup from her hands.

Lily jumped before realizing it was the new salesman, Mr White. 'You could say that, sir,' she replied, doing her utmost to be polite. One never knew how friendly these men might be with the management. The few times she'd seen him before, he'd been with the area manager. He looked extremely smart with a sharp crease in the trousers of his pin-striped suit, his fair hair slicked back from his high forehead, and a thin moustache covering his top lip. Lily thought him very much like the Hollywood actors she'd seen at the pictures, and had caught him watching her a few times from across the shop floor when he'd been in the teashop with Mr Grant. They could be related for all she knew, so best not to blot her copybook. 'A Nippy is prepared for anything,' she smiled, continuing to walk towards her workstation, where she could see a couple of diners being seated.

'I wonder, Miss Douglas, if you could advise me?'

'I'll do my best, sir,' she replied, keeping an eye out for Miss Butterworth, who would no doubt give her a telling off for chatting when she should be working.

'I'm staying in the area for a couple of days while I familiarize myself with the local teashops. The food in my hotel is awful. I wondered if you could recommend somewhere for dinner, and perhaps some entertainment afterwards?'

Lily raised her eyebrows. 'Why, there's nowhere better to eat than here,' she said, wondering if this was a way for management to catch out the Nippies if they recommended other establishments. 'As for entertainment — I'm not quite sure what you mean?' She blushed, aware that the conversation might not sound as innocent as it should.

'My God, I'm doing this all wrong,' he blustered, turning a delicate shade of pink. 'What I mean is — would you care to have dinner with me, and perhaps dancing afterwards?

I assume there is somewhere in Ramsgate to dance, now that the government has lifted restrictions?'

Lily laughed out loud before clamping a hand to her mouth and checking to see if Miss Butterworth had heard. 'I happen to know there is a dance at the Coronation Ballroom this evening. There are plenty of places to eat nearby.'

'Does that mean you'll join me?' he asked tentatively.

Lily thought for a moment; he seemed a decent sort. 'I'd love to,' she replied with a gentle smile, and they quickly made arrangements before she hurried to her workstation. As she served her customers Lily had a bounce to her step and felt quite cheered. He looked like a gentleman who could be trusted — and he had a good job. He could be the ideal person to fit in with her plans to get away from George. It was only as she headed to the staff quarters for her meal that she remembered she'd promised to go to the pictures with Rose. Whatever could she do? She hated to let her friend down. Deep in thought, she didn't notice Tom White watching her thoughtfully from the open door of the office as he ran a finger across his moustache and smiled to himself.

Collecting a plate of stew and a cup of tea, she went to the table where Katie was already seated eating egg on toast.

'There you are, Lily. It's not like you to be late for your food. I only have fifteen minutes left. Rose hasn't arrived yet. Twice I've had to tell other Nippies that these seats are taken. I noticed your accident with the soup,' she grinned. 'I'm surprised you didn't tip the rest over the head of that obnoxious child.'

Lily chuckled. 'I was so close to doing just that. I think that's why I've been overlooked as a manageress of my own teashop. No one could trust me not to lose my temper.'

Katie looked serious for just a moment. 'You're not jealous of Rose, are you?'

'My goodness, no. I think it's marvellous that Rose will be running the Margate branch. With a bit of luck, perhaps we could work there with her? What fun we'd have.' Lily grinned as she began to eat her lunch.

'I don't think I could move to Margate,' Katie said, 'not with the wedding and everything to plan. I like Ramsgate — it's been my home for many years. I'm not one for wanting to change jobs and move from town to town; I'll stay here, and we can meet up whenever possible. That's if you decide to go,' she smiled. 'By the way, did you hear about, Minnie, that new Nippy? It seems she was a little too friendly with one of the RAF lads that came in. There was a complaint, and old Butterworth hauled her over the coals and gave her the sack. Do you think she was really on the game like the girls are saying? She also seemed over-friendly with that Mr White the salesman when I walked in on them in the staffroom a few days ago, but perhaps he was talking to her about work? Lily . . . did you hear me?' Katie prompted, noticing that Lily was staring across to where Rose was collecting her meal.

'Sorry, Katie — I've just got to have a quick word with Rose. I won't be more than a minute,' she apologized, and left the table to head over to Rose.

'But I wanted to show you a picture of bridesmaids' hats. I thought we could have a go at making them . . . Well, I never,' Katie huffed, and bit into a slice of cold toast.

Rose could see Lily heading towards her and steeled herself to tell her friend she wouldn't be able to go to the pictures with her that evening. Knowing her friend had been so down earlier that morning, and then noticing the problems she'd had with a customer, she felt as though she'd be making Lily's day even worse. Had Lily had words with her stepfather, she wondered? He was known as a lazy man, and he drank too much; but Lily's late mother had always kept him in check. In those days, before she was taken poorly, she had provided Lily with a happy home.

'Rose, can you spare me a minute before you sit down with Katie? I've got something I want to say to you.'

Rose felt her stomach lurch. Was her friend going to tell her why she was so miserable first thing this morning? She placed her tray down on an empty table. 'Hurry up, though, I don't want my stew getting cold,' she grinned, trying to keep the atmosphere light while knowing that after whatever her friend was going to tell her she would be disappointing her even more.

Lily took a deep breath. 'I'm sorry to let you down. But that new salesman, Tom White, asked me to go dancing, and I didn't like to disappoint him and then I remembered . . . ' Lily stopped her awkward explanation as Rose began to laugh. 'What's so funny?'

'Would you believe, I've been plucking up courage to tell you that nice army captain has invited me out to dinner. It's most likely his last day in Ramsgate before he gets shipped off God knows where.'

Lily started to laugh. 'What a silly pair of whatsits we are! We can go to the pictures another time, can't we? Johnny Johnson can wait. Another day, another B movie,' she laughed. 'Come on, let's go and finish our food. Katie will be wondering what we are up to. She did pull a bit of a face when I dashed off just now.'

⋆   ⋆   ⋆

'You work very hard, I think,' Anya said as she finished polishing the brass doorknocker while Flora scrubbed the doorstep of the guesthouse. 'This house is always, what you say — spick and span? Although I have not known anyone clean while it is snowing before.'

'Yes, that's the right word,' Flora answered. 'I like to keep busy, and cleaning keeps my mind off of this war. I even forget the snow,' she smiled.

'But you join in with so many things to do with the war. This . . . RAP, it takes up much time, and you dash here and there helping people, all for this, what you say . . . war effort?' Anya stretched her arms above her head before brushing a stray hair from her face.

'ARP,' Flora corrected her with a smile. 'As I

said, I like to keep busy. Being busy stops me worrying. I keep thinking back to the last war and how people suffered. I'd hate to see my Rose, as well as all her friends, suffer in any way. Any little thing I can do to help others fight this war and bring it to an end is good enough for me.' She dipped her scrubbing brush back into the rapidly cooling water in the galvanized steel bucket, then stopped to think for a couple of seconds. 'I don't often talk about my past, and I've not always done the right thing. If I'd been a good girl, I wouldn't have had my wonderful daughter. But I've always followed my heart. I feel you are holding something back, Anya?'

Anya looked Flora in the eye. 'I have something to be afraid of. I think I go no further. I stay here at Sea View, and fight the war with my new friends.'

Flora gave her a big hug. 'You think too much, Anya. Why not take one step at a time — face one little thing and then another, eh?'

'Then I will do little things too. Put all our little things together, and we have one big thing. Hitler will not like that.'

Flora roared with laughter. 'You are certainly a tonic, Anya.'

'I thank you, I think — if I knew what this tonic was. But tell me, why do we clean and scrub outside in the dark?'

Flora stood up and looked about her. The night was coming in fast. 'Why, I'd hardly noticed, we'd been chatting so much.' She threw the water from the bucket into the street. 'Time to stop, I think. Everyone will be wanting dinner.'

'That is good for me,' Anya said, tucking her polishing cloth under her arm. 'Come, I will make the cuppa. Look how British I am becoming — and I shall not forget the one for the pot this time,' she laughed.

The two women entered the hall as Rose dashed downstairs. 'Mum, have you seen my clean pair of stockings? I can't find them anywhere.'

'If you mean the ones you left hanging in the bathroom, they were full of ladders, so I put them in my sewing basket. I was going to repair them when I sat down later.'

'Oh no, I don't have any others; and Ben's collecting me in half an hour. I can't wear those horrid work stockings, and I so wanted to look nice,' she said sadly.

'Go and start the cuppa,' Anya ordered her. 'I have what you want,' she said before hurrying upstairs.

Rose followed Flora through to the kitchen and did as Anya had ordered, while her mum put away the bucket and cleaning clothes. There was a box of vegetables on the kitchen table. 'Another gift?' she asked.

'Mildred dropped them off earlier. She said she swapped them for some fish before she took the rest to market. That woman doesn't stop bartering, but she's a godsend. Why, she even left some fish for us as well. Once I've had my tea and warmed up I'll be making a tasty pie for our dinners.'

Rose grimaced. 'I'm glad I'm going out to dinner — yuck, fish,' she said, turning up her nose.

'You'd eat it if you were hungry,' Flora tutted. 'So what's this sudden interest with your army captain? Is it serious?'

Rose poured boiling water into the teapot and put the knitted cosy over the pot. 'Oh Mum, he just asked me out to dinner. What with me going off to London for my training, and him off to fight the war, he said it would be a nice way to say goodbye. That's all.'

'But you don't know when you're going to London, do you?'

Rose looked a little shamefaced. 'I heard this afternoon. It's arranged for the day after tomorrow,' she said gently, seeing the hurt look on her mother's face. 'I was going to tell you, honest. What with rushing about getting ready for this evening, I'd not got round to it.'

Flora wasn't one for arguments, and she didn't wish to fall out with Rose. She'd brought her daughter up to be honest, and she believed they would have discussed it at some point that evening. 'Leave your bits and pieces out for me, and I'll have them rinsed through ready for you to pack. We can't have you off to London not looking your best, can we?'

'Oh Mum, what would I do without you?' Rose said, giving her a hug.

'You're going to have to learn to do without me once you're living in Margate,' Flora replied, trying hard to smile. It would break her heart not to have Rose living with her, but she was proud all the same that her daughter would be the manageress of a Lyons teashop. It was a much more secure life than the life of a singer, going

121

from venue to venue and meeting all kinds of people. She should know.

'Where is that cuppa? I am parched,' Anya said, handing Rose a slim cardboard box.

'I can see you're learning your English from Mum,' Rose laughed, and she took the box and carefully opened it. 'Oh my gosh — I can't take your silk stockings. Look, Mum. Please tell Anya she can't do this.'

'It's most generous of you, Anya. Are you sure this will not leave you without stockings to wear?'

Anya waved her hand to dismiss their comments. 'It is nothing; I have more. They were something not stolen from me on my journey. I hid them in lining of my suitcase, as they are good for the bartering. I learn this after I left Poland. Not all people are honest. You have all been good to me; now I can be good to you,' she said as she started to pour tea into the cups.

'Speaking of being good — Rose, have you asked about a job for Anya yet?'

Rose was about to speak when there was a knock on the door. 'Oh my goodness, it must be Ben. I must go and put on my stockings! Mum, can you let him in? And please don't cross-examine him. His intentions are honourable.' She stopped to kiss Anya on the cheek. 'You are a lifesaver. Ask Mum about the Sallys,' she added as she dashed off.

'The English are a strange race,' Anya murmured as she poured milk into her cup. 'But I do like them a lot.'

6

Lily stood outside the Coronation ballroom, tapping her foot impatiently. Shining a torch onto her wristwatch, she could see Tom was twenty minutes late. That's not a good start, she fumed to herself, clutching her coat closer to her body. I should've worn a cardigan — if I'd known he was going to be late I could have taken longer getting ready.

She stopped tapping as she recognized him sauntering up the road, seeming not to have a care in the world. I shouldn't have suggested we just went dancing, she said to herself, stubbing out a cigarette with the tip of one of her best shoes.

'There you are,' she said, trying to keep her voice light. 'I was a little early,' she added, hoping he would acknowledge how late he was. Instead he simply held out his arm. She took it without another word as they joined the queue going in to the dance.

'So, what's keeping a girl like you in Thanet?' he asked once they were inside, and he'd placed a small glass of sherry in front of her.

Lily wrinkled her nose. She wasn't one for sherry, but it was her fault for saying she didn't mind any drink that was on offer. She took a sip, trying not to gag. 'Habit, I suppose. That and a lack of opportunity. I could ask the same of you,' she hit back.

Tom laughed. 'This job will take me around the country. I don't plan to be a salesman for long. There are opportunities out there for a man like me, and I'll be grabbing them while the others are away at war.'

'What's your excuse for not joining the services?' Lily asked sharply. 'Don't you want to support your country against the Nazis?'

Tom looked hurt. 'In a flash,' he said, 'but I have a weak chest that would stop me fighting. My doctor advised against it.'

Lily wasn't daft; she had heard this excuse bandied about on more than one occasion. 'You could be a pen pusher, or do something where you didn't exert yourself. I know a chap who had polio as a kid, and they put him in the Pay Corps,' she threw back at him.

He sighed as if he'd heard these words before and slowly pulled a pack of cigarettes from his pocket, lighting one without offering them to Lily. 'People need to eat. I have a job; I visit the Lyons restaurants and tearooms to make sure they don't run out of food. If that's not helping the war effort, I don't know what is,' he said, standing up. 'Do you want to dance?'

Lily knocked back the last of the sherry and went to join him on the edge of the dance floor. Cigarette in hand, he pulled her close and they joined the throng of dancers as the band started to play a foxtrot. He wasn't a bad dancer, and she noticed some admiring glances from other women. Perhaps the evening wouldn't be so bad after all.

When they sat down again, Lily looked him

square in the face and said, 'I'd leave Ramsgate if the right offer was there. I'd quite like an adventure.' She smiled, reaching for the cigarettes he'd left on the table.

Tom gave her a look that suggested he knew what she meant. 'Stick around and see what happens,' he said, giving her a crafty wink. 'Do you want another one of those?'

'No, I'll have a gin this time, thanks,' she replied, and watched as he headed to the busy bar. Perhaps Tom would be her ticket away from Ramsgate and her stepfather?

George had been home when she'd popped in quickly after work to get her clothes, and she could tell without a second glance that he'd been drinking as usual. As she'd headed to the stairs without acknowledging his presence, he'd bellowed after her, 'What does a man have to do to get some food around here?'

Lily had ignored him and rushed to her room, quickly wedging a chair against the door handle to stop him forcing an entry. Anticipating that George would be home, she'd already had a quick wash at work. There was no way she was stripping off to wash at the kitchen sink — not after what had happened the other evening. She pulled her one good dance dress from the wardrobe. She'd saved hard for this dress, and although it was now a year old, it was still stylish and attracted glances from men when she wore it. The green crêpe de chine clung in all the right places and swirled around her ankles when she danced. She felt like a million dollars, just like those American film stars, when she went dancing — so the last thing she wanted was for George to launch himself at her and damage this dress, as he had before. Her previous best dress was now in the dustbin; she couldn't bear ever to see it again, let alone wear it — even if it could have been repaired.

Checking her make-up in the dressing-table mirror she had taken from her mum's room after she died, she thought hard as she reapplied red lipstick and added a few hairpins to her already neat hair. First turning off the light, she pulled back the blackout curtains and pushed hard on the warped frame of the sash window. Looking round the small bedroom, she spied a small chalk fairing that George had given her after a trip with her mum to Dreamland in Margate. She'd always hated the small ornament with the saying 'Honour your father' etched on the front. With one hefty throw, it flew from her hand out into the dark back garden and crashed against a wall, causing a lone dog to start barking and a neighbour to shout out in fright.

Straight away the back door banged open as George staggered out into the night, swearing loudly for all to hear as he tried to work out what the commotion was. Lily took this as her cue to grab her coat, and with her best shoes in her hand she belted down the stairs and out the front door before George could come in again. She was halfway down the street before she stopped to put on the shoes and catch her breath. She was laughing for all she was worth, but stopped suddenly, thinking she'd be for it when she got home later. Hoping vehemently that George would go out to the pub and have a skinful so she'd be safe for the night, she had headed off towards the dance hall with a spring in her step.

'What's up with you? You look miles away,' Tom said as he returned with their drinks.

'Nothing much,' she smiled back. 'I was just thinking I could do with a bag of chips later. My treat,' she added, in case he thought she was a gold digger. If only he knew what she'd really been thinking . . .

'Why not? Perhaps we could take them back to my hotel room. It's perishing cold out there.'

'Why not?' Lily replied, returning his knowing look. 'How about another dance?' she said as the lights dimmed slightly and the band started to play a waltz.

⋆　⋆　⋆

Flora put down her sewing bag and blinked several times. When she could move, she would put the kettle on for a cup of cocoa. She'd overdone it a bit today, what with going down to check the ARP entrance to the underground tunnels and having a chat with fellow wardens. There'd been talk about painting the edges of pavements white so that people didn't fall in the blackouts, but she'd soon put paid to that when she had asked who was going to volunteer to do such a thing, and where the money was coming from?

Some of those councillors are full of hot air, she huffed to herself. Then to come home and

127

decide to clean the doorstep and polish the brass fittings was a bit on the daft side. Thank goodness Anya had offered to help. She was a godsend around the house, and willing to learn. Even now she was upstairs with Miss Tibbs, learning how to use a sewing machine to make herself a skirt. Last week it had been knitting lessons. Whatever would she do next?

It was unusual to be alone in the evening, as there were usually one or two of the residents popping in for a chat or to make themselves a drink. Flora kept an open house for her paying guests and insisted they use the kitchen as much as they wanted, with her only presiding over breakfast and dinner, if it was required. It was a system that had worked for many years, back to when she first ran the guesthouse — before General Sykes had taken up residence as her main guest. It was nigh on fourteen years now since she'd lost her husband in the tram crash just down the road. She sighed. Whatever had made her think of Ron after all this time? It had not been the right thing to marry for friendship, but at least Rose had grown up being able to call someone Daddy. She must be feeling unsettled, what with Rose moving on to pastures new. Who'd have thought she'd be a manageress in charge of her own shop while she was still in her twenties?

Delving deep into the bag that held her knitting and darning equipment, she pulled out a bundle of faded cards held together with a piece of ribbon. Picking carefully at the knot, she pulled away the string and laid each one on her lap, opening one delicate card to reveal a photograph of herself in the days when she was younger than Rose. She lifted one closer to her face to look again at the young woman bending to collect flowers thrown onto the stage by admiring young men. 'Dear General Sykes,' she whispered to herself. 'What glorious times we had, until it all went wrong.' Whatever happens, history mustn't be repeated, she thought as she gently placed a kiss on the fading image before carefully placing the cards back where prying eyes would never find them. At least we have our Rose.

Flora jumped as someone rapped on the front door. It was gone eight o'clock. Whoever could it be? Please don't let harm have come to Rose, she prayed as she hurried along the hallway to pull back the blackout curtain and switched off the light. 'Hang on a minute; I'm just opening the door,' she called as again there was a sharp knock on the stained-glass insert in the top half of the door.

'Mrs Neville? I'm sorry to bother you so late in the evening. I'm Sergeant Miller, one of the army's billeting officers. I'm here to see what rooms you have available to put up some of our men?'

Flora opened the door wide and allowed him to step inside, followed by a young corporal with a clipboard. She'd heard from fellow landladies at a WVS meeting that she'd have a visit from them before too long.

'You do realize we have mainly ladies living here?' she asked with a pleasant smile. 'I'd not like them to feel uncomfortable with uncouth men sleeping under the same roof.'

The officer listened politely. 'There are many home-owners in the same position as you, Mrs Neville. The men we will place here, if there is room, are family men and quite respectable.'

Flora nodded politely and led the two men through to the kitchen. 'Would you like a hot drink? I was about to put the kettle on the hob. Please do sit down.'

The men sat down at the table, and Flora outlined who was living in the house, listing their names and how many bedrooms she had free. 'At the moment we are full up. However, my daughter, Rose Neville, is about to leave home. She's to be a manageress of the Lyons teashop in Margate, and will be living nearby,' she added proudly. 'I intend to move my guest, Anya Polinski, from the small box room into Rose's bedroom. So I can offer the small room to one gentleman officer.'

The corporal scribbled frantically, trying to keep up with what Flora had to say, while Sergeant Miller listened attentively before speaking. 'Would it be possible to see these two rooms,' he asked, 'along with the two rooms rented by Mrs Hannigan and her young daughter? Oh, and the rooms belonging to your other guests — Miss Tibbs, Miss Dalrymple and Mr Cardew?'

Flora frowned. 'I'm sure that would be possible. Would you mind if I went to check with the ladies first? My daughter is out at the moment, but I'm sure she wouldn't mind you

130

looking in her room. Here, drink your tea while I pop upstairs. Hopefully Mrs Hannigan hasn't put young Pearl to bed yet. It wouldn't be right to disturb the child when she has school tomorrow. As for Mr Cardew . . . he is a bit of a recluse, so possibly will object to his rooms being viewed.'

'A recluse, you say?'

Flora felt flustered. 'It's only what I call him. He rents one bedroom at the top of the house, and I allow him use of the attic room as he likes to bird-watch. He's no trouble most of the time, as we hardly see each other.' She wasn't about to mention the concern she'd felt about the man since Rose had mentioned his nocturnal walkabouts.

The sergeant agreed, and she left them with their tea and a few biscuits she'd hurriedly put on a plate.

As Flora climbed the stairs to the second floor, she removed the wraparound pinny and the scarf she'd tied around her hair whilst cleaning. She wasn't one to answer the front door in such apparel, and blamed the tiring day she'd had for her lapse of presentation. Tapping on the door to Miss Tibbs' room, she was quickly invited in. Miss Tibbs and Anya were busy pinning a paper pattern to a length of navy-blue worsted material.

'Have you come to help us?' Miss Tibbs enquired. 'Here, let me clear a seat for you.'

'I would love to have helped,' Flora said, taking in the many ornaments around the room placed on shelves and most available surfaces.

'But it's Anya I'd like to speak to, if I may?'

'Do you have the problem?' Anya asked after removing several pins from between her lips.

'No, not a problem as such. It's just that we have the army billeting officer downstairs, and he wishes to look at some of the bedrooms. He would like to look at yours, if he may?'

'The army wants my bedroom?' Anya asked, going slightly pale.

Miss Tibbs patted her arm. 'No, my dear, they won't take your room. I'll make sure of that. They will have me to contend with first,' she reassured her, before turning to Flora. 'They won't take dear Anya's room, will they?'

'No, of course not,' Flora said. 'It's just that as we plan to move you into Rose's room shortly, the army may decide to put somebody into your room. Accommodation is in short supply at the moment with so many men stationed in the area. Most of the guesthouses have empty rooms, as it is out of season. People mostly come to Ramsgate in the summer. Not that we expect many to visit this year,' she sighed. 'The ideal situation is that they put these men into the vacant rooms until the summer season starts. I am fortunate in that I have long-term guests in this house but even so, they wish to check availability. Does this answer your question, Anya? No one intends to kick you out, be assured of that,' she smiled.

Miss Tibbs looked thoughtful. 'I'd much rather have some of those handsome RAF chaps from the Manston airfield staying here. Do you think we could ask, Flora dear?'

Flora chuckled. 'I'm afraid it doesn't quite work like that, Miss Tibbs, although I must say I agree with you. Can you spare a few minutes now, Anya? The sooner we sort this out, the better.'

Anya stood up to follow Flora, who was already going downstairs to knock on Mrs Hannigan's door. 'I think I too would like a pilot to live here,' she whispered to Miss Tibbs.

Sergeant Miller went first to Rose's bedroom and paced the length and breadth of the room as his corporal wrote down what was said to him. Flora was pleased to see that Rose had left the room tidy, as sometimes there were clothes lying all over the place when she was rushing off somewhere in a hurry. They then did the same in Anya's smaller room, although only the sergeant went in. He called his measurements out to the hall, as the room was too small for them all to fit inside.

After that Flora took them to the two rooms that Mrs Hannigan rented, making many apologies for interrupting her evening, while Anya went downstairs to the kitchen. Flora joined her once she'd shown the two men to the door and checked the blackout curtain was back in place.

'I have been thinking,' Anya said. 'I am very comfortable in my room; it feels like home to me. We should let the army move into Rose's room. I believe the war is more important than me sleeping in a larger bed, don't you think?'

Flora, who was finishing her now cold tea, tried not to splutter as she imagined a whole army living in her back bedroom. Her feelings

133

were that Sergeant Miller had already made this decision, but it was nice of Anya to offer. 'Thank you, my dear. Shall we wait and see what's in the letter before we decide? I just hope that Mrs Hannigan and Pearl aren't inconvenienced, as I feel Sergeant Miller will request they give up one of their rooms. They keep themselves very much to themselves, as does Mr Cardew, and that's as it should be. They are able to treat the house as their home and do as they please.'

'I have yet to meet this Mr Cardew. Where did you say he sleeps?' Anya asked.

'At the very top of the house. He has his own staircase that leads from the first floor. Years ago, it would have been where the servants slept.'

'This house had servants and now you work alone caring for the people here?' Anya said in wonder. 'Then I help you more. You should not be servant to us all. It is not right,' she added firmly with a serious look on her face.

'Oh Anya, you do make me smile. It is not as if I wait hand and foot on all my guests. Most clean their own rooms, and I only supply breakfast and dinner if it is required. It is nothing like the old days, when General Sykes lived here. Then I did have to work a little harder.'

Anya raised her eyes with interest. 'You were proper servant then?'

'I preferred the title 'housekeeper' in those days. But we did have a lady coming to do odd cleaning jobs. My husband was also alive then, so he helped.'

Anya thought about this and nodded her head slowly. 'It was good setup but still you were

134

servant to another. Now you are boss lady,' she grinned.

'I suppose I am, and in a way that is why I worry about you all, from the elderly Miss Tibbs down to the youngest guest, Pearl Hannigan. You are all like family to me.'

'I meet little Pearl and she is . . . what you say . . . delightful. I should like a daughter like her one day, when war is over.'

'Don't wait too long, as age creeps up on us and then it is too late.'

'First I have to find husband. He is here in Kent somewhere. Then we live as man and wife again and the babies come along,' Anya said, placing a hand on her stomach. 'If he still wants me as wife.'

Flora watched the sadness flit across her face. 'You had a child, Anya . . . ? Please don't answer if you don't wish to. But anything you tell me I will not repeat.'

Anya gave her landlady a smile. 'You are a good woman, Flora, and I wish to share my story with you.'

Flora sat quietly and listened as Anya told how her family had perished as the Nazis invaded Poland. The shock of finding both her parents slain had caused her to lose her much-wanted baby. Her husband, Henio, had been a pilot in the Polish air force. Word had reached her just before the invasion that he was no longer in Poland, and that she should leave her beloved country — but it was too late. The night her parents and siblings perished she had been in a village close by, arranging to travel with another

135

pilot's wife to France, where they'd hoped to meet with their husbands. Going home to say goodbye to her family had been the biggest shock of her life. The house had all but gone, and only bricks and rubble remained. Neighbours had pulled bodies from the destruction, and they managed to bury their loved ones before fleeing. Anya had only the clothes she stood up in, but she knew that somewhere in the remains of the building was her father's cashbox. It took a day of searching before she came across it. The money inside enabled Anya and her friend to bribe and beg their way out of Poland to head for safety. They'd headed to Paris, where her friend Marta's father and mother-in-law lived. The news was not good. Marta's husband was a prisoner of the Germans, although it was thought that Henio was still well and in the air force.

'Through word of mouth I discover he could be in Kent, at a place called Manston near Margate. Marta's family helped me find a person who would arrange papers for me to reach London. It has been a long journey, but I am almost there. I plan to go to this place and see him.'

Flora couldn't believe what she'd heard. For a woman to come all this way after losing her child was heart-breaking. 'You are to be admired, Anya. Not many women would undertake what you have done. If I can help in any way, I will do so. Perhaps we could write a letter to the RAF at Manston and ask for their help?'

'No, we cannot do that!' Anya shouted,

looking frightened. 'There is something I have not told you.'

* * *

'Thank you for inviting me,' Rose said as Ben helped her into her coat. 'It was a lovely treat to be waited on rather than the other way round.'

Ben waited while she did up the buttons on her best coat and checked her scarf was tucked in properly. 'Shall we walk along the harbour front rather than take the direct route?'

'I'd love to. I may have been born here, but I never tire of seeing the sea. Even if it is dark and there's snow in the air,' she added, thinking it was a daft thing to say.

'I know what you mean,' he said as they both said goodnight to the waiter who was holding open the door for them. 'I'm a London boy born and bred. I'm used to seeing the river Thames, and that's as good as the sea for me. There's something about looking out over water, especially when you're alone and able to think.'

'I agree. I don't think I'd be up to working on a boat, like Mildred. She's one of our ladies at the guest house,' she added, seeing his enquiring look. 'Her father left her his fishing boat and she goes out in it in all weathers. Would you believe she even helped drag a mine out of the sea the other day?'

Ben took her arm as they crossed the road and walked over to the iron railings circling that part of the harbour. He held onto her as they gazed out to sea. The tide was in, and they listened as it lapped against the boats moored nearby. 'I could almost imagine there was no war and we were a couple on our holiday, taking a walk,' he said.

Rose closed her eyes and took a deep breath. She felt the same, but in her mind she was married to this handsome man. She could feel the warmth of his arm through hers and her heart beating fast in her chest. 'Shall we sit down?'

They sat companionably side by side, not saying a word and both deep in thought, until Rose shivered. 'You're cold,' Ben exclaimed and put his arm around her, pulling her into the open fold of his army greatcoat. 'Better?'

'Much,' she mumbled as she breathed in a mix of warm wool from his uniform and the scent of his shaving soap and cigarettes. She could stay here forever.

'I have to leave early tomorrow morning,' he said right out of the blue.

Rose froze. She had known he would have to leave Ramsgate soon, but his words still caught her by surprise. 'Will I see you again?' she asked in little more than a whisper.

'I was going to ask you when you would be in London for your training. If it is soon, I could take you dancing — or to see a show?'

Rose felt her heart start to beat so fast she thought it would burst. He wanted to see her again. 'The day after tomorrow, I catch the early train. Lyons have arranged a place for me to stay, and I have to report to an office in the Strand for further instructions. As I'm needed as soon as possible, they are bypassing the longer training period, but I'll be learning the job at Orchard

House. I'm rather scared by the whole thing,' she added honestly.

'Then we can definitely meet. Give me the name of your hotel and we can make arrangements,' he said.

Rose laughed. 'Nothing so glamorous as a hotel; I'm to stay in a kind of hostel for women who work in Lyons and nearby department stores. I have the feeling we may even be chaperoned,' she giggled. She felt a rumble of laughter come from Ben.

'Then we shall have to behave and have you home on time,' he laughed.

Rose felt inside her handbag and pulled out the envelope containing her instructions, given to her that afternoon by the area manager. 'Here — you will need my torch in order to read this, but be careful as we have some rather officious ARP wardens around here. One of them is my mum, but she's not on duty this evening. She does love to shout at people if she sees a light, though . . . '

'And so she should. One chink of light showing in this town could guide enemy aircraft to pinpoint not only where we are, but also help them find the airfield at Manston,' he said, as he quickly scribbled down the details of where Rose would be staying in London.

'Oh my goodness. I'd never thought of it like that. Do you really believe they will send over planes to bomb us here in Kent?' she asked with a shiver.

Ben turned off the torch and put his arms around her, pulling her close. As she looked up into his face, trying to distinguish his features, the moon came out from behind a cloud and she could see the passion in his eyes. 'You've no need to be frightened,' he said as she raised her face to his. 'I'll take care of you,' he added before claiming her lips.

Rose felt as though time had stood still, and if it hadn't been for the voices of men on a nearby fishing boat she'd have been happy to stay there with Ben for eternity. She reluctantly pulled away. 'I think I should be going home. It'll be getting late, and Mum will start to worry,' she said as she stood up and straightened her coat.

'I'll walk you to your door,' Ben said as he took her hand and they crossed back over the road to head up Madeira Walk. 'Does your mother always wait up for you?'

'No, I'm old enough to look after myself, but she fusses like a mother hen at times. We only have each other, as Dad died when I was ten years old. I don't like her to worry about me,' she said, feeling embarrassed that she'd even mentioned Flora.

'That's good. Everyone should have someone to worry about them,' Ben said.

'But who worries about you?' Rose asked, realizing she knew very little about the handsome army officer.

'I'm old enough not to need someone worrying about me.'

'We are never too old for that. Perhaps I could worry about you . . . even a little?' she added.

'I'm the person who should do the caring and the worrying. I've had enough experience of

140

that,' he added with a touch of bitterness in his voice. 'That's why they made me a captain in the army,' he added, trying to lighten the atmosphere.

'I shall worry about you all the same. You can't stop me,' she said defiantly. 'May I ask where you will be going after you've been to London? I take it you will be shipped out somewhere?'

Ben took a deep breath. He'd been dreading Rose asking. 'I can't say. To be honest, it's still not one hundred per cent decided. I'll find out more in a few days. All I can say is, it will be sooner rather than later.'

Rose was quiet for a few minutes as they crossed the road and walked towards the guesthouse. 'Then we'd best make the most of our time together in London,' she declared in a defiant voice.

Ben started to laugh at the determination in her voice, but stopped dead in his tracks. 'Did you see that?'

'No — what are you looking at? I can hardly see what's across the road.'

'Look up at the attic window of that house. Wait until the cloud passes over, and we may see it again. There you are . . . '

'Oh my,' Rose declared, as a glint of something was caught in the moonlight before the cloud passed over again. 'Yes, I saw a flash of what looked like light on glass. But it was most likely the moon on the windowpane,' she suggested.

'No, that wouldn't happen. It's something smaller behind the window, like a mirror. Perhaps even a flashlight. Look! There it is again. Whose house is it?'

'It's the attic window at Sea View . . . my mum's house,' Rose whispered.

They both stood looking up at the window until Ben broke the silence. 'Whose room would that be?'

'No one sleeps there, but Mr Cardew's room is just below it, and Mum allows him to store his things up in the attic.'

'What kind of things would those be?' he asked thoughtfully.

'I have no idea. I assume they're his boxes and suitcases from when he moved in. I don't know the man very well — he's not one for joining us for dinner. Mum says he's rather shy, so she takes a tray up to his room most evenings when he's home. He is a bit of a night owl, though. I can hear him moving about long after I'm tucked up in bed. Should I mention this to Mum?'

'No . . . I feel it's best to keep this between ourselves. We don't want to worry anyone, do we?'

Rose agreed. But for the second time that evening, she was starting to worry.

7

Flora looked at Anya's stricken face. 'Have you not told me the complete truth, Anya?'

The Polish woman slowly shook her head. 'I fear I will be put into prison if anyone should find out,' she said as her voice started to break, before she put her hands over her face and cried. 'I just wanted to find my Henio and to know he was alive and safe. I had to get from London to here at any cost.'

Flora went to the woman and put her arms about her. 'So you hid in a lorry and the man stole most of your possessions; there is nothing wrong with that,' she said comfortingly.

Anya rubbed the tears from her eyes with her fingers. 'I did not tell you all. This man, he gave me false papers for travelling. My friend Marta, the person I left Poland with, her family arranged it and told me to be very careful. I had to meet him in London and hand him money. My travel papers are, what you say . . . fake.'

Flora frowned. 'Are you telling me you are not Anya Polinski? I've seen your identity papers, and that is the name on them. I don't understand. We showed them to the sergeant at the police station and he didn't say anything. I'm totally confused.'

'The policeman was a fool. He did not look close.'

Flora had to admit the man had been caught

at a busy time; there had been someone else at the station desk reporting his chickens stolen from his garden, and he had caused a great deal of fuss. 'Can you tell me what is wrong with your identity papers? Is there false information on them?'

'Not at all. I am Anya Polinski, and I do come from Warsaw. There was no time to apply in the normal manner. Marta's papa said he knew a man who knew a man, and I had my papers much quicker than others who were waiting. Marta joked and told me the words, wink wink, which I did not understand. It was meeting this strange man in London who used the same words that made me understand something was wrong, and my papers were not right . . . I could be arrested.'

Flora started to chuckle. 'My dear, I don't think you have to worry. It seems to me that your friend's papa simply greased a few palms — I mean, he paid someone to hurry up with your identity paperwork. They are not fake or illegal.'

The two women were still laughing when Rose joined them.

'Hello, love, did you have a nice evening? I thought you might have brought your friend in for a cup of cocoa,' Flora said.

'He had to get off,' Rose said, looking distracted. For all their closeness, she had no idea where Ben was staying. Their goodbyes on the doorstep had been hurried due to the thought that someone may be watching at the attic window. A polite kiss goodnight and a whispered confirmation to meet the day after tomorrow in London was all they'd had time for.

'Oh my, I complete forgot to tell Anya about the Sally job,' Flora said, clapping her hand to her mouth. 'My goodness, I'd forget my head if it was loose.'

Anya shook her head in despair. 'Do not forget, I am foreigner. You are talking rubbish — and who is Sally, and what is wrong with your head?'

Rose giggled. 'I'm making cocoa. You can explain all of that, Mum.'

Flora gently explained that she had simply meant she was forgetful.

'Then say you forget, don't confuse matter,' Anya scoffed. 'So who is this Sally?'

'Sally is the name given to the ladies who sell baked goods at the front counters in the Lyons teashops.'

Anya thought about the proposition and nodded. 'When do I start?'

'You will have to have an interview, and then there is the training,' Rose said as she put a tray of drinks down in front of the women and joined them at the kitchen table.

'Will I wear the dress with the wrong thread colour?' Anya asked, looking slightly affronted. 'I do not like dresses with wrong thread.'

'You lost me now,' Flora said with a confused look on her face.

'It's the red thread we have to use to sew the white buttons onto our dresses, Mum,' Rose explained. 'It's part of the design of the uniform, Anya,' she explained. 'I agree it's a daft notion, but our bosses made the decision, so who are we to argue?'

'I would argue,' Anya said stubbornly.

'You won't have to wear the same uniform, so there's nothing to worry about,' Rose said with a smile. 'Your uniform would look much smarter,' she added, hoping to tempt Anya. 'Shall I tell Miss Butterworth you would like an interview for the Ramsgate teashop?'

Anya's face took on a stubborn look. 'No, I thank you, but I will work with you in Margate. You will be manageress, so you will give me interview.'

'Then you will have to wait until I return from my own training in London and have started my job as manageress,' Rose said, wondering if in fact there was a vacancy for a Sally at the Margate teashop.

'Then I will go to the teashop in Ramsgate and see Miss Butterworth. I need job now, not in future,' Anya said, finishing her drink and standing up. 'I will wash cups and lay table for breakfast. You,' she said nodding at Flora, 'you will go to your bed now. You work too hard, and will end up in your grave before you are old. Then there will be no more forgetting of your head,' she said, shooing Flora from the room.

Rose laughed. Anya was like a breath of fresh air at Sea View.

'As for you,' Anya continued, taking the cup from Rose's hand, 'you go to bed too and dream of the man you like to kiss.'

'What? How did you know . . . ? I mean . . . ' Rose stumbled over her words.

It was Anya's turn to laugh. 'Lipstick smudged and your eyes shine brighter than the stars. Off to your bed for happy dreams,' she commanded.

Anya watched Rose walk out of the kitchen and head towards the stairs. 'One day the stars will come back to my eyes and there will be much smudging of lipstick,' she said to herself before making a start on the washing-up.

★ ★ ★

Lily wriggled her toes and sighed. The bed was warm, and she did her best to snuggle beneath the blankets to avoid a bright light. On losing the battle she peeped above the bedclothes; perhaps she'd left the lights on the night before? No; it was the early morning light, through open curtains that framed a window she didn't recognize. Rubbing sleep from her eyes, she peered about her. This most certainly was not her bedroom, and no wonder the bed was so comfortable — it was not the narrow, hard bed she slept on at home. Gradually her memory of the night before came back to her, and she blushed in shame. Feeling beneath the sheets, she was mortified to find she was as naked as the day she was born.

'So you've woken then? You've missed breakfast. I've got to get a move on. I'm due at the Ramsgate teashop at nine, and it's nearly that now. Hurry up and get dressed; we've got to vacate the room by ten. I only paid for the one night.'

Lily was puzzled. 'I thought this was your room — the one you lived in while you worked down this end of the county?'

Tom laughed. 'As if I'd take every woman I met back to my lodgings! My landlady would soon let Lyons know I was up to no good. Impressions count in this business if you want to climb the management ladder,' he said, tightening his tie and taking his hat from the hook behind the door. 'Thanks for a pleasant night. I'll see you around.'

Lily burst into tears. 'What do you take me for? I'm not that kind of girl, I thought you liked me. This is the first time I've ever done anything like this,' she sniffed, wiping her eyes on the back of her hand.

'You could have fooled me,' he mocked. 'I could tell, you know; I'm not daft,' he added before leaving the room.

Lily fell back onto the pillows and sobbed her heart out. 'But it was my first time,' she mumbled. 'The first time I thought somebody loved me, and the first time I'd agreed to be loved and not had to fight off my awful stepfather.' She cried silently for some time before falling asleep. A loud knock at the door startled her awake. 'Who is it?' she called out.

'Madam, it's ten o'clock. I need to come in to clean the room.'

'I'll . . . I'll just be a few minutes,' she replied, hurrying out of the bed and searching for her clothes strewn around the room. Shoving her stockings into her handbag and pulling on her coat over her dance frock, she didn't stop to check her make-up or even to run a comb through her hair. Passing the maid on the landing, she did her best to look the other way as the woman tutted and hissed the word 'prostitute' at Lily's back.

Lily fled, looking neither left or right, trying hard not to make eye contact with the staff or other guests as she hurried away from the hotel and towards the teashop. She felt so ashamed of herself, and the maid's voice rang in her ears. A thought buzzed around in her head as she gave a manic laugh: how could she be a prostitute when money hadn't changed hands?

'My goodness, Lily, whatever has happened to you?' Katie asked as her friend hurried through the teashop into the staff area, indicating that Katie should follow her.

'Why are you wearing your clothes from last night?' she asked as she closed the door after them so as not to be seen by others. She looked at her friend's pale face as Lily pulled open her locker, dragging out items of her uniform, before the penny dropped. 'Oh no, you never . . . you never stayed out all night . . . with a man?'

'I can't explain now. I'm over an hour late, and I must already be in Miss Butterworth's bad books. Where is she? I expected her to jump on me the moment I walked in the door.'

Katie was worried for her friend, and knew she would have to wait to hear her tell the full story, so there was no point in asking questions now. 'You are safe. She's been holed up in her office with Mr Grant and Mr White since nine. Rose is in there too. I overheard Mr Grant say that Rose could do well by learning what happens in these meetings for when she starts her new job. If you hurry and get dressed you may not have been missed — I've been covering your workstation

149

this morning. I signed you in as well,' she grinned.

Lily stopped and quickly gave Katie a kiss on the cheek. For her young friend to have done such thing was brave. 'Blimey, Katie, you're becoming a bit of a rebel,' she said with a weak smile. 'I'll repay the favour one day, not that I can see you doing what I did last night, at least not before you and Jack married.'

Katie look shocked. 'You mean you . . . you never did?'

Lily nodded her head. 'I've already wished I hadn't. It's all a big mistake, and not worth losing my job over. You wouldn't happen to have a pair of stockings in your locker, would you?' she asked, knowing the ones in the handbag weren't fit to wear and would soon be in the dustbin.

'You're in luck. I did some darning at the weekend and there's a spare pair washed and ready in case I need to change them at work,' Katie replied, opening her locker. 'I hope you don't mind stockings with the toes stitched up?'

'Katie, you are a lifesaver. Now, if you could cover for me for another five minutes I'll be out on the floor and working twice as hard. I owe you the biggest favour going for this.'

'Knowing you still have a job and will be my bridesmaid in a few weeks' time is good enough for me,' her friend smiled.

'Jack said yes?' Lily asked, a big grin covering her face.

'He did, and is very grateful for all you both suggested. He is going to speak to his captain today. I just hope and pray he's not shipped off overseas before the wedding.'

Lily gave her a quick hug. 'I'm sure he won't be,' she said, holding up her hands to show her crossed fingers. 'Now, I must finish getting dressed before Miss Butterworth finds us in here, or we will both get the sack.'

Lily was as good as her word and worked like a Trojan, even covering a couple of Katie's tables when Miss Butterworth wasn't looking, as questions would have been asked. She turned her back when Tom appeared in the teashop on his way to the front door. It was easy enough to pretend she was busy collecting dirty plates and loading a tray. If she'd seen any form of expression cross his face when he looked at her, she wouldn't have been accountable for her actions.

'Where were you this morning?' Rose asked when she joined the girls for their midday meal.

'I was late,' Lily said as she prodded a sausage with her fork. 'Katie covered for me, so everything is all right. She has news about the wedding,' she added quickly, just in case Rose was going to ask for more details.

'I'm going to walk up to the vicarage this evening and ask Reverend Peterson if he will marry Jack and me. I just hope there is time.'

'I think you can get a special licence,' Rose said. 'Didn't one of the Sallys do that recently?'

'It was Christine. She's on duty at the moment. I'll go back to my workstation early and see if I can catch her eye and ask her about it,' Lily said. 'I'm the closest to the counter staff to be able to have a few words without Miss

151

Butterworth telling me off.'

The girls chatted excitedly about the wedding and what the two bridesmaids would wear, until Lily checked the time and headed back to her customers.

'Rose, do you mind if I ask you something?' Katie said as Rose started to collect the dirty plates from the table.

'By all means; is it about the wedding?'

'No, it's Lily. I'm so worried about her. She didn't go home last night — and she was in quite a state when she arrived for work. I had to lend her some stockings. I hate speaking out of school, but she's so dear to me, as are you; I'd hate anything to go wrong in her life.'

Rose sat down, looking worried. 'She was out with Tom White last night. If she was with him, why did he come in to work on his own? And so much earlier than her?'

'I don't know; she didn't tell me,' Katie said.

Rose knew it had taken a lot for innocent Katie to say these few words.

'I'll see if I can have a word with her, but as I'm going off to London tomorrow morning, there may not be time. I'll do my best,' she promised, seeing the fear in her friend's eyes. 'You are not to worry about a thing. Just enjoy organizing your wedding. You must go to Mum for anything that worries you. She's itching to see me walk up the aisle, so you're doing me a favour by letting her practise on you,' Rose laughed. 'I just wish I didn't have to go to London for my training at the moment and miss all the fun.'

'Write to me as soon as you arrive, and I promise to keep in touch to tell you everything. Our main problem will be finding something for you and Lily to wear as my bridesmaids. I do wish we had more time in that respect. I saw a lovely dress pattern that would double as a summer dress once we get some nice weather.'

'Did you know Miss Tibbs is teaching Anya how to sew? Why not ask if the pair of them would take on the job of making the dresses? Anya is such a lovely lady, and I reckon she would be delighted to get involved with your wedding. Shall I ask her when I get home this evening?'

Katie's face lit up. 'Oh, would you? I'd be too embarrassed to ask. I'm sure Anya is very nice, but she frightens me a little. Now she has settled in she seems so confident, and a little forthright with her comments.'

Rose thought Katie was spot on with her impressions of their Polish friend. 'She fits in very well at Sea View and is a great help to Mum. I'm hoping she decided to have an interview to be a Sally. She would be perfect, especially as Lyons like taller girls to work behind the counters.'

'If she gets to work here, I'll help her all I can,' Katie promised. 'It's going to be so sad not seeing you every day once you're living and working in Margate. So much is changing in our lives,' she added wistfully.

Rose gave her a quick hug. 'The changes are going to be so exciting. You will be a married woman and will have a husband to care for, while I'll just have a teashop to look after,' she said.

Katie laughed. 'I don't know which will be

153

harder work. My Jack can be so untidy at times! His landlady is always telling me how she has to nag him to tidy his room. I hope the navy will teach him a thing or two. Now, this is enough chatting — we must get some work done. Come along, Miss Neville. Do you realize this is your final afternoon working as a Nippy?'

'Gosh, I'd never given it a thought. I'll miss wearing this uniform.'

'Really?' Katie said in amazement.

'Haha, I was joking. At long last I won't be told off for my dress being the wrong length, or having a button missing.'

'You'll have to dress extra smart once you are a manageress,' Katie said as they left the staffroom to head back to their workstations.

'I'll be fitted for my manageress outfits while I'm at Orchard House having my training. I'm told I will be able to bring at least one outfit home with me by the end of my training period — rather like we did when we went up to London for our Nippy training.'

Katie shivered. 'Rather you than me,' she replied. 'Do you remember how frightened we were to be in London? We hardly left the hostel unless it was to go to Orchard House for our lessons. I'm not one for London, especially now we're at war. Why, anything could happen.'

'It could happen here too, though. There's no knowing what Adolf will get up to, is there?'

Katie shivered. 'Let's talk about something else. Did you hear about the customer who tried to leave without paying this morning? Thankfully that Mr White caught him at the front door.'

Rose smiled, but Katie mentioning Tom White had reminded her about Lily and her escapade last night.

★ ★ ★

'Goodnight, Miss Neville. I wish you well with your training,' Clarice Butterworth said as she held open the door. 'I will have left by the time you return to Thanet. I hope our paths cross some time in the future,' she said, holding out her hand for Rose to shake.

Rose heard a slight snigger and knew it would be Lily, who had been helping one of the other Nippies to put up wooden shutters over the windows at the front of the teashop. Although the town had been free from attack so far, the staff at Lyons were ever vigilant. She ignored them and smiled at Miss Butterworth as she shook her hand. 'I'd like to thank you for recommending me for the position. I hope I can be as good a manageress as you have been.' Clarice Butterworth nodded and glared past Rose to where Lily stood. 'Believe me, there was very little choice,' she said before entering the teashop, closing the door and pulling down the blinds.

'That put you in your place,' Lily laughed as she looped her arm through Rose's and fell into step beside her. They fought their way along the icy pavements down the street towards the harbour, where Rose would turn off to head up Madeira Walk.

'At least the snow has stopped,' Rose said. 'I just hope the trains will be running tomorrow. I don't fancy standing about at the station waiting to see if there is one heading up to London.'

'I'd rather have your problem than mine,' Lily said.

Rose stiffened. Was Lily going to tell her what had happened last night? 'What problem is that?' she asked, dreading what the answer would be.

'Why, waiting on people all day long who only want to come in out of the bad weather and then only order a cup of tea and a bun. Then there will be the people moaning that we don't have enough baked goods on sale — they have no understanding that if the roads are full of snow, the delivery vans can't get down here from Cadby Hall with fresh supplies of food. Then of course old Butterworth will have us out the front of the teashop shovelling snow off the pavements. I call that a cheek, and nearly told her so as well. I could hardly feel my fingers to serve my customers after half an hour outside. I swear I have frostbite.'

Rose smiled to herself. Lily had been quick enough to volunteer for clearing the snow when Miss Butterworth had asked the Nippies during their afternoon tea break. It was best to ignore her complaints when she started. 'Why don't you come back to Sea View for some dinner? We could chat to Miss Tibbs and Anya about the wedding dress and the possibility of them making our bridesmaid outfits. That's if you don't have to get back home for your stepfather?'

'Blow him. He's no doubt half cut by now, or off down the pub. Yes, I'd like to come back to your house, thank you,' she replied, losing some of her sarcastic tone. 'I don't always say it, but I'm grateful to you and your mum for looking out for me since Mum died.'

Rose steadied herself as she started to slip, and her grip tightened on Lily's arm. 'Phew — that was close. You must miss your mum a lot? I know I would, if it was mine who had passed away. You don't speak about it much. You know I'm always here to chat if you want to?'

'Yeah, I miss her, but not in the way you think,' Lily said slowly as they concentrated on walking up the steep incline of Madeira Walk and watching where to place their feet in the fresh snow that had recently fallen. 'She always managed to keep George from picking on me. She was a barrier for my safety. Now . . . now things are so different.'

'He must miss your mum,' Rose said, trying to pick her words with care. Lily wasn't one to talk about her feelings.

'Oh yes, he misses her in many ways,' she said before stopping to look back down the hill towards the waterfront. 'Ramsgate looks so different with a layer of snow. It's as if the town has been cleansed and is hiding all the bad stuff for a while.'

Rose stood close to her friend as Lily gazed out towards the water. She could see a single tear escape from her friend's eye, but somehow she felt that now wasn't the place or time to delve into what was bothering Lily.

They quietly turned and made their way further up the steep road.

'Look, there's an army lorry in front of your

house,' Lily said, grabbing Rose's arm in horror. 'Look at all the soldiers — some have guns! I wonder what's going on?'

Rose stood transfixed, staring at the scene in front of her. Her gaze was focused on Ben, who was talking to her mum on the doorstep when he should have been in London. Whatever was going on?

★   ★   ★

'Such a shame you missed all the excitement, dear,' Miss Tibbs said as Rose sat by her side in Flora's sitting room. They all had tea served in her mum's best cups and saucers. Rose could feel Ben watching her from across the room, which was making her feel just a little flushed. 'Why, we could all have been murdered in our beds if it wasn't for Captain Hargreaves. Who would have thought our Mr Cardew was a spy and living one floor above me! Whatever will my friends at the beetle drive say? I hope they don't think I was involved,' she twittered on.

'I'm sure they won't,' Rose said, patting her hand. 'If you've finished with your cup, I'll take it out to the kitchen.' She headed for the kitchen, grateful for its silence and cooler air. Flora had banked up the fire in the sitting room to the point the windows had been opened. Rose had so many questions flying around in her head; but above all, what was Ben doing drinking tea with her mum when he should be miles away?

'I'm sorry I couldn't warn you,' Ben said as he entered the room. 'It all happened rather quickly,' he added, placing a pile of crockery by the sink. 'I'll give you a hand with the washing-up.'

Rose tipped hot water from a kettle that had been kept warm on the hob into a large enamel bowl before sprinkling soap flakes. She carefully started to wash the cups and saucers. 'These were a wedding present to my mum and dad,' she explained as she placed each one onto the wooden draining board. 'They only come out on high days and holidays. You should feel honoured.' She smiled, thinking of her gentle father and how much he would have enjoyed Ben's company.

'Your mother is a very gracious lady. When we appeared on her doorstep to take Cardew away she didn't flap at all, but led us up to his room, and then knocked on the door to say she had bed linen for him. It made it very easy for us to enter and take him into custody.'

'Is this all because we spotted that glint of light from the attic window last night?'

'Yes. The local police were able to tell us who lodged in the house, and along with what you've said to me, it was thought best to take him into custody.'

Rose felt a little miffed. 'I didn't realize that when we were making small talk you were storing up all I'd said in case I was a danger to the security of this country.'

Ben put down the tea towel and took her by the shoulders, turning her to face him. 'Please don't ever think such things. I recalled our conversation about your mother's guests, and it worried me you could have someone dangerous in your midst. My thoughts were always for you.

Cardew was in with a dangerous crowd of people who have sympathies with the enemy. God forbid if you or your mother had met with danger . . . '

Time stood still as they looked into each other's eyes. Rose longed for Ben to kiss her, and she just knew he felt the same way.

Young Pearl Hannigan ran into the kitchen, breaking the spell, and Rose turned back to the washing-up.

'Rose, Mrs Neville said to put the kettle on again an' I'm to take in her best biscuit barrel — not the old one she uses every day,' Pearl added shyly when she spotted Ben. 'Could we also have a cloth dipped in cold water, as Mildred has a sore hand?'

'Whatever has she done?' Rose asked as she reached for a clean cloth kept behind a gingham curtain that covered a shelf below the sink.

'She thumped Mr Cardew,' Pearl said with glee. 'Just like that,' she added, punching the air like a seasoned boxer.

'She does pack a punch.' Ben grinned. 'He'll have a right shiner by the morning, which will add to his woes.'

Flora came out to the kitchen, leading a reluctant Mildred by the arm. 'You deserve everything you got,' she said sternly, making Mildred sit down at one of the hard wooden chairs set around the table. 'Why, you could have done serious damage to your hand — how would you have worked then?'

Mildred grinned. 'It was worth it even if I'd broken a few bones in my hand. Even if he isn't a spy, I never did like the man, so that punch is worth a little pain. Just to think a spy was in this house makes my blood boil! I had to do something. In fact, I think we should have done something earlier, as we were far too welcoming. You carrying his food to and fro, Miss Tibbs sewing buttons on his shirts, and me . . . well, I was the worst possible person, as I fixed his telescope, and Ben here told me he was using it to watch shipping movements,' she said, looking shamefaced. 'That's why, when he pulled away from the soldiers, I took my chance and thumped him as hard as I could — just in case he was going to make a run for it. I'm glad I did it,' she added, giving Flora a determined look. 'It's just a shame my fist made contact with the wall as well as his cheek.'

'The wall will survive,' Flora said, trying hard not to smile. 'I wish I'd had the chance to join you. Although grown-ups shouldn't do such things,' she added as she noticed young Pearl listening.

'What I'd like to know is how all this happened, and why you aren't in London,' Rose said to Ben. 'If this is the kind of thing you're going to get up to, I'll have second thoughts about going off and leaving you. Spies in the house, and Mildred here throwing punches — whatever next?'

'I too had expected to be in London by now, but after what we spotted last night as I walked you home, I thought it prudent to report back to the relevant authorities. I thought they would take over, but it wasn't to be. After liaising with local police I found that your Mr Cardew had a question mark against his name. He'd slipped the net while in another part of Kent — near Bromley,' he added, seeing Rose's quizzical expression. 'Even though Mrs Neville had notified the local police station that Cardew was one of her residents, it appears checks weren't made.'

'Oh my,' Flora said, looking flustered. 'Did I do something wrong? Is it my fault that a possible spy was left to roam Ramsgate?'

'No, not at all,' Ben assured her. 'Sadly these things happen.'

'It was more likely that lazy Sergeant Atkins wasn't doing his job,' Mildred huffed. 'It makes me wonder how many other foreigners are in this town who haven't been checked out properly?'

'I'm sure this was just a slip-up,' Flora said quickly, noting how Anya had turned rather pink-faced and averted her eyes. 'Besides, from what I could tell, Mr Cardew was British. If not, he was doing a pretty good job of pretending to be one of us.'

'So what happened next?' Rose prompted.

'Trust us to miss all the excitement because we were at work,' Lily said as she joined them in the kitchen. 'Hitler could invade and we would miss it just because we were busy pouring cups of tea for all and sundry.'

Young Pearl burst out laughing. 'That would be funny,' she said, enjoying the conversation.

'Time for your bed, young lady,' her mother said, taking her hand. 'Say goodnight to everybody.'

By the time Pearl had gone round all the visitors, politely making her goodbyes and kissing Miss Tibbs and Flora on the cheek, Rose was beyond agitated, desperate for more details about what had happened. 'Please tell me everything, or I shall burst,' she exclaimed.

'I was requested to bring my men to the guesthouse. They waited around the corner while I and a police inspector based at the station had a little chat with Mr Cardew. I'm not at liberty to say how the conversation went, but when Mr Cardew became agitated and it was obvious he was not innocent, we decided to bring him in while we made further investigations. It was while we were walking downstairs that he tried to give us the slip. Thankfully Miss Dalrymple assisting us with detaining him. After that, he went calmly with the inspector in the back of the lorry.'

Rose thought for a moment of all she had been told. 'Did you know this was going to happen, Mum?'

Flora nodded. 'Ben came in and spoke to me so that I was prepared. He did have the decency to ask if he and the inspector could go to Mr Cardew's room to speak to him. I thought it was handled very well, and no one seemed alarmed. Ben allowed me to inform the ladies who were at home so they were not alarmed.'

'So what will happen to Mr Cardew's property in his room — and would you want him back here after what's happened, Mum?'

Floor looked flustered. 'I hadn't given that any thought,' she said, looking towards Ben for help. 'He has only paid his rent up until Friday.'

'With the evidence we have already, I don't think Mr Cardew will be allowed to remain in

Ramsgate after this. My feelings are that he will be in custody but that's all I can say at this time.'

'But his things . . . ' Flora said.

'I shall arrange to have everything collected by tomorrow morning so as not to inconvenience you,' Ben said politely.

'You will have to let the billeting officer know that you have another spare room,' Miss Tibbs added.

Flora sat down, looking flustered. 'After this, I'm not sure I want another gentleman living in my house. Ladies seem much easier to get along with,' she sighed.

'Perhaps I can have a word with the officer in charge and explain what has happened. It could be that if you found another tenant very quickly, we could then consider this house full to capacity.'

For a moment Flora looked happy, but then her face dropped. 'Usually I would have a waiting list of people requiring rooms, or with the summer season approaching it would be holidaymakers staying here. But at the moment I can't name one single person to fill the rooms — and with Rose off to live in Margate before too long, I will have two rooms to rent out.'

'We could probably turn a blind eye to one small room being vacant, but two bedrooms is a different matter when we have to make so many sleeping arrangements at the moment,' Ben said.

Rose looked around the room and watched as the residents of Sea View tried to come up with an answer.

'I will move into Rose's room when she goes

to Margate,' Anya declared, 'but I wish to pay more money. I insist,' she added, as Flora started to protest. 'That box room is not large enough for one soldier to stretch his legs, so I'm doubting the army will want to use it.'

Rose suddenly thought of a solution that would suit both parties. 'Why don't you move into my room, Lily, and Anya can use Mr Cardew's room?' She smiled at her friend. 'I'll feel much happier about being away from home if someone is looking out for my mum — someone who's known her for many years,' she added quickly, just in case she had offended any of the tenants. She could see that Lily was interested by the way her face lit up. Whatever had been troubling Lily of late might be helped by having Flora nearby to care for her while Rose was away. 'Would you do that for me?' Rose asked.

Flora knew her daughter was up to something, but went along with the suggestion. 'It would be lovely to have you living here, Lily. Rose, you can have the box room when you come to visit and you can store your things in my room,' she said to her daughter with a smile. 'That seems to have sorted out everything nicely,' she added, giving another sigh.

Lily looked quite tearful as she accepted the offer of a room at Sea View. 'It will be like living with family,' she sniffed.

'There's just one more thing, Mrs Neville. May I ask your permission to drive your daughter to London tomorrow? It seems silly, with both of us heading in the same direction, for Rose to have to stand about waiting for trains in this awful weather,' Ben said.

'That is a very generous offer, Ben, and if Rose agrees then I agree,' Flora said, giving them both a big smile.

Rose groaned inwardly. She could almost see her mother making wedding arrangements and choosing an outfit to wear in church.

'I'll be here at nine, if that suits you?' Ben said, giving Rose a gentle smile. 'Wrap up warm, as the transport can be a little draughty,' he added, before wishing everyone good evening and taking his leave of them.

After he'd gone, while the others continued to chatter excitedly, Rose sat quietly with her thoughts. She felt as though her life was beginning to move in a new direction and, whether she liked it or not, she was being swept along on the crest of a wave to goodness knows where. But, as long as Ben was by her side, she didn't care one little bit.

8

'Whoops! Mind how you go. We don't want you having to walk down the aisle with a broken leg,' Jack said, putting an arm round Katie's waist to help her stay upright. 'Let's hope this snow eases off a bit before our wedding day.'

Katie stopped walking and turned to face him. He was only a couple of inches taller than her, so she could easily see his face even though there wasn't a street lamp or a light from a window to be seen. Perhaps it was the waning of the moon, or the pure white of the drifting snow. 'Our wedding day.' She sighed. 'Those few words sound magical. Aren't you excited? I know I am.' She linked her arm through his. 'Wasn't it splendid of the vicar to be able to fit us in so soon? In a few weeks I'll be Mrs Jack Jones. Isn't it just wonderful?'

Jack laughed and kissed the tip of her cold nose. 'It was indeed splendid of him,' he said, loving her even more for her enthusiasm. He didn't add that when Katie had gone to help the vicar's wife make tea, he'd told the vicar his ship would soon be sailing and he had no idea where they were heading or when they might return. The vicar understood immediately. He had known the young couple since the days when both were in the children's home, and he promised to move heaven and earth so that Katie could have her special day before Jack left.

'Now let's go and have a swift drink to celebrate us naming the day,' Jack said, steering her carefully down the path from the church towards the nearest public house.

The pub was quite full of sailors as well as airmen, and just a few army lads who were grouped around a piano singing loudly. Jack managed to guide his fiancée through the crowded bar to where there was a seat by the fireplace, with a dismal fire giving off just a little heat. Katie took off her hat and coat, stuffing her gloves into the pockets. She rubbed her hands together to help bring the circulation back. She couldn't remember the last time it had been so cold. Even wearing a woolly hat to bed and piling blankets and her coat on top, before cuddling up to a stone hot-water bottle in order to ward off the terrible chill, didn't help. She wished they would have more than that one small room in which to start their married life. First thing tomorrow she would begin searching for something better, somewhere Jack would be happy to return to when he came home on leave. Perhaps Rose's mother would know of suitable rooms?

'You're miles away,' Jack said as he returned with two halves of bitter and placed one down on the table close to where she sat. 'Cheers mate,' he said as a man pointed out a spare seat, and dragged it over to where Katie was sitting. 'So what were you dreaming about?' he asked before supping from his glass.

'Just that it would be wonderful to have a home of our own rather than my pokey, damp little room. It's not much of a place to start married life.'

'Katie, just to be married to you is enough for me. Once this wretched war is over we will have our own house and the family we've never known. Until then, let's be happy with our one little room.'

Katie sighed. 'I know you're right, Jack, but I can't help dreaming. If something comes up while you're away, can I take it?'

Jack laughed. 'Why not? But please do remember to write and give me the address, or I'll not know where to find you.'

Katie joined in with his laughter. 'I'm lucky to have you, Jack,' she said, leaning in to kiss his cheek. As she gazed over his shoulder she spotted a group of sailors starting to get rowdy. 'Are they some of yours?' she asked. 'It looks as though things are getting rough over there.'

Jack followed her gaze. 'No, I don't recognize them, but it looks like that old fool George Jacobs is up to his usual tricks.'

'What do you mean?' Katie asked, trying to look through the crowd to where the pub landlord was manhandling sailors away from the cause of the trouble and shouting for some of them to leave his pub before he called the police. 'That's Lily's stepfather.'

'I spotted him trying to grope a woman when I was up at the bar. He's his usual three sheets to the wind.'

Katie frowned. 'Oh, you mean he's drunk — why don't you say so, instead of using such a silly saying?' she scolded him. 'Lily lives alone with him since her mum died. I shouldn't think it's much fun living with someone who likes to drink. Don't think you are going to be heading off to the pub all the time once we are married,' she added pretending to scold him.

'I don't intend to when I have a pretty wife at home,' Jack said, still watching as George was hauled to his feet. 'Has Lily ever said anything about him?'

'No, but she's becoming more and more miserable these days. I thought perhaps she just missed her mum. I can be a shoulder to cry on for her, but apart from that I have no memory of what it would be like to have a mother, being as I had no recollection of having parents.'

Jack squeezed her hand. 'We have each other,' he said.

'I thank God for you being my friend from as far back as I can remember. Who'd have thought two kids from an orphanage would fall in love and marry?' she said, giving him a loving look.

'It won't be long before we have our own children — and then one day we will be grand-parents. It will make up for what we missed,' he said, giving her a tender smile. 'I don't know about you, but I can't wait.'

'I'd like to enjoy my children before I think about being a grandmother. Talk about wishing your life away,' Katie laughed. 'And I know I will be a better parent than that horrid man. Look at him now,' she exclaimed in horror, as they watched George trying to drag the woman he was sitting with by the arm towards the pub door.

'The man's a monster,' Jack spat out,

incensed. 'God knows what sort of life Lily has, living with him. I've heard talk he's not choosy who he goes with — and he'd put a woman in hospital rather than pay the going rate. Sorry,' he added, seeing Katie's shocked face. 'I shouldn't be saying such things in front of a lady.'

'I'm not shocked by what you've said. I'm afraid that's life. What has horrified me is realizing what a monster Lily is living with. She never really spoke about him when her mum was alive. Do you think he has . . . harmed her?'

'I'd not be surprised. Perhaps you and Rose could have a word with her,' Jack suggested. 'Talking woman to woman might help her share any problems she is having.'

'I'll do that. Rose is catching the mid-morning train to London tomorrow morning. I'll pop round and speak with her before I go in to work. It's my late shift, so I have time. It's best I speak with Rose first; then we'll know what to say before broaching the subject to Lily. She may hate us for asking, but I couldn't sleep nights knowing what that bully could be doing to her.'

★ ★ ★

'Have you packed all you need?' Flora asked as Rose dragged her suitcase to the front door, ready for when Ben arrived.

'Everything but the kitchen sink,' she grinned. 'I may only be going for two weeks, but I have no idea what is expected of me.' Rose didn't add that if Ben was to take her out for the evening it was important she had the right clothes to wear.

171

She wouldn't want to embarrass him, and she'd heard that Londoners could be very posh, especially when going to the theatre or dancing.

'Now, do you have your gas mask? I know what you girls are like for leaving them behind.'

'You've asked me that already, Mum. I also have my torch, a clean handkerchief, change for the telephone, and I'm wearing a clean pair of knickers. Are you happy now?' Rose laughed. She checked her wristwatch. 'Ben should be here by now; I wonder what's held him up? It's a long drive to London, from what I've been told. I've never travelled that far in a car before, and with it still snowing I must admit to being a little worried.'

'Why don't I make us a cup of tea? We can drink it in the front room and watch from the window, so you're all ready when Ben arrives. And I've made you some sandwiches for the journey — there's plenty for the two of you.'

Rose gave her mum a quick peck on the cheek. 'You think of everything. There wouldn't be a slice or two of cake as well, would there?'

Flora grinned. How could she forget her daughter's sweet tooth? 'I've wrapped two slices of the Bakewell tart you brought home from work the other day. I've put them on the top of the parcel of sandwiches, so be careful,' she said.

They'd not quite reached the kitchen when there was an urgent knock on the door. 'I didn't hear a vehicle pull up. Open the door, love, and I'll still make that tea. Ben's bound to want one before you set off. It's nigh on perishing out there,' Flora said, hurrying down the long passage.

Rose checked her hair in the mirror of the hall stand and licked her lips. There wasn't time to touch up her lipstick. Pulling back the blackout curtain they kept closed during the day to stop any cold draughts, she quickly opened the door with a bright smile pinned to her face, which faded somewhat when she saw it wasn't Ben standing on the doorstep. 'Hello Katie — you don't normally come visiting this time of the morning. I thought you'd be at work?' she said, ushering her friend inside and closing the door. 'I see there's been a fresh fall of snow overnight,' she added, noticing the deep virgin snow that lay down the road and across the park. The only footsteps marking it were Katie's, as even the milkman and postman had yet to visit the street.

'I'm on a later shift today,' Katie said as she stamped her feet on the hall mat before pulling off her headscarf and woolly mittens. 'I'm glad to have caught you before you set off for the station. However are you going to get your suitcase up there?' she asked, noticing the suitcase propped up by the wall. 'Are the trains running?'

'Ben's driving me to London, thank goodness — otherwise I don't think I'd have reached there by train.'

'Is he really?' Katie said, raising her eyebrows. 'Have I missed something here? I didn't realize you knew him so well.' She smiled with a mischievous glint in her eye.

'Don't you start. Mum's as good as got us walking up the aisle. I like him. Between you and me, I like him a lot, but it's early days. Come down to the kitchen and warm yourself up. So

173

much happened here last night. Would you believe Mr Cardew has been arrested? They think he's a spy,' she said excitedly as they headed into the kitchen. 'Mum, it's Katie — get another cup out,' she called.

'Hello, hello, my love,' Flora said, giving Katie a quick peck on the cheek. 'Do you have news about the wedding?'

'I do, the vicar has been so kind and understood the situation. It's two weeks tomorrow. I do hope you'll be back, Rose,' she said, looking anxious.

'I'll make sure that I'm back, even if it's the night before,' Rose promised. 'Miss Tibbs and Anya said they'd be happy to make the two bridesmaids' dresses, and it seems wedding dress alterations are almost finished. You're going to make a beautiful bride.'

Katie wasn't one for accepting compliments, and laughed off the remark. 'If you're going to be away, how can we fit you for your dress?'

'You don't need to worry about that. Miss Tibbs has my measurements from when she made me a dress to wear at Christmas. Lily and me are about the same size, so she can try it on if need be. What I was wondering was how you felt about your bridesmaids having dresses that would double up as summer frocks? It wouldn't be so expensive, and we'd get so much more wear out of them. Miss Tibbs was telling us that the fabric shop didn't have the stock they usually hold, and things could get worse if this war goes on too long.'

'Food rationing has started, so God knows

what will be in short supply next,' Flora said as she placed a hot drink in front of the girls.

'If that's what you want, then I'm happy,' Katie said, appreciating Rose's point about the expense.

'And we want to pay for our own dresses,' Rose added, raising her hand to fend off the look on Katie's face. 'No arguing,' she continued quickly as Katie started to protest. 'Lily and I discussed it last night. It can be our way of chipping in towards the wedding. Our dance shoes will be suitable, and Mum suggested we both carry the bibles we were given on the day we left school. What do you say to that?'

Katie's eyes sparkled with delight. 'That's a great weight off my mind,' she said, taking a sip of tea. 'However, you mentioning Lily reminds me of why I came to see you.' She started to explain what she'd seen in the pub the night before, and also what Jack had said about George Jacobs. 'So you see, I do believe that is why our Lily has been so miserable lately. I'm also worried that is why she came into work so dishevelled. I dread to think what he's been doing to the poor girl.'

Rose and Flora listened in horror. 'It would certainly explain a few things,' Rose said. 'However, with what happened here last night we may have solved the problem, and Lily should now be safe. Mum, would you tell Katie about last night while I go into the front room to see if Ben has arrived?'

As Rose pressed her nose against the cold window, trying to see down the road through the frosty panes, she could hear hoots of laughter from the kitchen. No doubt Flora was explaining about Mildred's participation in detaining the spy. As a lorry pulled up outside and Ben climbed out, Rose felt comforted that Katie was happy with her wedding arrangements while Lily was safe upstairs in the room vacated by Mr Cardew — even if it was against his will. Although his property was still in the room, Flora had quickly changed the bed linen and Lily had gratefully fallen into bed wearing one of Rose's flannelette nightgowns. Today Flora had promised to accompany her to collect a few possessions and carry them back to Lily's new home at Sea View guesthouse.

★　★　★

Rose screwed up her face in concentration, holding onto the steering wheel while staring ahead at the snow-covered road.

'That's it, Miss,' the soldier closest to her open window called out.

'You do know I've never driven a motor vehicle before,' she replied, surprised that her voice wasn't quaking in fear.

'Well, the engine isn't running and we are still in this snowdrift, so you've nothing to worry about yet,' the soldier replied, putting his shoulder back against the side of the army lorry and shoving with all his might as Ben gave the command to push.

There was a resounding cheer from the six soldiers as the lorry lurched forward out of the drift.

'You can hop down now, Miss,' the same soldier said as he half lifted her from the hard leather driver's seat down into the snow, which came up to her knees and over the top of the wellington boots loaned to her by Mildred. They'd seen better days, but had kept her feet dry up to that point.

'Oh blast,' she said, wondering how to remove the freezing snow before it soaked into the thick socks she'd used so that her feet fitted the larger-sized boots. She looked pleadingly at the soldiers. 'I'm stuck,' she declared. This was the final straw . . .

When Ben had entered Sea View earlier that day, he'd taken one look at Rose's attire before advising her to go and dress in something more suitable for travelling in an army lorry. She'd been astounded. Before he had time to explain there was a knock on the door, which she opened to find two corporals who immediately saluted when they spotted Ben. 'We are ready whenever you and the young lady are, sir,' one of them said.

'Thank you, Corporal,' Ben said. 'Take Miss Neville's suitcase out and we will be with you shortly.'

Rose watched as the soldier took her suitcase down the footpath. She felt so disappointed. Any thoughts of a romantic journey up to London alone with Ben were dashed.

'I'd hoped to be able to drive you, but the weather is closing in and we might well have been stranded before we reached London,' he explained. 'The lads have orders to collect an important piece of equipment, so it made sense to go with them. It will take a lot to get caught in

177

the snow with that vehicle.'

Rose nodded. 'I can see that. Thank you for still including me in your plans. I don't want to put anyone out. I still have time to catch the train,' she offered.

'The trains are all cancelled, so I'm afraid it's me and the lorry — or stay here in Ramsgate.' He grinned.

Rose couldn't be upset for long. At least she'd have time to spend with him before they parted company. 'I'll be just a few minutes changing into some warmer clothes. Go to the kitchen and say hello to Mum. Katie's with her, and there might be some tea left in the pot,' she called, hurrying upstairs to find socks to pull on over her stockings. She dug into the wardrobe and pulled out a thick tweed skirt she hadn't worn in a while. 'Not exactly stylish, but it will keep my legs warm,' she said to her reflection in the mirror before rifling through a chest of drawers for a cardigan that would fit over her jumper. She glanced at her reflection one more time to check her hair. 'You'll not win any beauty competitions, Rose Neville,' she grimaced before hurrying downstairs.

Mildred was in the kitchen and getting on like a house on fire with Ben, who was holding a large china mug that hadn't been in use since her dad had been alive. 'You can borrow my wellington boots. I have another pair; it will save your shoes getting wet and spoiling,' she told Rose with a smile. 'Your young man will understand why you aren't your usual smart self,' she added.

Rose was mortified and felt her cheeks start to

burn as she spotted Ben grinning. 'Thank you, Mildred; it's very kind of you. I'll make sure to bring them back at the end of my training. I'm sorry I won't be here to help with the wedding plans,' she apologized to Katie, 'and for not being able to help move Anya into Mr Cardew's old room,' she added as she hugged Flora. 'If you put my things into the box room, I'll sort them out when I get back.' Life was moving on at a fast pace, and as she prepared to leave home it was suddenly becoming clear to her that nothing would ever be the same again.

★ ★ ★

Ben stepped in and lifted Rose off her feet, leaving the wellington boots still buried in the snow. He carried her with ease to the rear of the lorry and carefully placed her down. Even with them both wearing numerous layers of clothing to fend off the cold, Rose swore she could feel his heart beating close to hers. With six soldiers watching, it still felt intimate. Her boots were passed to her, and after shaking out the powdery snow she was soon as snug as before.

'Time for a hot drink and some food, I should think,' Ben said, nodding to the men.

'Mum packed sandwiches and cake, if you'd all like some?' Rose offered, knowing that it wouldn't go far with so many hungry men to feed.

'Save them for later,' Ben smiled as the soldiers set to with a spade. They dug out an area of snow until they had a flat part of the road where they set a paraffin stove. Soon they had a kettle on the boil, and a frying pan busy sizzling fat sausages and sliced onion.

'Can I help?' Rose asked, feeling she should be doing something.

'You stay in there and keep yourself warm, Miss,' one of the soldiers said while another passed her a blanket to wrap around her shoulders.

'I must say, this is so much more fun than it would have been travelling by train,' she smiled at Ben as he appeared with a map.

'We can't offer you the same service you give at Lyons, but I can assure you Corporal Jenkins is a very good cook,' he said before going back to studying the map once more.

'I 'ope I can keep up the standard of service once we are over in Fr . . . ' the soldier started to say before faltering.

Rose knew he had spoken out of turn and would be in trouble if he had said where the regiment would be posted. 'I'm sorry, Corporal, I didn't catch a word you said. Everything seems muffled when I wear this headscarf. Did you ask for my help?'

'No Miss, I wondered if you wanted onion in your sandwich?' he replied, giving her a grateful smile.

'That would be super, thank you,' she grinned back. 'I am impressed with how you cope in such conditions.'

'We have to cope, Miss. Sometimes we can be feeding 'undreds,' he said, before a cough from Ben had him put his head down and get on with the cooking.

'We are a little over halfway through our

180

journey,' Ben said, looking up at the brooding sky. 'There's plenty more snow up there. We'd best eat and be on our way, or we'll never get to London before nightfall.'

Rose impulsively reached out and touched his arm. 'Please don't be angry with the corporal. He meant no harm, and I'm to be trusted — unlike Mr Cardew,' she added with a wry smile. 'I can't thank you enough for including me in your journey. I'd have been in real trouble if I couldn't get to London to start my training course tomorrow morning.'

Ben nodded. 'It'll go no further this time — unlike Cardew, who will be going to prison if his actions are deemed not to be in the interests of this country. But rest assured, if it turns out he was simply a foolhardy man the authorities have told me he will be moved away from Ramsgate to save any embarrassment. The ladies of Sea View will have no reason to ever see the man again. I informed your mother that the last of his possessions should be removed today. I hope that gives you some peace of mind?'

'It does, thank you,' she replied, realizing her hand was still on his arm and pulling it back quickly. 'This war is already affecting so many people I know. This talk of it being over quickly — some say Christmas — what do you think?'

'I can't see it finishing any time soon. I fear things will get darker . . . much darker,' he said, his eyes taking on a distant look. 'We can only hope our loved ones can cope.'

'Are you going to Fr — are you going away soon?'

'Very soon, and I'm afraid that's all I can say. These few days in London will be the last I see of Blighty for some time, I would think. For many reasons, but especially one, I wish it wasn't so,' he added with a bleak smile.

Rose took a shuddering breath. She felt as though someone had walked over her grave. Raising the tin mug of hot tea she just been handed, she said, 'Until we meet again. And I hope it will be soon.'

'We have a few days before we need to think about saying our goodbyes. I intend to make them memorable days that I can look back on.'

'I look forward to that,' she replied as their quiet moment was broken by the arrival of their food.

It was early evening as the army lorry drove down the Strand. 'Look — I can just see Lyons Corner House,' Rose said, more than a little excited. 'Orchard House, where I will be training, is close by. I just need to find my way to where I'll be staying,' she added, looking in her handbag for the piece of paper with the address. 'Thank you so much,' she said to the lorry driver. 'You can drop me here.'

'I'll do no such thing, Miss. The Captain has already given me the address, and that's where I intend to drop you off. We can't have you wandering around the streets of London with it starting to get dark, let alone have you disappearing in another snowdrift.'

Rumbles of agreement came from the back of the vehicle, where the other soldiers sat alongside Ben.

'That's very kind of you,' she said, ignoring the jokes she could hear about losing her boots in the snow.

The journey into London had been long and arduous, and more than once they'd been stuck in the snow. The men had insisted she remain in the cab of the lorry while they put the vehicle back on the road.

They pulled up outside a four-storey house several streets away from where she would be working, and Rose was helped down from the lorry while her suitcase was unloaded from the back. Ben joined her on the pavement, carrying his own bag. With shouts of good luck ringing in her ears and promises of visiting the Margate tearooms when they were back in Thanet, they disappeared into the still falling snow.

'Thank you so much for getting me here; you have a good team of men,' she said as she went to pick up the suitcase. Ben beat her to it and despite her arguments walked to the front door of the establishment and gave the closed door a sharp knock.

Rose stood nervously as they heard footsteps approach from the other side of the door. From the outside the building did not seem inviting. She hoped it would appear different from inside.

'I'm Miss Rose Neville. A room has been booked for me by a Mr Jones at Orchard House . . . the Lyons training school,' she added as a short woman dressed from head to toe in black stood at the open door, glaring at them.

'Your room has been cancelled,' the woman replied with a stony stare.

Rose frowned. Surely this couldn't be so? 'The room is just for me.' She explained, wondering if the woman thought Ben was to stay too. 'Captain Hargreaves has been kind enough to bring me to London, as the trains aren't running from Kent.'

'There is no room for you; you should have been notified by your employers. My establishment is closed for the foreseeable future due to water damage. I wish you a good evening,' she added before closing the door on the couple.

'Oh dear, whatever can I do?' Rose said, suddenly feeling tired and just a little tearful. 'Orchard House will be closed by now; I can't even go there to ask for advice.'

Ben picked up her suitcase. 'You can come home with me, at least for tonight,' he added before heading to the pavement and hailing a taxi.

'But I'm not sure this is appropriate . . . ' she said as he ushered her inside and gave directions to the driver. 'What would people say?'

'People can mind their own business. I can't very well leave you freezing in the street when I have a perfectly good flat only a mile away from here. Tomorrow is soon enough to sort out this mess. For tonight, you will be fed and given a warm bed to sleep in. Do you think your mother would approve?'

Rose knew her mum would be delighted that Ben was helping her daughter. She seemed to be more than a little enamoured of the man, from what Rose had witnessed that morning. 'My mum will trust me to do what is right.' She added a little primly, 'Thank you for coming to my rescue.'

'It's my pleasure,' he replied before leaning back in the seat as silence fell for the remainder of the journey.

When the car pulled up at the pavement and the car door opened by a uniformed doorman, Rose was stunned into silence as she entered the impressive Victorian building. She thought Ben's home would be better than her own, but never envisaged such opulence. Deep pile carpets felt soft beneath her feet, whilst large oil paintings adorned the oak-panelled walls of the entrance hall. She followed Ben, and a young porter who'd been called to take the luggage, into a lift where a metal door was pulled shut and they were taken up towards the top of the building. Ben unlocked one of the two doors outside the lift, and the porter deposited the luggage on the floor. 'That will be all, thank you, Albert,' he said, slipping the lad a few coins.

'Will I ask Mrs Benton to come up and cook for you, sir?'

'No need to bother her this evening; we will go out to dine. Breakfast for half past seven in the morning, if you would let her know.'

The young porter touched his cap and left them alone.

'You can close your mouth now,' Ben grinned as he took off his overcoat and helped Rose from hers.

'But this is . . . it's . . . '

'It's my mother's, and yes, it is rather grand. That's my mother for you,' he smiled, watching her look about in awe.

'Are you sure your mother won't mind me staying here?' she asked, very aware of her wellington boots and old tweed skirt and the headscarf she'd just pulled off and stuffed into her pocket.

'She would welcome you into her home, if she were here. We all use this as our bolthole when in London. Now she's gone back to Scotland to wait out the war the place is often empty, unless my sister's in town.'

Crikey, if this is a bolthole goodness knows what her proper home is like, Rose thought to herself as she looked round at the ornate mirrors and posh upholstered chairs. Her mum would be putting covers on everything in case anyone left a mark. 'You are Scottish? I can't detect an accent.'

'No, but my mother is, and she's extremely proud of her roots and will always have her say. I can see similarities in your mother.'

'Oh yes, Mum will always have the last word,' Rose laughed.

Ben grinned as they looked at each other in companionable silence, both thinking of their mothers, until he slapped his leg in annoyance. 'Here's me inviting a guest into our home and not even offered you a drink. We usually have some sherry, or there's a drop of gin if you prefer it?' he said, opening the pull-down door of an ornate walnut cabinet.

'You may think me daft but I'd much prefer a cup of tea, if you don't mind — and is there somewhere I could wash my hands and powder my nose?'

186

'I'm so sorry,' he said. 'I'm not much of a host, am I? Let me show you to the guest room and you can get settled while I find the kitchen and a teapot. I don't know about you, but I could do with a bite to eat. It's been a while since we had that sandwich by the roadside. What say you get yourself dressed up and we go out to eat? There may even be time for a spot of dancing.'

Rose's eyes lit up. 'I'd like that, thank you.'

Ben showed her to the guest bedroom and pointed out the bathroom across the short passageway. 'Help yourself to the toiletries. There should be plenty of hot water,' he said before leaving her to settle in.

After closing the heavy drapes and putting on the light, she quickly opened a few doors and looked inside a large chest of drawers. There was plenty of room for the clothes she'd brought with her. She unpacked her dance frock and gave it a quick shake to remove a few creases before hanging it on the wardrobe door while she undressed. Pulling on a robe she found hanging behind the bedroom door, she grabbed her soap bag and hurried to the bathroom, locking the door.

Ben was right — there was plenty of hot water. Rose ran herself a bath, scattering in a handful of lavender-scented bath salts. Pinning her hair up, as there wouldn't be time to towel it dry, she stepped into the soothing water and lay back, luxuriating in the warmth as gradually she felt the chills of the day leave her cold limbs. After five minutes she reluctantly stepped out and towelled her warm skin dry on a fluffy towel she found in the airing cupboard. Cleaning her teeth before tidying the room, she hurried back to her bedroom and dressed quickly, thanking God she'd packed her best underwear and stockings.

Sitting at the stool placed in front of a three-mirrored dressing table, she ran a brush through her hair, applied a little rouge to her cheeks and dabbed perfume behind her ears. After adding some lipstick to her lips, she fastened a string of pearls around her slender neck. They'd been a present from her mum when she'd turned twenty-one, and she'd only worn them a few times in the past couple of years as they were saved for special occasions. This was most certainly a special occasion. Slipping her feet into her dance shoes, she gave a quick twirl, checking her image in the full-length mirror inside the wardrobe door. Satisfied that she'd scrubbed up well, she went back to the drawing room and stopped in shock when she saw Ben standing there in a dinner jacket and crisp white shirt. He was always smart in his uniform, but now he took her breath away.

He gave her a wry look. 'Are you any good at tying these things? I'm all fingers and thumbs,' he said, holding up a bow tie.

'Hmm. It's been a while, but I used to help the General when he was getting himself done up for one of the functions he attended. He was a lovely man, and I do miss him. He lived at Sea View for as long as I can remember. He was such a gentleman; it's rather sad to think that he was down on his luck. He said I had nimble fingers, but I'm not so sure they are as nimble now I'm an adult. I'll give it a try, though. Bend down a little,' she instructed him. After one false start caused by realizing how close she was to him and forgetting what to do in the heat of the moment, she found she remembered, and deftly knotted the black silk tie. Ben stood up straight as she cocked her head to one side, checking it was knotted properly. 'You'll do,' she said, stepping back and giving him a smile. It was fatal to be so close to him. She could almost feel the electricity crackle between them. She felt herself weakening as she looked at his lips, longing to kiss him. Giving herself a mental shake, she stepped away. 'I thought you were making us a cup of tea?' she asked, not daring to look at him. 'Or have you spent too long working out how to tie that thing?'

'Tea is ready, madam,' he bowed, before going to the kitchen and returning with a tray containing teacups and teapot.

Rose found herself giggling. 'You look like one of those waiters they have in posh hotels. Perhaps I'd best pour, in case you spill it,' she said. 'I've had more training than you have.'

Ben sat in a nearby armchair and watched as she stirred the tea before pouring the amber liquid into two cups. 'Milk and sugar?' she asked, noting that the milk jug and sugar basin matched the teapot. She made a mental note to tell her mum how delicate the china was, but then thought better of it. Flora would want to know what she was doing alone with Ben. Although her mum seemed to like him, she was rather old-fashioned and might well go bonkers if she

189

knew her daughter had spent the night alone with a man without a ring on her finger. To be honest, Rose felt the same way — but she couldn't ignore the small thrill of excitement she felt at being alone with Ben.

'Just milk, please,' he said, bringing her back to her senses. 'You looked miles away for a moment.'

'I was just thinking about how they're getting on back home with all this snow. I'm glad I've brought my heavy coat with me.'

Ben put down his cup and got to his feet. 'I'll just be a minute,' he said, hurrying away.

Rose sipped her tea thoughtfully. Ben had put a light to the logs in the large fireplace, and there was a warm glow as they crackled. Part of her felt she could happily stay in this evening and relax, but a growl deep in her stomach reminded her she was hungry. She spotted a gramophone in an ornate wooden cabinet in the corner of the room. She would have loved to browse through the record collection and listen to some music. Perhaps there would be time later, she thought as Ben returned . . . 'Oh my goodness,' she gasped, as he wrapped a fur stole around her shoulders.

'It will keep you as warm as your coat, but will look so much better with your dress.'

'Is it . . . is it real?'

'It's real,' he said, keeping his hands on her shoulders just a little longer than necessary before returning to his tea.

'It's beautiful,' Rose said, rubbing her cheek against the soft fur. 'Are you sure I can borrow it?'

Ben watched as her eyes sparkled and shone in delight. 'My mother would have offered it to you a long time before I thought of the idea. She has several in her wardrobe.'

'Gosh,' was all Rose could think to say.

9

'You didn't have to come out in this horrid weather. I could have collected my clothes on my own,' Lily said to Flora and Mildred.

'Nonsense. You'd not have managed on your own,' Flora said. 'Many hands make light work, you know.'

'I may as well tag along, as the boats are going out today,' Mildred said from beneath her muffler and the large hood of her duffle coat. She didn't add that she'd heard things about George Jacobs, and wasn't going to let her land-lady go to his house without some protection. She'd been relieved to know that young Lily was to become one of the inhabitants of the Sea View guesthouse.

'I'm grateful to you both,' Lily said loudly, her voice competing with the wind as they turned the corner of the road to face the turbulent sea. She had her fingers crossed inside her mittens that George would be out at the pub. He usually would be at this time of the day. She was embarrassed enough to have these two women see her home, let alone her drunken sod of a stepfather.

As they approached the small two-up, two-down terraced house, Flora noticed the untidy patch of garden and faded net curtains that hung limply at the windows. The woodwork needed a good going-over with a cleaning cloth, as even with the snow falling against the panes she could see a layer of dirt. Flora couldn't blame young Lily, who spent long hours working at the teashop and must have still been grieving for her mum.

'I do apologize for the mess,' Lily said as they stepped over the threshold straight into the front room. Looking around, she added, 'I think he's out somewhere. Let's go straight up to my bedroom and get my things.'

The two women followed Lily up the narrow, steep stairs. What carpet remained on the steps was threadbare and frayed. She opened one of the two doors at the top of the staircase, and they followed her in. 'This is a lovely room,' Flora said. As she looked around she could see that Lily had made an attempt to create a comfortable resting place for herself. 'Where shall we start?' she asked, pulling several folded sacks from her shopping bag. 'Is the bedding yours? I can strip the sheets and pillowcases and fold them up in here,' she said waving the sack. 'It's quite clean. Do you have any others? If we keep them separate, we won't need to wash both sets,' she explained, as Lily nodded and pulled other sheets from a drawer. 'You can use my sheets at the guesthouse as they all go off in the bag wash to the laundry, but it would be handy to have your own for future use. Think of them as starting your bottom drawer,' she smiled.

Lily grinned. 'Thank you for helping me. I'd not have thought to take them with me.'

'Shall I start on your wardrobe while you sort

out your knick-knacks?' Mildred asked as she reached up to the top of the wardrobe and pulled down a suitcase, blowing off a layer of dust before flicking back the latch and opening the lid. 'Shall I put everything in?'

'If it will fit,' Lily said gratefully, marvelling at how careful Mildred was with her possessions considering she was rather clumsy at times.

The women worked in companionable silence for a while until Lily wrapped the last of the few figurines that had belonged to her mother inside a pillowcase and gave a look around the room. 'I think that's everything,' she said. 'Let's get out of here before . . . ' She stopped speaking as they heard the front door creak open and heavy footsteps cross the floor downstairs.

Mildred noticed a look of fear cross Lily's face. It confirmed her worst suspicions. Feeling a rage grow inside her, she picked up the suitcase and turned to the others, saying, 'Follow me and don't be frightened.' Striding down the stairs, she stepped into the front room. She found George looking at Lily's coat, which she'd left draped across the back of a chair.

'What the hell are you doing in here?' he said, taking a step backwards. He recognized Mildred Dalrymple, and knew she was a force to be reckoned with.

'I'm helping young Lily remove her property from this house. If you've got any sense, you'll sit down and keep your mouth shut,' Mildred said between gritted teeth, not taking her eyes from his. 'I've heard things about you, George Jacobs, that I'm none too happy about.'

George sat down a little fearfully. 'I hope you ain't taking anything that doesn't belong to you,' he said as Lily and Flora came down the stairs and stood beside Mildred.

'I'm leaving more than I'm taking, so count yourself lucky. There is a letter going in the post to the landlord telling him I no longer want the house from the end of this week. The rent's paid up to date, so it's up to you to get in touch with him to find out about taking up the tenancy. I'm returning my key to him as well,' Lily said, feeling brave because her friends were by her side.

'Is there anything you need from down here?' Flora asked.

'No, I've got what I came for. Anything of Mum's that was down here he's either smashed or sold. Come on — let's go.' Lily opened the door and ushered them out. Turning back to her stepfather, she gave him a last cold look before leaving the house where she had been born and stepping bravely into her future. She did her best to ignore the flicker of disappointment she felt at not being able to comply with her mum's last words and take care of her stepfather.

Outside on the pavement, Flora made to go back to help Lily, but Mildred put out a hand to hold her back. 'Let it be for now,' she said. 'We must make sure to be on hand if the girl needs a shoulder to cry on.'

Flora nodded in agreement and did her best to force a smile onto her face as Lily joined them. 'Come on — let's get you home out of this cold. I don't know about you, but I could do with something to eat. I have a few crumpets in the pantry. We could toast them by the fire.'

Lily linked arms with Flora. 'I can't think of anything better.'

★ ★ ★

Rose gazed in awe at her surroundings. She'd been speechless when Ben had taken her to Claridge's to dine, but this exceeded her wildest dreams.

To know that a waitress from Ramsgate was dining with the cream of society had been so frightening she could have fainted with the shock. At any moment she had expected those around her to guess she was an interloper and point at her, declaring she should not be there. Her worries had soon evaporated, though, when she found the waiters respectful and charming. Before too long she was at ease in the elegant surroundings, and it helped that she was sitting opposite the most handsome man in the room. They dined on roast duck and drank champagne. If only Katie and Lily could see her now, she'd thought as a delicate dish of peach ice cream set in a bowl of ice was placed in front of her.

She had expected to go back to Ben's flat after the meal, but no, he'd hailed a taxi and they had headed off into the night, stopping outside a club. They'd been shown to a table at the side of the dance floor as a band the size of an orchestra had gently played dance tunes, some of which she recognized and had in her record collection. This was nothing like Silvano's band, she thought to herself as she sipped even more champagne and hummed along to the songs.

'Thank you so much for treating me to such a wonderful evening,' she said to Ben after they'd clapped at the end of the song. 'It is a dream come true to be able to hear such a superb orchestra play the songs I've always longed to sing.'

Ben, who had watched Rose close her eyes and sway to the tempo, could only agree. 'I've never had the urge to sing with a band, but I can see the appeal in performing in front of an appreciative audience.'

Rose looked again at the throng of people on the dance floor and answered. 'They are an appreciative audience. I shall remember this night for the rest of my life while I'm running the teashop and living out my days in Thanet.'

'Do you not have any dreams that will take you away from your home and job?' he asked gently as he reached out and held her hand.

'I've often dreamt of a different life. But nothing will come of it, especially now we are at war and must all do our bit.'

'Tell me, Rose. I promise I won't laugh or pull your leg,' he prompted her.

'Well, it's this! My dream is in this room,' she sighed, with her eyes sparkling.

'To dance and dine in splendour?' he asked, a little surprised. Somehow he had expected more of Rose than the other women he'd met, many of whom simply wanted the good life on the arm of a man who could afford to pamper their every whim.

'Oh no,' she gasped, looking shocked. 'I've had a wonderful time with you this evening, but that's not what I meant at all. In another lifetime I'd have sought out my dream to sing for my living, and tour the world with bands and orchestras such as this one. I so admire the singer Helen Forrest, and I've often wondered what it would be like to be able to entertain people and make them happy.'

'That is a worthy dream. I can't see what's stopping you?' he said as his thumb gently rubbed the palm of her hand.

Rose laughed out loud. 'Oh Ben, you have no idea how hard it would be to up sticks and follow my dream — although I did have an offer to do just that,' she said with a gentle tease in her voice. 'But it isn't to be. I live in a world where I have responsibilities — and a good job to look forward to.'

Ben ignored her talk of work and focused on the chance she'd missed to sing for a living. 'You did — when was this? Why didn't you take up the offer? I just know you would have been a success. I've only heard you sing the once, but you're as good as Helen Forrest any day of the week.'

'Ben, you were there when it happened, although you only saw the aftermath of my answer. It was Silvano offering me the chance to join his band as a singer. He was getting ready to tour with ENSA.'

Ben recalled the rather seedy-looking man who'd fronted the band the evening he heard Rose sing. 'Why did you say no?'

She gave a deep sigh. 'There were strings attached, and I'm not that kind of a girl. I know women who would have jumped at the chance, but it wasn't for me.'

Ben watched the sadness in her eyes and wished he could do something to cheer her up. 'Let's dance, shall we?' he asked as the band struck up a lively foxtrot.

Rose closed her eyes as Ben held her to him and steered her through the crowded dance floor. The gentle pressure of his hand on her back and the subtle scent of his cologne conjured up all kinds of feelings. She could have stayed there, on the dance floor in his arms, all evening. All too soon the music came to an end, and after joining in with the clapping they returned to their table. Ben replenished their champagne glasses.

'I have to leave you for a few minutes,' he said, leaning close so she could hear him above the chattering crowd before placing the briefest of kisses on her cheek.

Rose sat in a dream as she looked around at the chandeliers hanging from the high ceiling and the opulent wall curtains that shut out the ugly world outside. She would cherish this evening for as long as she lived.

When Ben returned he took her hand, encouraging her to stand. 'I have someone I'd like you to meet,' he said, leading her down the side of the dance floor to the edge of the stage. 'Mr Ross, this is Rose Neville, the young lady I spoke to you about.'

Fernando Ross turned to Rose and shook her

hand. 'My friend here tells me you are a singer, and have sung on stage with bands?'

Rose nodded. It was a thrill to meet and be able to speak with such a grand person. Perhaps he would be able to give her a tip or two on how to improve her singing? 'Yes, sir. Nothing as grand as yours, but I've sung since I was a child. My mother is always saying that I would perform at the drop of a hat,' she said.

'And your favourite singer is Helen Forrest?'

Rose clasped her hands together in delight. 'Oh yes, I've admired her for so long — I try to style my singing on hers. Have you met her?'

'Many times,' he answered, giving her a benevolent smile. 'I wonder, would you like to sing for me?'

'Me sing for you?' Rose almost shrieked as her voice went up several octaves. 'I would love to — but I'm only in London for a short while, and I have . . . some training to complete during the day,' she confessed, not liking to say she was a Nippy.

The conductor raised his hand to stop her excited chatter. 'I mean right now, when my musicians have finished their break. Come with me and we will discuss the music,' he said, leading her by the elbow to the rear of the stage where he started to go through a pile of sheet music.

Rose, apart from feeling shocked at the speed of what was happening, felt a growing excitement building up inside her. She loved to sing, and this was an opportunity worth grabbing with both hands. Watching the titles on the sheets of music as he went through them, she caught his arm and said, 'I know it's not a dance tune but I'd love to sing this, if I may? It means something special to me — and I would think to many other people here this evening.'

Fernando went over to have a word with his musicians and came back to Rose with a broad smile on his face. 'Stay there, and I'll introduce you after the next number.'

Rose answered his smile with her own broad grin. She'd never felt so excited in her life. She watched as the musicians struck up a waltz and the dance floor filled with couples moving to the beautiful melody.

All too soon it finished, and Fernando turned to the microphone and raised his hands to silence the enthusiastic dancers. Faces looked up to the stage, waiting to hear what he had to say. He got straight to the point. 'For many here this evening, there is sadness as they are seeing off loved ones and may not be together again for a while. To sing you on your way, we have a very special guest: Miss Rose Neville.' He turned to the side of the stage and started the applause as Rose hurried up a short flight of wooden steps onto the stage, waving to the crowd as she joined Fernando. He kissed her cheek in welcome and turned to the orchestra, raising his baton.

Rose listened as the strains of music filled the room swaying slightly as the music reached her soul. She took a deep breath and holding the microphone stand she sang her heart out.

'*We'll meet again . . .* '

She closed her eyes and imagined she was

alone with Ben, singing the words only to him — hoping that when the blue skies did drive the dark clouds far away, she would see him once more. The words hurt her deeply, as she knew she was saying goodbye to him publicly before he went overseas. It was easier to sing what was in her heart than to tell him privately. They'd not known each other long enough for such intimate words.

As the song came to an end and she opened her eyes, she was surprised to see not one person dancing. The crowd had come to the edge of the stage to listen, and as one they burst into spontaneous applause while Rose took a small bow. Fernando called her back to take another bow, and again he kissed her cheek. 'Come and sing for me anytime you are in town,' he said so only she could hear. Flushed with excitement, she whispered her thanks, her eyes seeking out Ben. The table where they'd been sitting was empty.

Worrying where he could be, she hurried down the wooden steps from the stage and found him waiting there for her. Without uttering a word he pulled her into his arms and swung her round before setting her on her feet. 'You were wonderful,' he said gently before claiming her lips. When they broke apart he looked into her eyes. 'I felt as though you were singing to me alone.'

Rose waited for a few seconds until her heart stopped beating so fast. 'I was . . . I was singing just for you,' she murmured.

Before they could speak again, Rose found

herself surrounded by people congratulating her on her singing. A few of them thrust cards into her hand, which she put into the pocket of her dress. By the time they reached their table and sat down there was fresh champagne waiting for them in an ice bucket, compliments of the owner of the club. Rose drank the chilled liquid greedily, ignoring the bubbles as she quenched her thirst. She was already drunk on the excitement of her performance, and no amount of champagne could make any difference to her exuberance.

It didn't seem long before the last dance of the evening was announced and she fell into Ben's arms, exhausted but happier than she'd ever felt before. 'Thank you,' she whispered close to his ear, as the main lights were lowered and a million lights glittered from a silver mirrored ball hanging from the ceiling. 'Thank you for giving me such a wonderful evening. I don't have the words to express how I feel.'

'Seeing you so happy is the best gift I could have. It's not every day a guy has his girl sing for him,' he replied, his breath so close to her ear that it made her tingle from head to toe.

His girl, she thought to herself with a contented sigh.

Outside, the snow was still falling hard and fast and they could hardly see where the pavement ended and the road began. A doorman whistled for a taxi, holding an umbrella over their heads until they were safely inside and the door was closed. Ben gave the address to the driver and the vehicle pulled away into a stream of slow-moving traffic.

'Oh dear, I hope the snow hasn't damaged your mother's lovely mink stole,' Rose said, trying to brush the slow-melting flakes away.

'Don't worry about it,' Ben said as he put his arm around her. She snuggled close, the warmth of his body making her feel sleepy.

'It was wonderful, wasn't it?' she said as her eyelids started to droop and she fell asleep. Ben smiled as she slept like a child in his arms. He knew he was beginning to fall in love with his beautiful Nippy, and that meant he would have to explain something to her before they became any closer . . .

'Hey, come on, sleepyhead,' he said a few minutes later, giving Rose a little shake. 'We're home.'

Rose woke and rubbed her eyes. 'My goodness, I didn't mean to fall asleep on you,' she apologized. 'You must think me an absolute bore.'

'Not at all. I could have dropped off myself, if I didn't have to instruct the taxi driver,' he said as the door was opened. He helped her out of the vehicle and led her carefully over the snowy pavements into the building, where the night porter was ready to take them in the lift to the top floor.

Rose could only lean against Ben as he kept his arm around her waist. She wasn't going to pull away, as her head felt rather light after an evening of dancing and sipping champagne, and she rather liked being close to him.

Inside the flat, she went straight to the open fire that was glowing brightly after staff had been in to bank it up, while Ben put a record on the gramophone player before pouring two brandies into crystal glasses and handing her one.

Rose started to protest that she wasn't one to drink spirits, but one sip of the warming liquid changed her mind. Ben slipped the stole from her shoulders and placed it onto the back of an armchair before removing his dinner jacket.

Rose was about to thank him again for taking her out for the evening when the record started to play on the gramophone. 'Oh, it's Helen Forrest singing 'Deep Purple',' she said in delight. 'I simply love this song, don't you?'

Ben slid a free arm around her waist. 'I believe I love you more,' he said as his lips came down on hers. She could taste the brandy on his lips as she returned his kisses until he pulled away and took her drink from her, placing both glasses on a small side table.

Rose wanted to say that they hardly knew each other, and so much more — but her heart was ruling her head as she took the few steps and reached out for him.

'I believe I love you too,' she answered.

Ben groaned as he lifted Rose in his arms and carried her to a nearby sofa where they continued to embrace, each kiss becoming more passionate than the last. All thoughts of what he had intended to tell her were completely forgotten.

As the needle on the gramophone record crackled and bumped at the end of the song, Ben leant back and took Rose's face in her hands. 'If I don't stop now I can't be responsible for my actions,' he said, taking a deep breath.

'I don't want you to stop,' Rose replied in a trembling voice.

'Are you sure?'

'I'm more than sure,' she sighed, holding out her arms to him.

★ ★ ★

'Miss Douglas, please pay attention. There's a customer waiting to place his order,' a sharp voice exclaimed, making Lily jump. 'Clarissa Butterworth must have allowed these girls to run rings around her,' her new manageress tittered provocatively to the man by her side. 'Would you care to take tea in my office before you leave for your next appointment, Mr White?'

'It would be my pleasure, Miss Roberts,' Tom said, giving Lily a backward look and daring to wink at her.

'Please, you must call me Dorothy now that we will be working so closely together,' Miss Roberts' shrill voice floated out to Lily as the office door closed.

Lily closed her eyes for a moment and sighed. Tom White had been in and out of the teashop for the past few weeks, blowing hot and cold. She wished he didn't lodge so close to the Ramsgate teashop, so she didn't see him so often. Most of the time, he either gazed straight through her or gave her suggestive looks. Well, she wouldn't stand for it. He'd treated her like dirt, and if rumours were to be believed, he had treated other Nippies in and around Thanet in exactly the same way. She just wished she'd known before she'd let him take advantage of her. If she said it to herself enough times, she thought, she might just start to believe that he had taken liberties with her. Deep down, though, she knew she had responded willingly to his suggestion of going back to his hotel room. There was a name for girls like that; and right now, if anyone found out, they'd be calling her the same name.

'Miss, can we have two cheese rarebits please, and a pot of tea for two?'

Lily wrote down the customer's choice and walked to the counter to hand over the order with her head still in the clouds. She had a lovely room now at Sea View, and it was time to turn over a new leaf and forget about her stepfather and the arrogant Tom White.

'Buck up, Lily, or you'll have the new boss down on us like a ton of bricks,' Katie hissed as she hurried past with a heavily laden tray. 'I thought old Butterworth was bad enough, but this one's even worse. Goodness knows where Lyons find these women! Thank goodness Mr Grant saw fit to put Rose up for management training and promotion.'

Lily grinned. Trust Katie to bring her to her senses. She'd best buck up, as she didn't have time to step into Miss Roberts' office after work for a telling off. Rose was coming home on the six o'clock train from London, and after tea with Flora they would be having the final fittings for their wedding attire. Who'd have believed that young Katie would be the first of them to marry?

she believed as she greeted a family who had hurried into the teashop out of the cold and led them to a table. Although there was no longer as much snow falling from the sky, it was perishing cold. She'd taken to wearing two pairs of stockings to work and a thin jumper under her Nippy uniform. With her workstation being close to the front of the shop she was forever feeling the cold, what with the door opening and closing as people came in to buy bread and cakes or sit down for a meal.

'Miss, is everything on the menu available?' enquired the mother of the family she'd just seated.

'To my knowledge it is, madam,' Lily replied politely. 'I've not been told otherwise.'

The woman beamed. 'I'm so relieved. It is my daughter's birthday and this is our family treat. My husband joins his regiment tomorrow,' she added with a little wobble in her voice.

'Then we should make this a very special meal,' Lily said, reaching for the tariff card to advise them. 'Would you like sandwiches and cake — or perhaps you were thinking of a main meal? I can recommend the sausages and mash, it's my favourite.' She smiled at the children, whose eyes lit up at her words. 'We also have trifle, and there's jelly if you prefer; although perhaps the adults would like one of our hot puddings and custard? Would you like me to bring you a drink while you decide?'

'Thank you,' the mother said, giving Lily a grateful look. 'We don't often go out for our meals, and I was a little nervous. You've helped us so much. I would like a cup of tea — how about you, Bert?'

'Tea would be very nice, thank you,' the nervous man said, giving Lily a small smile. 'Perhaps orangeade for the children, as this is a special occasion?'

'I'll get those for you now, and take your order when I return,' Lily said as she noted their requests on the pad attached to her waistband by a cord.

'Gosh, it must be hard seeing your husband off to join the army and being left behind with the children, not knowing when or if he will return,' Lily said as she stood alongside Katie, who was also waiting for a drinks order to be completed. 'My family on table ten are having a meal together before he leaves to join up. I don't think they dine out much, so this is something of a special occasion. I do feel for them.'

'At least she has children,' Katie said quietly. 'My wedding could be for nothing if Jack doesn't return.'

'Me and my big mouth!' Lily said, realizing how insensitive she had been with her comment. 'I only have to open it and I put my foot straight in. I'm sorry, Katie. However, if Jack doesn't return — and I'm sure he will,' she added quickly, 'at least you will have the memory of a beautiful wedding. And two glamorous brides-maids,' she finished, trying to make her friend smile.

Katie placed a pot of hot coffee onto her tray. 'I'll try and remember that, especially the glamorous bridesmaids part,' she grinned. 'Don't mind me. I'm just nervous about the wedding. I think it's allowed! I'll feel happier when Rose is back with us and I know her dress fits.'

'You're worrying unduly,' Lily said. 'Unless she's been tucking in to all the Lyons products while she's been training, it will fit perfectly. Miss Tibbs said it would, and I have no reason to doubt her.'

'It will be strange to have our Rose a fully fledged manageress. I hope it doesn't turn her head and make her start to boss us about away from work,' Katie joked.

'She could never be as bossy as that Miss Roberts. We'd best look sharp, as here she comes,' Lily whispered, looking past Katie towards the manageress's office as Miss Roberts appeared, followed by Tom. 'See you later,' she added as she grabbed her tray and headed back to her customers.

'So what's it to be?' she asked after placing the drinks in front of the family.

'The children have chosen sausage and mashed potato,' the father said. 'My wife would like the meat pie with potatoes and cabbage, and I will have the curried meat and rice, if you please.'

'Those are fine choices,' Lily smiled as she noted down the meals.

'I must say, it's a treat not to have to cook for the family for once,' the wife said.

'If I had a penny for every lady who said that to me, I'd be as rich as a king,' Lily chuckled.

'My husband was wondering how Lyons manages to provide such a varied menu now that we have rationing? The business he owns is already experiencing shortages and restrictions. We have a greengrocer's business on the other side of town,' she added proudly.

'From what I understand from our previous manager, who had the same concerns as yourself, it seems restaurants and cafes are not affected by the recent rationing announcements. But who knows what will happen if this war should continue?' Lily answered, aware that young ears were listening. 'I would have thought that in your line of business, you would have been in a reserved occupation,' she asked.

'Oh, my Bert has ideas about volunteering to sort out Hitler and end the war,' the wife said with a hint of bitterness in her voice. 'I'll be running the place single-handed from now on.'

'My landlady is in the same position. We've handed in our ration cards and she does the best she can for us. Flora's even been told she has to put up a few soldiers as she has a spare bedroom going begging now my friend . . . that's her daughter . . . is moving to Margate to be manageress of the teashop on the seafront,' Lily said, letting her tongue run away with her regardless of not knowing these people from Adam.

'That must be Flora Neville? Why, I've known her for years. We are both helping out the Air Raid Precaution unit here in town. We've got quite friendly during the meetings, and when we walk the tunnels to make sure there haven't been any fresh rock falls.'

Lily shuddered. 'I hope we never have to use

them,' she said with feeling.

'My dear, I don't think we should be talking about such things. You never know who is listening,' Bert said, glancing left and right. The children copied him.

'Be like Dad,' the little boy announced as he drained his glass.

'And keep Mum,' his sister added.

Lily did her best not to laugh. 'That's very wise advice.'

'Please send my best wishes to Flora. And will you tell her it's doubtful I'll be able to get to the meetings, now I'm alone running the shop? Seeing as this one here has decided to put his life on the line for King and Country,' the woman tutted.

'Now, Gladys, there's no need to speak like that. We did have a discussion about this.'

'Yes, and you then went down the pub, had a drink and went and signed up when you didn't have to,' she threw back at him. 'Just remember that while you're having a whale of the time with your mates, Muggins here has got to hold the fort,' she glared.

Lily noticed the children weren't at all worried by their parents bickering, so perhaps they had grown up with it. 'I'll get your meals ordered,' she said, slipping away before things became any more heated.

She placed the food order and went to serve another customer with tea and toast before cleaning down a vacant table and setting it ready for the next customers. Turning to head to the kitchen to collect the family's tray of food, she was stopped by Tom White.

'I've been trying to get you alone,' he said in a low voice while holding onto her arm so she couldn't leave. 'Come to my hotel this evening and we can carry on where we left off last time.'

Lily wriggled free, managing to control her anger enough not to send her heavy tray crashing down on his head. 'I wouldn't touch you if you were the last man on earth,' she hissed. 'The way you ignored me after last time we — the last time I made the mistake of getting too close to you — was not the behaviour of a gentleman. So you can crawl back in your hole, and stay away from me.'

'You'll do well not to cross me,' he snarled. 'It's no good acting all innocent and lily-white now. I could tell you'd been round the block a few times.'

'What do you mean? I'd never been with a man before,' Lily hissed back, doing her utmost not to alarm the customers sitting close by. 'I've a mind to report you to head office for how you're acting. It seems I'm not the first Nippy you've enticed to your room, from what I've heard since you took me there.'

Tom White looked puzzled for a moment, then laughed in her face. 'You can keep lying all you like, but a man can tell, and it wasn't the first time for either of us. Don't even think about reporting me, Lily, or you will find life around here very uncomfortable indeed,' he said, heading back to Miss Robert's office with a furious expression.

'Are you all right, my dear?' the nice lady at

table ten asked Lily when she approached with the family's food. 'I couldn't help but notice that man stopping you. He seemed angry about something.'

'It's nothing,' Lily said, forcing a smile onto her face although she wanted nothing more than to sit down and sob her heart out. 'It's a chap from head office, and he can be a bit of a bully at times. Don't worry — I can handle him.' She slid a plate of hot meat pie and vegetables in front of the woman. 'Please do enjoy your meals.'

'Before you go, would you mind passing a message to Flora for me? She mentioned that a Polish lady who lives with her is looking for work. Would you tell her I'll be needing someone to do a few hours every day now my husband's not at the shop? It's Peabody's the grocers, in case she's forgotten where I am.'

Lily said she would do just that and hurried away, but not before she heard Mrs Peabody putting her husband straight when he dared to question her employing someone.

10

Rose placed her hand over her mouth, doing her best to stifle a yawn. It wasn't yet midday, but she felt as though she'd been at Orchard House, the head office of J. Lyons, for a full day. Although the talk about managing staff was interesting and she'd been taking down notes, she couldn't stop thinking back to earlier that morning.

Rising early so as not to wake Ben, she'd dressed and collected her suitcase. If she hurried, she could be at Orchard House early and sort out her accommodation before beginning her first day of training.

'Were you going to love me and leave me?' a sleepy voice said as she put on her coat.

'I've left a note,' Rose smiled. 'You looked so peaceful, I didn't want to wake you.' He pulled her into his arms for a long lingering kiss. 'Can I see you this evening?' she asked.

A shadow crossed Ben's face. 'I'm afraid I won't be here.'

Rose felt as though her heart was about to stop beating. 'Oh — I thought we had more time . . . '

'I'm afraid not, my sweet. I'll be travelling with my regiment by this evening.'

She felt tears prick her eyes. 'Is this the end of the magic?' she whispered. 'Is what happened

215

last night to be the only time we spend time together?'

'No, never!' he exclaimed, almost shaking her as he forced her to listen to his words. 'I love you, Rose, and last night was just the start of our love. I want to show you my world, share secrets with you . . . ' His voice started to falter.

'Secrets?'

'Now's not the time,' he said, taking an envelope from a side table. 'I've put details here of how you can write to me. You will, won't you? I can explain more about my life and my plans in my letters.'

'I'll write and give you my new address, but you can always reach me if you write to Sea View,' she said, fighting back tears. 'I've seen people saying goodbye to loved ones as they head off to war, and now I know how much it hurts. I feel as though my heart is being ripped out.' She reached up to touch his face and ran her fingers through his unruly hair before picking up her suitcase.

'Can you wait while I shave and pull on some clothes, so I can accompany you? What about breakfast?'

'I daren't, or I'll be late,' she said, wishing she could stay with him for longer.

'I'll phone down for a taxi then I know you will arrive safely,' he said, reaching for the telephone. 'I can at least walk you to the lift . . . '

'Miss Neville, I asked a question,' the instructor said. Rose was shaken from her reverie by the sound of polite tittering from the other women in the room.

216

A girl sitting to her left discreetly pushed her notes in front of Rose, and she was able to give the correct answer before thanking her fellow student with a grateful smile.

The following days saw Rose studying hard as she learnt about the duties of a teashop manageress and the official paperwork, as well as taking a refresher course on the duties expected of all her teashop staff. She was reminded of how Nippies needed to have the ability to add up the prices of tariff items correctly, and of how good deportment and a pleasant disposition were essential. At times it felt as if her head was about to burst with so much information.

It wasn't all work; on some evenings, along with her fellow trainees, Rose went to the theatre or the cinema. It was only as she stood on the station platform at Charing Cross, ready to travel home, that she realized just how much she had grown up during the past fortnight — and how, with Ben now in her life, her future looked bright.

★ ★ ★

'Oh, you really shouldn't have done this,' Flora said, running the silky scarf through her fingers. 'You were in London to learn how to do your job, not to go shopping for presents for us all. You must have spent a fortune!'

Rose laughed. 'I knew I wouldn't be able to keep this a secret. One of the women who was training alongside me brought them in. Her dad works on a stall in the East End of London.

217

Honestly, they didn't cost that much money, and when I saw them I just knew you'd all love them as much as I did. Look — I'm wearing a blue one,' she said, opening her jacket to show the peacock-blue scarf draped over her jumper.

'I shall wear mine to the wedding,' Miss Tibbs said, as the other women of Sea View agreed.

'You must tell us all about London,' Joyce Hannigan said. 'I've never been. Mr Hannigan always promised to take me when he was over his illness, but it was never to be. Did you go to the theatre — and what about the dancing? I've heard there are clubs for such things,' she said, her face glowing with excitement.

'Joyce, Rose was there to work, not to enjoy herself,' Flora scolded. 'She probably didn't draw breath from all that learning, let alone visit dance halls and theatres.'

'I did go dancing once,' Rose said, her eyes taking on a faraway expression. 'It was so lovely, and I was asked to sing with a band that was large enough to be an orchestra. And on another evening I went to the theatre and saw a comedy with songs, called *Somewhere in England*. Will Hay was in it, would you believe? It was funny.'

Pearl came over to lean against Rose. 'I missed you, but thank you for my dolly,' she whispered. 'I'm glad you are home.'

Rose kissed the young girl's cheek. 'I missed you too, poppet.'

'You must tell us more about London,' Joyce said, her hands clasped together.

'Now, Rose, you must unpack, and you girls have to try on your gowns for tomorrow. At this

218

rate you'll be walking up the aisle with tailor tacks holding the frocks together. Now be off with the three of you. Perhaps, Mildred and Joyce, you'd help me with the washing-up this once? I have a million things to do before tomorrow — I don't know where to begin,' Flora interrupted, running a hand through her hair.

'I will be down in two of the ticks once I have helped Miss Tibbs with the dresses. You must not do the panicking,' Anya said. 'In the short time I am here you and Rose are my family, and I will help my family as much as I can,' she added, making Flora smile with gratitude. 'As for this — ' she stroked the forest-green scarf around her neck — 'I thank you with all my soul, for I have never owned anything so beautiful. I am eternally in your gratitude,' she said, pulling Rose to her in a bear hug.

'That goes for me too,' Mildred said gruffly as she looked at the pink scarf she held in her large hand. 'I'm not one for fripperies as a rule, but this means a lot; thank you. I will wear it tomorrow when we celebrate the young couple's wedding.'

Rose felt quite touched that her small gifts meant so much to the ladies of Sea View. She couldn't speak, for she knew she would start to cry.

'Come along,' Lily said, grabbing her arm. She could see that her friend was fighting back emotion. 'I'll race you up the stairs,' she said, and the three girls raced from the dining room along the hall and up the staircase, just as they had when playing together as children.

★ ★ ★

'You look as pretty as a picture,' Anya said, as Katie twisted and turned in the dress lent to her by Miss Tibbs. 'No one would know it was so old, and it fits you to perfection. What do you wear to cover your face?'

The girls started to giggle. 'Do you mean a wedding veil?' Lily asked.

'That is what I mean,' Anya said. 'Did I say something funny?'

'No, bless you,' Rose smiled. 'It was thinking of Katie having her face covered as she walked down the aisle that made us laugh.'

'But she has a point,' Rose said. 'Katie cannot walk down the aisle without a veil and headdress.'

'I'd be honoured if you would use mine,' a timid voice said from the doorway, as Joyce Hannigan walked in carefully carrying a white box. She laid it on Miss Tibbs' bed and took off the lid. 'This was mine when I married Mr Hannigan ten years ago,' she said as she pulled out a long white lace-edged veil and shook it out. 'It's as good as the day I was wed,' she said, with a tear in her eye. 'It was the happiest day of my life, apart from when our Pearl came along. There's a headband of silk flowers that my mother hand-stitched to go with it.' She passed the veil to Rose before delving back into the box and producing the delicate headdress, as the women all gasped at the intricate details in the stitching.

'Oh, it's beautiful, and — and you would allow

220

me to wear it for my wedding?' Katie asked, almost unable to speak.

'I would have offered my gown as well, if it hadn't been pulled apart to make a christening gown for Pearl. I still have the rest of the fabric, as I couldn't bear to part with it.'

Anya looked at Miss Tibbs, and the two women nodded at each other. Anya spoke first. 'It is only right, with Joyce being so good as to lend you of the head cover, that little Pearl is part of the wedding — do you not think?'

Katie nodded enthusiastically. 'I'd thought of asking her to be a bridesmaid, but with so little time and no money for dresses I felt it best not to mention it. Now I feel awful,' she said sadly.

Anya clapped her hands. 'We have the time; that is, if Joyce will trust us with the material from her dress?'

Joyce beamed. 'Pearl will love being part of the wedding. She has never been a bridesmaid before. I'll fetch the fabric now.'

'Are you sure about this? The wedding is only twenty hours away,' Katie said with a trace of anxiety.

Miss Tibbs shrugged her shoulders. 'My dear, it can be done with ease. Anya will help me with the cutting and then I shall do what I can this evening and finish the dress tomorrow. There is one stipulation.'

'Anything at all,' Katie said.

'You need someone to walk you down the aisle tomorrow, and I would like to offer my services. It is a little unusual, but those of us without family should stick together at times like this.'

221

Katie fell into Miss Tibbs' arms and sobbed. 'I'd be delighted.'

'I thought Miss Tibbs had a sister?' Lily whispered to Rose.

'Me too — I wonder what happened to her?'

Lily's lips twitched as she fought off a laugh. 'God only knows. I don't think Miss Tibbs knows what truly happened in the past, or what she has made up.'

★ ★ ★

'It's as good a day as it can be at this time of year,' Flora said as she stood inside the church door. 'No snow, and the choir boys have done a good job clearing the steps so the bottom of Katie's dress won't get mucky.'

'Jack told me that he and his mates swept the paths this morning before they headed to the pub for some Dutch courage,' Rose said, shivering even though she still had her best coat draped around her shoulders. The snow in the churchyard and on the roof might look pretty, but it was damned cold, she thought to herself.

Flora looked alarmed. 'I do hope they only had the one. We don't want drunken sailors in church, do we? Now, I'm going to take my place in the pew. Mildred is a little uncomfortable wearing a dress, and I don't trust her not to pop home and come back wearing a boiler suit. That was a joke,' she added, seeing the shocked look on her daughter's face. 'I must say, I feel quite honoured to be thought of as the mother of the bride. It's good that everyone pulled together for poor Katie and Jack, what with them both being orphans,' she added, reaching into her handbag for a clean cotton handkerchief.

'Friends are as good as family any day; better, in some cases,' Lily said, thinking of her stepfather. 'Before I forget — a Mrs Peabody came into the teashop yesterday. She and her husband own a grocery shop?' she added, as Flora didn't seem to recognize the name. 'Mr Peabody is off to join the army today, and she said as how you told her that Anya was looking for part-time work.'

'Oh, of course. Gladys Peabody. She'll be run off her feet with Bert leaving her. I'll let Anya know, although she was really interested in working at Lyons with you girls. Now I must be off. I'll take young Pearl here and have her sit at the back of the church until Katie and Miss Tibbs arrive. The poor child looks frozen to the bone,' she said, taking Pearl's hand and leaving the two friends alone.

'Now we're alone, can I ask why you've had a smile on your face ever since you returned home?' Lily asked.

'I have no idea what you're getting at,' Rose said. 'It's a happy occasion and I have a new job to look forward to, that's all.'

'So Ben's going away hasn't upset you at all? I thought the pair of you were getting close?' Lily asked as she looked up the road to see if the bride was in sight.

'I don't know what you mean,' Rose said quickly.

'Aha! I wondered if he was the reason for your

smiling face. I take it you two became a little closer . . . ?'

Rose felt her face start to burn at Lily's words. Even though they'd been friends since childhood, she was embarrassed to reply. Allowing a couple to step past them into the church, she wondered to herself how much she should tell Lily about her intimacy with Ben. Some things couldn't be shared with others. 'I don't think this is the right place to be discussing such things,' she hissed, as another of Katie's guests passed them with a greeting.

Lily raised her eyebrows in amusement. 'So something did happen. Who'd have thought it?' she grinned. 'Did you, erm . . . ?'

'If you must know, I have strong feelings for Ben, and he's a real gentleman. He's kind and thoughtful, and I feel good being with him. But he's gone away, and goodness knows when I'll see him again — so what's the point of imagining what could be?'

Lily just smiled thoughtfully as Katie and Miss Tibbs arrived in a car. It had been loaned for the occasion by one of Mildred's many contacts, and was driven by Jack's old school friend. The girls sprang into action, helping their friend prepare for the slow walk down the aisle to marry her Jack.

The service was beautiful, with some of the Nippies who weren't on duty coming along to watch the bride wed her groom, as well as people who'd cared for both Jack and Katie when they lived in the children's home. Jack's side of the church was filled with people he knew from when he was training to be a carpenter, as well as the smartly dressed sailors.

When it came time for the vicar to ask who gave Katie's hand in marriage, it was not Miss Tibbs, who had led her down the aisle, but Rose and Lily who spoke out, causing much mirth amongst the congregation.

After the register had been signed, the blushing bride and groom walked up the aisle as man and wife. They exited the church just as the snow started to fall once more. One of Jack's sailor friends produced a Box Brownie camera, and the guests huddled together for a few quick photographs before they froze in their finery. Then came the rush to get back to Sea View to toast the bride and groom.

The rest of the day went by in a flurry of fun and laughter until it was time for Katie and her husband to head off for a weekend in Broadstairs before Jack had to leave for his ship. There were tearful goodbyes amongst the girls, as all three knew their lives were moving in different directions.

The residents of Sea View collapsed in Flora's living room once the last guest had departed, looking round them at the leftover food and piles of washing-up that were calling for their attention.

'I suggest we change out of our finery before we make a start on all of this,' Rose said. 'Why don't you leave young Pearl where she is, Joyce? It would be a shame for her to wake and be alone,' she said, nodding to where the youngest bridesmaid was flat out on the settee.

'She can't be very comfortable,' Flora said. 'That old settee is as hard as nails and it's seen better days. I'll get a blanket and see if we can make her a little more comfy.'

The women all departed to their respective rooms to return in their day clothes with sleeves rolled up, ready to do battle with the washing-up. They laughed when Mildred appeared in her boiler suit. 'What's your problem?' she sniffed. 'It's clean and it's comfortable. I was glad to get out of that dress, I can tell you. It'll probably be the first and last time you'll see me in one.'

'You looked very nice,' Flora said, shushing Lily, who was still laughing. 'I hope we have a photograph from Jack's friend to show how good we looked in all our finery.'

Mildred looked horrified. 'I never want to see myself in a dress, so please don't put it on show.'

'It's all right, Mildred. You were with me at the back. Remember, the sailor man asked for the tall people at the back, so we stood with the men,' Anya reminded her.

'Thank goodness,' Mildred huffed as she picked up a heavy tray of crockery to take to the kitchen. 'Who's washing and who is drying?'

Rose followed her to the kitchen, carefully carrying the remains of the wedding cake, which had been provided by Lyons. Putting it on the table, she picked up a tea towel and started to dry the plates as the affable older woman placed them on the draining board.

'We don't seem to get much time to chat these days,' Mildred said. 'Remember all the times you came out on my boat and helped me bring in the

226

fishing nets? It seems an age ago.'

'It does. There's nothing better than the wind in your hair and sea-spray in your face. I must do it again soon.' Rose smiled wryly.

'You know I'll have to get permission from the powers that be. They don't let just anyone on a boat these days. You might be a spy,' Mildred said as she placed another load of tea plates into the bowl and added more hot water from a kettle slowly whistling away on the nearby hob.

'I think we've had our share of spies in this house. Have you heard any more about Mr Cardew? I've not had a chance to ask Mum.' Rose knew that if anything had happened in the seaside town, Mildred Dalryple would be the person to know about it.

'It seems your young man was right to call in the coppers. Cardew was up to no good. They've got him up in London now, and from what I've been told he'll spend the rest of the war locked up so that he doesn't get up to any more mischief.'

Rose ignored the mention of Ben, although it was good to hear him referred to as her young man. 'It's a bit tame to say Mr Cardew was up to mischief. I'd say it was a bit more than that.'

'He was talked into it by some chaps he knows at his bird-watching club. Cardew sang like a songbird in a gilded cage when he was carted off. Bloody good riddance to him! Thankfully they knew other residents weren't involved. Imagine if you'd come home from London and we'd all been arrested for working for Hitler?' she guffawed.

227

'It doesn't bear thinking about,' Rose joined in with the laughter. 'Imagine Miss Tibbs as a spy!'

'What's going on out here? I can hear you across the other side of the house,' Flora said as she joined them. 'I need my broom; there are crumbs all over my best rug.'

'Mildred was updating me about Mr Cardew,' Rose explained as she passed her mum a pile of dry plates. 'These are the ones that go back into the dresser cupboard.'

'What a daft old bugger,' Flora said. 'He should have kept to his bird-watching. Then, of course, it meant the billeting officer coming back, as he'd heard we had another empty room. It took all my powers of persuasion to convince him that young Lily was moving in, as he said she wasn't homeless and could go back to living with her stepfather. I'd no sooner move her back there than dine with Adolf Hitler. Being under the same roof as that George Jacobs is not good for any young woman,' she all but snarled.

Rose, who had tried not to go to the house since Lily's mum had passed, had to agree. George had always made her feel uncomfortable. 'Does that mean you'll have to give up the box room?' she asked, although she had a feeling she already knew the answer.

'I'm afraid we will have to, my love. We could store anything you don't want to take with you in my room. I have plenty of space.'

Rose felt a little miffed. She felt she'd lost her place in her own home, where she could hide away from the world if need be.

Flora could see she was upset. 'I suppose we

could put another bed in with Lily,' she said thoughtfully.

Rose nodded glumly.

'When do you expect to be able to move into your rooms in Margate?'

'I could have moved in today, but with the wedding and just getting home last night, it was all too much of a rush. I start at the teashop the day after tomorrow. I can always catch the bus to and from work for a while, until I've moved into my rooms.'

'We can't have you doing that,' Mildred said as she emptied the dirty water from the washing-up bowl and dried her hands on her overalls. 'I don't have to return the car to my friend until tomorrow afternoon, so we can move you to Margate tomorrow morning if you like?'

'That's very good of you, Mildred,' Flora beamed. 'With all this talk about petrol and God knows what else being rationed, it's very good of your friend to lend his car to run Katie to the church and now to help our Rose move home. We must make sure to pay something. What do you say, Rose?'

'It's very kind of you, Mildred, and yes, I insist on paying him for this,' Rose said, feeling as though everything and everyone was colluding to kick her out of her home.

'She wouldn't hear of it. We help each other out all the time. Think of it as my contribution,' Mildred said.

'A woman car owner? Fancy that,' Flora said, looking surprised.

'Do you really need all of this?' Lily said as she pulled a box covered in dust out from under Rose's bed. 'I wouldn't think you've opened it in years going by the muck on top of it.' She pulled back the flaps and peered inside. 'Why, they're all your books from school. Why ever have you kept them this long — shall I put them on the rubbish pile?'

'Oh no, don't do that,' Rose exclaimed, leaving a pile of knitted toys she was sorting out for Pearl and rushing to where Lily was sliding the box to the door to be taken away. 'I have such happy memories of school, and my exercise books have all my stories and poems in them. I'd like to share them with my own children one day.'

'You plan to have some, then?' Lily asked, pulling the box back.

'Oh yes, one day, when I have a nice home and I'm married.'

'Lizzy Soames who was in our class already has two nippers and not a husband to be seen,' Lily said as she brushed the dust from her skirt.

Rose screwed up her face in distaste. 'Just imagine not being married and having children. How she can hold her head up, I don't know. As Mum would say, she's no better than she ought to be. Katie and I crossed the road the other day just to avoid her.'

'It's not catching, you know. You have to . . . you know . . . before you can carry a kid.'

Rose's face dropped so much that Lily

thought it would hit the floor. 'I was right! You and Ben did . . . ' She stopped speaking as she saw tears forming in her friend's eyes. 'Oh Rose, he didn't force you, did he? I'll swing for him if he did.' Lily rushed to her friend's side to put an arm around her shoulders.

'No, it's nothing like that. It was wonderful, and he was a true gentleman.'

'So he didn't put pressure on you?'

'Gosh, no. If anything, I encouraged him.' Rose started to grin.

'Why, Rose Neville. You are going to get a reputation like Lizzy Soames if you carry on like this,' Lily joshed.

'What's all this laughter for? You've not been helping yourself to the leftover sherry, have you?' Flora asked as she stood in the doorway.

Lily raised her eyebrows at Rose as they both wondered how long Flora had been there and if she'd heard anything. 'We were just having a laugh about Rose's school books. She wants to keep them, and I'm for throwing them on the bonfire,' Lily said with a grin. 'She can't take everything with her to Margate.'

'I'm not. I'm giving some of my dolls to Pearl. She can have the baby doll with all the clothes Miss Tibbs made for her, and also this golliwog. I have two, so one can stay here. But this I'm taking with me,' Rose said, carefully opening a long cardboard box and lifting out a delicate china doll wearing a long pink silk dress. There was a small bunch of wax flowers attached to the doll's ribbon waistband.

'Oh, she's beautiful. You've never shown her to

231

me before,' Lily said as she gently stroked the doll's long chestnut hair.

'It was a special gift from General Sykes for my birthday. Mum only let me have it in my room when I was old enough to look after it. I named her Genny after the General,' she said, giving the doll a cuddle before wiping her eyes. 'Gosh, I do miss him. I know it's a silly thing to say, but I have better memories of him than I do of my dad.'

'With them passing away in the same year, it would have been confusing for a ten-year-old's memories. Would you mind if we packed her up carefully and stored her in the cellar where it is safe? It would be such a shame if she was damaged if there is an air raid. Goodness knows what will happen in this war, and as Ramsgate was bombed in the Great War, it could happen again.'

Rose passed the doll to her mum, confused by the emotion she saw on Flora's face. 'But we should give these other dolls to Pearl,' she said, trying to lighten the sad atmosphere.

'That's very generous of you. The child doesn't have much in the way of toys, poor little cock. She's woken up and running around as bright as a button after sleeping for a few hours. I don't know where they get the energy, I really don't.' Flora rubbed her back. 'As for these boxes of books — would you both be loves and take them into my bedroom? You can slide them under my bed out of the way for now. After that, come along downstairs. Mildred is making cocoa and we have some leftovers to eat, if you're hungry?' She turned to head back downstairs.

'That sounds good to me,' Lily said. 'Come on, Rose, grab the other end of this box and we'll get it moved. I could do with something to eat.'

The pair of them managed to move the heavy box across the landing to Flora's bedroom, and almost dropped it by the bed. 'I'll go and get the other bits and pieces while you push this out of the way. I don't feel right being in your mum's bedroom — some things are private,' Lily said, dashing off.

Rose got down onto her knees and started to push the box under her mum's bed. The large walnut bedstead with its iron frame was familiar to her, as she had hidden underneath it many times — and once, having caught her hair on the springs, had had to call for help from her mum, even though it was Flora she'd been hiding from. She gave the box a hefty push but found something was stopping it from sliding all the way under. Shuffling in beside the box, she found an old suitcase and grabbed the handle before wriggling back out, being careful not to snag her hair.

Leaning back against the bed to catch her breath, she looked at the case beside her. Whatever could it be, and why was it tucked away so far back under Flora's bed? It wasn't the one they used on the odd occasion they travelled away from home. There was something inside, she could tell by the weight. Clicking open the metal catches, she found a small leather attaché case inside and pulled it out onto her lap. The smaller latches on this case refused to budge, and Rose was dismayed to find it was locked. Quickly shoving the larger case back under the bed with her box of books beside it, she got to her feet and sat on Flora's bed, wondering where her mum would have kept the key. She was so curious to know what was inside that not for one moment did she think it was wrong to try and open the case. After all, they didn't have any secrets.

Rose looked around the room. The wardrobe was too high to be able to place a key on top, unless she'd used a chair to stand on. Her mum wasn't keen on having her feet off the floor, as it made her dizzy. Hadn't she said as much many times, when asking Rose to clean the downstairs windows? No, it would be somewhere close by . . . She checked the drawers in the tallboy, but found only clean clothes. Turning to the dressing table, she opened the two small drawers at each side of the mirror but found only a home-made necklace of shells that Rose had given to Flora one Christmas long ago, and a bundle of photographs in a fading envelope. Rose smiled. She'd seen these many times in the past when Flora had told her young daughter about a friend who'd worked in the music halls. The one long drawer had very little of interest, holding mainly handkerchiefs and scarves. She was just about to hold her hands up in defeat when she spotted a small china bowl with a domed lid. Decorated with a painted sea scene, it bore the inscription 'Greetings from Ramsgate' and was no different to the ones their guests had taken home as souvenirs in the days when Sea View accepted holidaymakers. Smiling at the thought her mum kept such a thing, she lifted the lid and pulled out a long chain. At the end of the chain was a key — a key small enough to fit the lock on the attaché case.

Rose went back to the bed and sat down, unlocking the small case as fast as she could, such was her need to know what was inside. Pulling back the lid, she stared in dismay at the contents. Paperwork. After all that effort, all she could see was an envelope and a few sheets of paper. Lifting them out to look for anything of interest, she found a pretty brooch and a ring underneath. Why would her mum hide such things? Surely such pretty trinkets would have been worn on a special occasion — an occasion like Katie's wedding? Absent-mindedly slipping the ring onto her finger, Rose looked briefly at the couple of sheets of paper before putting them to one side to read afterwards. That just left the envelope. She slid the single page of stiff white paper out, and started to read. As she did so, she felt her blood run cold. Surely this couldn't be right?

'You had no right to look into that case, let alone read my correspondence,' Flora said from the open door.

'And you had no right to keep such a thing from me,' Rose spat back. 'How could you, Mum, how could you? It states here that General Sykes is my father and he owned Sea View . . . '

Flora went to take a step closer to Rose, but she shrank away. 'After what I've read here, I don't want you to get near me, let alone touch me. If what I've read is true — and going by the name on the letter heading, it seems to be true enough — how do I even know you are my real mother? All these years I've felt sorry for Katie because she's an orphan, and I could be as alone in the world as she was. Just get away from me!' Rose cried out as Flora reached out to her.

'Darling . . . no good could come of you knowing, so that's why I kept the past a secret.'

Rose glanced to where the letter lay on the bed. The words and the embossed heading were ingrained in her mind — she knew she'd never forget that page of words, not if she lived to be a hundred years old.

'Rose, let's go downstairs and have a cup of tea in the kitchen. Everyone's in the living room, so we can talk in peace.'

Rose laughed out loud. 'Tea? Is that your answer to this?' she shouted back, pointing to the offending sheet of paper. 'I'm sorry; it is too late for such niceties. I'm going to my room, and tomorrow morning, first thing, I'm leaving. And I don't want to see you ever again,' she cried, pushing past her mum to leave the room. Seeing the ring on her finger, she wrenched it off.

'That was meant for you. I should have given it to you on your twenty-first birthday, but I was too afraid to rake up the past,' Flora said. 'Please take it now and let's not have us fall out,' she begged. 'We only have each other.'

A silence fell as Rose took several deep breaths to calm herself. She placed the ring on the green silk bedspread. 'I can't take it. Not at the moment. I need to think about what you've told me. General Sykes is my father? But he must have been so much older than you . . . '

'Love is no judge of age,' Flora said gently, kneeling down next to her daughter and trying to take her hand. 'There is so much to explain.'

Rose shook her head slowly. 'Can we leave it for now, Mum? I feel as though my past life has been built on shifting sand. So much has changed and I can't think straight. Perhaps another time, if I feel I can accept what you tell me,' she said, her voice little more than a whisper.

Flora looked at Rose, and felt as though she'd lost her daughter. Rose's eyes had taken on a distant, sad look and her body shrank away from Flora as if she couldn't accept what she'd found out.

'I'm sorry I kept this from you, my love. I never meant to hurt you. I did love your dad.'

'I do have one question. Where did you meet . . . the General?' Rose couldn't quite bear to call the lovely old man her father.

'It was during the last war — when I worked in the music halls as a dancer,' Flora said, knowing this too would be a shock for Rose. 'He wanted so much more for you, but . . . '

Rose backed away, shaking her head. 'I can't listen to any more of this. I'm going to bed, and I'll be off to Margate first thing, as I have a lot to do. Mildred will be helping me to move, so there's no need for you to come.'

Flora knew then she'd lost her daughter as she watched Rose walk from the room and cross the hall to her own bedroom before locking the door. 'What have I done?' she asked herself. Sinking onto the bed, she put her face in her hands and allowed the tears she'd held back to fall.

★ ★ ★

'Are you sure you don't want me to stay and help you settle in?' Mildred asked as she looked around the large living room. 'I must say, you have a lovely place here,' she added, looking at the pale-faced young woman. She was no fool, and had noticed something was amiss between Rose and her mother.

Rose wanted nothing better than to say yes and have the company of the much-loved older woman. Mildred could be relied upon to cheer her up whatever had happened, but she wasn't ready to have the plain-speaking woman tell her to kiss and make up with her mum once she explained why they'd fallen out. Deep in her heart Rose knew she should be sitting down and listening to what Flora had to say; but today, still deep in shock at finding out her father wasn't who she thought he was, she just couldn't take any more surprises. That'll teach me to poke about in Mum's belongings, she chided herself. She'd been awake most of the night, going over what had been said and trying to make sense of it all. Having finally dropped off to sleep at daybreak, she'd woken to a knock on her bedroom door.

'Rose, there's some breakfast on the table for you,' Lily had called loudly. 'I've got to go to work now. Good luck with the move, and sorry I couldn't be about to help.'

'Please tell Mum I'm not hungry,' she replied, and pulled the covers back over her head.

'A penny for them?' Mildred said now, pulling Rose back to the present.

'I'm sorry, Mildred. My head is all over the place, what with moving and starting the new job tomorrow,' Rose said, hurrying over and giving her friend a big hug. 'I can't thank you enough for helping me today. I don't know what I'd have done without you.'

Mildred's face turned red. She wasn't one for compliments. 'I'd do the same for anyone at Sea View. Now, shall I put the kettle on while you sort out some of these boxes, or would you rather I pushed off and left you to it?'

'I do need to visit the teashop. Mr Grant will be there, and he said he'd show me around. With their manager leaving to join up sooner than expected, they're a ship without a rudder just now.'

Mildred grinned. Any reference to the sea, and she was happy; Rose using one of her favourite sayings made her smile. 'Then I suggest you scoot off down there, and I'll unpack your bits and pieces and make up the bed.'

'Do you mind? It would be such a great help to me. I'll pick up some food while I'm there, and we can celebrate my new home. I promise I won't be long,' Rose said, grabbing her coat and hurrying out of the door after giving Mildred a quick peck on the cheek.

Mildred set to making up the bed with the

lavender-fragranced sheets Flora had packed for her daughter. She found an airing cupboard, where she placed another two sets and a spare blanket followed by towels and a table-cloth. She was aware that there was a frostiness between mother and daughter, but whatever had caused this rift, Flora had still provided Rose with everything she needed to set up a cosy home.

The first-floor flat was set over a shop only a couple of hundred yards down the road from the Margate teashop. The landlord had left basic furniture, and the linoleum-covered floor and heavy drapes at the tall windows were of good quality. 'Lyons have done her proud,' Mildred muttered out loud as she placed the empty sack that had held the bedding by the door ready to take back to her van, which was parked out in the street. She stopped to look out of the middle window at the scene below. People were scurrying along the street, taking care not to slide on the slushy pavements. Snow had stopped falling, but the sky was still a steel grey in colour. Out at sea, she could see a large navy vessel the same colour as the sky. As it was late morning the fishing boats were mainly back in the harbour. Her own small boat, the *Saucy Milly*, was moored at Ramsgate, where she'd left her one deck hand with a list of chores. She tried to ignore a group of soldiers who were rolling out barbed wire and placing sandbags around a gun emplacement. With such a grey scene, her mood dropped. What was to become of them here on the Kent coast? She'd been born not far from here, in the seaside town of Broadstairs, and it was a worry that this small clutch of villages, towns and farms based on the island of Thanet could be at risk from the enemy only twenty-odd miles across the English Channel. 'We'll beat the buggers,' she said out loud as she tucked a box of Rose's childhood toys under one arm and lifted her suitcase to take into the bedroom so Rose could unpack later. She'd spotted a mop, bucket and other cleaning items in the small kitchen, so she'd give the flat a quick going-over as a surprise for when young Rose came back to her new home.

Rose had a spring in her step as she left the flat to head down the staircase and out into the street behind the shops. It was so good of Mildred to stay so she could go to the teashop and see her new domain. She'd already been there once with Lily and Katie for tea, when Mr Grant first offered her the position of manager; but she had kept her head down, not mentioning her impending promotion, so that she could watch how the shop was ticking over. However, today she would be crossing the threshold as the new manageress and, with that in mind, she had worn a smart navy woollen dress in order to look the part. In her suitcase were two new suits provided by Lyons, and she had also purchased a tweed skirt and white blouse while in London. She was reminded of the General telling her that 'clothes maketh the man,' and at that moment she knew exactly what he meant. She didn't wish for her new staff to think her posh or a snob, but she was aware she had to remain a little apart from them in order to maintain her authority.

241

Entering the teashop, she was pleased to see that business was brisk despite the dismal weather. The office was set back a little from the front of the shop, where, as in most Lyons teashops, there was a counter where the Sallys sold their goods. Rose was a little dismayed to see that a Nippy was helping out there, rather than covering her group of tables.

'Ah, Miss Neville,' Mr Grant said as he spotted her. 'Welcome. Come this way and I'll go through the outstanding paperwork with you before we look around the teashop.'

Rose was aware of glances from the Nippies as she followed him into the office. The paperwork had been kept in order, and as her training at head office had been thorough, there was nothing that she needed to enquire about in that department. 'I wondered about staff. Are we short of Sallys at the moment? I only ask as I spotted a Nippy serving behind the counter.'

'Hmm, yes — we have had two of our Sallys leave recently, which means you will have to contact head office and ask for new staff to be allocated to this branch. It may be a while, but not to worry — I'm sure you will handle the situation. I've heard good things about you from our trainers at head office. Now, we do have a small problem. I've been informed that the wrong order of loaves has been sent to us. Whatever can we do with one hundred extra loaves of bread?'

Rose thought for a moment before speaking. 'Leave this with me, Mr Grant. I'll have the kitchen staff prepare bread pudding as well as individual dishes of bread-and-butter puddings.

Perhaps we could have some sent over to the Ramsgate branch?' I'll also have the staff take a loaf each home as well, she thought to herself, knowing that this would start her off on the right foot with all of them.

'Excellent, Miss Neville; you have certainly come up with a good idea. When this afternoon's delivery van arrives, have them take the food over to Ramsgate.' Mr Grant checked his watch. 'I will have to leave shortly, but I'll be back in a few days. Perhaps we could lunch together to discuss how you find your shop and staff?'

'Thank you,' was all Rose could think to say. How strange that only a month ago she had been one of the Nippies, and he would have been snapping his fingers at her to bring him more tea. As if on cue, he waved through the door at a passing Nippy and made that exact demand.

My life is changing more than I ever expected, she thought to herself.

11

May 25th 1940

Rose looked at the eager faces of her team of Nippies. After only a few months, she was proud of how she'd whipped the group of women into shape. Each one looked smart and was keen to work hard for the company.

'Ellen, would you please stand in on the front counter this morning? We are still short of a Sally. I'm hoping to hear from head office about a replacement very soon. Dora and Jean — as it is going to be a warm day, I suggest you guide customers up to the terrace for afternoon tea unless the air becomes too bracing. I have some paperwork to do before I get on with anything else, as Mr Grant arrives for his monthly inspection today. Please be vigilant and let us show him we have the best Lyons teashop on Thanet, shall we?'

The Nippies grinned enthusiastically and went about their duties as Rose retired to her small office at the back of the teashop. The room may have been small, but Rose had gone through it with a fine-toothed comb so that she could lay her hands on what was required without digging through piles of old files and paperwork. There was a pleasing smell of lavender-perfumed polish in the room, and she sighed with pleasure as she sat behind the polished oak desk and started to open the small pile of letters in front of her. Good, she thought to herself as a small missive from Orchard House informed her that a newly trained Sally would be starting work shortly and had been instructed to be at the teashop today at ten o'clock to meet her. She turned the paper over, but there was no mention of a name. 'That's a good start,' she muttered as she worked through the envelopes, making a note where necessary and pulling out folders to check figures for the stock sheets and order forms. She would need to hand those over when she had her meeting with Mr Grant and the salesman, Tom White, who she saw more often as he visited the teashop every few days and mainly got under her feet. Fresh food and shop stock still came down from head office, but paperwork had to be completed properly — otherwise they could end up short of tea, or have too many teacakes if the wrong box was ticked. She automatically thought back to how she'd rectified the problem of the wrong delivery of loaves on her first day in Margate and gave a big grin, thanking God that her quick thinking had impressed Mr Grant.

Rose worked on, aiming to have her desk cleared before the second post and long before Mr Grant arrived. She would then be able to devote her time to what he had to say without worrying about clearing her workload. A knock on the door had one of the Nippies bringing in a tray upon which was a small teapot and a plate with a toasted teacake.

'Why thank you, Jenny,' she smiled. 'Just what I need.'

The young Nippy quickly placed the tray on the desk and withdrew backwards, almost bobbing a curtsey. Rose sucked in her cheeks to try to stop herself from laughing. 'I'll bring the tea tray back, as I need to visit the kitchen,' she said to the departing girl. Not so long ago, she had been doing exactly the same thing when Miss Butterworth was the manageress at the Ramsgate teashop. By now, the girl would be hurrying to the kitchen to warn the workers that their manageress was on her way. She hoped that in time, the Nippies would relax even more when in her company.

Rose had just finished wiping crumbs from her mouth with the white napkin that had been placed on the tray, when there was another knock on the door. 'Enter,' she called, drinking the last of the tea in her cup.

It was the same Nippy, who again bobbed a curtsey. 'Miss, there's a lady to see you. I've put her at an empty table near the door. Shall I bring her here?'

'No, I'll come out to see her,' Rose said. With Mr Grant due anytime soon, at least he could use her office if he arrived while she was speaking to the woman. It was about time the new Sally got here, too, so she could have a quick word and assign her to the Nippy who'd been put behind the counter for the day to show her the ropes.

Young Jenny took the tea tray and backed out, bobbing as she went.

'Oh, Jenny, there is no need to curtsey. You are no longer working in service,' Rose smiled, trying not to laugh as the girl curtsied again and left the office in a hurry.

Rose was relieved to have a new staff member to serve customers with bread and cakes in the little sales section of the tearoom, with its tidy counter and shelving. Like the Nippies, all Sallys were trained in how to present baked goods for sale and how to serve customers at the counter. Every time she had to move a Nippy to that section, it meant a workstation wasn't being covered, and the tables had to be divided up between the remaining Nippies on duty. Rose knew the problem would get worse as so many younger women were moving into the services now, while others were keen to work at munitions factories because the money was so good.

Nodding hello to a few of her regular customers as she walked to the front of the tearoom, she stopped in surprise as a familiar voice called out to her. Turning, she saw Lily sitting alone. Rose glanced over to where she had been told the new Sally was sitting, and could see a Nippy serving her tea; so it seemed as if she could spare a few minutes. She hurried to see her friend, first giving her a hug before she sat down opposite her at the small table for two.

'Oh, it's so good to see you, Lily,' she said, waving her hand to a Nippy who stood nearby surveying the tables. 'Tea for my guest, please, Jane. Would you like something to eat?' she asked her friend.

'Not for me, ta,' Lily said, pulling her coat closer around her.

'Are you cold?' Rose asked, looking towards where the May sun shone brightly through the window.

'Just a bit,' Lily threw back at her while reaching for a pack of cigarettes. 'So, how's it going being the boss of your own teashop?' she asked as she struck a match against the side of the box and lit the cigarette with shaking hands.

Rose frowned. She could see there was something wrong with her friend, and felt guilty for not finding time to meet up so much since taking on her new responsibilities. 'I'm sorry not to have seen much of you since I left home. It's been rather busy,' she added, looking round the crowded room and thinking she should be carrying out her duties rather than sitting drinking tea, even if it was with a good friend.

'Everyone's all right, if that's what you was going to ask me?' Lily said pointedly.

'I know. Katie and her Jack visited and had tea here before he went off on his ship.'

Lily gave her a look that spoke volumes. 'That was two months ago,' she said.

'Gosh, was it really? How time flies,' was all Rose could think to say.

'Miss Tibbs has had a bad chest infection, and your mum's been busy what with the RAF lads taking her empty room,' Lily added, watching to see Rose's reaction to the mention of Flora.

'RAF? I thought the army was taking her room?'

'All the soldiers have left the area so the RAF took over. Seems there are quite a few of them over at Manston these days. I'm surprised your boyfriend hasn't told you,' she added, stubbing out her cigarette as the Nippy arrived with their tea.

'I've not seen or heard from Ben since I was in

London,' Rose said, looking sad. 'He could be anywhere for all I know.'

Lily was stony-faced. 'And meanwhile you hide yourself in work and ignore your family and friends.'

Rose was shocked by her friend's outburst. 'I haven't . . . I mean . . . I didn't mean to,' she said, floundering over what to say.

'Your mum has been deeply affected by you rushing off like you did. She's scared to come and see you in case you cause a fuss. She's lost weight and sits around most days staring into space. We've all mucked in, but it isn't the same as it used to be.'

'But she has her ARP work and helps out with the WRVS. I don't understand?'

'Oh come off it, Rose. We all know the ARP wardens are mostly twiddling their thumbs these days, waiting for something to happen. They've even said ARP means ''Anging Round Pubs' as they aren't busy now most things are organized in the town.'

Rose felt her face twitch with a smile. She had heard people say that about the ARP wardens, which she thought was a little unfair. 'That doesn't sound like Mum at all.'

'Well, believe me, it is just like your mum. She misses you, Rose, and whatever it was you fell out over, you need to see her and talk things through. I'd give my right arm to be able to see my mum and talk with her . . . especially right now,' she added, picking up her cup with her still shaking hands. Tea slopped into her saucer.

'Lily, what's wrong?' Rose said, taking the cup

from her hand as tears started to fall down Lily's cheeks. 'Please, you've got to tell me.'

'I can't, not here,' she sniffed. 'It's not the right place to talk about my problems.'

Rose thought for a moment before reaching into her pocket and pulling out a key. 'Here, go to my flat and wait for me. I usually take my midday break here, but I will come home and we can have a chat.'

Lily took the key, and after Rose instructed her where to go she gave her a quick hug and left the teashop. Rose stood up and brushed her skirt down. She was worried about her friend, and had decided immediately that she couldn't ignore whatever had brought Lily to Margate. It was bad enough not speaking to her mum — and as the weeks turned into months, it was becoming harder to face going home to see her. At least there was a new Sally to work in the shop, she thought as she went to the table to invite the woman to accompany her to the office.

As she approached the table, she spotted Anya. Please God she hadn't come here to give her a talking-to about not visiting Flora? Rose still felt upset and angry, and wasn't ready to discuss it with anyone else today. As she walked toward the Polish woman's table she looked around her. The teashop was filling up fast and there was a queue at the counter, with people buying supplies. Wherever was that new Sally?

'Hello, Miss Neville. You look very smart — just as the manageress should do,' Anya said, holding out her hand to shake Rose's.

Rose leant over to kiss Anya's cheek. She was

250

very fond of the woman. 'Hello Anya, what brings you to Margate? Not that I'm unhappy to see you,' Rose said.

'No — no kisses, you must be professional lady,' Anya said sharply, ducking away from Rose.

Rose was puzzled. 'Is there something wrong, Anya?' she asked as she sat down next to the woman.

'I am here to work. You must call me Sally. I am no longer Anya the friend when I am working here.'

Rose grinned as the penny dropped. 'Don't tell me you are to be our new Sally?'

Anya nodded solemnly. 'I am telling you.'

'Why, that is splendid. But what happened to the job at Mrs Peabody's grocery shop?'

'A better person has the job. I arranged it for her.'

'But why?'

'Joyce is much suited for the job, and she can take young Pearl with her as she plays with Mrs Peabody's children. It makes Joyce happy to earn the wage. I wish to have a fulfilling job with Joe Lyons, but not to be waitress, as I am too clumsy,' Anya explained patiently. 'I went to London to learn how to be a Sally and serve customers.' She looked around the teashop, her eyes stopping on the window display close to the counters. 'I soon sort out and make it look good,' she said. 'You may call me Sally Polinski from this day forward,' she added with a twinkle in her eye.

'That's wonderful. I received a letter from head office, but they didn't put the name of the new Sally. Does this mean you have moved to Margate?' Rose asked.

'No, I have the bicycle Mr Cardew left in the garden shed. I am told he will not need it where he has gone,' Anya said seriously. 'I will ride the bike to and from your teashop each day. Mildred, she say she will collect me when she has the use of the motor van. She has it quite often, as she has a good friend. It all works out well.'

Rose remembered that the official letter had stated the new Sally would be working part-time each day, so there was no need to worry about Anya cycling in the dark. 'There is also a bus that runs between the towns, if the weather should turn bad.'

'Rain it does not worry me,' Anya said.

Rose doubted that much bothered Anya, as she was such a strong character.

'Let me show you the staffroom and where everything is kept; then you can change into your uniform and start to learn the ropes. Welcome on board, Anya,' Rose said. It was good to know that at least she would get to hear from Anya about how her mother was getting on, even if she wasn't yet prepared to visit or speak with Flora.

★　★　★

'You'll never guess who my new Sally is?' Rose exclaimed as she burst into the front room of her flat overlooking the beach, before grinding to a halt as she saw her friend sobbing into her hands. 'My dear Lily, whatever is the matter?' she asked, rushing over to sit beside her.

252

'Oh, Rose, I'm in such a mess,' Lily said as soon as she could speak properly. 'I have to do something that I know you will hate me for. In fact, everyone will hate me.'

'No one is going to hate you, Lily. You are a good person, and always will be. Let me get you a drink to calm you down,' Rose said, going to the sideboard and taking out a half bottle of gin. She poured a generous amount into a glass. 'Here — drink this. It will help calm you down.'

Lily knocked back the gin in one gulp and gave a shudder. 'Thank you; I needed that. I'm sorry for being such a mess, but I couldn't tell anyone about my problem, and it's been eating me up inside. I've got a big favour to ask you, Rose.'

Rose felt terrible. If she hadn't cut herself off from everyone at Sea View these past months, she would have been able to help her friend with her problem — whatever it was. 'I will do all I can to help you,' Rose said sincerely.

'I wondered if I could transfer to the Margate teashop and stay with you? It would be better if I wasn't in Ramsgate for a while.'

'You can stay with me for as long as you like. I have a small spare bedroom. The flat came furnished, so there's a single bed already in there, and a chest of drawers for your bits and bobs. You can use my wardrobe if you need to hang anything up. How will you collect your possessions from Ramsgate, though?' she asked, hoping Lily wouldn't want her to go to Sea View to help collect her things. She wasn't ready to face Flora just yet.

'I have a suitcase with me. I hoped you'd say yes,' Lily said with an apologetic look.

Rose grinned. 'It'll be just like old times with us working together. I've been more than a little lonely here on my own. I can't really ask any of the Nippies to come to the pictures, what with me being their boss.'

'It won't be quite like the old days,' Lily said as she stood up, slipping off the heavy coat she had been wearing since they met in the teashop.

'Oh my goodness,' Rose said, placing her hands to her mouth. 'You . . .'

Lily looked down to the swell of her stomach. 'Yes, I have a little visitor on the way. Any chance of another glass of gin?'

Rose sat down with a thud on one of the wooden chairs set around the dining table, shocked by her friend's revelation. 'I don't think joking about it will help,' she said seriously. 'And drinking gin isn't any good for a baby.'

'Believe me, I'm not joking. I've heard the old wives' tales too. I've downed enough gin to sink a battleship to try and get rid of this, so I don't think another glass will make the slightest difference.'

Against her better judgement, Rose poured another glass. She thought briefly about having some herself, but knew it wouldn't be a good idea when she had an afternoon of work ahead of her. 'Here you are, but when this bottle's gone there'll be no more alcohol in this flat. We have to think about your child from now on — we don't want you getting sozzled and falling over, do we?'

'There's not going to be a child,' Lily said, taking a gulp from the glass. 'I've got the address of someone who can help me get rid of it.'

Rose thought of Katie and her Jack, who had grown up in a children's home 'Surely you can try to keep it? You know what Katie used to tell us about all the babies in that orphanage. It's no life for a little kiddie.'

'It won't be in an orphanage. The woman I'm going to see will help me to lose it,' Lily said defiantly. 'That's why I've come here. If I'd stayed at Sea View, someone would have tried to stop me. As it was, your mum kept giving me strange looks because I wore my coat so much. If she hadn't been so distracted worrying about you, she'd have noticed I was expecting.'

Rose didn't know what to say. At that moment, she wanted her mum more than anything in the whole wide world. She didn't know how to help her friend — and who, for goodness' sake, was the father of the child?

★   ★   ★

'The news isn't looking good,' Mr Grant said as he turned the page of his newspaper, almost knocking a cup out of its saucer.

'I just wish I was able to get over there and help our lads,' Tom White said pompously as he helped himself to the last biscuit on the plate.

Rose was beyond fed up with the area manager and his sidekick using her office for their meal breaks when she had so much to do. 'Have you not thought about joining up?' she asked Tom.

He looked as though Rose had attacked him as her few words hit home. 'Don't think I wouldn't like to, Miss Neville. However, my services are required here as I'm in a reserved occupation, besides having certain health problems,' he said in a weak voice.

'I see,' she said, giving him a hard stare. He glanced away. 'If you have finished your tea, gentlemen, I need to use my office to speak to several of my staff.'

'Can you not use the staffroom while we do our business in here?' Tom White asked indignantly.

Rose hadn't seen any work being done, unless it was inspecting the pies and cakes they'd consumed.

'It's rather delicate and not something to be discussed in a staffroom,' she said pointedly.

'You might have a word with that Lily Douglas while you're at it. I'm surprised she was allowed to have a transfer to this teashop, what with it being the most important in the area,' Tom White said. 'I've heard she doesn't have a very good reputation with the, er . . . men,' he added, seeing Rose start to glare.

'Miss Douglas is one of our best workers. I have no qualms about her working here,' she answered, trying hard to keep her temper. Although not aware of what went on, Rose knew that Lily had fallen out with the man at some point. 'I'm more than happy to conduct my business with my staff in front of you both, but must warn you it is of a delicate nature to do with female health. I'm sure you won't mind, though, having health problems yourself,' she said pointedly in Tom's direction.

The two men had jumped to their feet and picked up their belongings before Rose could draw breath.

'Perhaps you would take your tea tray with you? My staff are too busy to wait on fellow staff members,' she said to Tom, who gave her a hard stare and left without lifting a finger to clear up his mess. 'I didn't expect it any other way,' she muttered to their departing backs. I've a mind to hand him a bundle of white feathers, she fumed to herself as she indicated to a passing Nippy to take away the tray.

'You seem to be in a bad mood,' Lily said as she took a seat in front of her friend's desk.

'Ignore me. I'm fed up with that horrid man Tom White. Thank goodness most men aren't like him, or Hitler would be landing on our beaches this very minute.'

The smile dropped from Lily's face at the mention of Tom's name.

'You really don't like him, do you? Has something happened between you?'

Lily shrugged her shoulders. 'He means nothing to me anymore. I won't be getting near him again in a hurry, believe me.'

'That's the spirit,' Rose said, all the time wondering how they'd fallen out. 'Now, what was it you wanted to speak to me about?'

'I wondered if I could go early? I have an appointment.'

'Of course you can,' Rose said. She'd been nagging Lily all week to see a doctor to check everything was fine with her pregnancy. 'Perhaps I . . . ' She got no further, as the door burst open and Tom White charged in. Lily gave her a quick nod and hurried from the room.

'I insist you dismiss that damnable woman serving behind the counter,' he all but shouted at her.

'Mr White, my counter staff are nothing if not professional. Please explain yourself.'

'That foreign one. She told me off and said I should mind my manners. Does she not know who I am? She was rude, and I insist she leaves the premises right now,' he demanded.

'I think it best to call the Sally in so she can explain her side of what happened,' Rose said with a sigh. She'd really wanted to chat with Lily before she left for the afternoon, and perhaps offer to go with her for the appointment. She was due a few hours off, and her staff were more than capable of coping if an emergency should arise. Opening the office door, she waved to Anya, beckoning her to come to the office.

'You wanted to see me, Miss Neville?' Anya said, ignoring the red-faced Tom.

'Yes, Anya. Would you please take a seat? Mr White here tells me you were rude to him. Would you explain what happened?'

Anya took a seat, placing her hands in her lap. 'This man, he barged in front of the queue. I told him to wait his turn.'

Rose looked to Tom to explain himself.

Tom's face grew redder than before. 'I am management. This woman should not tell me what to do.'

'Manners they cost nothing,' Anya spoke clearly to Rose. 'My lady customers they have been waiting patiently. He should not push them and ask for free food.'

Rose raised her eyebrows and looked to Tom. 'Free food? All staff should pay for their purchases, Mr White,' she said coldly.

'I am management,' was his reply.

'Miss Neville she pays for her purchases and she is senior to you,' Anya told him without expression. 'I simply do the Sally's job and follow Mr Joe Lyons rules that I was taught at Sally school. If I am wrong, then Miss Neville she should give me the sack,' Anya directed at him.

'Mrs Polinski is correct. I must request that in future you pay for your purchases, and treat our customers with respect. Thank you, Anya, you may return to your counter.' Rose waited for the door to close after Anya and turned to Tom, her eyes blazing with anger. 'Don't you ever act that way in my tearoom again, or I'll speak to head office and have you removed so fast you will find yourself out of work and signed up for the army. Do you hear me?'

Tom's mouth opened and closed like a goldfish. 'I'll take this further, mark my words,' he finally said. 'I'll not have any woman talking to me like that.'

Rose took a step closer to him, and stared angrily into his face. 'Lyons teashops have a reputation for perfection in catering. No employee acts as you have done in my teashop. Do you understand me?' she hissed.

He stepped backwards, lost for words, as Mr

Grant entered the office. 'Ah, Tom — let us be on our way. Thank you once more for making my job easy, Miss Neville. You run a tight ship, yes, a tight ship,' he repeated, as he glanced out the window towards where a grey battleship was heading out to sea.

Tom White followed Mr Grant from the office, but turned back at the last minute. 'Don't cross me, Miss Neville. Or you won't like the outcome.'

Rose took a deep breath. There was something about that man she really didn't like. She wasn't one to listen to rumours, but there were so many stories doing the rounds involving Tom White and female members of the Lyons staff, and she wasn't happy about it. Especially as her gut feeling was that Lily had been involved with the man in the past. Surely he couldn't be . . . ?

Giving herself a mental shake, she went out into the teashop to check that everything was in order. What Lily did in her private life was none of her business. Rose liked to walk through the teashop and onto the upper terrace that looked out over the sea. It must have been a wonderful sight before the war, to look out over the sands with families enjoying the sun and their time together.

With the sun out and warm on her face, she felt good. She could cope with people like Tom White — and so far, the war hadn't caused too many problems in her small world. Apart from the newspaper headlines and Pathé News, Rose felt the war had hardly touched her life so far. Thinking of Ben, her heart lurched a little, but the pain of him not being in touch since that blissful time in London was fading fast. He couldn't have thought as fondly of her as she'd thought of him. She refused to think about Flora and her deceit — that was blocked from her mind. It didn't occur to her that she was blocking out the most painful parts of her life.

Picking up several newspapers that had been left on tables vacated by diners, she placed them on a rack for the use of new customers. The news reports were still full of Mr Chamberlain resigning, along with complicated explanations about the war overseas. France was mentioned, and she thought of Ben for one fleeting moment before dismissing him from her mind.

Looking around, she could see the roof terrace part of the teashop was ticking over nicely, and she hurried back downstairs to look for Lily. She had a gut feeling that her friend was going to visit a doctor. Rose had begged Lily to see a doctor before making a decision about the baby. Perhaps this was where she was off to? Rose thought accompanying her friend would be the supportive thing to do. Collecting her coat from the office, she instructed a couple of Nippies on their duties before saying she would be going out for a while and asking if they'd seen Lily.

'She left about five minutes ago, Miss Neville,' one of the Nippies answered.

Rose nodded her thanks and hurried from the teashop. She would soon catch up with Lily, she thought, walking away from the seafront and threading through the back-streets to where she knew the local doctor lived and had his surgery. Turning a corner, she spotted Lily's royal blue coat and matching hat up ahead. 'Lily,' she called out, but her friend couldn't have heard her.

Not to worry, Rose thought. The doctor's house was not far, and she should be able to reach Lily by then. She leant against a wall briefly, trying to catch her breath, before once more setting off at a fast pace. She could see the front garden of the doctor's house, so it wasn't far now.

What happened next had Rose doubting herself. Lily walked straight past the house and headed across the road, down a side street. Rose shook her head in disbelief as a nagging worry filled her head. This was confirmed as she turned the corner and saw Lily standing on the pavement, not moving.

This street was made up of run-down houses without gardens. The house Lily stood in front of was possibly the worst one in the street. As Rose picked up speed, ignoring the need to stop and take a breath, she saw her friend look at a scrap of paper in her hand before checking the house number. She raised her hand and knocked on the door.

'No ... no ... ' Rose called out, her breathless voice going unheard. 'No, please don't do this,' she started to sob. 'Please don't kill your baby.'

12

Rose caught up with Lily just as the door opened a crack. 'Don't do it, Lily. Please don't do it,' she begged.

Lily ignored Rose and stared towards the door as it opened wider. 'I was told to come along to see you this afternoon,' she said without any form of expression on her face.

'Please, Lily,' Rose said as she reached her friend and clung to her arm.

'You was told to come on yer own,' the woman muttered, ushering Lily inside. 'I don't want no trouble on my doorstep.'

Rose hung onto her friend and forced her way into the house as the door started to close. She'd heard about women who helped young girls when they were in trouble, and she didn't want her friend to suffer. But she also feared for the baby she'd begun to think of as a real person. Surely Lily wasn't going to get rid of her child? Rose took deep breaths, trying to calm down. She had to keep a clear head if this baby was to be saved. 'Lily,' she whispered. 'Let's go home, eh? We can talk about this properly indoors. This isn't the answer . . . '

Lily spun round to face Rose. 'What? You mean we can chat about it over a cup of tea and everything will be all right?' she said, looking distressed. 'You've got no idea how I've worried about this and thought about the future and what people will say when they see me with a baby . . . his baby. I feel sick even thinking about it.'

Rose knew it was the time for plain talking. 'Lily, it could be me just as easily. I'm not as squeaky clean as you seem to think. I know how it can happen,' she added, thinking fleetingly of that magical night with Ben before he walked out of her life.

Lily gave a harsh laugh, sounding like an injured animal caught in a trap. 'This was no lovers' tryst, believe me,' she snarled. 'I want rid of it, and I would have done it before now if I'd known where to go for help. Do you think I'd have carried it for so long, covering myself up in loose clothes and keeping my coat on, if I could have been rid of it months ago? Don't make it worse for me than it already is,' she pleaded. 'Please, Rose, I need you to help by not trying to stop me. If you can't promise me that, you should go home right now.'

Rose looked around her at the hallway with its peeling wallpaper and torn linoleum flooring. There was a smell resembling boiled cabbage and cats that almost had her gagging as she took each breath. How could she walk away and leave her best friend to face whatever was about to happen? No; if Lily was determined to go through with this, then Rose would stand by her.

'I'll stay,' she said, dreading what was about to happen. Abortions were only every talked about in hushed words. This was not something she had ever expected to experience, even if it was only by holding her friend's hand.

The woman pointed for them to enter a room, which turned out to be the kitchen of the house, giving Rose a wary look as she took the envelope of money held out to her by Lily. Rose wrinkled her nose at the stench. It seemed stronger in this room.

'You can wipe that look off yer face,' the woman snarled at Rose. 'The table's clean, and that's all that matters for her. You can drink that before I get started,' she said to Lily, sliding a half bottle of whisky across the table along with a chipped cup. 'I'll be back in a minute.'

Lily lifted the bottle to her lips and grimaced at the strong taste. 'Why do people drink this stuff?' she said, trying to make Rose smile. 'I thought women in my position were supposed to drink gin and take hot baths?'

'I wouldn't know,' Rose said sadly.

'Believe me, it doesn't work. I tried it twice,' Lily said. 'All I did was waste the hot water.'

'I don't know how you can be so light-hearted about this,' Rose snapped.

'I'm most definitely not doing that,' Lily said, taking another swig from the bottle. 'I'm truly not.'

Rose looked around the room as Lily continued to drink. She could only think that the idea was to get Lily so drunk she wouldn't feel any pain. Apart from a cracked sink with a tap over it and a small stove in one corner, there was just a wooden cupboard with an assortment of items laid out on top. She stepped closer to look and gasped in shock, backing away.

'What's up?' Lily asked.

'I think these are what she's going to use to . . . to help you . . . ' Rose whispered, feeling as though she might be sick at any moment.

Lily stepped round the table and looked closer. 'But that's a knitting needle, that's a crochet hook . . . and is that a hatpin?' she asked, swallowing hard. 'I don't know what the rest are, but they look dirty. And the crochet hook is rusty. Surely she isn't going to use them on me — is she?' she asked Rose, who couldn't find the words to answer.

They both looked in silence before Rose reached for the whisky and took a gulp. 'I don't think this is a very good idea, Lily,' she said, looking fearful.

'I've got no choice.'

'You do have a choice, and you have friends who will support you. Whatever happened when you fell pregnant with this baby, it shouldn't make you decide to be rid of the child. It is still a human being and deserves to live. I know I'd be honoured to be an aunty, and I'm sure Katie would too,' she said gently, taking her friend's hand and giving it a squeeze. 'We'd never question what happened or judge you for thinking this was the right decision.'

Lily looked towards the door. 'I don't think she'd take well to me legging it,' she said warily.

'What's she going to do — call a copper?' Rose asked. 'They'd lock her up before she stuck that hatpin in her bonnet. Come on. Let's go home.'

'Hang on just a minute,' Lily said, picking up the envelope from where the woman had left it on the table and tucking it into her pocket. They both hurried from the room and let themselves out into the street, where they started to run.

'Oi! Where the hell do yer think yer off to with me money?' the woman bellowed from the doorway. 'You drank me whisky as well, you thieving bitches!'

The two girls ran as far as the corner of the road before leaning against the wall to catch their breath. 'I know I shouldn't laugh considering what I've done, but this reminds me of when we almost got caught when we went scrumping as kids,' Lily said, giving Rose an apologetic look. 'I'm sorry for dragging you into my problems. I suppose I'm going to have to go back to Sea View with my tail between my legs and hope Flora will take me back in, and won't be shocked by my condition.'

Rose noticed that Lily had not mentioned going back to live with her stepfather.

The loud beep from a vehicle made both the girls jump. As it pulled up alongside them, the window was rolled down and a familiar voice boomed, 'What are you two up to?'

Rose leant into the car. 'Hello, Mildred, we could ask you the same. Have you been delivering fish?' she asked, wrinkling her nose.

'I've just finished. Are you off home, or back to the teashop? I fancy a cuppa, but wouldn't be welcome in my work clothes.' Mildred grinned, knowing how the young girls disliked her choice of work.

'We are on the way to my flat. You are welcome to join us,' Rose said with a grin. One of the things she missed most about living at Sea View was chatting with Mildred.

'Jump in, then,' Mildred said, clearing a pile of papers off the long front seat. 'It's unusual to see you both together . . . and hurrying out of that old prostitute's house. I've heard she offers other services these days. As I doubt Lyons have started making deliveries, can I ask what you were up to?' She didn't take her eyes off the road as they set off towards the seafront.

Both girls fell silent until Lily nudged Rose to say something.

'Well . . . ' she started to say, without knowing what words to use or how to explain Lily's predicament.

'I've got all day,' Mildred threatened. 'Unless you want me to drive through to Ramsgate and get your mum involved?'

Lily gave Rose a sideways look and sighed. 'It's my problem, and I'll share it with you, Mildred. Can we go to Rose's flat, please?'

★ ★ ★

'That went down a treat,' Mildred said, brushing crumbs from the front of her navy-blue dungarees. She'd removed the pullover she always wore when out on her fishing boat, as even she knew it was rather ripe. 'I've got a bit of news for the pair of you, but first I want to know what games you are playing at. Does it have anything to do with that?' she asked, nodding towards the bulge under Lily's Nippy dress.

Lily gasped and put her hands across her

268

stomach. She'd forgotten to cover herself up as she'd started to do in the past weeks, assuming Mildred wouldn't notice.

'Sit yourself down and tell me everything.'

Lily did as she was told, but didn't know how to start to explain.

'Let's start with: you are expecting a baby. And you went to that woman's house to get rid of it, eh?'

Lily nodded her head before bursting into tears. Rose hurried over to comfort her.

'There's no need for tears. I'm here to help you,' Mildred said. 'I'd like another cup of tea, though. That sausage roll has left me a bit dry.'

Rose hurried into the kitchen to squeeze another cup out of the pot. She was a bag of nerves, wondering what Mildred had to say — and worse still, what she would say to Flora when she went home to Sea View.

'You know that woman could have killed you?' Mildred said, not unsympathetically.

Lily sniffed into her handkerchief. 'I didn't know what was going to happen. One of the Nippies at the Ramsgate teashop gave me the address . . .'

'So you told us all you had been transferred to Margate, so as not to cause concern for the people at Sea View who care for you?' Mildred asked. 'But you forgot one thing.'

Lily frowned. 'Did I?'

'Yes. Some of us have experienced what you are going through, and were watching.'

Rose's eyes opened wide. 'Oh my goodness. Was it my mum, or perhaps Joyce? Don't say it was Miss Tibbs?'

Mildred gave a belly laugh. 'No, it was me.'

'You?' both the girls asked in unison.

Mildred looked affronted. 'Why are you so shocked? I have had men friends, you know. There was a time when I was planning to marry. Oh, yes; I was considered a bit of a catch in my time, what with my father having his own boat. I hope you aren't laughing at me,' she said, seeing the two girls look at each other, although she had a kindly twinkle in her eye. 'It was me who called it off when I found out he was stealing from my father. I sent him packing, I can tell you. Then I found I was expecting his child.'

'Oh, Mildred,' Rose said, thinking how the poor woman had lived alone without a family of her own.

Mildred raised her hands in mock horror. 'Good God, girl, don't you be feeling sorry for me. It was a long time ago, and I'm more than happy with my lot. My point is, I panicked, and I went to someone like that woman you visited — and she nearly killed me with her dirty knitting needles. My old dad was beside himself with grief at losing his grandchild and nearly losing me, his only living relative. He blamed the chap I should have married. He should have blamed me, because I was too much of a coward to ask anyone for help, preferring to visit a butcher.'

The girls fell silent as they digested Mildred's words.

'Did you never meet another man you wanted to marry?' Lily asked quietly, feeling sorry for the woman she'd never once thought of as someone who'd carried a child.

Mildred shrugged her shoulders. 'Who'd want a barren bride? What that woman did to me left me unable to carry another baby, let alone conceive. I did meet someone else, but that's another story — and a long one.'

Lily's face dropped. 'I don't understand.'

'My dear, you wouldn't, because you are an innocent who doesn't know what goes on in this horrid world. Women like the one you met today are just after your money. Once she put dirty instruments inside you and cut your body, God only knows what would have happened to you. In a way I was lucky, because I survived when so many poor women don't.'

'I thought they wanted to help me and people like me,' Lily said, shaking her head. 'This is so hard to understand. The Nippy who guessed my problem and gave me that woman's details said she was a good person who helped girls who were in trouble.'

Mildred looked across to Rose, who sat stony-faced, and raised her eyebrows. Rose nodded slowly, knowing what the older woman was trying to convey without words. Rose knew she would have to track this girl down and have her removed from the employ of the Lyons company, for God only knew how many other young women she'd sent to the abortionist. Time enough to find out who this person was. First, she must make everything right in Lily's world.

'Lily, there are people who do help women — and not just because they've made a mistake with a young man they've only just met,' Mildred explained sympathetically. 'Some wives just can't bear to have another child when they have so many mouths to feed, and hardly any money coming into the house. They know who to go to for help. Sadly, for the likes of us, we chose the wrong person to turn to. You were lucky you had Rose to stop you from going through with this. I like to think someone was looking down on you today in your hour of need. I'm not a religious woman, but we all need a guardian angel at some time in our lives. Yours could have been your mum stepping in to help,' she smiled gently, not expecting Lily to all but explode.

'My mum?' she cried. 'You think my mum helped me? Bloody hell, Mildred, she could have done it sooner than this if she wanted to help. For some reason she loved that old bastard, and wouldn't listen to the stories of his womanizing. After she died he thought I was an easy target. I should have killed him when I had the chance. That poker was inches from my hand. I could have ended it — but like a silly cow, I thought it was doing wrong, not knowing his rotten seed was already inside me and ruining my life. Oh no, I went on thinking I could keep out of his way through some stupid misguided loyalty to my dead mum, who on her deathbed begged me to keep a roof over his head after she'd gone.' Lily collapsed back into the chair she'd leapt from in anger only seconds before. 'What a bloody, bloody fool I've been,' she sobbed into her hands. 'A bloody, bloody fool.'

'Perhaps your mum didn't know what he was like?' Mildred soothed her as she rocked Lily in her arms. The look Rose gave her told her that they both knew the man was a drunk and a troublemaker.

The distraught girl gave a shuddering breath as she tried to stop her heartrending sobs before hiccuping a hysterical laugh. 'Good try, Mildred, but Mum knew what he was like. She even paid off a few women who banged on our door, as she said they were telling lies. She didn't want anyone blackening our family name. I'm surprised an angry husband never bumped him off one dark night and threw him into the harbour. He deserved it.'

Rose didn't know what to say to help her friend. Her own mum had warned her more than once not to go to Lily's home, and now she knew why. 'Perhaps the baby isn't his?' she suggested, knowing that regardless of Lily's home life, she liked a laugh with the men.

'Thanks for that,' Lily said, cuffing her eyes with the back of her hand. 'What do you think I'm like? I've only ever been with one bloke, and he laughed at me when I said I hadn't done it before. He made me feel like a dirty tart. I didn't even know until then that what that bastard had done to me meant I'd not be able to walk up the aisle in a white dress.'

Rose enveloped her friend in her arms and they both cried together. 'Can I tell you something, Lily?'

Lily raised her swollen, tear-stained face and looked at Rose without saying a thing.

Rose felt embarrassed as Mildred was in the room and listening intently. 'I can't wear white at my wedding either, so we are a right pair, aren't we?' She tried to smile, but also felt saddened by what she'd said. She wasn't a church-goer, but she'd never lie in church, and wearing a white gown with all it meant was as good as a lie any day.

Mildred wiped her red face with a handkerchief. 'Well, we are a right trio, aren't we? Not a white frock to be worn between us. Think of the old girls tittle-tattling about this,' she smiled. 'What I can't understand is how the pair of you didn't know what you were doing. Don't you read books? Even those women's magazines mention what goes on during the wedding night.'

'I only look at the fashion pages,' Lily said with a weak smile, 'and the last book I read was when I was at school.'

'But Flora would have explained what was what, wouldn't she?' Mildred asked, looking at Rose's red face.

'No, she just told me I wasn't to go bringing shame on her by doing things I oughtn't to.'

'Well, I'll be . . . ' Mildred said, shaking her head. 'What about when you go to the pictures?' she asked, turning back to Lily.

'Clive Danvers is too much of a gentleman to take advantage of his lady friends. It has to be true love. And then all we see is him smoking a cigarette afterwards,' Lily said seriously.

'He is the spy from the films we like to watch. Johnny Johnson is our favourite actor,' Rose explained.

Mildred was lost for words until she started to see a small smile pass between the two girls. 'Oh, you two. You had me going there for a minute,' she huffed. 'Can't you take anything seriously?'

'I'm sorry,' Rose said. 'We shouldn't have done that. I know I don't want to make light of the situation. However, I'll say this now: whatever happens, I'll welcome this baby — whoever its father is — because it is your baby, Lily, and we are like sisters. Let's make some plans and have no more talk about getting rid of it, shall we? I reckon Katie will say the same as well.'

Mildred went out to the kitchen to put the kettle on, but called out, 'This war will do you a favour. With you being over here away from Ramsgate, we can make up a bit of a story to explain the baby.'

'But I won't be able to work before too long, and I wouldn't expect Rose to support me or put me up here. It wouldn't be right, what with her a manageress at the teashop. Perhaps I should move away and make a fresh start rather than bring shame on you all,' Lily said with a resolute look on her face.

'Oh no you won't,' Rose and Mildred said at the same time.

'I've got an idea,' Mildred continued, 'and once you've drunk this tea I've just made, you are both going for a short ride with me.'

'Not to Ramsgate,' Rose said quickly. 'I'm not ready to speak to Mum yet and I don't want to bump into her too soon.'

'No, I'm not taking you to Sea View. I'm going to show you my little secret. It's something I've kept to myself for many years now. It's time I helped you girls out. You'd know soon enough if anything happened to me. I've been putting my house in order for a while now, and it's about time I explained everything.'

Rose and Lily looked puzzled at Mildred's words, but didn't argue with her as she raised her hand to indicate it wasn't open for discussion.

'Do you mind if I just pop down to the teashop? I told them I'd only be gone a couple of hours, and it's about that now,' Rose asked. It felt much longer, what with everything that had happened, but she wanted to check all was well before she left the shop again. She had capable staff, and knew it would be in good hands for a while.

'Be off with you now, and we'll be waiting when you get back,' Mildred said as she carried a tea tray into the room.

★ ★ ★

'Miss Neville,' one of the Nippies called as Rose entered the teashop. 'Miss Neville, there's a message on your desk to contact head office as soon as possible.'

'Thank you Janet; have there been any problems while I've been out?' she asked as she took off her coat and hurried to her office, nodding hello to a few of the people enjoying afternoon tea. It wasn't usual for head office to make a telephone call to the tearooms, especially when Mr Grant had been there earlier that day. He would normally have been the person to impart information from head office.

Rose waited patiently as the person on the other end of the telephone line went to find a Mrs Burgess who wished to speak with her. She flicked through the few letters that had arrived in the afternoon post. There was nothing that couldn't wait to be dealt with in the morning.

'Ah, Miss Neville, thank you for your patience,' a pleasant and efficient older voice said down the phone line. 'I thought I would let you know about something important that has been decided here at head office.'

'That's very kind of you,' Rose said, her interest at once piqued by the idea of something out of the ordinary happening.

'You've probably seen the newspaper headlines over the past few days about our lads over the Channel?'

Rose had to agree she'd seen the news reports, although she wasn't one for reading the newspapers; anything important typically reached her by way of her customers or the Nippies. She'd caught part of the Pathé News when she'd been to the pictures with Lily the other night and been shocked to see the enemy had invaded Holland and Belgium, and were bombing all the airports. It made her think of Anya and how she had escaped to England — and then, of course, Ben . . .

'Are you there?' Mrs Burgess asked with an edge of impatience.

Rose came back to the present with a start. 'I'm sorry, I couldn't hear you for a minute,' she apologized. 'You asked if I'd seen the newspapers? Yes, it's awful, isn't it?' she said, trying to show she was aware of what was going on even though she hadn't seen today's paper.

'Terrible, but at least we can now help the war effort, and that is why I wanted to speak with you rather than send a letter. Speed is of the essence if we are to be ready to help our brave lads.'

Rose, trying hard to keep up, was confused by what was being said. How could they help the war effort down here in Margate — apart from helping to raise money for the troops' parcel fund that the girls all supported at the teashop?

'Our vans should be with you some time tomorrow. It will mean your teashop as well as the Ramsgate branch being short-staffed, but what else can we do at a time like this? I just wanted to warn you before I clock off and head home for the night. I'll be back in touch once I have more information. Goodbye . . . '

Rose bid the woman goodbye, not understanding a word of what she was talking about. 'Oh well, I'll find out tomorrow,' she said aloud. 'Now to see what Mildred is up to.' After speaking to the senior Nippies, she checked her handbag and hurried off to meet her friends, who she found standing by Mildred's vehicle waiting for her to arrive.

Rose climbed in beside Lily and they headed eastwards along the coastline. 'Are you sure we aren't going to Ramsgate?' she asked, a worried expression crossing her face.

'I said we weren't, and you are going to have to trust me,' Mildred replied as she changed gears, causing the ageing vehicle to complain and shudder.

The two girls sat quietly as Mildred continued the journey, heading through Cliftonville and inland before joining the North Foreland Road. Lily gazed out of the window with unseeing eyes, her head resting on the cool glass, thinking about the future and how she would cope with a child and no means of support — not to mention the stigma of being unmarried. Meanwhile, Rose went over the telephone conversation she'd just had, wondering what Mrs Burgess had been talking about. They both came to with a start when Mildred pulled up beside a small flint-fronted house and told them to jump out.

'Why are we in Broadstairs?' Rose asked. 'Do you have friends living here?'

'It is my house,' Mildred laughed, seeing the looks on their faces but not explaining. 'Welcome to Captain's Cottage.'

'Have you moved out of Sea View?' Rose asked, wondering if there had been another falling out with her mum.

'It's beautiful,' Lily said, looking over the low brick wall at the garden bursting with colour, and then to the mullioned windows. 'I can see why you moved here. This is the kind of home I've dreamt about. I could live my days out in a place like this.'

'I never thought you were one for dreaming about lovely houses and living happily ever after,' Rose said, giving her friend a sad look. 'Not many people get to live their dreams.'

'Well, this here house has been a nightmare for me since I was a young girl,' Mildred said, digging into the pocket of her duffle coat and

279

pulling out a large rusty key. 'And I don't live here,' she corrected Lily. 'Come along indoors and I'll tell you about it. If we stand here much longer, the nosy neighbours will be out asking us what we are up to.'

Rose and Lily followed the older woman up a winding path and waited as she struggled with the stiff lock. 'This is the first time the house has been empty in ten years. It was left to me by my father and I had no wish ever to live here,' she said, giving the door a hefty shove before beckoning them in. 'I have no idea what we will find . . . '

'Oh, it's wonderful,' Lily exclaimed as she stepped through the storm porch straight into a small living room and turned around, taking in the open fireplace and blackened beams. 'With a little tender care this could be a very comfortable home. May I . . . ?' she asked, looking towards two closed doors.

'Be my guest,' Mildred said as she pulled the front door closed with a bang. 'These hinges need a drop of oil.'

Lily pulled back the first door to find a steep oak staircase. She turned to the next door, which took her down two stone steps to a room with a flagstone floor and a small bay window that overlooked a garden. She threw herself down onto the wooden window seat and gazed out. 'I could be happy in a house like this. You are so lucky, Mildred,' she sighed.

'Why would I be lucky? I hate the place and wish it had never been left to me. Why do you think I've lived at Sea View all these years with people I consider to be my friends? The lucky person is you, Lily, as I hope you will both be my new tenants and bring the baby up here?'

The two girls looked at Mildred in surprise.

'This war has had me thinking about my future, so I've been to see my solicitor and put my affairs in order. Oh, no, there's nothing wrong with me. I'm as fit and healthy as I've always been — but what with being out on the boat so much and not knowing what that monster Adolf Hitler has in store for us, I've had to think carefully about my life. I don't have any relatives who will inherit my belongings, and being so fond of the three of you, it made sense for me to consider you as the beneficiaries of my will. And to make sure you can enjoy part of it while I'm still around to watch.'

'The three of us?' Rose asked.

'The two of you, and Katie.'

The girls rushed to hug the older woman, who opened her arms and accepted their grateful thanks. 'I wish the house had been available earlier, so Katie could have made use of it as soon as she was married — but who was to know my tenant would give back her lease? She's headed north to join her son and daughter, as they feared for her down here on the coast,' Mildred explained. 'Let's go upstairs and see the bedrooms.'

The girls didn't need a second bidding and rushed up to the floor above, followed by Mildred, who was beaming from cheek to cheek. 'Who knew this house could bring joy again?' she muttered to herself.

'Look, there are three bedrooms,' Rose said, pushing open the doors — not wanting to point out that one was no more than a cupboard, as it would make her sound ungrateful.

'Don't be daft — that one's no use to man nor beast,' Mildred said as she caught them up. 'The previous tenant had some notion of me putting a bath in there. I wasn't going to do it for her, but for you girls it's a different matter completely.'

'An indoor bathroom!' Lily sighed. She had lived most of her life in a two-up, two-down where they'd had to drag a tin bath indoors and boil a kettle for hot water. It had only been for the few months she'd lived at Sea View, and then with Rose, that she'd enjoyed such luxury.

'I know a man who can get it done for me. There's a loo downstairs past the scullery and the outhouse,' Mildred said.

'You've got an outhouse indoors?'

Mildred laughed. 'The tenant before last bricked up the outside doors, and the attached outhouse and loo became inside rooms. Clever, eh? You'll have to take a look to appreciate it,' she said, seeing the girls' confused faces. 'Now I have one more surprise for you,' she grinned.

'It wouldn't be a millionaire looking for a Nippy wife, would it?' Lily laughed.

'If it was I'd be fighting you for him,' Rose said, as they watched Mildred open what they'd thought was a cupboard door. It was painted black, unlike the others, which were plain oak. Mildred disappeared inside. 'Follow me,' her muffled voice called back.

The girls went up a wooden spiral staircase

and found themselves in a light and airy attic room with windows on three sides.

'The view is wonderful,' Rose exclaimed. 'I can see out to sea and over much of Broadstairs as well. It's like our own private lookout tower. What can you see?' she asked, joining Lily.

'It's the garden. Look at the flower beds — and is that a vegetable plot?' she asked Mildred, who nodded. 'The baby will be able to lie out there in the pram and enjoy the lovely weather,' she sighed.

Rose and Mildred couldn't speak. What a difference a few hours had made to Lily's state of mind. Her life suddenly had a bright future.

'There's an Anderson shelter down the end of the garden. I know as I got the bill for it,' Mildred said as Lily went to look out at the sea, which was sparkling in the bright May sunshine.

'Mildred, are there usually that many fishing boats on this stretch of water?'

The two women joined her and watched as a row of small boats passed in convoy accompanied by navy vessels, all heading in the general direction of Ramsgate.

'I need to be somewhere else,' Mildred said as she threw the door key to Rose. 'I'd been warned that me and my boat would be needed in the next couple of days. You can either stay here and catch the bus back to Margate, or perhaps I can drop you off at Katie's place so you can tell her about the cottage — that's if you want it?'

Lily shrieked with laughter as she followed Mildred down the staircase. 'Want it? Don't talk daft. I've never wanted anything so much in all

283

my life. I'll never stop thanking you until the day I die.'

Rose held back, watching as the endless stream of boats passed by. She recognized a few of the fishing vessels that frequented the harbour at Ramsgate. She'd known the boat owners since she was a child — and wasn't that the pleasure steamer *Kentish Queen*? Ted Sayers and his daughter Gracie often stopped at Margate and Ramsgate, bringing trippers down from further up the Thames in north Kent. Something was going on here. She shivered as she watched until Lily called her to hurry up or she'd be left behind.

13

'Something is not right,' Anya said as she threw her cardigan across the back of the kitchen chair and started to help put plates and cutlery on the kitchen table.

'Have you not had a good day at work, dear?' Miss Tibbs asked from where she sat in an old armchair in the corner of the room, knitting a balaclava helmet.

'My work, it is good. I have never sold as much packets of tea in one day before. Some people they argue they want more, but I have to be strict and follow the law. No ration card, no tea!' she said, waving a handful of forks into the air. 'We all like our cuppa and I have to be fair. I will not be bribed.'

Miss Tibbs' eyes lit up. 'Someone tried to bribe you?'

'Yes, it was that horrid butcher man. He offered me sausages. I told him no thank you and his sausages are full of sawdust,' she grimaced. 'I had never heard such language. If Miss Rose had been in the teashop she would have sent him packing. In her absence I did the packing off of the butcher man,' she said.

'Well done, Anya. Joe Lyons has a loyal employee in you,' Miss Tibbs said, continuing to knit.

Flora carried a bowl of steaming cabbage and carrots to the table. 'You say Rose wasn't there?'

she asked, a worried expression crossing her face. 'Is she all right?'

'She is fine,' Anya said. She wasn't about to say she had a feeling something wasn't right, as both Lily and Rose had disappeared for most of the afternoon and that wasn't a common occurrence. She'd noticed a change in Lily as well, but did not say so. 'They had an afternoon off — those two work hard,' she added, knowing Flora would be proud even though she wouldn't say so. She exchanged a look with Miss Tibbs. The two women had spent hours in Miss Tibbs' room discussing how to get Rose and her mother back under the same roof to iron out their differences. So far they'd not had one good idea.

Flora, who was happy with Anya's reply, went back to the cooker and stirred a large saucepan. 'Anya dear, would you call everyone down for dinner please? Joyce and Pearl are out until late this evening, so it's just the two RAF men and the three of us. Then you can tell us what you think is not right,' she added to the Polish woman's back.

Anya returned as Flora started to dish stew onto dinner plates. 'They are on their way,' she said, taking her place at the table. 'That smells very good but only a little for me. They feed us well at the Lyons teashop.'

'It's only rabbit with lots of vegetables, but it's filling,' Flora said, wishing she could put more food on the table for her guests.

'You feed us very well,' Anya said, noticing Flora's downcast face. 'You should not worry so much.'

'There seems so much to worry about these days,' Flora replied, thinking of her daughter. Rose might be only a few miles away in Margate, but it might as well be the other side of the world, for the pair hadn't met since the day Rose had found out about her real father. Flora wished she'd never kept her secret from Rose, as now it could be too late to heal the rift. 'Come on in,' Flora said, jerking herself out of her reverie as she spotted the two men standing awkwardly at the door.

'Thank you, ma'am,' said the taller of the two as he stepped forward to hold a chair for Miss Tibbs. Then they both sat down, taking their plates of food from Flora.

'We have not met, as I have been at my work,' Anya said formally.

Flora made the necessary introductions and explained about the three absent residents. The men were impressed that a lady would be in ownership of a fishing boat.

'Mildred is a remarkable woman. She does many jobs that we would usually expect men to undertake. I'm sure you will get on with her when you meet. I don't know of anyone who hasn't.'

'Mildred told me she would be late,' Miss Tibbs said as she absent-mindedly picked pieces of cabbage from the front of her cardigan. 'She is going out in her boat.'

Flora nodded her head. She was used to Miss Tibbs' lapses of memory; sometimes she forgot a message completely, or shared it a day too late. 'I'll put a plate on top of her food and keep it warm in the oven. We may have fish tomorrow, if she is going out to sea.'

'France,' Miss Tibbs announced. 'She said she was going to France. It may be best not to keep her food in the oven, as it will dry out. She told me when she popped in for her spare water-proofs.'

'You've lost me,' Flora said, looking bemused. 'You say Mildred is going to France?'

'It is possible,' Anya said, putting down her knife and fork. 'I told you something is not right. There are too many boats in the harbour for fishing. Surely they don't all fish? There are also many sailors, and I found it hard to walk from the bus stop as there were people everywhere. Something is happening, I fear.'

'I'll walk down to the harbour after dinner and see what's happening. Eat up, everyone — it looks as though there will be leftovers, as Mildred won't be home. Now tell me, lads, do you fly planes? If you do, why aren't you living on the base at Manston?'

The two men looked at each other. 'No, we are what you'd call the backroom boys,' explained one, who had introduced himself as Ted. 'I'm in the stores and Nobby here is good with numbers and such like, so he's at a desk most of the time. With so many people needed, some of us volunteered to be billeted away from the airfield to make room for the pilots and ground crew.'

'I reckon we fell on our feet coming here,' Nobby butted in as Flora handed out dishes of steamed pudding and custard. 'We'll be sure to make extra contributions to the household. It's only fair.'

'There's no need. I wouldn't want anyone to get into trouble on my behalf. It's just nice to have two men under our roof.'

'Rather than a spy,' Miss Tibbs muttered under her breath.

Flora was surprised that Anya hadn't asked if there were any Polish pilots at the airfield. Perhaps she needed a little help? 'Do you have pilots of other nationalities at Manston?' she asked, trying to sound nonchalant.

'I'm not sure we should be talking about what happens at the airfield,' Nobby said. 'You might all be spies.' He laughed at his own joke.

'I am Polish, not German,' Anya said, giving him a stern look.

'I'm sorry; I wasn't meaning anything by it. I do know Polish people,' he added, giving Anya a wary look.

'You do?' Flora said. 'Do you know any Polish pilots?' she asked, pouring more custard into his bowl.

'I'm not sure,' Nobby said. 'Where I work, I don't get to see much of the pilots. They can be a little aloof as far as I'm concerned.'

'I've met a couple of them when I hand out spare uniforms,' Ted said, covering his bowl with one hand to refuse more food from Flora. 'Decent enough chaps. They've had a rough time, by all accounts.'

'Do you happen to know one called Henio Polinski?' Flora asked hopefully.

Ted frowned for a moment as he thought. 'The name doesn't come to mind, but I can ask about. Who wants to know?'

Anya rose to her feet and hurried over to the sink. She started to wash the plates, banging about so that she couldn't hear the conversation. She was still unsure whether Henio would wish to know his wife was in England.

'Thank you,' Flora said to the two men. 'It's for a friend.'

With her residents insisting on clearing away after their meal, Flora took her jacket and gas mask and headed out the door and down Madeira Walk towards the seafront. Anya was right. The place was buzzing with officious-looking sailors giving instructions to boat owners, while others passed out blankets and provisions. She spotted a friend from the WVS, and hurried over the road to find out what was going on.

'My dear, it has been on the radio. Any civilian with a boat over a certain size has orders to report to points along the coast. It seems our men are trapped on the beaches over there and need rescuing,' the woman said excitedly as she nodded somewhere out to sea in the direction of France. 'By this time tomorrow there could be hundreds of soldiers coming ashore into our little town. Isn't it thrilling? However, I do wish they'd let us get a little closer to the harbour wall so we can watch. It doesn't seem right, keeping us residents behind these barriers.'

Flora felt it was anything but thrilling. If what they were saying was true, then husbands, sons and fathers were in mortal danger not twenty miles away from where she stood. She gave a silent prayer as she watched the owners of so many small boats preparing to head across the

Channel to bring loved ones safely back home.

'Hello, Mrs Neville,' a quiet voice said close to Flora's side, pulling her from her prayers. 'I think we are watching something very important happening here.'

Flora turned to see Katie standing beside her, white-faced. She slipped her arm around the girl's shoulders. 'You could be right,' she replied, giving her a small hug.

'My Jack must be out there somewhere. Who knows — he could be trying to rescue our boys, just as these brave people are doing,' Katie said, not taking her eyes off the sea.

Flora had taken great strength from the words of Mr Churchill, the new prime minister, when he'd said: *Having received His Majesty's commission, I have formed an Administration of men and women of every Party and of almost every point of view. We have differed and quarrelled in the past; but now one bond unites us all — to wage war until victory is won, and never to surrender ourselves to servitude and shame, whatever the cost and the agony may be . . .*

'Everyone, including God, is on our side, Katie,' she said. 'Those boys will get home safely, if what we are watching is anything to go by.'

'It really makes you wonder what must be going on over there for all these people to rally with their tiny boats and go out to rescue our men, doesn't it?' Katie said.

Flora could feel the young woman trembling beneath her thin coat. 'Why don't you come back to my house tonight? I doubt many of us will get much sleep, but I can make you up a bed. And then we can come down early tomorrow to wave the boats off. I'm thinking there'll be ways for us to help before too long.'

'I'd like that, thank you,' Katie said as Flora tucked an arm through hers and they headed away from the harbour. 'I saw Rose and Lily earlier,' she added, knowing she was on dodgy ground mentioning her friend. 'They had some exciting news for me.' She filled Flora in on the generosity of their friend, Mildred.

Flora turned to look back at the many boats congregating in the harbour and beyond. Somewhere out there was Mildred, getting ready to set sail on a dangerous mission. If the woman could do so much for her daughter and friends then she, Flora Neville, needed to do the same and stop this awkward silence between herself and Rose. What had happened in her past needed to be put to bed once and for all, and only she could set the wheels in motion. All she needed to do was see Rose and talk with her face to face — which was a problem, as her daughter was still avoiding her.

⋆   ⋆   ⋆

Rose wiped her brow with a satisfied smile. She had asked for volunteers from amongst her staff to help hand out refreshments to the servicemen, and the plan had been a resounding success. Mrs Burgess at Cadby Hall had helped arrange for extra food to be sent down for the Nippies to give out to the tired and hungry men as they came ashore after their arduous journey across the Channel, escaping the dangerous beaches of Dunkirk. Everything was set for the early morning when they would head up to the station, where coaches and buses were collecting men from the assortment of boats in the harbour and taking them to extra trains, laid on specially to ferry troops away from the town. From her vantage point at the window of the teashop, Rose could see many boats filled to overflowing with soldiers waiting to disembark. At times she was surprised the small vessels didn't tip over, as it seemed they were top-heavy with men clinging to every possible part of the boat.

The delivery vans sent from head office would be available for the food to be moved to wherever it was required. Checking her wristwatch, Rose could see it was about time for them to set off. She was confident that Lily would do a good job overseeing the teashop during the day; despite her friend's objections, Rose was adamant that a long day on her feet handing out refreshments would be too much for the expectant mother. Anya too would be at the teashop, and would work all day helping out the remaining Nippies if required. Rose felt confident she'd left the shop in good hands. Straightening her Nippy cap and checking her black dress and crisp white apron were pristine, she was ready to go. Today she was not a manageress, but one of the Nippies standing side by side to serve the troops. The Margate workers would be doing the same job as Nippies from the Ramsgate teashop, and Rose was looking forward to working alongside Katie, who had been sent along to help make up the numbers. It seemed an age since the friends had last worked together. So much had happened since then.

Sending several of the Nippies on ahead on their bicycles, once she had checked they had their gas masks, she climbed into the front seat of one of the vans and directed the driver towards the railway station. She was informed that there would be extra food dropped off during the day, and if they ran short before the vans returned she could use the telephone at the station to ask for more to be sent over from either of the two teashops. Rose nodded, her mind already on the task that lay ahead.

Driving past the small jetty, Rose could see that weary men were being helped ashore from fishing boats. Some were walking towards the transport that would take them up to the station, while the injured were being carried on stretchers to a row of waiting ambulances. Already a number of boats were making their way back to the beaches of Dunkirk.

From the road leading to the station, where the Lyons staff had set up trestle tables, they could still see along the short coastline to where the men were being brought ashore. 'It seems to be never-ending,' she said to a WVS volunteer, who was handing out tea from an urn.

'It's been like this for most of the night, my love. I'm glad you're here, as we've nigh on run out of everything. I'm off to put my head down for a couple of hours, then I'll be back with my team.'

Rose could see how tired the woman was. 'We'll do our best to give refreshments to as many people as possible,' she assured her.

With a reminder not to forget the boat owners, who'd been told to come and get fed, the woman shut down the WVS van and disappeared into the crowd along with her helpers.

'Right,' Rose said to her girls. 'Let's get cracking, shall we? I suggest that we pile a selection of the pork pies and sausage rolls on each tray and have one Nippy carry them around, while a second follows with mugs of tea. Further up the line a couple of you can have trays of sliced cakes that can be held in one hand. Divide yourselves into teams of three, and let's see how it works out. I will need a few of you here to replenish trays and keep the urn going. These trestle tables are ours, so this will be our base while we do our bit for our troops and our country,' Rose said, proudly hoping she had said the right words to boost morale in her team.

'Who will hand out napkins and plates?' a young Nippy asked as her co-workers tittered.

'On this occasion we won't be worrying about such things, but I do want you to keep smiling and have a pleasant word for everyone. You may see some unpleasant sights,' she added, as an ambulance passed by and groans of pain could be heard, 'but you will remember at all times that you work for Joe Lyons, and we are here to make a difference. If you have a problem with that, please come and speak to me. Now, let's do what we do best. Smile and serve,' she said, ushering the Nippies to where there were already trays of food to hand out.

'Where do you want me, boss?' Katie said when she arrived some time later with a couple of her fellow workers.

'Oh, I'm so pleased to see you,' Rose said, giving her a quick hug and greeting the other women. 'Would you start replenishing these trays — and some of you help hand out the food and the mugs of tea. I need to let some of my girls take a short break.'

Katie nodded her head. 'Yes, I can do that, and please tell them to help themselves to changes of aprons if they're mucky. We've had our lecture about representing the company at all times . . . '

Rose laughed. 'I have to confess to giving my staff the same talking-to. Here, come alongside me and we can catch up with news while we slice these Swiss rolls. I'll have one of my girls telephone for more supplies when they go for their break.'

'What's it been like down here?' Katie asked as she wielded a large carving knife to tackle the sponge rolls.

'To be honest, it's hell. I've never seen so many injured or weary men in my life. God only knows what it's like on the other side of the Channel. The owners of the boats have been at it non-stop. I've been keeping an eye out for Mildred, but there's not been a sign of her so far. I do hope she's all right.'

'Fancy a woman going into war like that!' Katie said. 'From what someone said at our teashop, there are lines of soldiers wading out to get onto the smaller boats while enemy planes are coming in and firing at them. It's made me wonder if my Jack's over there.' She looked worried.

The two girls looked up as planes flew overhead, heading out to sea.

'It's comforting to know they're going over there,' Katie said as her chin started to wobble. 'They could be saving Jack's ship . . . '

Rose put down the cake she was about to slice and took Katie's hand in her own. 'Now, there's no need for all these tears. If your Jack is out there he's on a bloody great big ship, not bobbing about like a cork in a bathtub like these poor chaps. Come on, chin up!'

Katie swallowed hard and did her best to smile. 'Gosh, I don't know what came over me. I'm just feeling a little sorry for myself. I'll be fine in a minute. Let's talk about something else, shall we?' She picked up her knife and tackled the cake in front of her. 'Wasn't it truly wonderful of Mildred to give us her house? Why, I didn't even know she had one. What a dark horse she is. When do you think we can move in?'

'I can't think of any reason why you and Lily cannot move in as soon as we've sorted out some furniture,' Rose said, relieved that Katie's sadness had passed for now. 'I'm going to stay in my flat, as I need to be close to work. It will be preferable to cycling to work every day. You know what I'm like on a bike. Mind you, I'll be round every chance I've got to enjoy that lovely garden,' she added, thinking it would give more room for Katie and Jack as well as Lily and the baby when it came along. 'You didn't seem too surprised about Lily being pregnant,' she said as she handed a full tray of cakes over to a Nippy and started to slice up pork pies. 'We need more tea over there,' she called out to two of the women manning the tea urn.

'To be honest, I expected as much when she went dashing off to stay with you,' Katie said. 'I'm disappointed in her, as I thought she had more sense than to be so generous with her virtue.'

Rose smiled at Katie's old-fashioned words. 'I do think there is more to this than meets the eye. Can we just be kind to her for now, do you think? At the end of the day, there's a child on the horizon who we can spoil, and who will call us aunty. We also have Mildred's lovely house to enjoy. Whatever could go wrong?'

'I think of Lily as a sister, so I'll forgive her, whatever happened to put her in this situation. Do you have any idea who the father might be? You never know — he may offer to marry her . . . ?'

Rose just shook her head and didn't speak as Nippies arrived to replenish their trays. 'Perhaps in time we will know a little more, but it doesn't change what has happened, so we will have to live with things and be as supportive as we possibly can.'

'Miss Neville, there's a soldier asking after you,' one of the Nippies said, pushing through to the front of the queue, where staff were waiting for more food. 'He's over there by that bus that's just pulled up.' She pointed.

Rose felt her heart skip a beat. Could it be Ben? She'd not heard a word from him since that magical night in London. It seemed such a long time ago now. When he hadn't written, she'd put him to the back of her mind and decided that perhaps the romance she longed for wasn't to be. She left Katie in charge, and pushed her way through the crowd to where the lorry was parked as weary soldiers climbed aboard. Her heart plummeted as she searched the many faces looking for that one special person.

'Miss Neville? We thought you might be about. I hope you didn't mind me asking that other Nippy if you was here?'

Rose spun round on her heels as she recognized the familiar accent. 'Why, it's . . . '

'Corporal Jenkins, Miss. We shared that journey to London a while back when you helped us get out of the snow. I didn't expect to see you here — and still a Nippy? I thought as how you was off to London to be something important for Joe Lyons?'

'It's good to see you, Corporal Jenkins. It's good to see all of you,' she added, spotting other familiar faces. 'I'm a manageress now at the Margate teashop. I wore the uniform today as I'm down here helping out with my staff,' she explained, straightening her cap where it had come slightly adrift. 'Were you rescued?'

'Too right we were, Miss, and by a lady as well. You could have knocked me down with a feather when we was pulled out of the water and found the skipper of the boat was a lady. She treated us like royalty all the way home.'

Rose beamed. It could only have been Mildred. How many female skippers of fishing boats could there be? 'I believe that was my friend Mildred.'

'That's the name. She nigh on saved our lives. We'd been in the water that long I was turning into a prune. If we'd been in there much longer I reckon the Captain would have been a goner.'

Rose gasped. 'Ben . . . Captain Hargreaves . . . is he here?'

'We've just seen him off in an ambulance. He took one when a Stuka was strafing the beach, trying to pick us off. He'd pushed a few of us out of the way and copped it himself. He's a brave bloke — deserves a medal for what he did, and no mistake.'

The men around him mumbled their agreement.

'But where are they taking him?' Rose asked urgently.

'We was told he's heading for Dreamland at Margate. We thought they were joking, what with it being a funfair and all, but it seems parts are being used as a hospital with there being so many of us landing here. They're going to billet some of us there in the ballroom by all accounts, until they know what to do with us. That'll be a right old laugh,' he grinned.

Rose had heard from her customers that much of the area at Dreamland, a well-known fairground and amusement park, had been turned into facilities for the servicemen. She longed to see Ben but had responsibilities to see to first. 'Please, let me get you all some food and

300

a mug of tea before you head off. It's the least I can do after your arduous journey.' She led them towards where the Nippies were preparing the food and handed them over to one of her staff, saying, 'Give them plenty to eat, ladies. These men are heroes.'

'I've got news for you,' another familiar voice said.

'So it was you, Mildred, who rescued these men! Here, have a mug of tea and some food,' Rose said, grabbing the older woman by the arm and taking her to a nearby wooden bench. They both sat down, and Mildred knocked back the tea in one long gulp.

'I needed that,' Mildred gasped as she wiped her mouth on the sleeves of her overalls. 'I made some tea on board, but it wasn't as good as this. I'll have a bit of a rest and then I'll be back off again. You wouldn't believe how many of our lads are over there at the mercy of those bastards.'

Rose ignored Mildred swearing. No doubt she'd have done the same in her situation. 'Is it as bad as they are saying?'

'Depends what you've heard. If it's about our men in queues chest-high in the sea trying to reach the boats as the Germans shoot them out of the water, then yes, it's as bad as that. It takes a lot for me to cry, as you well know, but I do shed some tears when I see what this war has done to our men. I don't want to frighten you, love, but I think we're losing this war right now. It's going to take a lot more than that Winston Churchill spouting words for us to beat Adolf. However, I'll be back over there raising my fist at him and doing my best to get our lads back home.'

'I know you will, Mildred. Can you tell me if you expected this to happen? Is that why you made sure the three of us knew about the house?'

Mildred nodded. 'The last few days, we've been talking about the war getting closer to our shores — and if we had the chance, then we'd go and bring the lads home. I didn't expect all of this,' she said, looking at the hubbub in the usually much quieter town. 'It's busier than the height of the holiday season. We thought it would be a few of our fishing boats popping over there at the dead of night, not a bloody armada. That's one in the eye for Hitler.'

'I wish I could come with you and help,' Rose said wistfully.

'Now that would frighten Hitler. Imagine a Nippy at the helm of the boat speeding across the Channel? No, love, you stay here and do your bit with the food and drink. It's more than needed after the time these chaps have had. Did you know I had that Captain you were sweet on come back on my boat? He's been injured, but he'll live. He remembered me from when he came up to Sea View. He spoke fondly of you before he passed out. Seems he was confused as to why you'd never answered his letters.'

'I've never seen any letters,' Rose said, feeling bewildered and more than a little hurt. 'I've sent so many, even though he never replied. I gave my new address — but surely, even if they'd been sent to Sea View, someone would have passed them on?'

Mildred shrugged her shoulders. 'There haven't been any letters for you; and don't even start to imagine your mother would have hidden them. She liked Ben, and you know she loves you.'

Rose shook her head, trying to think straight. 'I'll have to ask him where he sent them . . .'

'That's between you and him. I'm only telling you what he said. Right — I'm off. See you when I see you,' Mildred grinned, slapping Rose on the back and heading off into the crowd.

⋆ ⋆ ⋆

Rose changed back into the suit she usually wore as manageress of the Margate teashop. She couldn't stop thinking that Ben was less than a mile away from where she was right now, and that he could be in pain and badly injured. There was no time just now to worry about what had happened to stop her receiving his letters. Lily had done well running the teashop, and by all accounts it had been a busy day. News was that troops were still being brought into Margate jetty as well as Ramsgate, so if head office could send more food she'd be out again tomorrow doing her bit. She'd make a telephone call first thing in the morning and let them know what it was like down here, and how their contributions were helping. For now, she only wanted to fall into her bed and sleep — but there was something she needed to do first.

Heading out into the night, she walked along the seafront in the direction of Dreamland. She could see weary soldiers disembarking from the

303

small boats, and wondered how long it would be before every man was home and safe. Following the beach away from the harbour, she headed towards the place where all holiday-makers spent some of their time while in the seaside resort. Whether they were enjoying the funfair, eating in one of the restaurants or dancing the night away in the ballroom, there was always something going on. For now the place had been taken over by the army, and she wondered whether it would be for the duration of the war, as she too enjoyed dancing and the entertainment at Dreamland. The facade of the main building looked sad and unappealing without the vivid display of lights that brightened it up in peacetime.

Approaching the main entrance, she was stopped by two soldiers at a wooden barrier that had been placed across the road. 'Sorry, Miss, you can't come in here. It's off limits to the public unless you have written authority. Do you have authority?'

Rose hadn't thought for one moment that she'd be denied entry. 'I don't. I just wanted to see someone who was brought here this afternoon. He's been injured and I just want to know how he is,' she pleaded. 'His name is Captain Benjamin Hargreaves.'

'I'm sorry, Miss. It's more than my job's worth to let a civilian in here. Why, you might be a spy or something.'

Rose laughed out loud. 'If I was a spy I'd not have asked to be let in by the main entrance, would I?'

'You never know, Miss, these spies can be crafty.'

'You could be right. By day I masquerade as the manageress of the Lyons Teashop up the road. Why, all my Nippies are undercover agents, don't you know?' she snapped back before starting to turn away. She was more than disappointed not to be able to see Ben after all this time! A few minutes wouldn't have hurt, would it?

'Hang on a minute, Miss,' one of the gatekeepers called as he flashed his torch into her face.

'Yes, that's her,' the other one muttered.

'You're lucky, Miss; my mate here was in your teashop last week and recognizes you.' He handed her a slip of paper. 'If you go down this path and turn left, you'll find someone to point you in the right direction,' he said with a nod.

Rose thanked them profusely, promising toasted teacakes for both next time they were in her teashop, and headed off in the direction they'd pointed out. After a couple of wrong turnings, she found herself at the door of what seemed to be a makeshift ward.

A nurse in a fancy white starched headdress and long white apron stepped into her path. 'May I help you?' she asked.

Rose handed the slip of paper she'd been given and said, 'I'm here to visit Captain Benjamin Hargreaves. He was brought in injured this afternoon.'

She waited patiently as the nurse checked a list she'd taken from a nearby table. 'Captain Hargreaves does have visitors with him at the moment. I would think they will be leaving soon, if you wish to wait? He's due to be transferred to the Royal Sea Bathing Hospital early tomorrow for an operation.'

Rose agreed and stood to one side as a porter pushed a wheelchair into the ward. No doubt it would be some of Ben's men visiting him. They all seemed on good terms with their officer, and like her, they would have wanted to know how he was faring.

A bubble of excitement crept into her stomach at the thought that soon she would be holding his hand, and might even be able to sneak a quick kiss. Until this moment she hadn't realized how much she had missed him and wanted him back in her life.

The door opened again as the porter left the ward, and she leant forward, trying to look through the closing gap. What she saw froze her to the spot. She could see Ben sitting up in bed, and beside him, leaning over and kissing his cheek, was a young, smartly dressed woman — and with her were two children. As the door closed, she heard one of the children call out, 'Goodnight, Daddy.'

Turning on her heel, Rose fled from the ward, not wanting to see the woman or the children — it was just too painful. What a fool she'd been, to think Ben was a single man without any family ties! Ben had used her. She could only count her blessings when she thought of how easily she might have ended up in the same predicament as Lily, after her one night of passion with the man she'd believed she truly loved.

14

'They are leaving us here to die,' Miss Tibbs wailed into her damp handkerchief. 'We will be murdered in our beds,' she added, looking up to see who was taking notice.

'Get over it, old woman,' Anya snapped. 'You think this is all personal against you? Then you are mad as box of frogs. The army goes away for a reason.'

Flora rubbed her fingers on her temples and sighed. The headache that had been threatening all day had arrived with a vengeance. She'd hoped that once they'd cleared up after their evening meal and gone to the sitting room to relax and listen to the wireless, she would start to feel a little brighter. 'Please, can you stop your bickering for a while? No good can come of it. The army is being moved out of Thanet because of the threat of invasion. No doubt plans will be made for civilians as well — so then you'll have something else to complain about,' she snapped.

Miss Tibbs was startled by Flora's words. 'Well, I've never known you be so sharp with me before. Perhaps I should pack my bags and leave. I'll not stay where I'm not wanted,' she said, slowly getting to her feet while dabbing her eyes as a fresh flood of tears threatened.

'Oh please sit down, Miss Tibbs. I'm sorry if

we appear sharp, but there's a lot to consider right now.'

'Life will go on,' Mildred said philosophically. 'As long as we can eat and don't get bombed out of our beds, then we will be all right.'

'What — even if the Nazis are marching along the seafront?' Miss Tibbs declared, looking horrified. 'Surely we should move out now and find somewhere to live away from the harbour. If the army's going inland, then so should we.'

'Where do you think we go to, old woman?' Anya said, turning on Miss Tibbs. 'I have been in this position before. I see my home and family burn to the ground. Do you see me having hystericals? Walk in my boots and then shed your tears.'

Flora frowned. Whatever was Anya saying?

'She means walk a mile in her shoes,' Mildred mouthed to Flora.

'I do believe we should listen to Anya, as she can tell us what to expect. Why don't we make a plan so we are prepared for whatever happens?'

Anya looked at the women who had become like family since she came to England. 'A plan is good. It will keep our minds from worrying, if nothing else. What do you want us to do, Flora?' she asked, giving her a slight smile.

'I suggest we share what we know is happening — and I don't mean tittle-tattle,' Mildred interrupted.

'What is the teetle-tattle?' Anya asked.

'Mildred means idle gossip. Things that we know are untrue,' Flora explained.

'I see.' Anya nodded her head slowly as she

digested what Flora and Mildred had said. 'So if I am told something while I am being a Sally at the teashop, it could be teetle-tattle?'

'It could, but then, it might also be true,' Miss Tibbs retaliated. 'How are we to know?'

'Then I suggest we share all our news each evening over dinner. That way we can decide what is true and what is gossip.'

'You've forgotten something,' Miss Tibbs said, warming up to the idea. 'What if we don't have any dinner to eat?'

'Now you are being daft and worrying over nothing,' Flora all but exploded. 'While the men of this country lay down their lives to keep us free, you are worrying about where your next meal is coming from . . . Has the butcher's shop closed? Has Mrs Peabody given up running her grocer's shop just because her husband has joined up? Times may be getting tougher now we have rationing, but we can do our bit by coping and keeping a smile on our faces . . . can't we?' she added, seeing the astounded faces in front of her.

Anya leapt from her seat and gave Flora a hug. 'You sound like the Churchill man — but promise me you never smoke cigar. They stink.'

Mildred snorted with laughter. 'Imagine if Flora was the Prime Minister. She'd be banging everyone's heads together and telling them they were bad boys for fighting.'

Even Miss Tibbs smiled as the other ladies of Sea View laughed. 'I'm still afraid, all the same,' she said in a quiet voice.

'There is no need. I promise to look after you,'

Mildred said. 'Now, I have a visitor coming to see us all, and what she has to say may be a little disappointing for some of you. So please be kind, and don't judge,' she said, 'or you'll all have me to answer to.'

'This all sounds rather intriguing, my dear,' Miss Tibbs said, brightening up at once at the suggestion something untoward was about to happen.

'You could say that I've been tidying up loose ends in my life, and this is one that still needs tidying,' Mildred said with a mysterious look towards Flora.

'Is this about you giving that house to the three girls?' Miss Tibbs asked, trying to find out what Mildred was up to.

'No, that's a loose end that has been well and truly tidied. Whatever you may think, I have no need for Captain's Cottage; and as I have no offspring, it made sense to hand it to Lily, Rose and Katie and see them enjoy it while I'm still around. It's called putting my affairs in order.'

'You are not going to die, are you?' Anya asked, looking worried. 'I would be sorry to see you not here anymore.'

Mildred grinned. She was getting used to the Polish woman's turn of phrase. 'I'm perfectly well, thank you. As I said before, I want to put my affairs in order while I can see people enjoy my money. I think of those girls as the family I never had, and if this war has taught me anything, it's that we should live for today. Now, I'm going to stand outside and wait for my visitor in case she has a change of heart about coming in.'

Flora watched Mildred leave the room, before looking to where Anya had picked up her knitting and was frowning at a dropped stitch. 'Anya, dear, Mildred's idea about sorting out the loose ends in her life made me think about you.'

'What do you mean?' Anya said with a frown. 'My life is here now. I have no loose ends in Poland. The Germans killed everything I hold dear.'

'But the reason you came here. You've done nothing to find your husband. You seemed to think he was at Manston, but with the threat of invasion now closer, chances are Henio could be moved away . . . Or worse,' she added, hoping not to upset her lodger.

'Take note of what Flora is telling you,' Miss Tibbs interrupted. 'Act now, before he is killed like the rest of your family.'

Flora held her breath, wishing the older woman hadn't spoken so tactlessly. Miss Tibbs could be a dear, but her ageing years meant she was sometimes a little blunter than necessary.

'I am frightened,' Anya said, ignoring Miss Tibbs' sharp words.

'Why would you be frightened?' Miss Tibbs asked, looking with concern at the sadness in Anya's eyes.

'Henio has new life now. Will he still want to know naive young woman from Poland? I think it better I stay here in Sea View and be with my new friends, and work as Sally for Joe Lyons and grow to be old maid like you,' she said. 'To be close to Henio is enough for me . . .'

'Did you not write to your husband at the

Manston airfield?' Flora asked. As far as she was aware, Anya had sent a letter months ago.

'No, the letter was not sent. It did not feel right, and now it will never be sent.'

Miss Tibbs looked distressed. 'But, my dear, he is your husband. He must be wondering what has happened to you?'

Anya shrugged her shoulders. 'I wish to leave things as they are. Now, who wants the cuppa or the cocoa?' she asked, bringing the discussion to an end.

Flora wasn't fooled for one moment. She knew that Anya had spoken to her of her fears about meeting Henio, but thought she still held a candle for him. Anya had travelled for hundreds of miles searching for Henio; to give up now was foolish. Had she lost her nerve? Perhaps it was time to step in and help the young woman once and for all.

Miss Tibbs struggled to her feet. 'I think I'll have an early night. All this upset has made me feel quite tired,' she said as she collected her knitting and book. The sound of voices in the hallway stopped her in her tracks. 'Perhaps I'll wait for that cup of tea after all,' she said, returning to her seat.

Flora's mouth twitched as she tried not to laugh. Miss Tibbs was not one to miss what was happening at Sea View. She had to confess to wondering who Mildred's visitors were herself. The smile left her face as Rose walked into the room, followed by Katie and Lily as well as a smiling Mildred. 'What a lovely surprise,' she managed to say, while trying not to make eye contact with her daughter for fear of what she'd see.

'The girls have some news to share with you,' Mildred said, stepping to one side as Anya walked in with a tray of teacups. 'Sit yourself down for a minute,' she instructed the woman. 'I think it best you all know at once. Where is Joyce? I don't want to have to repeat everything a second time.'

'She's working late, and she has young Pearl with her.'

Mildred thought for a moment. 'Perhaps it's for the best. This news isn't right for young ears.'

Flora frowned. What was Mildred going to say?

'I think it's best I take over, as it's my business that most of you won't be happy to hear,' Lily said, jutting out her chin defiantly.

Mildred raised her hand to stop Lily speaking further. 'I talked you into coming here, so I take full responsibility. What you are about to hear may shock you, ladies, but please keep your thoughts to yourself. I want no outbursts and no opinions. Do you hear me?' she said, looking towards Miss Tibbs.

'I'm sure we are all reasonable women,' the older woman said, looking slightly miffed.

'Oh, for heaven's sake,' Lily said, pulling off her coat so that everyone present could see she was pregnant.

The room fell quiet apart from a small gasp from Flora. 'Is this why you moved out?'

'I had my reasons for leaving Sea View and moving in with Rose, but it wasn't because of

313

bringing shame to you, if that's what you're thinking,' Lily said. 'I just wanted to be with my friend while I came to terms with my future.'

'It's not as if you could kick Lily out for bringing the guesthouse into disrepute, now, is it, Mum?' Rose said, as she sat down beside a quiet Katie and stared hard at her mother.

'Now is not the time for this, Rose,' Flora said. She had no wish for her daughter to air their differences in public. She desperately wished to be able to sit down and talk to Rose alone, rather than involve their friends at this stage. Rose didn't yet know everything about the past, and Flora's dearest wish was for her to understand and for them to be friends once more.

'A baby is such wonderful news. I wish you much joy,' Anya said. 'Miss Tibbs, you must show me how to knit a layette for the baby.'

Miss Tibbs simply sucked in her cheeks and stared at Lily's bare ring finger.

'That's right, I'm not married — and I have no wish to be,' Lily said, waving her ring-free hand in the air defiantly. 'There's worse things happen at sea. It took Rose and Mildred to show me I could keep the baby and bring it up with the help of my friends.'

'You would have had the child adopted?' Miss Tibbs exclaimed.

'No, I wouldn't,' Lily said, looking hard at the old woman and daring her to say more.

Miss Tibbs bent her head to study the cover of the book on her lap and kept quiet.

'I think it's very brave of Lily. And with Mildred generously giving the three of us her house, we know Lily's child will have a very good start in life,' Rose said.

So that's the reason Mildred made her decision, Flora thought to herself. 'When will you be packing up work?' she asked.

Lily shrugged her shoulders. 'I'll work for as long as I can, and Rose says I can transfer to being a Sally when carrying the heavy tea trays becomes a problem.'

'You cannot take my job,' Anya said sharply.

'There's plenty of work for everyone,' Rose said, giving Anya a smile. 'You've no need to worry.' The last thing she wanted was to cause unrest amongst her friends while her heart was aching over Ben.

'If you'd been here half an hour ago, you'd have been worried sick,' Miss Tibbs said, keen to add a little excitement to the discussion. 'Have you heard that the army are pulling back to St Nicholas? That means we will be alone here when the invasion happens.'

Rose gave her another hard look. 'Do you honestly think that Winston Churchill would leave us all at the mercy of the Germans? Deliveries are still coming through from Lyons in London, and I've not heard a thing about them closing the teashops down. Have you heard anything at the Ramsgate teashop, Katie?'

'Not a thing,' Katie said. 'And we are as busy as we've ever been. If people were that worried they would have started to move away from the area, wouldn't they? It's not as if they are being stopped.'

Anya reached for a newspaper on an

occasional table by the side of her armchair. 'People will be leaving soon. They will make me go as well. Look.'

Flora took the newspaper and quickly scanned the words.

'What's up, Mum?' Rose asked, forgetting for a moment that she and Flora were at logger-heads.

'It seems that all aliens will have to leave the Thanet area. I had heard about this down at the ARP centre. But I don't think it means you will have to go, Anya, or even be interned. Aren't the Polish on our side? Why, your husband is fighting for our country. You are not to worry,' Flora said, leaning over to pat the woman's hand. 'I'll have a word down at the police station and get it sorted out. They were very helpful when you first came to live with us.'

Anya nodded, but she didn't look convinced. 'I will be at work tomorrow bright and early,' she said, looking first at Rose before glaring at Lily. 'You can be my helper — but nothing more. Do you understand, Lilee?'

Lily laughed. 'Your job is safe, Anya, never you fear.'

'Do you think there will still be a dance at Dreamland tomorrow?' Katie asked. 'The army was organizing it and we've all had invitations.'

Mildred reached into the pocket of her overalls and pulled out a crumpled card. 'I was given an invitation, but I'm not one for dancing. Here, you have it,' she said, pushing it into Flora's hand.

'Oh, I don't know about that. I'm not one for

316

such occasions,' she said, seeing Rose look hopefully in her direction. 'But — yes, thank you, Mildred. I'll gladly take the ticket. Will you come too, Anya?'

'Why not? I may as well enjoy myself before the English army lock me up,' Anya said, in a tone that made her friends wonder whether she was jesting or not.

'It is going to be the Silvano Caprice band. He plays for ENSA now,' Katie explained. 'Rose used to sing for him,' she added, looking at Anya. 'Although I was surprised when you received that note asking you to sing with the band, Rose.'

Rose shrugged her shoulders. 'He needed a singer and I like to sing. I wouldn't read too much into it.' She smiled.

'I would like to hear you sing before I leave,' Anya said, looking sad.

Flora shook her head. She must find time to go down to the police station tomorrow, as she couldn't take much more of her guests and their problems — especially when she wanted more than anything to spend time mending bridges with Rose. 'My daughter has a beautiful voice. It will be a treat to hear her sing,'

* * *

'The place is packed,' Katie said as they pushed and squeezed their way through the crowd already standing on the dance floor, waiting for the first dance of the evening.

'Let us hope Hitler does not invade this

evening, as he will find most of the town in the one place,' Anya said loudly, trying to be heard above the noise.

'Always the cheerful one, aren't you?' Lily laughed. 'I for one intend to enjoy myself this evening. Hitler or no Hitler, I won't be out much when this little one comes along, so I'm making the most of things.'

'You cannot dance with men in your condition,' Anya said.

'Try and stop me,' Lily said, nudging an airman and dragging him to the middle of the floor as Silvano raised his baton. The band went into a rousing rendition of 'I've Got My Love to Keep Me Warm'.

'We must sit down before we get grabbed,' Anya said, steering Rose and Katie to where Flora was sitting at an empty table. They all sat down gratefully.

'How did you manage to get a table?' Katie asked.

Flora grinned. 'I said we were from the convent and here to save people's souls.'

The women shrieked with laughter.

'You look very pretty, my love,' Flora said, looking at Rose in a becoming red georgette dress decorated with a large white rose on the waistline.

'So do you, Mum.' Rose returned the compliment, thinking how young Flora looked in the navy-blue silk suit she'd worn for Katie's wedding. Perhaps she could be civil to her for the evening, if she really tried hard.

'Look, Rose,' Flora said leaning close. 'About

what you found in the attaché case. We need to talk . . . '

Rose raised her hand to halt the conversation. 'No, Mum, let's not talk about that. I'll talk about anything but that, so please don't say another word.' She looked up and smiled as a lad in an ill-fitting army uniform asked her to dance, and didn't look back as he led her to the dance floor for a foxtrot. When she returned to the table, Flora was no longer there. Rose looked around the room and spotted her in the arms of an RAF officer as they shuffled slowly around the floor.

'They look cosy,' Lily said, as she slid a glass of lemonade across the table towards Rose. 'You'd best drink this before you start to sing. If Silvano is true to form he won't offer you a sip of anything while you're up on the stage. What are you singing this evening?'

Rose dipped into her handbag and pulled out a scrap of paper. 'I'm starting with 'Smoke Gets in Your Eyes' and then going straight into 'You Made Me Love You'. What do you think?'

'The crowd will love them. Are you only singing the two?'

'You never know with Silvano. He could kick me off without a thank you after two songs, or I could be up there for half an hour. He did say he has the score for 'I Cried for You' and also 'Perfidia', so I've brushed up on the lyrics in case he throws them at me.' She didn't add that part of her wished she wasn't here at all, as singing romantic songs brought back thoughts of Ben that she was trying to bury deep down inside.

'I'll be bawling buckets of tears by the time you finish those songs. The words get to me every time you sing them.'

'That was fun,' Flora said as she arrived back at their table, her cheeks glowing pink from dancing.

'I'll be going to the stage now,' Rose said. 'Wish me luck.'

'Let's get closer to the front so we can see her,' Katie whispered to Lily as they watched Rose go up the short flight of steps to join Silvano Caprice on stage. He announced her as 'England's answer to Helen Forrest' before she went into her first song. Her lilting voice soared across the large hall as couples danced to the popular 'Smoke Gets in Your Eyes'.

'This takes me back to my younger days,' Flora said, almost to herself.

Katie turned to ask Flora what she meant, but Lily put a hand on her arm to stop her. 'Best not go there, love,' she whispered.

They cheered and whistled as Rose finished her first song and straight away started the first lines of 'You Made Me Love You'. The crowd stopped dancing and stood watching as Rose, her eyes closed, performed the song as if she was living the lyrics.

Silvano walked over to Rose and kissed her cheek as she bowed at the end of the song. 'Isn't she great, ladies and gentlemen? Would you like another song?'

The crowd cheered and clapped as Rose blushed. Having been so wrapped up in the words of the song, she always forgot that others were listening and liking what they heard. So many had danced with loved ones, or had happy memories of the songs, and that was some of the pleasure she felt when sharing them with others.

Silvano whispered in her ear before returning to raise his baton, and the musicians started to play 'I Cried for You'.

Katie gave a big sigh. 'I love this song — it is so sad.'

'You English are very strange. How can you enjoy a sad song so much?' Anya said as she sat down at the table.

'There's nothing wrong with having a bit of a cry along to a sad song. I often put on a record and have a bit of a wallow,' Katie said. 'This song reminds me of my Jack and how we danced together in the kitchen of our flat after our wedding. It was so romantic — but a bit on the chilly side, what with the windows iced up and the fire not having been lit. I'll never forget it,' she sighed with a dreamy look in her eyes.

Anya tutted and looked towards the stage. 'Rose is in another world too, going by the look on her face. Is she crying over some man as well?'

Lily watched as Rose brushed a tear from her cheek while continuing to sing. 'She never did hear from that Ben after they went to London together, did she?'

'He was a nice bloke,' Katie said. 'Didn't he come back injured from Dunkirk?'

'I've no idea,' Flora said, listening to the girls' chatter. 'No one tells me a thing these days. Her customers see more of my daughter than I do.'

'They seem to love her,' Anya said as she lit a cigarette. 'She should sing for a job rather than look after Joe Lyons' teashop for him.'

The four women watched as Rose came to the end of the song and smiled sweetly at the crowd, who once again clapped and cheered for more.

She turned to Silvano. 'Perfidia?'

He nodded and raised his baton yet again, leading the band into the first minute of the memorable melody.

Rose swayed in time to the music, watching as the crowd drifted from the front of the stage, gradually finding their partners and shuffling around the dance floor as much as the packed crowd would allow. Looking out over the audience, she frowned as she caught sight of a figure she recognized . . . Surely not? Was it Ben? She recognized the way he held his back so straight, and . . . So intent was she on looking at the upright army officer's figure on the far side of the dance floor that she almost missed her cue to start singing the haunting refrain of 'Perfidia' — one of her favourite songs of lost love. He was moving through the dancing couples until he stood at the edge of the stage, looking up into her face as she continued to sing.

How Rose ever remembered the words, she never knew, as her mind went back to the last time she'd seen him, what now felt like an age ago, in the hospital bed, with another woman leaning over to kiss him. After all she thought they'd meant to each other — he had another woman and also children. How could he? she thought, as she continued to sing the haunting melody. She steeled herself for the line she knew was coming, and stared down to him as she reached the part of the song that told of the singer finding her love with another woman. She thought her heart would break as she walked to the other end of the stage to sing down to a couple who, arm in arm, were swaying to the music. It was hard knowing he was there watching her, and it would be oh so easy to finish the song and go to him. But he had a wife, and children were involved. She wasn't the kind of person to break up a marriage. Not even if it meant spending the rest of her life alone until she was an old spinster.

When the song finished she slipped from the stage and hurried over towards her friends. She heard him call her name, but rushed through the crowd of dancing couples. 'Pass me my coat, will you? I've just seen Ben and I don't want to speak to him. I'm going to stay at Captain's Cottage tonight, if that's all right with you? Please don't tell Ben where I've gone. I never want to see him again for as long as I live.'

'I'll come with you,' Katie said. 'You'd best come too,' she said, passing Lily her coat from where they'd been left on an empty seat. 'I don't want to be walking the streets searching for you if there's an air raid.'

'You English women are mad!' Anya declared as she walked away. 'We have not yet had the hokey-cokey and you are leaving. Bah!'

★ ★ ★

Rose looked up at the sound of tapping on her office door. 'Come in,' she called.

The door was opened by a nervous-looking Nippy. 'Miss Neville, there's a policeman to see you,' she said, before ducking backwards and scuttling away.

'Come along in,' Rose smiled as the plain-clothes policeman held out his identity card. 'How can I help you?' She indicated the seat across the other side of her desk. The distraction was welcome; she had hardly been able to keep her eyes open today, after tossing and turning all night thinking of Ben. How dare he come to the dance and try to approach her?

'I'm Sergeant Thompson,' the policeman said as he took a seat before opening a notebook, checking what he'd written. 'I understand you have a Mrs Anya Polinksi working here?'

Rose's heart missed a beat. 'Yes, Anya works here. Please don't say something has happened to her husband?'

'I know nothing of her husband,' he said in a gruff voice. 'I'm here to inspect your personnel records and to ask how well you know this woman.'

'Why — what has she done wrong?' Rose asked, knowing in her heart of hearts that this had something to do with the internment of anyone not born in the country. Rumour had it that foreigners were being rounded up and moved away from Thanet. 'Do you think she is a danger to people just because she is Polish? I thought the Polish were not only on our side, but their people were fighting with our air force and our army. It would be very inconvenient to have Mrs Polinski removed from my employ at this time, as she is a hard-working and valued member of staff.'

Sergeant Thompson looked taken aback. 'Madam, I'm simply updating my records. Between you and me, I'm as concerned about this hounding of foreigners as as you seem to be. My eldest daughter is courting a fine young Polish man who works at Manston. He recently requested her hand in marriage. The wife would be none too happy to see him locked up for the duration. My life would not be worth living if that were to happen.'

Rose felt herself warm to the sergeant. 'Would you like a cup of tea and perhaps a slice of cake? It's no trouble at all,' she added as she saw him waver. 'I promise it isn't a bribe for you to think kindly of our Anya.' She grinned.

'It would take more than that, Miss Neville. A pork pie at least,' he laughed as she went to the door and called out to a passing Nippy to take the order.

Returning to her desk, she folded her hands in front of her and looked serious. 'I know you are here to ask me about Anya, and I can give you all the details I have about her. Head office has the same information as well, plus a record of her wages. However, if you wish to speak to the people who really know her, you need to visit my mother, Flora Neville, at the Sea View guest house in Ramsgate.' She quickly scribbled the address on a piece of paper and slid it across the desk. 'Along with some of the residents, my mother can tell you everything about Anya from the day she rescued her to what she had for breakfast this morning.'

'Sea View? That rings a bell . . . '

'It should do. A Mr Cardew was arrested there a few months ago on suspicion of being a spy — and before you say anything, he did not know Anya, and to my knowledge he never spoke to her. He was rather a recluse. You will find all our statements on your files.'

Sergeant Thompson nodded his head thoughtfully as the tea tray was brought in, and took a cup of tea from Rose before speaking again. 'Do you know much about Mrs Polinski's past?'

Rose explained what she had learnt while living at Sea View. 'Since taking over as manageress, I've been living in a flat here in Margate. Anya travels back to Ramsgate by bus unless she's offered a lift.'

Sergeant Thompson raised his eyebrows. 'Who would give her a lift?'

Rose gave a small laugh. 'No one of any importance. Mildred Dalrymple if she was passing, and sometimes one of our delivery drivers if they had a drop-off at the Ramsgate tearoom. You can dig as deep as you like, but Anya Polinski would never endanger this country's safety.'

He nodded his head slowly. 'I'm inclined to believe you — but of course I will have to make the usual investigations, you understand.'

'I do. But perhaps you could do something for me? It would also prove that Anya is not a threat to our country.'

'If I can,' he said, reaching for a tea plate containing a buttered scone.

326

'Anya came here to Thanet to look for her husband. She travelled from Poland, where she lost all her family in the invasion, after being told her husband had escaped with the Polish air force. She was told he was at Manston — but for the past few months she's done nothing more to find him. I feel she has lost her nerve,' Rose explained, not knowing that she had hit the nail on the head.

'Would you happen to have an idea why she hasn't tried to make any enquiries?'

'I don't know. My mother may know more. I know if it was me, I'd be banging on their door wanting to see my husband.'

'Perhaps it is better to travel in hope than to arrive?' he said thoughtfully.

'You could be right there. Knowing he is nearby may be comfort enough. She might be frightened of hearing he has died, I suppose — then she would know for certain she had lost everything.'

'What a situation to be in. What is it you would like me to do?'

'Would you be able to check to see whether Henio Polinski is at the airfield? And if he is, inform him that Anya is here?'

'You understand I can't go in there asking questions, as I could be locked up and have the key thrown away. However, if during my enquiries he should appear, then of course I will pass on the message.'

'And your daughter's boyfriend may just know something about him.'

'You are right. He might very well know this

young man. You would make a good detective, Miss Neville. Now, if I may see Mrs Polinski for a few minutes to complete my questions, I will then be on my way and leave you to your work,' he said, glancing to the magazine that lay open on Rose's desk. It showed an article about American bandleaders that Rose had been reading. 'I'm partial to a bit of Glenn Miller myself.'

★ ★ ★

'Mrs Neville?'

'Can I help?' Flora said as she opened the door a little wider, being prepared to shut it fast if the visitor did not identify himself. It was pitch black without the street lighting, and ten o'clock at night was rather late to be calling.

'I'm sorry to be knocking on your door so late at night. I'm Sergeant Thompson, based at Margate police station,' he replied, quickly shining his torch towards himself so Flora could see the uniform and also his identity card.

'Oh, please do come in,' Flora said feeling a little foolish. 'I'm sorry for keeping you standing on the doorstep like that. Come through to the kitchen and I'll put the kettle on,' she said, leading the way through the house.

'Please, there's no need to apologize. I understand why you would want to know who was on your doorstep at this time of night,' he said as he sat down at the kitchen table. 'This is a very cosy room.'

'I think so. Everyone gravitates to this room, even though I have a nice sitting room for my residents,' Flora said as she too sat down after filling the kettle and placing it on the hob.

'It's the same in my house — though in our street the front room is hardly used apart from high days and holidays,' he replied, not mentioning that for most residents the room was also used for laying out the dear departed.

'I've heard that's the case,' Flora smiled. 'With Sea View being slightly larger, I'm fortunate to have more rooms. I've often thought about moving to a smaller house, as it could be so much cosier and easier to keep clean.'

'It must be hard work,' he replied as he pulled out his notebook.

'So must yours, to be working at this time of night. What can I do for you?' she asked as the kettle started to boil. 'Carry on — I can hear you as I do this,' she said as she got to her feet to make the tea.

'It's about one of your guests: a Mrs Anya Polinski.'

'I thought this would happen, what with Anya coming here from Poland,' Flora said as she warmed the teapot before tipping the water into the sink. 'I'd bet my last breath on Anya being a good citizen, and will do all I can not to have her sent to an internment camp. We've been hearing about such things down at the ARP centre,' she added as she saw the police sergeant's questioning look.

'You're an ARP warden?' he asked as he made some notes on a clean page of the book.

'I was one of the first to volunteer in Thanet,' she said proudly.

Sergeant Thompson tried not to smile. His colleagues were often joking about the team of officious people who did very little apart from checking for chinks of light coming from buildings after dark. They seemed to have a loud voice on the local council, with one of their group known for making dire predictions about what would happen if Germany were to invade.

'I can see you are amused by our work,' Flora said as she placed a cup of steaming tea in front of him. 'Help yourself to milk.'

He apologized before looking through the notes in his book. 'Your daughter, Rose, seems to be of the same opinion as yourself about Mrs Polinski.'

Flora stiffened. 'You've spoken to my daughter?'

'Several days ago, when I went into the Lyons Teashop in Margate; has she not told you?'

'We don't speak very often. She no longer lives here. I'm not sure how I can help you, if Rose has already spoken,' she said, taking a sip of her tea.

'It was something she said about Anya Polinski's husband . . . ' He flicked through a couple of pages. 'Henio Polinski. An interesting name.'

'It's Polish for Henry,' Flora said.

'Do you know if Anya has made contact with him since arriving in this country?'

'She's never spoken of seeing him. I feel that if they had met, I would have been informed. You know she had a terrible time before she left her homeland, Sergeant? It would be so unfair if she were to be taken away from the only people she can call her friends.'

'I'm aware of her circumstances, as your daughter filled me in. I also spoke to Mrs Polinski,' he added as if he had said far too much.

'Then why ask me? Besides, I thought it was only male aliens you were locking up?'

He blanched at the directness of her words. 'I need to fill in a complete profile of the lady, and someone may give me information that another person forgot — or withheld.'

'I can vouch for her, if that would help? I just know that nobody living under my roof could be an enemy of this country.'

The police sergeant looked up from his notes and stared at Flora. The silence between them was palpable as she realized what she had said. 'Perhaps we'll forget you said that,' he replied.

Flora got up and busied herself checking the teapot. 'Would you like another cup?' she asked, knowing her cheeks were burning red. How could she have forgotten about Mr Cardew?

'Not for me, thanks. So Mrs Polinski, to your knowledge, has never made contact with her husband, or perhaps anyone else . . . ?'

Flora sat back down. 'No — and I do wish she would contact the powers that be at Manston and enquire. Even write a letter, so she knew for sure that he was safe and well.' She looked sad. 'I did ask her about it once, and she said she was afraid that after she had travelled all this way he would reject her. She seems to think he would have seen a new kind of life in the air force, mixing with the toffs who fly the planes. I've often wondered why they only pick posh people to fly.'

Sergeant Thompson nodded, but didn't say anything. He had often wondered the same thing.

'I wonder . . . No, it's wrong of me to ask you to do such a thing.'

He placed his notebook on the table and looked thoughtful. 'Were you by any chance going to ask me to find out whether Henio Polinski is based at the airfield?'

'Forget I asked you. It seems an awful cheek. I just thought that if he knew Anya was here, he might come to see her and they'd . . . '

'They'd fall into each other's arms, and all would be right with the world?'

'Goodness. Whatever made you say that?'

'My wife reads those weekly magazines with the soppy stories inside. She hides them where she thinks I won't find them.'

Flora hoped she'd put her copy of *My Weekly* safely out of the way of prying eyes. 'Loving someone isn't always soppy, Sergeant. Anya Polinski deserves happiness after what she's been through. I'll ask again. Will you be so kind as to enquire about Henio at the airfield? I did write a letter, but have not received a reply.'

'I'll see what I can do, Mrs Neville. You and your daughter can be quite persuasive, you know.'

'Rose asked you too?'

'She did, and please don't quote me, but I can't see what will be achieved by moving Mrs

Polinski away from Thanet. I'll do all I can to put in a good word for her and also enquire about her husband,' he said, making his thanks for the tea and heading out of the kitchen with Flora following.

They'd just reached the front door when it opened, and Anya walked in. 'So, policeman, you come here to arrest me?' she said, giving him a dirty look. 'You have nothing better to do with your time than to hound an innocent woman?'

'No, not at all,' Sergeant Thompson blustered, not knowing what to say when caught out by the woman he was investigating.

'We are letting out the light,' Flora snapped, pulling Anya inside and trying to close the door. Before she could say anything else an ear-splitting wail called out into the darkness, getting louder and louder by the second. 'It's an air raid,' she exclaimed, rushing to the bottom of the stairs to call up to Miss Tibbs, Mildred, Joyce and Pearl. 'Hurry up, ladies,' she called as doors started to slam closed and footsteps could be heard. 'You know what to do, but we must all keep together.'

'I must go,' Sergeant Thompson said, opening the front door.

'No. You are away from your home. I'll show you where to go,' Flora said, ushering the residents out in front of her. She picked up a bag she had left in the hall for just such an occurrence, along with a tin helmet with ARP painted on the front. The residents were all carrying bags and blankets.

'Do you have a shelter?' Sergeant Thompson

asked, feeling slightly relieved, as he had imagined for a moment that he'd be driving back to Margate through an air raid. Trust him to be away from home when the first raids hit the town.

Flora pushed him along the path and out into the street, where they joined crowds of people heading along the road. 'No, Sergeant Thompson, we are going down into the bowels of Ramsgate. You are about to join us in the tunnels that have been carved out under this town. Follow me — I know the way.'

15

August 24th 1940

Lily shivered and pulled a blanket close around her shoulders. They'd spent many hours in the air-raid shelter at the back of their home in Broadstairs already that day. It had been the same, night after night, for nearly a week. 'Are you sure it isn't a false alarm this time?' she asked. 'It's bloody miserable out there in the shelter. We've spent so much time down there lately, I'm on first-name terms with the spiders.'

'It's best we go down,' Katie said, helping Lily to her feet. 'I've made it as cosy as I can. There are candles, and I've made one of those flower-pot heaters we read about in your magazine.'

'I have a thermos of cocoa and the leftover sausage rolls from the teashop that we would have had for our supper if we hadn't been full up from the vegetable pie Katie made,' Rose added as she took Lily's other arm and with Katie's help pulled Lily to her feet. They headed out of their house and down the gravel path to the end of the garden. 'Mind the steps here,' Rose said, shining her torch at the short flight of steps that took them down into the Anderson shelter. Pulling the door to behind them, she quickly lit a couple of candles while they sorted themselves out.

'If there are any rats, I'm going back to the house and taking my chances,' Lily muttered as she heaved herself down onto one of the benches running the length of the shelter. It was padded enough to make a bed if they had to stay the night. A bunk bed was set into the other side, with an upturned wooden box between the beds forming a table.

'I'll sort out the hurricane lamp, and then we can save the candles for later,' Rose said as she fiddled with the temperamental light. 'Put your feet up, Lily — you don't want your ankles swelling, do you?' she said, helping her friend to manoeuvre in the small space.

'Thanks for reminding me,' Lily huffed. 'I feel like a beached whale as it is, and none of my clothes fit me anymore. I'm fed up with wearing matronly smocks over my skirts and dresses that won't do up. I'll be glad when I've had this kid and can fit back into my clothes again,' she sighed.

'It can only be a matter of weeks now,' Katie said. 'It would have helped if you'd gone to see the doctor,' she added, pulling out her knitting. 'At least we'd have had a proper date for this little one's arrival.'

'What's the point? Joyce and Flora have told me what to expect, and I have the name of a midwife who will come in when I'm ready to give birth. I don't want people fussing.'

'I've never known anyone not want to know when a baby is due or to plan ahead. If it weren't for your friends, you'd not even have any clothes or a pram. At least Mildred said she'd paint the

336

little bedroom, and Flora has a cot up in the attic that she kept from when holidaymakers used to stay at Sea View.'

'I didn't know Mum was so involved,' Rose said with a bitter tone to her voice.

'You've not been here to see her when she visits,' Lily spat back. 'Don't you think it's time for you both to kiss and make up? Why, a bomb could wipe out everyone at Sea View before you can say Bob's yer uncle, and then how would you feel?'

They fell silent. Thinking of Lily's words Rose tried to imagine what it would be like if her mum was to pass away before they'd had time to discuss what she'd found in the leather attaché case. Perhaps, she thought, it was time she allowed Flora a chance to explain what had happened in the past.

Katie was thinking of her Jack. She'd not seen him since just after their wedding day, and had hoped that she would be able to write to let him know she was expecting his child; but Mother Nature thought otherwise, so she longed for the day when he came home on leave. In his last letter he'd said how pleased he was about Mildred's kind offer, and mentioned how much he liked the sea and that he might well change career to become a fisherman once the war was over — that was if she agreed. Of course she did, she smiled to herself in the dimly lit shelter. She was still thinking of their future when a crash so loud it shook the foundations of their shelter made the friends jump out of their skins.

'Bloody hell, that was close,' Lily said, sitting

up and grabbing Rose for comfort. 'How far away do you think they are?'

Katie went to the door of the air-raid shelter and stepped outside. 'Oh my God, the sky is full of planes. I can see . . . '

'Katie!' Rose screamed, and pulled the girl's limp body back inside the shelter, quickly pulling the door to behind them.

'Was she hit — is she dead?' Lily asked with a sob. 'I couldn't bear it if . . . '

'No, it looks as though she just fainted. Something must have frightened her.'

'Isn't a sky full of German planes scary enough?' Lily asked as she shook Katie and rubbed her hands. Eventually she stirred and began to mumble incoherently.

'Katie, love, whatever's the matter?' Rose asked, putting her arms around Katie as she tried to stop Lily slapping the girl so much. 'Did you see something in the garden that frightened you?'

Katie nodded. 'I spotted something up near the house. It was when the searchlights swept over the sky and lit up the house for just a moment. I thought . . . I thought I saw someone. Do you think the invasion has started?' she asked fearfully, looking back towards the closed door of the shelter.

'It seems rather strange if it has. Surely they wouldn't invade while the Luftwaffe's bombing the daylights out of us?' Lily said. 'Perhaps it's one of those looters we keep reading about. They steal from damaged properties and when people are down the shelters.'

'Why, that's downright despicable,' Katie said, brushing herself down. 'I have wedding presents in the house, and I'll be damned if anyone's going to pinch them.' She reached for the door, opening it just as another crash came from nearby and shook them again.

'Come back in,' Rose begged. 'It's not worth getting killed for a few kitchen items and a set of flannelette sheets, is it? If you're that worried, I'll replace them myself. That's *if* the mysterious shadow was a burglar.'

'I've been called a few things in my life, but never a burglar,' a familiar voice came from outside the shelter. 'Watch out — I'm coming in.'

'Oh, Mildred! I've never been so relieved to see a familiar face,' Rose said as she turned up the light in the lamp after lowering it when the door was opened. 'Whatever are you doing out in an air raid?' She gave her friend a hug after shifting up on the bunk to make room for her.

'I'd dropped off some fish to friends, and we got talking. I was halfway home when the air-raid siren started to wail. I had the choice of coming to you or getting home and going down the tunnels. One look towards Ramsgate told me I should come here.'

Rose shuddered. She knew in her heart of hearts that the town where she was born, and where she'd lived a happy childhood, was where she should be right now. 'I hope everyone got down to the tunnels in time. The enemy planes seemed to be overhead seconds after the air-raid sirens had stopped.'

'It was quite a sight as I came along the cliff

road, I can tell you. I had to resist the urge to turn off the engine and sit and watch. Our guns are doing a valiant effort to blow them out the sky, but from what I could see, they are not effective. I just hope Manston had time to get their planes up and away from trouble in time. This must be the fifth day in a row the Germans have gone after the aerodrome.'

'So they are heading for Manston again?'

'From what I can see and hear, they are. Sadly Hitler didn't let me know what his plans were,' Mildred grinned, doing her best to cheer up the girls.

'I'm so glad we have our little house and this Anderson shelter,' Katie said. 'I dreaded going into the tunnels under Ramsgate. The one time I went with Flora, we'd only gone into the main tunnel a few hundred feet before I was feeling frightened. To have to go through that maze of tunnels and huddle together, not knowing what was going on outside, would scare me to death.'

'If it's that or die, you'd soon get used to it,' Lily muttered. 'I'm wondering if my stepfather managed to get himself to safety or not.'

Katie reached out a hand in the gloom and gave Lily's arm a squeeze. 'He probably did.'

'Not if he was pissed out of his skull, he wouldn't. Half the time he had no idea what he got up to while he was drunk,' she added bitterly.

There was silence in the shelter for a few seconds while they thought about Lily's words. 'You mean he knocked you and your mum about?' Katie asked, with a hint of anger in her voice.

'Yes, and more. Mum worked her fingers to the bone to keep a nice house and make sure the rent was paid on time. That lazy slob did nothing.'

'What I don't understand is, why didn't we know about this? We would sit side by side in school every day, and you were the best-turned-out kid — and you seemed to be the happiest,' Katie said. She reached for the flask and started to pour hot cocoa into the enamel cups they kept ready for times such as these.

'My mother was aware that people would talk if they knew our home was not a happy one. She decided that whatever happened behind our front door, we should keep a united front and appear in public as if nothing was wrong in our life. Granted George would stagger home three sheets to the wind, but as long as we carried on and the nets were kept white and the doorstep clean, then all was right in our little world. My mum would look at you and Flora and how you coped after your dad died, and decided that we should be the same: respectable, liked by the local community, and be as close as we could . . . ' Lily's words caught in her throat.

'Oh Lily,' Rose said with a harsh laugh. 'There was my mum flogging her guts out trying to be a pillar of the community as well. It's quite funny really, when all the time Mum was hiding a secret from everyone, and that included me. I do wonder why people are so quick to hide their real lives from others?'

'Because we are ashamed of our pasts, or perhaps we just want to make a fresh start,'

Mildred said, banging her empty mug down on the makeshift table. 'Just remember, you have a lot to be grateful for. Whatever secrets they had, or whatever they hid from prying eyes, was all done for the best — and it was for your benefit. Some kids weren't so lucky. Are you forgetting that Katie here never knew her parents? It's not just your generation, you know. I wasn't too lucky when they handed them out, either,' she added, but didn't elaborate.

'Don't feel sorry for me,' Katie said as her friends started to apologize. 'I've got a lot to be grateful for. I'm married to my Jack, and I know we will have a happy future together — once this war is over and done with,' she added, as the earth shook and they were nearly deafened by another explosion. 'We just need to get through this,' she continued cheerfully. 'But can you tell us what it is that your mum has done? Or would you prefer not to share it?'

'You always manage to look on the bright side, don't you, Katie?' Rose said. 'I wish I could.' She took a deep breath. 'I found out that General Sykes is my real father. All I know about the circumstances is that Mum met him while she was working on the stage.'

'Oh, that is so romantic,' Katie said. 'I barely remember the General, but he seemed very nice. One of the nicer nuns at the children's home told me that no one is completely bad, and I try to remember that whenever someone is unpleasant or if I feel they have secrets.'

'You're a good kid,' Mildred said in a choked voice. 'We could all learn from you.'

'I'm no angel, Mildred,' Katie giggled, embarrassed at the way the conversation had gone. 'Lily, can I ask you something?'

'Fire away; I'll answer if I can.'

'If things were that bad with George's womanizing and cruelty, why did you and your mum not leave him?'

The girls all ducked again, coughing because of the dust shaken up in the shelter, then waited for the noise to subside before Lily answered. 'I've often wondered why we didn't. Mum was a proud woman, and as I said before, she didn't want anyone knowing what went on behind closed doors. I asked her once why we didn't just pack up and leave. It was after he'd been free and easy with his fists when he came home from the pub, and Mum had lost her temper and thrown his dinner out the back door. She told me that when you married someone, you had to take the good with the bad. Besides, we had nowhere to go. Nan was alive at that time but mum would have died rather than gone cap in hand to her. When Mum first knew she'd made a mistake marrying George, Nan had told her she'd made her bed and now must lie in it. She certainly did that all right.'

'What a horrid thing to say,' Mildred all but exploded.

'She'd not had a good life herself,' Lily said, 'so Mum forgave her in time, and it was never mentioned again. If anything, it made Mum more determined to put a brave face on everything. Do you know, I think she loved George in her own funny way. She begged me, when she knew she didn't have long left, to stay and look after him. I couldn't really say no, could I? It took a lot for me to walk out when I did and come to stay with you. Then to have this house . . . ' She couldn't speak any more.

'Oh Lily, I reckon if Mum had known, she'd have given you both rooms at Sea View,' Rose said, giving her friend a hug. 'I can't believe you'd been going through that all these years, and we didn't know a thing.'

'It just shows my mum's plan to keep our business to ourselves must have worked,' Lily said, giving a short laugh. 'But I know she was grateful when I was allowed to stay overnight at your home and we slept top to tail in your bed, as the holidaymakers had taken all the spare rooms.'

'I remember that. We earned pocket money helping Mum with the breakfasts and pushing suitcases to the train station in an old pram. That was a lovely summer.'

'Oh yes, your mum wrote to the children's home and convinced them to let me stay as well for a week,' Katie said. 'Your mum is lovely, Rose. I wish things weren't so strained between the two of you.'

Rose felt terrible. Here were two of the most important people in her life, who hadn't had the best of upbringings, and she was the only one left with a mother and she was refusing to discuss their differences. She was starting to feel quite uncomfortable about the situation and didn't know how to answer Katie.

Lily, who could feel the tension in the air,

broke the ice. 'Blimey, I could do with a glass of beer or something. I'm parched after all this talking.'

Mildred rummaged through the pockets of the large mackintosh she was wearing over her overalls, and pulled out a bottle of brandy. 'Empty the dregs out of your tin mugs and we can have a drop of this to warm us up.'

'And I have sausage rolls,' Rose declared, making them all chuckle, thinking that when the opportunity arose she would try to make her peace with her mum.

★   ★   ★

'Hasn't the all-clear sounded yet?' Rose asked, waking from a troubled sleep. 'How long have we been down here?'

Katie switched on her torch and looked at her wristwatch. 'It's two o'clock in the afternoon. We've been down here for over twelve hours. I feel like hell,' she said, standing up and trying to stretch in the confined space before lighting one of the candles. 'How do you feel, Lily?'

'My ankles have swollen up like balloons, and I need a wee. Before you say it, I'm not going in that bucket again. If the pair of you hadn't caught hold of me I'd have fallen off last time.' She caught her friends grinning, and burst out laughing. 'You'd not have laughed if it had spilt all over your feet! Oh, I could kill for a hot cup of tea.'

'You and me both,' a grumpy voice came from beneath a blanket where Mildred had covered

345

herself and been snoring gently until the girls started to talk.

'Do you think we could risk going up to the house and replenishing supplies?' Katie asked. 'The enemy activity hasn't been around here for a couple of hours. I've been counting the time between explosions, a bit like we used to count the seconds between thunder and lightning.'

'What do you think, Mildred?' Rose asked the older woman.

'I think we'd be mad to attempt it, but I'm game if you are,' she replied. 'I suggest me and Rose go first, and see how the land lies.'

They all agreed, and Lily said, 'Do you think you could empty the bucket? It's starting to make me heave.'

Mildred roared with laughter. 'I'll take it with me. When you've worked on a fishing boat as long as I have, a bit of a smell is nothing.'

Lily placed a hand over her mouth. 'Please don't talk about it, as I can't cope even thinking about smells and the like. But if you can bring me back something to eat, I'll be ever so grateful.'

Rose collected the flask and the mugs, trying to remember the requests for candles from Katie, along with another ball of wool. They headed out of the shelter and hurried towards the house.

'I can see a few slates missing off the roof — and a back bedroom windowpane has gone,' Mildred reported as she looked up at the house. 'Not too bad, considering what we've been listening to. I'll go round to the front and see if there's any damage there.'

Rose let herself in through the back door while Mildred headed around the side of the house. 'Oh no,' Rose cried out as she looked through from the kitchen to the front room and could see Mildred standing where the front door used to be.

'Don't worry — it's been blown clean off its hinges. Half the front wall has gone, but apart from that we've been lucky. Others haven't fared so well. Three doors down have lost most of their roof, but at least it didn't catch fire.'

Rose shuddered. 'There but for the grace of God . . . ' she started to say, until she saw the thunderous look in Mildred's eyes.

'If there was a God, he wouldn't have allowed this to happen,' she spat out. 'I'll get some tools from the shed and secure the front while you sort out drinks and food for the girls. Then get yourself back down that shelter as quickly as you can. The all-clear hasn't sounded yet, so goodness knows what could happen before it does.'

Rose didn't need any second bidding, and quickly raided the cupboards. She gathered bread, a lump of cheese and the remains of a large pork pie she'd rescued from the teashop. Never had she been so grateful that they were allowed to bring home food that would have gone off overnight. Often she gave her staff the remaining food, but for some reason the pork pie had not been taken. She made a mental note to ensure all her staff had food to take home each night, even if she was a little over-generous with

Joe Lyons' stock. She hated to think of any staff going without if they had to put up with another night like this.

Thoughts of the teashop made her realize that she should have been at work, as it was a Saturday. She should at least be prepared to go in to check for damage once the all-clear sounded. Checking the gas was working and water ran from the tap, she put on a kettle to boil and rinsed out the mugs. Filling the thermos with cocoa and adding a little milk, she placed it into a shopping basket along with the food before making a pot of tea. There was just time to pop to the toilet while it brewed, and to wash her face in cold water. Feeling refreshed, she poured the tea into the mugs and took one through to where Mildred was hammering lengths of wood on the door frame to keep the heavy wooden door from falling.

'There's a hot cup of tea here,' she said. 'Can I give you a hand?'

'Best not to,' Mildred smiled while holding a couple of nails in her mouth. 'Take a look over there.' She nodded out towards the sea.

'Oh my . . . ' Rose said as she spotted five planes getting closer.

'They're not ours. Look like Messerschmitts to me, heading towards Ramsgate. Get yourself back down the shelter. I'll be there with you in a minute or two.'

Rose picked up Mildred's drink and hurried to the kitchen, where she placed the steaming mugs of tea onto a tray. Slinging the shopping basket over her spare arm, she hurried down the garden to the Anderson shelter, thankful her training meant she could carry a laden tray almost anywhere without dropping it.

Shouting to Katie to open the door, she passed through the tray and basket before hurrying inside.

'Any chance I can go to the house and use the loo?' Lily asked before the sound of enemy aircraft silenced her. 'Perhaps not,' she answered herself. 'Where's Mildred?'

'I'm right here,' Mildred answered, jumping down the few steps into the shelter and pulling the door closed behind her. 'Where's that cup of tea?'

Rose handed out the tea and explained to the girls what had happened to the house. 'Mildred has made some repairs to the door, but we'll have to find a builder to fix the windows and put the slates back on the roof.'

'Don't we have to get in touch with the council for help?' Katie asked. 'We've not had to think about this before.'

Mildred finished her tea and wiped her mouth. 'That went down a treat. There's something to be said about being stuck in an air-raid shelter with a group of Nippies. At least they make a decent cup of tea,' she grinned. 'It beats being down those tunnels in Ramsgate with Miss Tibbs wittering away nineteen to the dozen.'

'Wasn't she supposed to be going to stay with her niece in Guildford, away from danger?'

'She refused. Told Flora she'd not be able to sleep nights worrying about everyone at Sea

View. Flora's moved her and Anya downstairs and they are sleeping in the living room, although they both refused the use of the Morrison shelter. Flora must have the patience of a saint when those two start bickering.'

Katie, who had taken it upon herself to keep the candles alight, blew out a match and looked thoughtful. 'I wonder if Henio is safe? It feels as though I know the man, with us all wondering if Anya will ever see her husband again. I wonder if he is anything like we imagine him? I do hope he is safe.'

Rose nodded, thinking not only of her mum and the residents of Sea View but of the brave Royal Air Force staff over at Manston, especially Henio, the Polish pilot they all so wanted to meet. She looked towards Mildred, and even in the dimly lit shelter she could see the older woman was thinking the same.

★　★　★

'I want to go and see how my stepfather is coping,' Lily exclaimed, getting to her feet from where she had been resting on the sofa with her feet up as her friends cleaned up the mess in Captain's Cottage. 'Mum would never forgive me if something happened to him.'

Mildred was aghast. 'After what he's done to you?'

'I still hate the man, but I'd not wish anyone to be suffering after the night we've had. I'd just like to check, if that's all right with you all?'

Mildred nodded. 'But you aren't going alone.'

They had all finally staggered out into the late afternoon sunlight a couple of hours after the all-clear sounded. The air had tasted of dust, and there had been an acrid smell of burning that just didn't seem to clear. The girls had looked about them and agreed they'd been bloody lucky that their house had withstood more than others nearby.

'This house has been standing for a few centuries. It would take more than the Luftwaffe to damage it. The walls are two foot deep in places,' Mildred had said, patting the back wall as if it were a pet dog. 'I'll get as much repaired as I can myself and call in a builder to do the rest. You've not to worry about anything, or that little one is going to arrive red-faced and angry,' she'd told Lily. After this, Lily had slept soundly until she awoke and made her announcement.

'I'd like to go and see how everyone is down at Sea View,' Rose said. 'I can't help but worry about them,' she added, seeing a smile appear on Mildred's dirty face.

'I wonder how the teashops fared? We could all be out of jobs if they took a hit,' Katie said as she dragged a rug out the back door to give it a beating in order to remove the layer of thick dust. 'Wherever did this all come from?'

'The house took a bit of a pounding, and with the broken window and front door knocked off its hinges, debris would have blown in from the other houses,' Mildred explained. 'We'll soon have it spick and span, so don't you go worrying yourselves. As I said before, this could have been worse. We are alive, and that's all that counts right now. As for going through to Ramsgate, I don't know . . . '

'I could check on George at the same time,' Lily suggested. 'It would only take a few minutes. God knows if he even got down the shelter.'

'Knowing your stepfather, he was so drunk he would have slept through the whole day and not heard a thing. As for God, let's leave him out of it, shall we?'

Rose frowned. That was the second time she'd heard Mildred take offence when God was mentioned. Perhaps while others clung to their faith, she'd lost hers. People could be strange at times. 'Couldn't we at least try to see if we can get through to the outskirts of the town? We could walk the rest of the way,' she said, hoping that Mildred would agree.

Lily opened her mouth to say she didn't think she could walk very far. Too long sitting in one place down the shelter had made her legs ache. If she was honest, she'd prefer just to go to bed; but first she needed to put her mind at rest and know the old bastard was all right. She silently cursed her mum for giving her a conscience about someone she shouldn't care about.

Mildred looked between the three girls. 'I'm not going to get any peace until we've been to see that everyone is all right, am I?'

'I can stay here if there isn't much room in your van. It's not as if I have anyone to check up on, is there? I'd probably be in the way,' Katie said sadly. She wished she did have family to care for. The residents of the children's home

352

had been evacuated away from the seaside town for the duration, so she didn't even need to check up on the little ones either. 'Although I am worried about everyone,' she quickly added.

'There's room for you all. Lily will have to sit up front, and you two can climb into the back. You'll end up smelling a bit on the fishy side, but needs must.'

'You could check on the Ramsgate teashop while I look in on everyone at Sea View,' Rose said. 'I'll have to go into Margate later to see how my flat and the tearoom have fared. I do hope we'll be able to open up on Monday, if there isn't another air raid.'

Mildred looked up at the clock on the wall. 'I say we get cracking soon — then we can be back here by sunset, in case there's another raid.'

Lily groaned. 'Not another night down the shelter — please, not that. We've had months with nothing happening, then the bloody Luftwaffe can't keep away.'

'Give me ten minutes to tidy the shelter, then it will be ready for next time it's required,' Rose said, collecting the clean mugs along with a box of candles and matches to take down the garden to the Anderson shelter.

Mildred pulled out a drawer in the sideboard. 'You'd best take this piece of oilcloth to wrap the matches in. It'll stop them getting damp. There should be a piece of linoleum under the stairs. We could put it down on the floor of the shelter, and it would help control the dust,' she said, pulling out the rolled-up piece of faded flooring and following Rose out the back door.

Lily watched the pair of them leave. 'You know, there's something strange about Mildred owning this house and not living here.'

'Perhaps she enjoys the company of the people at Sea View. I'm not sure I'd want to live alone all the time. It must get very lonely,' Katie said. 'At least when I had my room over the chip shop, I could hear people most of the time. I found it reassuring.'

Lily was thoughtful. 'Then she gave the house to us, when she could have sold it and made a bob or two. I wonder if she thinks it's haunted or something?' She shivered and looked about her.

'I don't think so. She seems happy enough spending time here with us,' Katie said, picking up the carpet beater and starting to drag another large rug from the room.

'Then it must be something else, you mark my words.'

16

'Well, I'll be . . . ' Mildred said as she stopped the van and looked up ahead. Their journey had taken some time, as she'd had to weave her way around large potholes in the road. At one point they had stopped to help a woman whose chickens had escaped from her garden. Halfway round Wellington Crescent, Mildred came to a sudden halt.

'What's the problem?' Rose asked from the back of the van.

'We can't get any further forward. There are houses damaged at the far end and the road's a mess. Even to try and get through would mean us getting in the way for the rescue workers and Fire Service. I'm going to back up a bit and find somewhere to leave the van. We'll have to walk the rest of the way. Will you be all right with that, Lily?'

'I'll manage,' Lily said. 'Don't worry about me. I'm more concerned that Sea View isn't far from here, and it could have bomb damage too,' she said, looking ahead at the smoke spiralling from the back of the Georgian houses.

'We will soon know what's going on. Don't any of you start worrying just yet, will you?'

They all called out, 'No,' but the tension in the vehicle could have been cut with a knife.

'I hope you've all got your gas masks with

you?' Katie said, after they'd climbed from the van and straightened their clothing. 'This might be the time we need them,' she added before nodding her approval as her friends slung the masks, packed inside small boxes, over their shoulders.

'If you don't mind, I'm going to walk through to Mum's — I mean George's house. I'll meet you all back at Sea View,' Lily said, turning to walk away down a side street.

'Wait, I'm coming with you,' Katie said, receiving a nod of approval from Mildred and Rose as she hurried to catch up with Lily. She linked arms with her friend as they took a short stroll past a row of Georgian houses that didn't seem to have been touched by the destruction of the past days.

Turning a corner into the narrow road of small terraced houses, they stopped dead. 'Oh my dear God,' Lily screamed, and began to run as fast as her legs would carry her. 'There's nothing left . . .'

Katie grabbed hold of the sleeve of Lily's cardigan, trying to hold her back. 'Careful — it looks as though that part of the wall is going to come down at any minute,' she said, looking to where the front wall of the house had crumbled away, showing each room with hardly a stick of furniture out of place. It reminded her of a doll's house, opened up for all to look inside.

'Why is there no one helping?' Lily screamed, climbing over what had been the front wall.

'Most of them was down the tunnels,' a woman said from further down the road. 'A bloody good job they was too, or they'd all be stone dead if they'd stayed at home.'

Lily looked hopeful. 'Did you see my stepfather, George Jacobs, down there?' she asked, knowing that although the tunnels were like the catacombs of old, with smaller tunnels branching off the major one, neighbours were allocated places and small bunk beds close to each other.

The woman walked closer and peered at Lily. 'You look different to how you used to look when you lived here,' she said, staring at Lily's protruding stomach. ''Ere — are you expecting? Where's your husband? I don't remember any mention of a wedding. Your mum would have invited me if she was still here, God bless her soul,' she said, crossing herself.

'It was a very quick affair,' Lily muttered, not wanting to explain herself to this meddling busybody.

'In the army, is he? Our Daphne's young man was called up before we could arrange an engagement. I see you must have had time for a honeymoon,' she said again, looking at Lily's obvious pregnancy. 'Was it a nice wedding? Let me see your ring.'

Katie held her breath. This would be where the nosy woman found out that Lily wasn't married. If Katie had been able to without the woman seeing, she would have slipped her own wedding band onto her friend's finger.

'Here you are, you nosy old cow,' Lily said, pulling her left hand out of her pocket and waving it into the woman's face. 'Are you satisfied now you can see I'm legal? There's no gossip to be found here, so if you can't tell me where my stepfather is, would you please sod off up your own end of the street?'

'Well, I never. I was only trying to help. Your mother would never have spoken to me like that,' the woman stuttered, not knowing which way to look. 'If you must know, he wasn't down the tunnel. I know that as our Stevie slept on his bunk, seeing as he wasn't using it. He's probably lying drunk somewhere. We all know what he's like, so you don't need to put your airs and graces on in front of me like your mother used to. All of us up this road know she was no better than she ought to be.'

Katie sucked in her breath. Lily's mum had been the salt of the earth. There had never been any gossip about her in all the years Katie had known her.

Lily's face turned bright red, and she took a step closer to the woman. 'Why, you old cow,' she said, swinging her right hand back before punching her squarely on the chin. The woman stood looking puzzled for a few seconds before tottering backwards against a lamppost that was just about standing upright, then sliding down the post onto her backside.

'She'll be out cold for a while. Come on, let's go in and find George.'

'I don't think we should go in there,' Katie said as she watched Lily hitch up her skirt and climb over the pile of rubble that had once formed part of the front wall of the house. Lily didn't take any notice, but started to disappear

358

into the building. Katie looked left and right to make sure no one was watching her before lifting her own skirts and following her friend into what was left of her former home.

★ ★ ★

Rose looked up at the building that had been her home for so many years and where she had been born. She was relieved to see that Sea View was still standing, but it had certainly suffered. The gabled window of the attic was missing and most windows on the second floor had lost their glass. Plaster had come away in places and the beautiful tiled front path was cracked and pitted. Across the grassed area to the front of the guesthouse, she could see a large gap where two similar houses had stood. Her relief turned to sadness as she spotted an ambulance and men taking away a body covered with a blanket. That could so easily have been her mum. She could have died before they'd made their peace, Rose thought to herself.

'Mum, are you in?' she called as she carefully stepped over the cracked pathway and banged on the front door, which swung open on her touch. Treading carefully, she went into the hall, still calling out to Flora.

'Mind how you go, there's no knowing what damage has been done,' Mildred said from close behind her.

'I just want to know that Mum is all right,' she called back as fear gripped her stomach.

'I'm here, love,' Flora said as she appeared at

the end of the hall and hurried to hug Rose and then Mildred. 'We've been so worried about you all. Where are Lily and Katie?'

'They've gone to check up on George. You didn't happen to see him, did you?' Mildred asked.

Flora shook her head, looking concerned. 'No, but then he would go down the tunnels by a different route to us. There's no knowing where he was when the air-raid siren went off.'

'He could be sleeping it off somewhere,' Mildred said, and Rose and Flora agreed. They followed Flora down the few steps at the end of the hall into the kitchen, where they spotted Joyce, Anya and Miss Tibbs preparing a meal. 'There's no knowing with that man, but after what's gone on today it's only right that Lily checks he's not injured. I just hope she's careful. We don't want any harm to come to her or the baby. Now sit yourself down, and help yourself to tea. You look tired out. What's it been like over your way?'

Mildred filled the ladies in on how they had fared at Captain's Cottage and what damage they'd sustained. 'I'll give you a hand patching up here once I've finished this,' she said, tucking into the sardines on toast that had been put in front of her. 'I know a chap that'll sort out the damage, and he won't diddle you.'

'That's very good of you, Mildred, but I'm wondering if we'd do as well to just board the windows over for now. It's likely Hitler will send his bully boys back again tomorrow, and we can't keep patching up Sea View.'

'But what about the bedrooms, Mum?' Rose said, concerned for Flora's income, as she couldn't very well rent out rooms with boarded-over windows.

'I've moved downstairs,' Joyce said. 'There's no need for me to have that big room now that Pearl's been evacuated. Flora's put three beds in the living room, and it's been quite fun mucking in together with Anya and Miss Tibbs. It reminds me of when I went to boarding school,' she grinned.

'Miss Tibbs remind me of my husband. He snores too,' Anya exclaimed, giving the older woman a glare.

'Then swap with me,' Flora said, trying to stop the argument that was bound to start if the women bickered. 'You can move into the dining room and share with Mildred.'

'She snores louder,' Anya answered.

'Oh dear,' was all Flora could think to say.

Rose looked around the large kitchen. 'You could always move out Miss Tibbs' armchair and put Pearl's small single bed in here. I would think it would be warm and cosy on colder nights. That's if you aren't expecting Pearl back anytime soon?' she asked Joyce.

'I'm missing Pearl dreadfully, but she's safe in Tunbridge Wells with my sister and having a wonderful time with her cousin. I was invited to go with her, but I like working at the grocery shop with Mrs Peabody, and it means I can put in extra hours and do some volunteer work. If Pearl should come back, we can always top and tail in my bed — there's plenty of room. I don't want to put anyone out.'

'That's extremely generous of you,' Flora said. 'I must say, I miss young Pearl, as she brightened up the place and was such good company,' she added, looking to where Anya and Miss Tibbs were bickering over who snored and who didn't. 'Now, before we set to and do any more cleaning I say we have a cup of tea and something to eat. We can move that bed at the same time, while there are plenty of willing hands. Miss Tibbs, perhaps you'd like to get started while we move the furniture, and then we will all be down here on the ground floor? I'll sleep much happier knowing no one is upstairs, where the most damage seems to have happened.'

'I should think we'll be spending more and more time in the tunnels if these air raids continue. Do you know, I overheard someone in the shop saying they were going to move lock, stock and barrel into the tunnel as it was safer.'

'I'm not sure the authorities will allow that. Mind you, so many people have been inventive, using curtains and things to partition off a small area for their families. I've heard there are church services as well. Life in Ramsgate seems to be continuing underground just as it did out in the fresh air.'

'Talking of fresh air, I'm going to take those lavender bags I made with me next time we have to go down there,' Miss Tibbs said as she filled the kettle. 'What with the lavvies only curtained off by a piece of sacking and then those men a bit down the tunnel from us not seeming to bother about burping and passing wind, it can get right smelly at times. A few lavender bags just might just do the trick.'

Flora looked at Rose and they both giggled. 'I would think it will take more than a bit of lavender, Miss Tibbs, but no harm in trying. Rose, would you help me collect the blankets for the bed?'

Rose followed her mum, knowing that they would be alone and perhaps it was time to have a word and clear the air. 'Mum, about what we fell out over . . . ' she said as they pulled the blankets and sheet from what had been Pearl's bed.

'We didn't really fall out, dear, did we?'

Rose looked ashamed. 'Well, I got upset after what I found.'

'And I was annoyed that you had pried into my private papers.'

'I'm sorry. I shouldn't have been looking,' she said, biting her lip.

'It's quite understandable. I should have told you the truth about Sea View, and how I came to own it.'

Rose shook a pillowcase and folded it neatly. 'That's what confused me. Dad's name wasn't mentioned, and it was an old document. It named you and me, but I'd have only been a child, going by the date. And why was General Sykes handing it over to us, when I thought he'd just been one of your lodgers? I was upset to see such things, and you never having told me. As for my birth certificate only having your name on it — why would that be?'

★ ★ ★

'Wait for me, Lily, and be careful,' Katie said as she followed her friend into what would have been the living room, if there had been a front wall and more than half a ceiling remaining. What wasn't covered in dust had a layer of soot from where the chimney place had crumbled away from the supporting wall. If the girls had wanted to, they could have poked their heads through the hole in the brickwork and seen into next door.

'Here, I didn't know you had a wedding ring,' Katie added with a laugh. 'That wiped the smile off that nosy woman's face, but I'm not sure you should have thumped her like that.'

Lily waved her hand in the air. 'Good old Woolies. I bought it the other day, thinking I was bound to have problems with some old trout before too long. As for walloping her like I did, well, perhaps it was wrong; but she was asking for it, telling stories about my mum like that. It's a bit of a mess here, isn't it?' she added, seeming more worried about the house than the neighbour.

'Listen — what's that?' Katie said as the sound of a groan came from the back of the house.

'It sounds like George,' Lily said as she pulled an armchair aside and cleared a path to the kitchen. 'Here, give me a hand — this door seems to be stuck.'

Katie put her shoulder to the door and gave it a hefty shove, causing it to groan as it opened halfway. 'It won't go any further, but I think I can squeeze through,' she said as she forced herself through the gap. 'I can see the problem;

364

there's some rubble on the floor. Hang on a minute,' she added, kicking the mess out of the way. Grabbing the door with both hands, she pulled, and it opened enough for Lily to get herself into the kitchen.

'George, where are you?' Lily called as she carefully stepped over the brick rubble. A groan led her to the pantry, where he was lying on the floor of the walk-in stone cupboard.

'Get me some help. I can't move me legs,' he said.

'It looks as though the stone shelf came loose in the air raid and trapped him,' Katie said.

George glared at her. 'Stop with stating the bloody obvious and get me some help,' he growled.

Lily, who was about to lean in to help her stepfather, backed away as a wave of stale beer fumes hit her in the face. Putting her hand over her mouth, she heaved, but managed not to be sick. 'No wonder you weren't down the tunnels. You were blind drunk and probably didn't even hear the siren,' she shouted at. him. 'We ought to leave you here to die,' she said as a wave of anger flooded over her.

'I'll go and get some help,' Katie said. 'There were some soldiers up the road — one of them might just be able to come and give a hand. Don't you go lifting him, not in your condition. You might hurt the baby,' she said sternly before hurrying from the house.

George wiped a hand across his eyes, trying to clear a layer of dust. 'So you've got yourself in the club, have you? You always did have the morals of an alley cat.'

'Just shut up,' Lily spat back at him. 'Once Katie brings some help, I'm off, and I don't ever want to see your ugly face ever again. I only came as Mum would have wanted me to make sure you were all right. I owe you nothing after the way you've treated me.'

'I gave you a good home,' he muttered, wincing as pain shot through him. 'When I took on your mother and put a roof over her head, I never expected to be landed with a young kid as well. She kept that quiet.'

Lily was livid. She felt the blood pump through her head as she digested his words. 'You put a roof over our heads? I think you'll find Mum was already renting this place and putting food on the table. What she did wrong was to fall in love with you and become blind to what you was up to,' she shouted, kicking the stone slab lying over his legs, causing him to scream in pain. 'She paid for your booze, and your gambling, and got nothing in return — not even another child, which she always wanted. I've lost count of the number of times she'd promised me a baby brother or sister when I was growing up.'

'So you've had to provide a kid for yourself, have you? What poor sucker got tied up with you?' he snarled back, wiping a drop of blood from his nose. It left a pale red streak across his dust-covered face.

Lily couldn't believe what she was hearing. 'But this is yours. Don't you remember . . . ?'

George laughed loudly, prompting a fit of coughing. 'Me put you in the club?' he said, laughing again. 'Chance would be a fine thing. You picked the wrong mug, darling. I've been firing blanks since I was injured in the last war. If everything worked as it should, your mother would have had a dozen or more — and they'd have a few brothers and sisters wandering about this town with different mothers,' he chuckled. 'So don't you go blaming that on me,' he added, his voice growing weaker before he rallied with a little more strength. 'Not through want of trying though, eh?'

Lily couldn't believe what she was hearing. 'You mean all those years of Mum waiting for her monthlies and thinking there was something wrong with her, and you knew this all along? That was the one thing she wanted, and you couldn't even tell her the truth, you filthy piece of shit,' she screamed, kicking at his head until her feet grew numb and he stopped whimpering. 'You bloody bastard,' she spat out as she staggered back against the wall, panting. It seemed as if everything around her started to move, and she felt as if she might be about to faint. Grabbing at the damaged edge of the wall, she felt it shift in her hand — and then it crashed down around her, bringing down lath and plaster from the ceiling along with some large planks of wood. 'Not now,' Lily cried out, falling alongside George as everything went black.

'It's just up here,' Katie called out to the group of soldiers who had stopped clearing a collapsed wall from the road to help her. 'That house right there,' she said, stopping to catch her breath. As they hurried past her, there was a crash of falling masonry from inside.

'Oh no — Lily!' Katie cried.

'It's Katie, isn't it?' one of the soldiers asked. She frowned. 'Yes, but . . . '

'I'm Captain Hargreaves . . . Ben,' he added, as she looked puzzled. 'We met at a dance when you were with Rose.'

'I'm sorry, I didn't recognize you in the overalls,' she said, her focus still on the front of Lily's building. 'You all looked the same.'

'Guv, there's two of 'em in here. One's a goner and the other, well, she's in a bad way.'

'That's Lily. Please — you've got to help her. She's expecting a baby,' Katie explained, not knowing what to do.

'We will do all we can,' he reassured her. 'Don't you live not far from here?'

'Not anymore — we moved to Broadstairs. We're here to see if Flora — Rose's mum — is all right after the bashing the town's taken today. Lily wanted to check on her stepfather. That's him in there with her.'

Ben nodded as he listened to what Katie had to say. 'It might be a good idea for you to go to Flora's house and tell them what has happened. Lily may want people she knows to be with her.' And I don't want you to see anything that will upset you, he thought to himself.

'Yes, I'll go this instant.' Katie turned and started to run as fast as she could. It felt an age before she spotted Sea View and put a spurt on for the last few yards. As she banged loudly on the door, her legs gave way, and she sank to her knees on the step as the door opened. 'Please, you've got to come with me. It's Lily. I think she's dying.'

Mildred shouted to the other women for help as she lifted Katie to her feet and assisted her into the front room, laying her on Miss Tibbs' bed. 'Calm down, love, and tell me slowly what has happened,' she said as Rose appeared with a glass of water. Katie took a sip, and did her best to breathe slowly until she was able to speak.

'The army are helping, and I was told to come and tell you all as quickly as I could,' she added, after explaining what had occurred since they'd left Mildred and Rose. 'I thought she was all right, because I could hear her shouting at George as I left to find help for him. Something terrible must have happened to her. What if she's lost the baby?' Katie added, looking fearfully at the worried faces of her friends.

17

For Rose, what followed was a nightmare. They reached the remains of Lily's old home just as a stretcher was being loaded into the back of an army lorry. She froze, numbed by the horror of the scene, and it was only as someone shouted, 'We've found her,' that she realized the body under the blanket was not that of her dear friend Lily. She recognized the white-faced Lily as the ambulance crew, along with concerned soldiers, carried her away from the rubble and gently placed her into the waiting ambulance.

'This war's a bastard,' an older soldier said to no one in particular as he stood watching the ambulance head away.

'Where will they take her?' Rose asked. 'She's my friend,' she explained to the soldier, as he gave her a look that implied she was another nosy neighbour. He'd already had to see off one woman with a bloody nose wanting to know the ins and outs of the situation.

'I've no idea, love, but I'll find out for you. It might be a good idea if you let her husband know what's happened.'

'She doesn't have a husband, and her only family was her stepfather — who you brought out just before her. We, her friends, are all she has now,' Rose said as her eyes started to fill with tears. 'We need to be with her in case she wakes up.'

The soldier looked at the small group of women standing close by, the youngest woman sobbing on the shoulder of an elderly woman, while two middle-aged women hung on to each other, looking upset. Another woman he'd seen talking to his captain had just marched off at some speed, as if she had some kind of plan hatching. 'I'll go and find out,' he said as he patted her arm in a fatherly manner. No husband, eh? he thought to himself as he went over to his captain, who had gone into that house with his men, not thinking of his own safety. He thought of his own daughter safely at home and gave a shudder, hoping that she never found herself with child and without a man to stand by her.

'Mildred's gone to fetch the van,' Joyce said as she scrubbed her eyes with a balled up-handkerchief. 'She seems to know where they are taking Lily. I just hope we're in time to . . . ' She couldn't speak any more.

Rose nodded, unable to speak, as if she'd done so she knew it would be to talk about her friend being close to death — and most likely the baby, who they'd all looked forward to welcoming into their close-knit group, losing its life before it had taken one breath.

Flora looked at Rose, and they could see each other's thoughts. No words were needed. 'I'll see to Miss Tibbs,' she said, and went to help the old lady console Katie.

'I'm so grateful my Pearl is away from here and out of danger,' Joyce gulped. 'She wrote to me to say she was knitting a pair of bootees for Lily's child, and said it would be like having a baby brother or sister. I don't know how she is going to take the news . . . ' she said, before breaking into fresh tears.

'No one has died yet,' Rose said sharply. 'Lily wouldn't want us standing here talking about her as if she were dead. We need to be with her,' she added, looking to see where the soldier had gone. There was no sign of Mildred, either. Why was everything happening so slowly?

'Miss, the Captain said I could take you to the 'ospital in his car. He's tied up at the minute, but sends his regards.'

'That's very kind of him,' Rose said as she hurried to tell the others.

'I'll wait for Mildred,' Flora said when she was given the news. 'You go with the others, and let's hope we are there in time,' she added, looking sad. 'I've never taken to that George Jacobs. That's why I'm none too upset about him meeting his maker like he has.'

Rose felt the same, and not knowing what to say, she hugged her mother tightly. 'I'll see you at the hospital,' she said before hurrying to join the others, who'd by now climbed into the army vehicle. As they sped up the road they passed Mildred in her van, and Rose breathed a sigh of relief that her mum would soon be joining them. If only they'd had time to talk properly before Katie had come rushing back, and things were as they used to be before she opened that attaché case and found her childhood had been a lie. She would need to know the whole story before she could consider forgiving her mum for not sharing her secrets.

She leant back in the seat and tried to relax, knowing it would be a long day as they waited and prayed for Lily and her unborn child. Taking deep breaths and trying to ignore her nagging thoughts, she scanned the interior of the army vehicle. With Miss Tibbs, Katie and Joyce in the back, it was getting warm. She reached for the handle to open the window and noticed a card stuck to the dashboard showing the details of the army unit and the registered user. Her heart fluttered as she saw the name: Captain Benjamin Hargreaves.

Why was this man forever turning up in her life? With thousands of army personnel on Thanet, why was it that Ben was the one to keep crossing her path? Her life was more than complicated enough, with poor Lily at death's door and her mother having secrets. She didn't need the man she had fallen in love with, who had a wife and children, coming back into the picture. At that moment she could have stopped the car and run as fast as her legs would carry her, so she could leave her worries and fears far behind.

'If you head through those doors, you'll find out where your friend has been taken,' the soldier said. With grateful thanks ringing in his ears, he headed off, honking the horn of the vehicle as it sped out of the hospital grounds just as Mildred entered. Spotting her friends, she waved for them to wait for her.

'Look who I found,' she said as Anya climbed out of the back of the van, helped by Flora as the Polish woman moaned about the smell of fish in the vehicle.

Mildred ignored her and looked at the worried faces of her friends. 'Right, let's go and find out what's happening, shall we?' she said as she took charge of the worried group of women. Heading down a long passageway, she stopped by a desk where a nurse sat writing notes. 'Excuse me, miss; we want to know about our friend Lily Douglas. She was brought in a few minutes ago. She's injured and is expecting a baby,' Mildred added, hoping it would help the nurse to find her.

'If you'll all take a seat, I'll find someone who can help,' the nurse said, disappearing behind two heavy swinging doors.

The women sat on a row of seats and waited. No one spoke as they all stared ahead at the green tiles on the lower portion of the wall in front of them. The top half of the wall was painted cream and upon it were pinned signs about two visitors per bed, and only relatives being allowed on the wards. Rose was wondering what happened in the case of people like Lily, who had no living relatives, when the nurse appeared, followed by a doctor in a white coat.

'Are you all here for Lily Douglas?' he asked, looking along the line of waiting women.

A resounding 'yes' answered his question, after which Flora said, 'I'm her adopted mother and these are her two adopted sisters,' pointing towards Rose and Katie.

The doctor smiled, looking at the poster the women had been eyeing warily. 'I suppose you are the adopted grandmother and assorted adopted aunts?'

'I am nothing to her,' Anya said. 'I am from Poland and just live in Mrs Neville's house. I had no knowledge of them all being related,' she said, looking confused. 'But, I will not leave, so tell us what you have to say so we know if she is dead or alive if you please.'

'Anya is our very good friend and we all work together . . . ' Rose started to explain until Anya interrupted.

'For Mr Joe Lyons. They are all Nippies but I am a Sally. I sell the bread and cakes.'

'I'm Dr Gregson, and having examined Mrs Douglas . . . '

'It is Miss Douglas. She wears the wedding ring so people do not think she is the unmarried mother we all look down on . . . ' Anya explained.

'I'm sorry,' Rose said, embarrassed. 'Mrs Polinski's turn of phrase can be a little blunt at times. Lily is a good woman, so please don't be shocked by her lack of husband.'

Dr Gregson gave her a reassuring smile. 'Believe me, I'm not concerned by your friend's marital status. I'm more worried about her health, and that of her child at this moment in time.'

'Is she that ill?' Rose asked.

'She is very poorly, and we need to operate on her broken leg and arm,' the doctor started to explain. 'They were not straightforward breaks.'

'Surely that could hurt the baby?' Flora said, putting her arm around Rose, who stood looking shocked and not taking in what the doctor was saying.

'It might. Miss Douglas is a strong, healthy

375

woman and will survive, but we are not so sure about the baby.'

'Oh, the poor little mite.' Miss Tibbs started to cry.

'Can you not do something to save the baby?' Flora asked, as Katie tried to soothe Miss Tibbs.

'We can perform a caesarean to deliver the baby before we operate on Miss Douglas. I can't say this is something I've done before, but it should be straightforward. Individually the two operations are often successful, but it is whether Miss Douglas's body can cope with both at the same time.'

Flora knew that it would be down to her to make the decision, as Rose and Katie seemed too upset. She looked to Mildred, as she respected the woman's advice. 'What do you think, Mildred?'

'Lily has come to love the child she is carrying. If we were to ask the doctor to just repair her broken bones and let the baby take a chance on surviving the anaesthetic — and it died — would she forgive us?'

'No, I don't feel she would,' Flora said.

'Then it makes sense for the child to be delivered, followed by Lily's broken bones being fixed. Tell me, Doctor, how long would this operation take?'

Dr Gregson thought carefully. 'The team who will deliver the child and the team who will sort out your friend's injuries are different people. It is imperative the baby is delivered as quickly as possible. Depending on what they find when they start to work on Miss Douglas, it could be several hours after the baby is born before the other operation is finished. I suggest we say three hours before you can expect any news,' he said, looking at the row of women as they took in his words.

'Thank you,' Mildred said. 'Do we have to sign anything?'

'It is usual for the next of kin to sign a consent form.'

'Her stepfather was killed when Lily was injured. As I said before, I feel I'm her next of kin,' Flora said. 'These are her two friends from childhood. They are like sisters. It is all we can offer,' she said with pleading eyes.

'You sign the forms, Mum,' Rose said. 'Lily would want that.'

The doctor nodded. He was far too busy to worry about the intricacies of next of kin. 'I'll have the paperwork prepared and notify the operating teams. I suggest just a couple of you stay, as it will be a long night.'

'What if there is another air raid?' Katie asked.

'We have two underground operating theatres as well as shelters, so don't fear for your friend on that count. Now, if you'll excuse me . . . '

'What a nice man,' Miss Tibbs said as they watched him leave. 'I'm not sure I shall wait here for long, as the seats are rather uncomfortable,' she added, wriggling on the wooden bench to get her point across to the others.

'I suggest Miss Tibbs goes back to Sea View while just a couple of us stay and wait for news,' Flora said. 'Rose and Katie, will you stay?'

Rose looked up at the large round clock on the

wall of the waiting room. 'I should really go in to work. I have no idea of the state of the teashop. However, Lily is more important than a teashop.'

Katie got to her feet. 'I should make an appearance too, if only to see whether we have a shop left. I don't like the thought of no one being here, though.'

Flora clapped her hands together as if making a decision. 'The pair of you go to your teashops, then come back here when you can. I'm going nowhere. Now be off with you. Katie, you should go back to Sea View first as there is a letter for you from Jack. I put it inside my copper kettle on the dresser for safe-keeping. You can stop looking so worried. He wrote to me too, and may well be home on leave before too long,' she said with a smile on her face for the young girl.

'I'll sit with you — it will help pass the time with someone to talk to,' Joyce said.

'I must also go to work, or Joe Lyons will not be pleased with me either,' Anya said. 'So I accompany you,' she said to Rose.

'Then I'll drive you over to Margate. I can pop back to Captain's Cottage and get on with a few repairs. What say I come down to the teashop in two hours and bring you back here to see what's happening?' Mildred offered to Rose.

'That sounds like a plan,' Rose said, standing up and beckoning to Anya to follow. 'Will you walk Miss Tibbs back to Sea View before you go to work?' she asked Katie.

'I'll do that and read my Jack's letter at the same time,' she said, her eyes now shining with happiness. If you see Lily, will you give her my love?' she asked, biting her lip. 'I just can't bear to think of what she has to go through this afternoon. And that poor baby . . . '

'Now don't you start fretting,' Miss Tibbs scolded as she took her arm. 'We will take a brisk walk back to Sea View, and you can have a hot drink before you go to work. Remember to let me know what is happening.' She glared at the two women who were to remain at the hospital. 'No secrets, mind you!'

'Could you not drop these two close to the house? It will be quite a walk,' Flora asked Mildred.

'I was just about to suggest the same. I'll make sure we all know what is going on with Lily, even if it means driving back and forth for as long as is needed. I'll find the fuel for the van by hook or by crook. Come along, ladies,' she instructed, shepherding those that were leaving out of the room.

Rose held back for a moment to look at Flora. 'Mum . . . ' was all she could say, searching Flora's face for some sign that she knew how Rose felt.

'I'll ask to see Lily before she goes to theatre and tell her you send your love,' Flora said, reaching out to squeeze her hand. 'If you get the chance, please thank that young man of yours and his men for all their help in pulling our Lily out of that building. Katie told me he was there.'

'Young man — you mean Ben? Mum, he is nothing to me. He's been nothing since I found out he was married and had a family,' she said, looking wretched. 'I saw them together when he was injured,' she said, explaining quickly about seeing Ben at Dreamland.

Flora was shocked. 'He seemed such a nice young man. He still does,' she faltered. 'But let's forget about that for now and concentrate on what's going on through that door. There's plenty of time for other things later. I do feel we need to talk, don't you?'

Rose nodded, her head too full of emotion to say much more. With her eyes blurred with tears, she hurried away and through the hospital corridors, not seeing the man who was coming in the main entrance until she ran into him and started to apologize. 'I'm so sorry ... Oh — Ben.'

'Rose — I need to speak with you,' Ben said, reaching out to take her arm.

'I'm sorry, Ben, I have nothing to say to you. Please don't touch me. I need to go,' she said, snatching her arm away and hurrying to catch up with her friends.

Ben watched as Rose ran away. He felt as though she was running from his life, and had no idea why. He racked his brain for something he'd missed, but couldn't think beyond their few days together in London before he'd left for France. He'd written three letters declaring his love for her, but she hadn't responded. There had been many times after that when he'd picked up a pen to write again, and then put it down again. What was the point, when she never replied?

He walked on, deep in thought. He wanted to see how the young woman was faring who they'd dug out from the rubble of the house. Regardless of his feelings for Rose, he still had to do his job. He found the waiting room and took a seat, knowing staff were busy after a day of air raids and would come to his assistance when they were able. Deep in thought, he took no notice of his surroundings.

'It's Ben, isn't it — Captain Ben Hargreaves?' a voice asked from across the room.

Looking up, he recognized the woman as Rose's mother. 'Hello, Mrs Neville,' he said politely. 'I take it you are here because of Lily Douglas?'

'Yes, and this is my friend Joyce,' she indicated to the woman sitting close by. 'We are waiting for news, as Lily is going down for an operation on her arm and leg. They are going to deliver her baby as well. It's most worrying. The poor girl's had a terrible time, and she's not out of the woods yet.'

'The child is an added complication,' Ben murmured as he moved to sit closer to Flora so they could talk.

'Children are a problem all their lives. But then, you'd know that, wouldn't you?' she said pointedly.

Ben frowned. What was Flora getting at? 'I wondered if you could tell me why Rose is acting as she is. I thought we had an understanding — but since I came back from France, she has changed and won't speak to me.'

Flora looked at him and shook her head. 'Would it have something to do with your wife and children, by any chance?'

'But my wife is dead,' he said.

381

'Oh, my poor boy,' Flora interrupted, placing a hand on his arm in sympathy. Whatever had happened between Ben and her daughter, she was shocked to learn he had been recently widowed. 'Was it an air raid — did your children survive?'

Ben was confused. 'No — my wife died in childbirth, years ago.'

'But Rose saw her with your children when you came back injured from Dunkirk. You were in Dreamland at the time. This is so confusing; I just don't understand.'

'I think I'll see if I can conjure up a cup of tea,' Joyce said, not wishing to eavesdrop on what was becoming a private conversation.

'I wrote to Rose after our few days together in London, telling her about my past life, that I'd been married and had children. Knowing I had fallen in love with her, I wanted to give her time to think about what she would be letting herself in for if we were to marry. I thought that when she didn't reply, she had decided there was no future for us. But even so, I felt it wouldn't be like Rose not to at least reply to me. I knew her that well, at least. After sending three letters without an answer, though, I stopped writing . . . ' he finished, looking sad.

'From the little Rose has told me, she never received a letter from you. All she has is the memory of seeing you with two children and a woman she thought was their mother, in Dreamland.'

Ben slapped his hand on his forehead. 'What a bloody mess! If only she'd received my letters.

The first one explained my past life. I have nothing to hide.' He looked Flora in the eye. 'I truly love your daughter, and I want to be with her for the rest of my life. Do you believe me?'

Flora looked at the distress on his face and knew Ben was telling the truth. 'Why not make yourself comfortable and tell me everything — then I'll see what I can do to help you.'

Ben did as he was told. 'I was married at a very young age to my childhood sweetheart. We had two daughters, but the second birth was tough on Mary, and she died not long afterwards from a weak heart. Please — no sympathy,' Ben said, as Flora started to speak. 'I found out not long before our second child was born that my wife had not been faithful to me. It was the pregnancy that caused her death; however, I would never turn away a child, as her lover did when he found out he was to be a father. To him, it had been a meaningless liaison. The child should not be blamed for what happened; I love her as much as if she were my own. I just hope that Rose understands? The woman she saw would have been my sister, Ruth. She lives near Canterbury and the children are with her. We thought it best they were evacuated to the countryside.'

'Many men would turn a child away, while many others would support the ones they love even if they were not free to marry. I've learnt to my cost that keeping a secret is not good. It has caused a division between my daughter and me that I'm afraid may never be healed. However, my Rose is an understanding woman — and I know she has deep feelings for you. I would suggest biding your time, but in this war who is to know whether we have that precious thing called time?'

Ben looked crestfallen. 'Rose won't talk to me; believe me, I've tried. I never thought for one moment that my letters had never arrived, but that's the price we pay in wartime. With my injury healed, I doubt I'll be in the area for much longer. I just wish I could speak to her properly — even if only to hear that she no longer wishes to know me.'

Flora pondered what Ben had told her. 'My daughter can be headstrong. Would you be able to come back in a couple of hours? Rose will be returning to see Lily once she has been to the Margate teashop. Now is not a good time to look for her there — she's preoccupied about Lily, and will also have her work to do. Once we know the outcome with Lily and the baby, though, she might just be in a better frame of mind to listen to you.'

Ben took Flora's hand and shook it. 'Thank you, I'll do that,' he said as he bid her farewell.

Flora watched him leave, hoping fervently that her daughter would also listen to what she had to say. So much depended on Rose listening to her loved ones and making the right decisions.

★ ★ ★

'I spotted you talking to your young man as you left the hospital,' Mildred said as Rose climbed into the seat beside her after they'd dropped off

Miss Tibbs and Katie at Sea View. 'Do I take it you are stepping out with him once more?'

'He's not my young man. If you want to know, he has a wife and children,' Rose said, staring straight ahead as Mildred drove towards Margate. They had to avoid roads that were shut off, as firefighters and the army worked on bomb-damaged roads and buildings.

Mildred shook her head in disbelief. 'He doesn't seem to be the kind of man to chase after women when he has a wife already. Are you sure?'

'My eyes did not deceive me. I saw her, and his two daughters.'

Mildred braked hard and swore loudly as an army lorry shot out of a side road. 'That's hard to believe,' she said. 'Perhaps if you listened to what he has to say it would at least clear the air, and you wouldn't appear to be so upset. From what I could see, he didn't seem to be in a happy frame of mind either. And come to that, you still need to clear the air with your mother as well.'

'She is like bear with sore head,' Anya grumbled from where she sat in the back of the van. 'Whereas I smell like a fish. Why do you not clean out this van, Mildred?' she asked.

'What's the point? It would soon smell just as bad,' Mildred grinned. They all liked Anya and her funny ways.

'As long as Miss Neville does not mind her Sally smelling like fish, then I am happy,' Anya called back, grabbing the side of the van to support herself as the van went over a hole in the road.

'Mum and I will talk properly as soon as we

get the chance,' said Rose wearily. 'But as for Ben, he is part of my past, and I'll not go back there again.' A dull pang of regret struck her heart as she spoke.

'Thank you for the lift,' Anya said, as Mildred helped her from the back of the van. 'Do not worry about collecting me from work this evening. You have much to do helping those who are the friends of Lily. I will find my own way back to Sea View by bus.'

'Don't be daft, woman, there's not likely to be a bus that can get through this evening. Besides, Flora would have my guts for garters if she didn't know all her friends were safe where they should be. I'll take you back to Ramsgate when I collect Rose. I'm sure, under the circumstances, Miss Neville will allow one of her staff members to leave early,' Mildred said, using the name that Anya preferred to use at work when addressing Rose.

'Miss Neville is fine with that,' Rose smiled before kissing Mildred's cheek. 'What would we do without you, Mildred?'

Mildred gave a big grin and sounded the van horn loudly as she drove away.

'That woman is like big child,' Anya huffed as they entered the teashop. 'But I like her very much.'

'Oh Miss Neville, thank goodness you're here!' One of the Nippies rushed up to Rose as she crossed the floor of the teashop, stopping to speak with diners she recognized. 'We've been so worried about Lily. We heard she'd been hit by a bomb . . . please tell us she hasn't died.'

Rose, who was used to news travelling fast in the small town, found a small lump forming in her throat at this evidence that despite the shame usually associated with Lily's situation, people really did care for her. In the few months Lily had worked at the Margate branch, she had become a firm favourite with staff and customers. 'No, Jennie, Lily is still very much with us, but as she requires an operation to repair her broken limbs, they are going to deliver the baby early. Perhaps you would let your fellow Nippies know and ask them to keep her in their prayers. I promise to let everyone know as soon as we are told more,' she said with a reassuring smile.

Entering the office, she closed the door behind her and leant against the wall. It was going to be hard holding herself together while wondering what was happening with her dear friend.

'Miss Neville?' her assistant said as she tapped on the door and entered carrying a tray.

'Oh Phoebe, thank you so much for opening up the teashop and holding the fort,' Rose said. 'I don't know what I'd have done without you today.'

The Nippy smiled. 'At least we've survived the air raid — and as we've only been open a few hours since the all-clear, there's not much that has happened to cause problems. I've just heard about Lily, and I hope you don't mind, but I've said a little prayer for her.'

'That's very kind of you, Phoebe. She could do with as many prayers as possible, as could her baby,' Rose said as Phoebe passed her a cup of tea. 'Now, what has happened here? Has today's delivery got though?'

'Yes — and we've taken Ramsgate's delivery as well, as the van couldn't reach them. With us opening late this evening, and so many people wanting to get out and stretch their legs after spending hours in their-air raid shelters, we'll soon use up the food. That's if the Luftwaffe aren't planning another visit. Tell me, was it bad in Ramsgate?'

'Pretty awful, but thank goodness for the tunnels under the town where many of the locals could take shelter. Lily's stepfather died in his house, as he never took refuge when the sirens went off. Lily was injured when she went to find him.'

'My goodness — it doesn't bear thinking about,' Phoebe said, shaking her head. 'Something strange happened here an hour ago. One of the Nippies came to find me to say she thought the Germans had invaded and were asking after Anya.'

'Oh no, not that again,' Rose sighed. It used to be funny, but at the moment she couldn't laugh at the joke. 'I thought people were used to our Anya and her being Polish. But who was the man?'

'Joan said he was a Polish airman — but of course some of the younger Nippies didn't believe that, and were checking their gas masks were to hand. At least it was an opportunity to remind them they should all be wearing their masks on the back of their uniforms, attached to their belts.'

Rose nodded her agreement. But deep inside, a glimmer of hope had begun to form.

18

Anya was on her hands and knees, sweeping crumbs from the floor behind the counter. 'Why these other Sallys cannot clean up after themselves, I don't know,' she grumbled. 'I smell of fish and have hole in my stockings from kneeling, and now there will be vermin to contend with. I sometimes think my life was better when I was fleeing from Adolf Hitler. I am nothing but the skivvy around here,' she muttered to herself.

'Excuse me, love, there's a queue here waiting to be served. I'd love to put a bit of food in front of my old man before the air-raid sirens go off again, if it's all the same to you. This man in front of me has been waiting for ages to be served.'

'You English think I am at your becking and calling all the time. Why you not wait for a while? Unless you want rodents running around your feet if I don't sweep away this mess,' she huffed, brushing her hair away from her face with one hand as she stood up while straightening her skirt with the other.

'Please may I have some babka?' a gentle male voice requested.

Anya turned with a scowl on her face. 'You foolish man, what makes you think Joe Lyons would sell such things?' she said before bursting into tears, rushing out from behind her counter and throwing herself into his arms.

'Oh my beautiful Anya, I have missed you so much,' he said, covering her face with kisses.

'I thought you were lost to me,' she whispered. 'Who would want a simple Polish girl when you have the English roses to choose from?'

'You are the most beautiful woman in the world to me, my Anya. We must never be parted again,' he said, kissing her lips.

'Your English is much better, Henio,' she whispered when she could speak. 'How did you find me?'

'A kindly policeman spoke to my commanding officer, and a lady called Flora Neville wrote to me. I went to her house, but she was not there. An old lady told me where I could find you — and here I am,' he said, swinging her round before kissing her soundly.

'Some of us only want a loaf of bread, not a bloody song and dance,' the lady in the queue complained, while others cheered.

'Anya, take the rest of the day off,' Rose said as she joined the couple. 'I'll get someone to take over your duties. You must be Henio,' she smiled, holding out her hand. 'You have no idea how pleased I am to see you.' The man stood as tall as Anya and his hair, as dark as hers, held flecks of steel grey even though he could only be in his early thirties.

'Miss Neville is the manageress, and one of the good friends I have made since coming to this country. Come, I take you back to Sea View for the cuppa. We drink nothing else. I have become very English. I can do the hokey-cokey, and I like Winston Churchill. Come, husband, we have much catching up to do,' Anya said, as one of the Nippies handed her her coat and bag. She and Henio left the teashop, followed by cheers and claps from those who knew her.

'At last, some happy news,' Rose said with a huge grin on her face as she stepped behind the counter to serve the waiting customers.

The time shot by in the teashop as Rose tried to do her own work and also help out her staff. They were two people short, what with Anya's unexpected departure and poor Lily having her operation. Rose only wished that she too could leave the teashop and rush to Lily's side. Every minute, she found herself praying for her friend's survival. Whatever work she was doing, Rose's eyes kept going to her wristwatch as she counted the minutes and wondered what was happening at the hospital. She was deep in thought when her office door burst open and Tom White staggered in, his suit covered in dust and a small cut on his cheek. 'Mr White — whatever has happened to you?' she asked, trying not to laugh as he collapsed into a chair, sighing deeply.

'I was very nearly killed!' he exclaimed. 'Get a Nippy to bring me a drink and something to clean up my suit.'

'Was it the air raid?' she asked, starting to stand up to help him.

He gave her a glare. 'No. I was attacked by the husband of one of the Nippies in the road outside. He accused me of carrying on with his wife.'

Rose sat back down and folded her hands in

front of her on the desk. 'And have you?'

'She didn't tell me she was married. I do believe I will have a black eye,' he said, as he gently touched his cheek and winced. 'Perhaps the Nippy could get a cold cloth for it? Well, hurry up and call someone before I start to bruise.'

Rose gave a harsh laugh. 'Why not go to the staffroom and sort yourself out? I have work to do here, and you are holding me up. My friend Lily is in hospital and I need to be with her. I don't wish you to hold me up any longer than necessary. Oh, and stop bothering members of my staff. They are not your playthings. I have your number, Mr White, so watch your step.'

Tom White got to his feet and glared at Rose, but kept quiet as he left.

When Mildred appeared in the teashop, Rose ushered her into the office and ordered sandwiches and tea.

'You need to have something inside you, with all the running about you are doing for all of us,' Rose told her sternly when Mildred tried to refuse.

'I grabbed a bite when I popped back to Sea View for a wash and to change my clothes. It doesn't do for someone to be wandering about the hospital in old overalls and a sou'wester,' Mildred said, looking embarrassed to be seen in a tweed skirt, knitted jumper, lisle stockings and stout shoes. 'I also met Henio. What a delightful chap, and such a happy ever after — just like those daft films you like to go and see at the pictures.'

Rose didn't like to say that they'd all spotted

Mildred in the stalls on numerous occasions, sniffing into a large white handkerchief. It was a secret they'd keep until such times that she agreed to go with them to see a weepie. 'We could all do with a happy ever after at times. I'm hoping Lily gets her happy ending after what she's gone through today. How about you, Mildred?'

The older woman shrugged her shoulders. 'I'm happier than I've been in a long time. Just to see you girls making use of Captain's Cottage. It pleases me a lot to see it being turned into a home.'

'You've never said why you don't want to live there yourself. Did something happen there to make you unhappy?' Rose asked, as a Nippy brought their tray in and left it on the desk.

'It was a long time ago. I'm not one to rake over old times — but perhaps if I tell you, you'll understand a little more about me. But it may shock you.'

'I feel I know you very well, Mildred. Nothing would shock me about you.'

Mildred took a gulp of tea and placed her cup back on the saucer. 'There is more to what I started to tell you about my earlier life after my fiancé died. I returned to live with my father at Captain's Cottage and to recuperate, but he kept introducing me to young men. I wasn't interested, as I was still grieving for the life I had lost. The one thing we shared was a love for the sea, and I managed to convince him to let me join him on the fishing boat. In a way, that was the only time we got on well together. He was thinking of retiring, and I was to have the boat put into my name.'

'So that's how you got to have your own fishing boat. How exciting; and to be able to carry on your father's business,' Rose said, before noticing the troubled look on Mildred's face.

'It didn't become mine until he died,' she said. 'I told him something that shocked him so much, he had a seizure at Captain's Cottage. He died less than a month later.'

'Oh, no. The poor man — and poor you, for going through that after all that had happened in your life.'

Mildred shook her head. 'No, I told him that I had a lady friend and was going to move in with her. He took off his leather belt and beat me relentlessly, and to within an inch of my life. The names he called me are unrepeatable. I took the beating and just looked him in the eye. It was then he collapsed,' she said, wiping her eyes with one of the familiar large white handkerchiefs she always carried. 'Until recently I couldn't enter Captain's Cottage without seeing my father with his hateful expression, raising his belt to me. I still carry the scars.' She put her hand to her heart.

Rose felt the tears running down her cheeks and made no attempt to wipe them away. 'At least you had your friend,' she said gently. 'She must have helped console you?'

'No. It is my biggest regret that I turned my back on the one person who could have brought love into my life. That is why I cannot stand by and see you fall out with your mother, and why I think you should listen to what Ben has to say.

Grasp love and happiness while you can, or you will regret it for the rest of your life, Rose.'

'I will,' Rose promised before wiping her eyes and leaving her seat to give this wonderfully generous woman the biggest hug she could. Did it matter that her friend had found love with another woman, if only for a short time? 'Don't forget we all love you, Mildred. You are part of our family now, so please, don't ever feel you are alone.'

*   *   *

Rose entered the hospital waiting room with trepidation. 'Has there been any word yet?' she asked her mother.

'Not a word. If it wasn't for Joyce finding somewhere to get us a cup of tea, we'd not have left this room since you were all here. I'm almost ready to hammer on that door and ask what's going on,' she sighed. 'It's long past three hours now.'

Rose dug into a shopping bag she'd brought with her and pulled out a box full of sandwiches. 'Here, help yourselves. Mildred and I had ours before we left the teashop. I have some bits and pieces of broken cake and biscuits and there's a flask of cocoa. Oh, and a few sausage rolls. We have an excess of them, as the delivery couldn't get through to the Ramsgate teashop. How did you get on, Katie?'

'Oh Rose, I don't think we will be opening for a few days. The place is a mess. No one in their right mind will be going in there for a meal until they've mended the broken windows and cleared up all the muck and dust,' Katie said.

'So that's why you'll be coming to work for me from tomorrow. I had Mrs Burgess from Cadby Hall on the telephone just before we left. I assured her we could take on every available Nippy from the Ramsgate teashop — although a few would have to cover Sally duties, as we are one short at the moment. I particularly asked for you.'

Katie grinned. 'Thank you. It will be just like old times.' Her face dropped. 'Or it would be if Lily was with us.'

Mildred looked at their sad faces and made a decision. 'I'm going to find out what's happening,' she declared, and barged through the doors marked 'private'.

They held their collective breath and waited for someone to send Mildred back through the doors with a flea in her ear, but nothing happened.

'They've probably kicked her out the main entrance,' Miss Tibbs said with just a hint of glee in her voice.

'I doubt it very much, as she'd come back to let us know. She looked quite impressive in her proper clothes. I'd not want to cross Miss Mildred Dalrymple,' Flora said.

They all jumped as the door to the outside passage opened and then relaxed as Anya walked in, followed by Henio. 'Why you all look at me like that?' she demanded. 'I only bring the husband to meet you all. Henio, this is most of the people I know since coming to England,' she said as she introduced each of them to her husband.

'I'm so pleased to finally meet you,' Flora said as she patted the seat next to her so he could sit down.

'I must thank you for looking after my wife, and for writing the letter. If not for you we might never have seen each other again,' he said, taking her hand and placing a gentle kiss on the back.

Flora watched as he returned to his wife before turning to Rose, who was now sitting next to her pouring out cocoa. 'He wrote to you . . . '

'Henio?'

'No, Ben; he told me he wrote to you while he was in France. He's a good man, Rose. Please don't disappoint him.'

'It's too late. I have nothing to say to him,' Rose said, getting up to hand out the hot drinks and ignoring Flora's pleading looks to sit down and talk more.

Another ten minutes passed in silence before Mildred returned. 'I've seen her,' she declared, before bursting into loud sobs.

'Oh no, please don't say something's gone wrong and that's why they've not spoken to us,' Flora said, getting up to wrap her arms around the inconsolable woman.

'I've seen the baby,' Mildred said as she blew her nose with a loud honk. 'A little girl, and such a small scrap of a thing, but they say she's full of life and she'll pull through even though she's still a bit on the small side. A nurse is on her way to take you through to see Lily, and one other visitor can come,' she added, looking at Flora's puzzled expression. 'You are the next of kin, are you not?'

'Oh, of course,' Flora said, remembering how she'd insisted on being the person to be contacted. She hadn't wished for Rose or Katie to be the ones to hear bad news if things had gone wrong. 'Who would like to come with me?' she asked.

'You go, Rose. I'm happy enough to sit here knowing Lily and her baby have pulled through,' Katie said. 'Besides, you know me. One drop of blood and I'll be fainting at your feet.'

'If you are sure?' Rose said, standing up as a nurse appeared and called out Flora's name.

'Come along, love,' Flora said as she took Rose's arm. 'Let's go and tell Lily how she gave us all a scare. Just remember, she has lost a member of her family today as well as gaining a new one.' Not that any of us will mourn the passing of George Jacobs, she thought to herself.

They followed the young nurse down a long corridor that sloped downwards into the cellars of the hospital. They could hear voices and movement behind some of the closed doors they passed. 'It's as if they'd moved the whole hospital underground,' Flora said in awe.

'Quite a lot of it,' the nurse replied before stopping at a door and ushering them through. 'Lily, we have visitors for you,' she said brightly before turning to Flora and Rose. 'She is still very groggy after the long operation, so you can only have a few minutes with her. I'll let you take a peep at the baby afterwards. We've all fallen in love with the little mite already.' She smiled before leaving them alone.

Rose pulled two wooden chairs close to the

bed so they could talk without Lily having to move. Her friend looked pale against the white sheets, and Rose marvelled at what she must have gone through since they'd last met. A cradle contraption covered her legs, and that in turn was covered with a blanket. One arm lay on top of the covers, encased in white plaster of Paris.

Lily's eyelids fluttered before opening, and she gave a weak smile. 'Hello, you two,' she said. 'I hope you don't mind if I don't get up.'

'Stay where you are,' Flora answered quickly before realizing that even in her weak state, Lily was joking. 'You've given us a right old shock, young lady,' she smiled. 'All your friends are outside and worried stiff about you. Miss Tibbs is having to knit twice as fast now that the baby has arrived.'

Lily's face shone at the mention of her child. 'She's beautiful, and none the worse for being on the small side,' she whispered. 'I'm so grateful to you for talking me out of . . . ' She looked to Rose, who nodded her head, as she understood what her friend was trying to say.

'It all turned out for the best,' she reassured her.

'Something strange happened while I was being rescued,' Lily murmured, looking confused. 'I could have sworn that nice Captain Hargreaves helped me. I must have been hallucinating, as you sent him packing, didn't you?'

Flora spoke before Rose could even open her mouth. 'You weren't hallucinating, as it was his team of soldiers who came to your rescue. I've spoken to him today. Of course, Rose here knows better, and still won't have it out with him about what happened between them,' she huffed.

'Mum, please, now is not the time. We don't want Lily upset,' Rose begged.

Lily did her best to laugh, but it came out as a weak cough. 'You have to be nice to me as I nearly died, so will you please make your peace? Flora, what really made Rose leave Sea View so quickly? I don't want to go to meet my maker without knowing . . . '

She stopped speaking as the nurse came in carrying Lily's baby. 'I thought you'd like to see her,' she said as Rose and Flora bent over to look at the sleeping child.

'Oh my, she's so tiny. Her face is like a little screwed-up rosebud,' Flora sighed.

Rose frowned, being careful not to let Lily see what she was thinking. There was something familiar about the baby's face. Rose could swear there was a likeness to Tom White. The little angry face reminded her of Tom's expression at the teashop earlier, and there was a similarity with the shape of the nose . . . Didn't Lily go out dancing with the man the night she was out with Ben, and didn't she seem upset the next day? She swore then to watch that man closely in future.

The nurse took the baby close to Lily so she could give her daughter a kiss, and they all watched as the nurse took the baby from the room.

'As I was saying about meeting my maker . . . ?'

Rose scoffed at Lily's words. 'Talk about milking it for all it's worth. You are not going to die . . . are you?' she added uncertainly.

'Don't argue. Just tell me — and no one's to

storm out,' she said, as fiercely as her weak voice would allow.

'Oh, well, if you insist,' Rose sighed, thinking perhaps it was only fair to let her friend know what had happened. 'As you know, I found some information in Mum's attaché case under her bed that made me question who my parents are. Are you happy now?'

Flora shook her head. 'Oh, Rose, I am your mother, so please don't ever think otherwise.'

'But that letter — and the jewellery . . . '

'I will explain from the beginning. That's if Lily is strong enough to listen. I don't want to tire you,' Flora said, giving Lily's good hand a squeeze.

'Fire away,' Lily said. 'If I doze off, please wake me, as I don't want to miss anything.'

Flora took a deep breath. 'Some of this you already know, but I will start from the beginning. It started when I was a young woman. Like our Katie, I grew up in an orphanage but dreamt of singing and dancing on the stage. Yes, just like you,' she smiled at Rose's astonished look. 'You have seen some old pictures of what I said was a friend. It was me; I'm sorry I lied. I was quite good at what I did; and oh, how I love to perform,' she said with a faraway look in her eyes. 'It was a magical time for me. But like all good times, it would change. I too met a young army captain, and we fell in love. Unlike you, my love, I was so infatuated I did what all good girls shouldn't do, and I ended up expecting his baby . . . '

Rose caught Lily's eye and knew they were both thinking the same thing. Rose's liaison with

Ben could have ended the same way.

' . . . But he was a good man, and made provision to care for me.'

'Why didn't he marry you?' Rose demanded, feeling uncomfortable that the story was too close to home.

'He was already married, and his position meant he could never leave his wife and children. He wanted me to be thought of as a respectable woman, and purchased Sea View to give us a good home and a way of making a comfortable living. Moving to Ramsgate and a new life meant I'd never be thought of as a good-time girl who sold her favours.'

'You never did, though. You simply fell in love,' Lily said, enthralled by what Flora was saying.

'You mean I have siblings?' Rose gasped. 'But what about Dad?'

'Never think for one moment that the man I later married, who you knew as your dad, didn't love you. He was devoted to you until the day he died.'

Flashes of her young life kept rushing through her mind as Rose did her best to understand. Flora was right; the man she thought of as her dad had indeed been like a true father to her. 'What happened with my real dad?'

'He stayed in the army, but his wife and one of his children died in the influenza outbreak in 1918. The other child, your half-sister, went to live with her maternal grandparents. By then I was married and settled here, and was content with my life. I always cared for him, even when he became a grand general. We would correspond, so he knew all about you. Then he became ill, and with no one close to care for him, we brought him to Sea View . . . ', Flora said, watching to see if Rose had understood. 'I never had any secrets from the man I married, and he became a good friend to the General.'

'So my real father was truly General Sykes?' Rose said. She'd adored the man, who had spent many hours teaching her to read and talking about his journeys. 'I couldn't believe what I'd seen in those papers, but now it makes sense . . . also how kind he always was towards me.'

'Yes,' Flora said, feeling a great weight fall from her shoulders. 'The papers you only glimpsed, and the two pieces of jewellery, are from him. We both decided the house should go to you — and the jewellery is from his mother, who was the only person he told about you not long before she passed away. You see, he never wanted to have secrets, and he would have been greatly distressed by the mess I've made of all of this. We had such plans for you, Rose. We wanted you to have a good education and train for a decent job.' She laughed as she thought of something. 'Do you know that the day I went to London to see the solicitor, after the General died, I stopped at a Lyons Corner House. I remember thinking that at least my daughter would never have to be a waitress — but things didn't go to plan.'

Rose smiled and reached for Flora's hand. 'What happened, Mum?'

'His investments came to nothing. But at least we had a roof over our head and could make a living from Sea View. We were luckier than most. You may not recall, but he died within months of your dad's accident, and suddenly it was just me and you.' Flora watched Rose's face to see how she was taking the news.

Rose felt confused with so much information buzzing round in her head. 'Why did you never tell me?'

'It was his wish that I inform you of the part he played in your life on your twenty-fifth birthday. He wanted me to say that Sea View was your house — your inheritance. I was supposed to give you the ring and the cameo brooch when you turned twenty-one, as gifts from him as a friend. I forgot about the jewellery — I'm sorry. He thought he was leaving you a rich young woman, and until the day he died I helped keep up that belief.'

'You must have loved him very much,' was all Rose could think to say.

'Just as I love you — and I know you love Ben. Please, Rose, give him time to explain . . . '

'It's a beautiful story, and it shows how much everyone loved you to keep up the pretence. You are lucky to have had two dads, when I only have that old bastard George Jacobs to remember,' Lily sighed.

Rose couldn't have felt guiltier if she tried. 'Lily, you know he didn't survive, don't you?' she said gently.

'He was a goner before the roof caved in,' Lily said without an ounce of remorse. 'It's just me and my baby daughter now.'

'And your friends. You have all of us, whether

you like it or not,' Rose said, getting up to lean over the bed and give Lily a kiss on the cheek before turning to do the same to Flora. 'I'm sorry for acting as I did and not giving you a chance to explain, Mum.'

Flora nodded. 'There's no need to say sorry. I've not gone about things as I should have done.'

'Will the two of you stop going on about yourselves. Don't you realize I'm the sick one in this room and should be having all the attention?' Lily said, making them all laugh.

'I've been thinking about a name for the baby. I want her christened Rosemary Flora — that's if they will christen her in church, what with . . . '

'The vicar will have us to answer to if he objects,' Flora said.

'Rosemary was my mum's name, so it is fitting she is remembered. But as you've been like a mum to me as well, her second name will be Flora, if that's all right with you?'

'It sounds delightful to me,' Flora beamed.

'I want her everyday name to be Mary, otherwise we will be confused with Roses popping up all over the place,' Lily smiled.

Rose and Flora broke into song simultaneously. '*But it was Mary, Mary, long before the fashions came. And there is something there that sounds so square — it's a grand old name . . . *'

They all started to laugh until Flora stopped to listen. 'It's Moaning Minnie. Hitler's not letting up today, is he? Now what do we do?'

The nurse burst into the room. 'Ladies, you need to get to the shelter as fast as you can. Lily and the baby will be safe down here,' she said, ushering them from the room.

'Don't forget to speak to Ben,' Lily called as they kissed her before hurrying away.

★ ★ ★

'I hate this place. It is cold and damp. I would rather be facing the Germans and fight them as we did in Poland than die down this hole in the ground,' Anya said as she shivered against her husband.

'Anya, living down these tunnels has saved many lives. Be thankful there was an entrance close by the hospital or we'd be out there right now, ducking the bombs and praying we survive the night,' Miss Tibbs scolded her. 'Besides, now your husband has found you he may be whisking you away from Ramsgate to somewhere new and safe.'

Anya looked up at her husband in the flickering half-light of their part of the tunnel. 'Will you be whisking me away, Henio?'

'Not any time soon, my sweetness,' he smiled down at her questioning face. 'I am here to help the RAF fight the Luftwaffe. It needs every man we have to win this war. Would you like me to whisk you away?'

'No, I too wish to fight and will do my bit, as they say, helping Mr Joe Lyons feed the public. I like Ramsgate and would like to live here forever,' she said, bringing that conversation to an end. 'Rose,' she called out, 'why don't you sing to us and cheer everyone up. Tell that old sod down there on his piano to play something nice you can sing to.'

Rose had been sitting with Flora, trying to catch up on all her mum could tell her about her real father. 'I don't want Sea View, Mum. I will always think of it as home, but with Mildred being so generous and giving us Captain's Cottage to share, I don't need to own another property. It will always be yours,' she said as Flora gave her a loving hug.

'We can talk about it when the time is right,' Flora said. 'What I'm more concerned about is that you speak with Ben and clear the air. He told me about his wife and children . . . '

'So he does have a wife?' Rose said sadly. 'I wasn't wrong after all.'

'Oh, but you were wrong in so many ways — and you most definitely need to clear the air, even if you decide there's no future for the pair of you. It's not my place to tell you what he said.'.

Rose was thoughtful for a while. 'I believe it's too late for that. I rebuked him again earlier this afternoon, when I saw him at the hospital. He's probably sick to death of me,' she said as her voice broke with the emotion of pent-up tears. 'It's far too late to make amends now.'

Flora pulled her daughter close and hugged her. 'It's never too late. You will find an opportunity to speak again. I can feel it in my bones — please believe me,' she said as she rocked Rose back and forth, allowing her to cry while silently cursing the Luftwaffe for coming over when they did. She'd hoped Ben would keep his word and return to the hospital as she'd requested, but the best-laid plans . . . 'Anya is right — why not wipe your eyes and give us all a song? I know I'd enjoy hearing you sing.'

Rose wiped her eyes. 'I promise that if I see Ben again, I'll listen to what he has to say. What song would you like me to sing?'

'Sing from your heart, Rose. You never know who is listening.'

'I'll do it now, or Anya will never stop shouting at me,' she grinned, getting up from the wooden bench she was sharing with her mum and all her friends. She headed over to where, as strange as it seemed, a piano had been placed in the tunnel and an elderly gentleman was playing his heart out. There were crowds of people listening to him in that part of the myriad tunnels running under the streets of Ramsgate.

Climbing around children playing on the floor, and stopping to say hello to people she knew, Rose finally reached the pianist. She leant in close to the man to discuss what she could sing, and he nodded enthusiastically before running his fingers over the keys to introduce the song.

The people fell silent as familiar chords sounded out and echoed through the tunnel. Rose took a deep breath and started to sing. She thought only of Ben as the words came out clear and strong.

Women who were waiting to hear news of husbands who were far from home reached for their handkerchiefs as Rose sang the opening bars of the well-known song 'I'll Be Seeing You'. She sang for them all as her words of lost love accompanied the old piano. As the clear notes reached the end of the song there was a break in her voice as she told of looking up to the moon and seeing the face of her loved one. There was not a dry eye in that part of the underground tunnels.

Rose couldn't speak as the friends and neighbours in their part of the tunnel cheered out and shouted for more. She wasn't sure she could sing again, having poured her heart and soul into the first song, but she knew it would cheer up everyone deep underground in those tunnels while the war raged overhead. Bending close, she tried to listen to the pianist's suggestions but was aware of someone standing close by. She could smell his cologne and shivered at his closeness. 'Ben?' she asked, half turning round, afraid in case her wishes were just dreams.

'Rose . . . please . . . ' he all but begged as she turned fully to face him.

'I was singing that song for you, Ben,' she whispered, as they became the only couple in the world and everything around them dissolved.

'We need to talk,' he said, taking her hand and leading her a little way away from the crowded area.

'I'm so sorry I didn't give you time to explain. I feel a fool for running away from you all the time,' she whispered as he held her close and told her of his life before they met. She listened without questioning his words until he fell silent and she reached up to brush his lips with her own.

'I want to spend the rest of my life with you,

Rose Neville. That's if you can accept my young family? We come as a package. Does that bother you?'

'Nothing bothers me at all now I have you by my side,' she said, and reached up to kiss him once more. 'I trust you, and I'll love you until the end of time. It took my mum and my friends to show me what an idiot I've been. We've wasted enough time, and I've been a fool. Please forgive me?'

'There's nothing to forgive,' he said as he swept her up in his arms, giving a jubilant thumbs up to Flora, who stood cheering along with their friends. 'No more secrets,' he said.

Acknowledgements

There are so many people to thank. First and foremost my agent, Caroline Sheldon, who is always at hand to advise and support me when I have my wobbles. What would I do without her? My publisher, Pan Macmillan, who has been so generous with contracts for further books and behind me as I write my sagas. My lovely editor, Caroline Hogg, and the equally lovely Louise Davies, who is standing in for Caroline during her maternity leave — it is great to be able to work with you both. I mustn't forget Jayne Osborne, who is always there at the end of an email. I have the most wonderful publicists — ED PR Ltd, who do their utmost to let the world know about my books and Bethan James, who looks after me. I must mention Annie Aldington who does such a wonderful job narrating my audiobooks, bringing 'the girls' to life. The covers of my books are so true to the time of the stories. A big thank you to Mel Four and the team who are behind the production of all my books. Thank you all.

Writing is never a solitary occupation, whatever our readers imagine. In this day and age we are only a password away from the many groups of readers and fellow writers. Thank you to the readers of The Saga Girls, Readers and Writers and Bloggers group for your continued support. A very special thank you goes to a very secret group of saga writers, The Strictly Saga Girls. We share secrets, cry on each other's shoulders and cheer each other on, as well as share successes. I couldn't do without any of you xx

I must give a shout-out to my students at The Write Place creative writing school. I've known many of you for a good number of years and have cheered you on as you climb that ladder to writing successes. Long may your successes continue and long may the celebration cakes appear each week!

Last but not least, my long-suffering husband, Michael. He is always there to put up with my moaning and to remind me of my deadlines and to stop watching *Tipping Point* and *The Chase* and to get on with my work.

From reports we read in the newspapers that show our dream job it appears I am living the dream, as 'writer' is always at number one. Lucky me! Thank you all for keeping this writer in work and cheering her on xx

A Letter from Elaine

Dear Reader,

Thank you for reading *The Teashop Girls*. I do hope you've enjoyed the story and have made friends with Rose, Lily, Kate, Flora, Anya and Mildred. I had fun writing this story, as it brought back so many memories for me — not that I was around during the War, I hasten to add.

As a child in the fifties and early sixties my family would take its annual holiday in Ramsgate, Kent. Like so many people back then my father was not a driver, so the trip would be by Margot's Coaches from nearby Crayford. It wasn't a pleasant experience for me or my sister, as we didn't travel well. However, the thought of going to the seaside for two weeks would outweigh any feelings of sickness. Spotting the sea for the first time would have us screaming in delight. Fortunately Mum discovered we could travel from Slade Green to Ramsgate by train, and also send the large family suitcase on ahead. That case was full of matching outfits, as Mum was a very good seamstress. Sundresses, party dresses and knitted cardigans were lovingly made so we looked as smart as possible for those two weeks. Our holiday, like many other families', was always taken in the last week of July and the first week of August as holidays were governed by factory shut-downs.

Arriving in Ramsgate, we would be met by

lads with various versions of carts made from old pram wheels and planks of wood, who would transport our cases to the boarding houses for just a few pennies. Those lads must have done well in the summer months. Looking back, those large houses were like palaces to a small child. They had an underlying odour of furniture polish and tasty food, and everywhere I looked there would be knick-knacks with 'a gift from Ramsgate' printed on them — no doubt gifts from parting guests. We would take something similar back for Nan each year. We always had the family room for the four of us — five after my brother arrived when I was seven — and this was our first experience of bunk beds. Such fun!

Our days were spent on the beach before heading back to the boarding house for an evening meal. We would wash and put on one of our special outfits, and other guests would tell us how sweet we looked. All I can recall was my red sunburnt shoulders itching under a yellow seersucker dress. After dinner we would walk down to the sea-front and perhaps sit in a pub garden or go to the amusement arcade to spend some of the pennies we'd saved. I always lost my money, whereas my sister came away with a bulging purse. My friends will tell you that any time we visit the coast on a writing retreat, I make a bee-line for the amusement arcade to relive my childhood memories.

Something that has stuck in my mind is the walk back to our lodgings after the exciting day. For a young child it was a steep climb up Madeira Walk, but we were able to stop and watch the lights and the magical waterfall that bordered the walk. No wonder that the walk is mentioned in *The Teashop Girls* more than a few times, or that Flora runs a guesthouse in that seaside town.

Margate, where Rose manages her teashop, is a different kettle of fish. For me it has always been the place for a day trip, whether with my siblings or taking the Brownies when I used to help out the local pack. A morning on the beach before chips for lunch, and then off to Dreamland for an afternoon of fun. My favourite was the water caves, as to this day I simply hate the fast rides.

When researching the Lyons teashops I was delighted to find that there had been one in Ramsgate, although these days the building is a public house. In Margate the teashop with the beautiful veranda looking out to sea has gone, although the building remains. Walk round the back of the shops and a sign can just about be seen over what would have been one of the entrances into the teashop. What I would give to have been able to enjoy afternoon tea in one of those iconic Lyons teashops. As it is, I can just about recall the Lyons Corner House on the Strand, although by then it was self-service and some of the magic had gone.

Do you have memories of Lyons teashops, or perhaps holidays on the Kent coast back in the fifties and sixties? Please pop over to my Facebook author page and we can reminisce about those golden days of our childhood.

Until next time,
Elaine xx

We do hope that you have enjoyed reading this large print book.

Did you know that all of our titles are available for purchase?

We publish a wide range of high quality large print books including:
Romances, Mysteries, Classics
General Fiction
Non Fiction and Westerns

Special interest titles available in large print are:
The Little Oxford Dictionary
Music Book
Song Book
Hymn Book
Service Book

Also available from us courtesy of Oxford University Press:
Young Readers' Dictionary
(large print edition)
Young Readers' Thesaurus
(large print edition)

For further information or a free brochure, please contact us at:
Ulverscroft Large Print Books Ltd.,
The Green, Bradgate Road, Anstey,
Leicester, LE7 7FU, England.
Tel: (00 44) **0116 236 4325**
Fax: (00 44) **0116 234 0205**

Other titles published by Ulverscroft:

A GIFT FROM WOOLWORTHS

Elaine Everest

As the war moves into 1945 the lives of the women of Woolworths continue. When store manager Betty Billington announces that she is expecting a baby, her life is about to change more than she expects. Freda has fallen in love with a handsome Scottish engineer. Maisie loves being a mother and also caring for her two nieces, although she still has her own dreams. When her brother appears on the scene he brings unexpected danger. Meanwhile Sarah dreams of her husband's return and a cottage with roses around the door. Will our girls sail into times of peace, or will they experience more heartache and sorrow?

WARTIME AT WOOLWORTHS

Elaine Everest

Freda leaves the safety of her hometown to go in search of her distant mother. But when she arrives, it's the scars of war that greet her. Ruby is a kindly soul, looking out for every-one — none more so than the cantankerous Vera. But when Vera's home is under threat, Ruby realizes something must be wrong — what is she hiding? Maisie is devoted to her young family and to Woolworths, but her happy life with her RAF officer husband and baby daughter leads her to think of the family she left behind . . . With families separated by war, will the Woolworths girls be able to pull together?